RUDE BOY
USA

RUDE BOY USA

USA

VICTORIA BOLTON

Copyright © 2015 Victoria Bolton
All rights reserved.
Hairummat Books, White Plains, NY
Cover Concept and Design by Victoria Bolton

ISBN: 1518754333
ISBN 13: 9781518754333
Library of Congress Control Number: 2015919011
CreateSpace Independent Publishing Platform
North Charleston, South Carolina

ACKNOWLEDGEMENTS

First, I would like to thank God for giving me life so I can have dreams that enabled me to put a story like this together. It's finally on paper and out of my head.

To my Mom, I love you. Thank you for making me and giving me your strength. I watch you handle things like a champion every day.

To my best friend, Lisa Holmes. Thank you for putting up with my shenanigans for all of these years.

Thank you so much for my editing and publishing team for being patient with all of my questions and changes.

To my extended family and friends, thank you for all of your support.

Last but certainly not least, thank you to those who I mused to create this story. You have inspired one heck of a story.

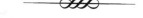

PROLOGUE

In the middle of the night in a trashy abandoned lot in Harlem, New York, there were four men. Three of them had arrived together as a team. The fourth man, Sammy, was their victim, and they had tied up his arms and legs. Sammy was not associated with the others. He had stolen money from the leader of the group. Sammy would not divulge details of the theft. His silence did not help his situation as each of the three men took turns beating him until they got him to talk. One of the three men turned to the others. "He looks young. He looks very young."

One of the men responded, "He looks old enough to go to war. Nobody cares how young you look when you are in a war."

Sammy continued to taunt them back. "You guys are fucking trash," Sammy said to the men, and he spat on one of them.

The man Sammy spat on told him, "Watch your god-damn mouth!" Sammy ensured them that they would never get information from him and said they could kiss his ass. The three men looked at each other. They began torturing and pistol-whipping Sammy in return. Irritated, the man who Sammy spat on got the idea to stuff money in Sammy's ass and mouth for being greedy and talking too much shit. He had warned the tied-up man to watch his mouth, and this was the consequence of ignoring that warning. Once they were finished with him, they put a plastic bag over his head, tossed him in the trunk of an abandoned car in the lot, and closed the trunk.

A fifth man rode up in a car. He got out to see the damage that the three men had produced. They opened the trunk to show him. The fifth man's face showed his objection. "Was this necessary? Are we wasting money now?" the gentleman said to his three associates.

One of them said, "It's theater."

Another associate added, "He asked for it. He asked us to do this. He told me to kiss his ass. He likes money, so…" He shrugged.

The last associate added, "It's only two hundred dollars in singles. It looks like a lot, but it isn't." The fifth man looked down at the body and slammed the trunk shut.

"Fine, we will discuss this back at the office," he said. He and his three associates got in the car and headed back to Midtown Manhattan.

Chapter 1

In the middle of a block in busy Midtown Manhattan full of shops and stores stood a silver building just twelve feet wide. Distinctive architecture decked in superior aesthetic treatments surrounded this place. Professional pedestrians, as well as regular shoppers, walked up and down the block every day. The noise of cars, police sirens, fire trucks, ambulances, and human voices filled the street twenty-four hours a day. There was no other place like Nineteen West Forty-Sixth Street. This location was noted not only for its unique size but also for its occupants, the Chimera Group. The Chimera Group consisted of a group of men who many residents, as well as law enforcement in the city, speculated were into organized crime, but this was never outright proven. Their involvement in organized crime may have been true on the inside, and to those who knew the inner workings. The sign on the outside of the building—which bore the Chimera Group's name and a symbol that consisted of a hybrid animal made with a lion's head, goat's middle, and snake's tail—indicated a high-class and highly successful investment company. The company's logo confused many people. It represented the people who ran it. It comprised the parts of more than one faction, and the philosophy of such a mixture was wildly imaginative, implausible, and dazzling. Bernie chose the name not only because he found the symbol appealing but also because he wanted to pay tribute to his half-Greek heritage and his obsession with Greek mythology.

The multiracial Chimera Group consisted of four main impeccably groomed men who wore the sharpest of mohair Tonik suits. Each one's background gave the boss the ability for broad outreach to the city. They were sales representatives, but they were not the typical door-to-door peddlers; they sold futures to the residents of New York City and the surrounding areas. "Give us your money; we will invest it, and you will reap the rewards in due time." It was hard to believe that many people fell for this line, but they did. The economic environment and future market forecast of the late 1960s did not seem promising. Hard-working, blue-collar residents needed a plan for their future, and these men provided hope, on paper. Wealthier clients had it easier; they were more willing to take risks, as they had more funds to spare.

Bernie Banks (born Bernard Rhodos), the founder and CEO of Chimera, prided himself on the company's layout, which consisted of four main men: him and three associates who did the footwork while he stayed at the office. At times, the office resembled a boiler room with lots of phone calls, alcohol, smoking and occasional visits from scantily clad women on call. He saw the company's logo as a representation of the associates who worked under him. Bernie was a tall man in his sixties with short, thinning hair. He had a salt-and-pepper beard that was medium in length. His face was endearing and pleasant with a slight tan. From looking at him, one could not tell his profession. He wore suits and glasses on occasion, and he was of average weight. Still handsome in his advanced age, he had no problems attracting women. Bernie was a World War II veteran who served honorably until he was court-martialed for assault on an English citizen. The Englishman had physically assaulted a fellow black soldier who served with Bernie in the European Theater of Operations. The two beat the guy to a pulp as a response. The black soldier continued to beat him until the man passed out. The man ended up dying a week later from a brain hemorrhage. The black service member was later convicted of murder and executed at Shepton Mallet. Bernie served two years for assault. He felt that the black soldier had just been defending himself; racism had led to the unjust execution by hanging. He felt that he would have reacted the same if he had been the one attacked.

In the early years, he began his business in his apartment with one helper, and it eventually grew into a multimillion-dollar empire for a time. He had spent his entire life working and saving so that he could attain his current situation. He built his reputation on good communication. He was the one in the company who only dealt with the big dogs. The other three men dealt with the general public unless there was a problem. The other men operated as supervisors, with helpers to assist them. Each man was in charge of a borough. One man worked the Bronx and Harlem. Another man worked in Brooklyn, and one other in Queens and sometimes Westchester. Bernie dealt with downtown and Staten Island. All four also made their presence known in Midtown Manhattan if need be.

Bernie associated with the other Mafia groups, whom he considered lesser to Chimera in their innovation and style. He also dealt with law enforcement, making sure that he kept in good standing with them by paying off large sums of money to keep himself and sometimes his associates out of jail. He also made deals with judges and those involved in the courts. Obtaining funds from the public was not an easy feat, so Bernie had to go through other channels to get money. While the other three men kept their trail clean by working with the mostly legal aspects of Chimera, Bernie headed the illegal part, which included forced protection services, labor racketeering, loansharking, extortion, money laundering, illegal gambling, and, in extreme cases, an occasional robbery. Bernie made sure to inform whoever worked for him that robbery was not a tactic to use unless necessary because it would result in more payoffs to law enforcement for cleanup. That would mean less money for the company.

The employees of Bernie's three junior associates split the robberies and other petty crime. Those guys had nothing to lose if they did not complete the assignments; they were the uninformed scapegoats. Those people consisted of young men in their twenties who had no other direction to go but the military. For many of them, it was a choice of organized crime, jail, or Vietnam. Most of them did not do much but sit around all day, play cards, smoke, and drink before they started working for Bernie. No women were working in Chimera. Bernie and the others felt that this setup was no place for a woman, as the environment was incredibly misogynistic and the guys could be assholes with their daily conversations about the opposite sex. Chimera was a male culture based on power.

Due to their unique racial makeup and financial success, Chimera became so successful and popular that people in the underground began to refer to the group as the Rude Boys. Their style was a tribute to the most sophisticated subculture of the young street gangsters popular in the United Kingdom and Jamaica. The States had seen nothing like them before now. They were clean-shaven and debonair, with their Ray-Ban sunglasses, immaculate loafers, and sometimes porkpie or trilby hats. When trends turned more to longhaired, Afrocentric, and club flashy, they kept their suited style. Visually, Chimera comprised the coolest people in town. In name recognition, they were second only to the Ambrosino family in New York, the highest ranked crime family. The Ambrosinos had thirty crews and over a thousand members. They ran a dangerous operation. To them, murder was just part of the business and life. To date, it was rumored that the family as a whole had committed over one hundred and fifty murders, all ordered by their boss, Enzo Ambrosino.

———

Ben Berardi, a second-generation Italian American, joined Chimera because he just needed a job. He had served in Vietnam briefly before coming to work at Chimera full time. Ben was a tall, slim, but muscular man with dark hair, thick brows, blue eyes, and a classically handsome face with a faint scar down his cheek. He got that scar as a child when he fell off a bike and cut his face. Ben's grandparents adopted him because his mother was mentally ill and admitted to an institution, where she could not keep custody of him. His father decided he was not ready for a family and abandoned Ben's mother and him. The details of their relationship were kept secret, but Ben knew that both of his parents had the same last name. When he asked his grandparents about this, they would not give him a clear answer except to say it was a coincidence.

Ben was Chimera's number three man. Bernie considered him special because he had been raised in very similar circumstances, losing both parents at a very young age. Bernie had a way of sympathizing with other people's plight, as his family persecuted his mother. Her sin lay in not being the obedient Jewish woman that her parents wanted and in having a child out of wedlock with a Greek immigrant. Ben idolized James Bond and Al Capone. He saw himself as a hybrid of both men. His job at Chimera involved elements of both. Ben walked like Bond, attempted to act like Bond, and had the mobster ambition like Capone. In his mind, he nailed it, but in reality it came off as trying too hard. The guys would tease him and tell him that he should be Scarface instead because of his old injury. He would quickly correct them and make sure they referred to him as Capone instead because he was the greatest ever to do it, according to Ben. He was sensitive to their taunts, and he felt at times as if he was being bullied.

Bernie also served as a counselor to Ben, who had substance abuse problems. Ben had attention issues as well as mood swings. His grandparents never sought help for these matters when he was a child. They did not want to come to terms with the fact that his mother may have passed on some of her mental-health issues to him. Ben never received a medical diagnosis, although most would consider him bipolar. He dealt with these problems unmedicated. His grandparents felt that seeking divine intervention would better help him. He used alcohol and drugs as a coping mechanism for his frustration, as he claimed that they made him concentrate and calm down. Bernie kept an eye on him, knowing a drug user would not make good snap decisions when it came to business affairs and bookkeeping. Bernie considered drugs a nasty business despite other families' active partaking in those activities. Bernie wanted him to succeed, but Ben needed a lot of guidance.

Ben had been jailed for drug dealing, robbery, and petty larceny, which supported his drug habit, and he also got into trouble while serving in the Army. Ben would claim innocence and say that he was just being profiled by law enforcement because he looked like a typical gangster. Bernie had to pull strings to have him released. One such incident involved Ben being arrested for sticking up a shopkeeper in lower Manhattan and beating him with a pistol. The case made it all the way to a jury trial. Bernie had to give kickbacks to several jurors to make sure they found Ben not guilty. Bernie paid some of them off immediately, and others he promised to pay off later. Ben was in charge of making sure the people who helped him maintain his freedom received compensation.

Ben shadowed Bernie in many of his actions on and off the field. Ben was very sensitive about Bernie's criticisms of him. Bernie was not mean to Ben, but if he thought Ben's drinking or actions became a distraction, he would curb him. If Bernie thought Ben was falling off the wagon, he would scorn him. The comments hurt Ben, but he understood why Bernie was criticizing him. If anyone else told Ben something in the same realm, even if it were for his own good, he would tell them to go fuck off. Ben treated Bernie like a father. Ben's desire to inherit Bernie's empire provided the driving force behind his work at Chimera. He wanted to be the one to bring the group to the number one spot. He had always admired the well-known Mafia groups in New York and other cities, and he felt that his Italian heritage was the key to bringing the group higher. The Cosa Nostra in New York was heavily embedded in Sicilian culture and history. They viewed outside groups as frauds and invaders of their culture. Bernie wanted to see Ben succeed, and he would often pull Ben aside for talks. Bernie used his past experiences as a way to get to Ben.

"Benjamin, I want you to listen to me. Stop fooling around. It's time to straighten out. Start planning your future. I won't always be here to bail you out," Bernie would often tell him.

"I know, I know," Ben would answer.

"You are causing too many problems, unnecessary problems, all over the place. Here is how you will fail. Control yourself. Jail isn't Neverland," Bernie told him.

"I'm listening. I promise. I am not going back to jail. I cannot fail. I'm here," Ben said.

"Make your promises count. Bernie knows; don't argue." Bernie ended.

Ben walked with a sense of entitlement, and he felt that his fellow associates were secretly holding him back. Because of this, Ben continued with his drug use but hid it cleverly from the others in the group. He went from using lightweight drugs such as cannabis, which was popular at the moment, to taking harder narcotics when he enlisted in the army. When he utilized them, he timed each hit so it would not affect his day job. He graduated from smoke to needles. Despite these issues, Ben was a team player for his protection, and he would be until it was no longer convenient for him.

The number four man was Jerome Dexter. Jerome was a tall, dark-brown, slim black man from Harlem, New York. Jerome came from a two-parent home of respected members of the local community. Optimistic about his future, his family had sent him to college. His parents started saving for his education once they learned that his mother was pregnant with him. When other black middle-class families were fleeing Harlem for Queens and other boroughs with better education and housing, the Dexter family stayed and saved their money for their investment in Jerome.

Jerome was smart enough to succeed, but he felt that his overbearing parents pushed him into things that he did not want to do. He never had a say in his future. They wanted him to be a scientist because his father, James Dexter, who worked at the Freedom National Bank, felt that the community needed representation that resembled them, and science was the future. He could be a great inventor, they hoped. Jerome was bored with furthering his education by the time he graduated from high school, of which he was valedictorian. He attended Fisk University, but because of a lack of discipline and a penchant for the southern women in Tennessee, he flunked out.

Disappointed in his outcome, Jerome's parents made him leave the family home to fend for himself, and he had to do so until he got his act together. Jerome slept on various friends' and relatives' couches and maintained odd jobs to support himself. At one such job, he worked as a busboy at a diner on 116th Street, where he met John, a gentleman who was already working for Chimera. They hit it off immediately, and John, feeling that Jerome could be a good subworker for Chimera, sent him to drop off a package. John promised that if he did so and made it back safely, he would receive a generous reward. Jerome did not know what John meant by that, but because he needed the funds, he decided to do the job. That package turned out to be a bomb, which he delivered at a rival's doorstep. It was a Trojan-horse attack. Bernie had friends that were connected to the Weathermen, and he asked John to find someone to do the job. Bernie did not want to put any of his people at risk.

The Weathermen were a group of people whose supporters stretched nationwide. They took their name from a Bob Dylan lyric, "You don't need a weatherman to know which way the wind blows." They consisted of advocates of the black-power movement and individuals strongly opposed to the Vietnam War. The FBI also knew them as the Weather Underground. The nationwide group was small, no more than five hundred people, but the smaller groups spread throughout the country. They intended to create their separate political party to overthrow the government. They considered themselves the new left. This group was known to use aggressive tactics to get their message across to the media and government. The group felt that America needed to change its values. Male hegemony, white supremacy, fascism, high unemployment, inadequate education, and terrible treatment of blacks and poor women were the real issues, not some unjust war overseas.

The Weathermen also organized some of the anti-Vietnam War protests that occurred on college campuses throughout the country. They bombed a few high-profile government sites as a way to protest the United States' actions in several parts of the world. A private sector of the Weathermen was located in Greenwich Village, where Bernie would go and get help with weapons if necessary, including guns and sometimes bombs if they needed to send a stern message to a rival. Bernie also had a younger girlfriend, Gina, who was active in the Weather Underground. Gina was a five-foot-eight red-head with feathered shoulder-length hair. Her face had faint signs of freckles, and she kept her eyes lined and lashed heavily and her lips glossy. Gina stood out in not only looks but also personality and skill. She was the local Weather Underground chapter's chief bomb maker. She had a dominant personality, and she idolized Fidel Castro. She was Bernie's direct connection to the group, in which he charmingly referred to her as "Red." The Weathermen and Chimera were secret allies in the local area, and they often used each other's services. Gina partook in her separate activities separate from the underground, and these helped serve her and Bernie's personal agenda. Gina organized a couple of bank bombings and armored truck robberies to obtain funds for the both of them. She had been successful, as she was never caught in these activities. Gina and Bernie dated casually, and he enjoyed her company and sex, but Gina saw Bernie as something to do for the time being. In her mind, he was too old for them to consider having a future as a couple.

The package delivery that John gave to Jerome was successful. When Jerome later discovered that he had become a bomb-delivery boy, he had second thoughts about associating with John. John was impressed with his work and his attention to detail; to make it up to him, he recruited Jerome to Chimera and offered him a generous salary for his services. It was an offer that Jerome could not refuse since he was working for below minimum wage at the time. Jerome did so well at Chimera that he eventually moved up the ranks. Jerome used his family's reputation to gain the trust of those in the Harlem and Bronx communities. He succeeded enough that, under the guise of working for a reputable company, he was able to get his place. Jerome soon regained the respect of his parents. He was a single guy who enjoyed the ladies and still partook in the nightlife, but with Chimera he became a flashier version of himself. He hung out with John the most, and they formed a brotherly relationship.

Last but not least, John, a tall, slim, and athletic fair-skinned black man, was not only the most popular and most productive of the three associates, but he was also Bernie's favorite. Bernie considers John, a son of his. Bernie championed John because he did not need supervising. He knew how to lead and be productive with high confidence, which also mixed with his moody yet alpha-male traits. Everyone in the public nicknamed him the Conqueror. Bernie saw John as beneficial to the future of the company, and this was how he became a made man. When John entered the room, everyone took notice. He had a signature call of three quick whistles in succession. He used it to let everyone know that he had arrived. John was one of the first people Bernie recruited into his new business. John also hoped to succeed Bernie in Chimera, as Bernie had no heirs to whom he could pass along his fortune. John was never concerned about this, as he was too busy working to be a legend in the city. His name, freedom, and reputation were important to him.

John LeBlanc, a New Orleans native, had moved to New York City a year after high school in search of a different, urban city life. He had recently married his wife, Edina, a white Bronxville socialite who was in her second year at New York University. John left New Orleans because he felt he needed to get away from the area where he grew up. Downtown New Orleans was a cultural dream, with the many jazz clubs and a great nightlife filled with wealthy whites and rich blacks, but the outskirts homed poverty. Many poorer blacks and those of Creole descent struggled to make ends meet. As a kid, John had a paper route to earn money for himself. His pay entirely depended on tips, as his boss would often not pay him for his work. John had an easier time making small change because of his light skin tone, which made white residents feel at ease with him. John, who had a younger brother from a different father, had to work to help the family when he became a teenager.

Edina was a liberal arts major whose parents sent her to school to find a husband, but until she succeeded, she was to be educated so she could take over the family business. Edina was an average-height, bottle-strawberry blonde with layered hair. She had a high-pitched young valley voice that was typical of the college crowds. The location of New York University enabled Edina to meet those who were outside of the Jewish community in Westchester and, to her family's dismay, experiment with different activities that other students partook in, activities that were not culturally acceptable. Edina was seeing a boy, a fellow Jewish man named David. Both of their families expected Edina and David to marry. Although Edina carried many of the values that her family instilled in her, she was open to experiencing new people. She enjoyed the fact that New York had a vast transportation system, and she often traveled to other boroughs with friends to check out the other spots in the city.

John met her at Half Note, one of the few clubs that safely integrated without too many racial incidents. It had great jazz music. Edina had come in with friends to hear some music when she met John, who was also there to check out the scene. Not having had many interactions with black men, Edina decided to take a chance. She introduced herself to John, whom she felt was the nicest looking black fellow she had ever seen. Not long after meeting and sharing a few drinks, John had her in bed.

That one-night fling resulted in a pregnancy. Edina was not ready to be a mother, but she loved John so much, even after knowing him such a short time, that she decided to keep the baby. Her parents, who were Jewish traditional-ists, were outraged that their daughter would commingle with a Negro man, and they threatened his life. Her family demanded that she give this child away and never see him again. She refused, and they demanded that he marry her or else. He decided that he liked living and went on to marry her, to the disdain of his mother back home in Louisiana. She did not attend the ceremony. Shortly after they wed, Edina miscarried, but they remained married. She was never able to conceive again.

Edina introduced John to Bernie. Her family owned a delicatessen in Brooklyn, and Bernie's family owned a small grocery store, Banks Grocers, in Brooklyn just a block from the deli. Edina's family would frequent the store for sup-plies, and the two families became good friends. Edina had been a very young girl when Bernie, who was in his twen-ties, worked as a stock boy and kept the store clean. Bernie's family hoped that, if the business became successful enough, they would be able to expand into other areas. Bernie was training to take over the family business, but he had no real interest in managing a chain of grocery stores. The lifestyle of a store manager was not flashy enough for him. When his grandfather, who owned the Banks grocery store, passed away suddenly, and his grandmother became too ill to run the business, she officially turned it over to Bernie, as she felt confident that he could handle the store. Bernie had other ideas as to which direction he wanted to go, and he decided that he wanted to be just like the men who wheel and deal on Wall Street. He decided to start an investment business in which he would take money, put it in the stock market for other people, and do all of the work for a cut. At the time, the market was still recovering from the crash in the 1930s. It eventually stabilized, so more affluent people were willing to invest in their futures by the 1950s and early 1960s. To start this business, Bernie decided to sell the store, much to the dismay of his grandmother and other family members, who felt that the family had invested too much time and just give it up. The selling of Banks Grocers caused so much discord between Bernie and his family that the stress caused his grandmother to have a stroke. He did take care of her financially until she passed away.

When Bernie moved away for a time after selling the store to a community investor, his and Edina's families did not see each other. The two reunited when they ran into each other at a social event. Edina informed Bernie, much to his dismay, that the old building that once housed the Banks grocery store had been torn down and replaced by a residential building. This was the only time that Bernie felt some guilt over his decision to branch out on his own. He decided to make sure that he worked hard enough that his own business would succeed, as his grandfather had with the store. Edina asked Bernie if he had any connections that could offer John employment as he was just living on her wealth with no direction. She had risked her reputation for him, and she felt that he needed to pull his weight. Bernie had just opened Chimera, and he offered to pay John for his help. Bernie felt that John's look would appeal to a broad range of nonwhite people in New York and could garner him some business, his looks were non-threatening. Bernie hired him as a favor to Edina's family. John and Bernie forged a father-and-son-like relationship as John's ability to appeal to people made him popular, and he became a star in the company. Bernie appreciated that John's popularity resulted in lots of money for the business, so much that they were able to set up shop in Midtown Manhattan, a prime but expensive location.

John spent many hours and days at Chimera as an escape from his home life with Edina. Despite public appearances, John and Edina had marital difficulties. She mourned her inability to conceive and wanted John to show more sympathy for her struggle. John cared for his wife, and he tried his best to show it, but on the inside, he was unhappy; he felt trapped. He never intended his relationship with Edina to go past one night, but because she seemed so enamored with him, had money, and became pregnant (and because her family threatened his life), he stayed with her. This gave Edina a sense of power over John, and she often reminded him of how much he should appreciate her. To win his affection, she often showered him with gifts. One particular gift was a high-powered camera. As a kid, John had loved art and photos. He had wanted to be a newspaper photographer but had never fully pursued it. John would take pictures of things he felt could double as wall art. He also enjoyed wine. Introduced to it growing up in New Orleans, he had drunk a little on occasion, but he developed a taste for expensive wines once he married Edina and had access to better quality bottles. John wanted to start his own wine business, as he had developed a passion and a small collection of various wines. He wanted to stand out and have his signature flavor, but he had been unable to produce one.

John let out his frustrations about his home life in the form of extramarital affairs. He went after and had sex with any attractive woman within reason that would let him indulge. His job allowed him plenty of opportunities to meet numerous women, many of them homemakers who were home during the times he would visit. Because John was a handsome man, many women took him up on his offer of his dick for their business. John laid his hat in many places. Women were crazy about John. Part of the reason was his charm. He was rather affectionate when he felt at ease with a person. John made sure to be careful each time he had a fling with a woman. He had mastered burning the candle at both ends. No feelings, and he would not do anything that would make her attached to him. He did not have these rules out of respect for his union; he did not want another Edina.

One was enough, and if he could get out of the marriage without things going south for him quickly, he would. At the time, society still considered their marriage taboo and frowned upon it. They would not make everyday public appearances like regular couples. That meant there were no trips to the park, movies, or even extra hand holding in public. He feared verbal and physical attacks, especially after the incident where someone smashed their car window and left a note. They suspected that it had been Edina's ex-boyfriend, whom she left for John. Her ex-boyfriend did not take the split very well. Someone looked through a cracked window and saw John and Edina having sex the night they met, and the person recognized Edina. Word got back to her boyfriend and the neighborhood, and the threats began. All of this stayed with John, and he would admit to friends that despite many years of marriage, he had never been in love. He considered himself immune to real feelings.

When their shouting matches got out of control, John would leave altogether for a few days or weeks at a time. John leased a small apartment in a luxury high-rise on East Eighty-Third, which was cab distance to the office. He found more dignity in sleeping in his separate space than he could get spending time on a couch at home. He forbade Edina from stepping foot in the apartment. He would only return to the marital home when she begged, or they had to make social appearances as a couple.

None of the small issues with the men's personal lives prevented the success of Chimera, which was duly noted by the Ambrosino family. The Ambrosino family felt that Chimera was encroaching on their territory and needed to be kept at bay, as the competition for funds and customers in the city and outlying areas was cutthroat. The Ambrosino family did not like the idea of a group of people they considered mongrels (because of their multicultural makeup) outshining or outselling them in any manner and dividing the profits. Therefore, Chimera was not officially included as part of the Commission. The two groups often exchanged verbal jabs, which became heated at times. Members of the Ambrosino family would taunt Chimera and call them faux gangsters. John, as the mouthpiece of the group, would inform them that the Ambrosinos were no threat and that Chimera was the real deal. They would do the threatening. Except for when one person from either group stepped out of bounds, then it turned violent. Until then the rivalry mostly stayed verbal.

There were very few conflicts within Chimera. Bernie wanted to keep in tradition with the other five families of New York. Chimera was the unofficial sixth family. Before John, Jerome, and Ben became official members, Bernie introduced each of them in a ceremonial swearing in. John was the first, so his swearing in placed him at the top of the three under Bernie. This made John the official underboss of Chimera. Bernie pricked John's finger and dripped his blood onto a photo of the Catholic Saint John. Bernie then set the picture on fire while John held it. Bernie made John repeat, "I will burn like him if I betray my family." John had to repeat this until he could not hold the paper any longer. The photo continued to burn until it turned into ash. If John betrayed anyone in the family, he would burn like the Saint Bernie had set on fire. When the fire burned out, John took the ashes and rubbed them against his skin. Bernie repeated this ceremony with Ben, with John present. Bernie used a photo of St. Benedict. For Jerome's swearing in, with John and Ben present, Bernie used a picture of Saint Martin de Porres. Bernie made sure the Saints were particular to the men he was swearing in. When the ceremony ended each time, Bernie would tell the new member to be at ease. Bernie considered the three men his sons. He never had children of his own, so he felt the need to keep these men on the right track. They were his legacy and a reflection of all of his hard work. Swearing them in kept things in order. That meant Chimera became their number one priority. They were on call at all hours and would be busy for now on. Whatever each man earned, they earned for everyone. No one was allowed to walk away from Chimera. The only way out of the family was death.

Bookkeeping was always an issue in the company. There was a book for show and a book with real numbers, which Bernie kept to himself. They showed the first book to customers who demanded to see the progress of their investments. John, Jerome, and Ben had copies of this book. Bernie tried his best to make sure the numbers in it made sense. Although the other three knew the majority of the company's workings, Bernie did not divulge all the details, as he felt that some things needed to be secret. He reserved that information for the brain of the operation. Expenses from the business ran high, and often they had to dip into the contributions that clients made, especially during slow periods in the economy. When clients demanded payment, the company paid from this pot. When they ran short on occasion, Bernie went into the gambling profits. He wanted to keep from dipping into the gambling pot as much as possible. For that reason, he asked the guys to push investors not to withdraw their money early. This gave the business time to bring in new customers and new funds to keep the cycle going. This plan worked for years with very few mishaps. Then for some reason, Bernie miscalculated one customer's payback from a gambling bet, and unfortunately, one of his guys paid the price.

Chapter 2

*T*he daily routine starts. Get out the measuring tape and make
sure everything is still the same as it was yesterday. Thirty-six
by twenty-three by thirty-six. Yes, it is still the same despite that
meal from the night before. Tail fluffed ears tidy, and glossy yel-
low bunny uniform sharp. There will be no demerits today. Celia
Jones was ready for another night at work in the Playboy
Club Manhattan. Celia was a beautiful five-foot-three fire-
cracker. Celia has curves in the right places that turn heads
wherever she walks. Her hair always coiffed to perfection.
Sometimes she wore it flipped and other times she wore it
curly. It all depended on her mood for the day. Many people
had described her look as a brown-skinned, brown-eyed version of young Elizabeth Taylor.

East Fifty-Ninth Street was just as jumping as the rest
of the city, but the opening of the Playboy Club made it

more attractive. The club employed a variety of bunnies. You could pick your flavor. If you loved strawberries, they had a few redheads; if you liked vanilla, there were plenty of blondes and brunettes. If you were into chocolate, however, your options were limited to just two women. Celia was one of the two at the club and one of the most sought after women due to her exotic looks and great personality. Celia found working at the club brought excitement into her life. The atmosphere provided socialization and great music, which she loved because she was also an aspiring musician.

The club enforced strict rules. A bunny was there to look beautiful and serve. She could not fraternize with "keyholders" or any other employees. The keyholders were the clients who frequented the club. Only those who were connected or invited earned a key. The members were mostly men who went to the club for the environment, drinks, and eye candy. Interactions between the bunnies and keyholders are restricted to the drink and meal orders. Members could only identify bunnies by their nametags, except for Celia. They often referred to her as the "chocolate" bunny or "the black one." Celia and the other black bunny had different shifts, so they rarely interacted. For safety reasons, the club did not permit bunnies to give their last name, home address, or phone number to keyholders. The club rewarded Celia with bonuses for her attention to the rules and willingness to work extra hours. Following the rules was not an easy feat for Celia, especially given the attention her looks alone received.

A prominent black doctor from Harlem named Dr. C. Smith, frequented the establishment. People in the city knew him as a brilliant and respected surgeon, the doctor of many well-connected people in Manhattan, despite his race. Even with his success, he did not have much luck in the dating world. His career as a doctor did not help him because he was very unattractive physically, and the women he wanted did not see him as a suitable partner despite his wealth and reputation. He had many dates, but the women could not stand more than one night with him. Much like the other patrons, Dr. Smith went to the Playboy Club mostly to drink and look at the women. He had small hopes of meeting a woman who would find him good enough to marry. He did not socialize much with the other keyholders because, despite his status, he was still considered to be an outsider during nonwork hours. He was dark brown and overweight, and he was holding on for dear life to the last two hairs left in the middle of his head. He had a protruding belly and gap in his teeth so wide that you could kick a football between them. His teeth were clean but distracting.

He had a nice disposition, and he would passively offer small talk to Celia. She knew that he was flirting with her. He thought Celia was beautiful, but she kept it professional, as the rules told her to do. Celia was not above breaking the rules, but despite the plethora of wealth and celebrity at her workplace daily, she never caved into pressure from any the keyholders. Some other bunnies took the opportunity to find themselves a husband and were promptly dismissed for doing so once they succeeded. Dr. Smith did not tempt Celia. She was not attracted to him. She never thought of herself as being shallow, but she had her limits. If she caved into him simply because of his money, or because of his friendly personality, she knew that she would be miserable. She would never sleep with a man like this. She also felt that Dr. Smith spent too much time at the club, as doctors were supposed to be on call at all hours. How good could he be if he was always drinking? He always excused his presence in the club by saying he had his practice and could be flexible. Celia told the other bunnies about this man and asked that if he got too flirty with her, one of them would go over and make a distraction so she could walk away. The bunnies looked out for one another, as most of them had problems with unwanted advances from a few overzealous keyholders. This way the environment stayed professional and keyholders did not violate the rules except in extreme cases. Celia often tag-teamed with Rose, a fellow bunny who wore the pink uniform. Rose was also her roommate.

Rose was also an aspiring musician who worked at the Playboy Club. She parted her straight, blond hair down the middle, had blue eyes, and was of average height. She was quite ordinary looking but became more attractive once she put on makeup and the bunny suit. Rose and Celia hit it off when they met each other in the bunny dressing rooms and began discussing their plans for the future. When they met, both women were looking for their apartments. They became such close friends that they decided to live together.

They settled in an apartment on East Sixty-Second Street. The place was ideal because of its proximity to the club and location in the Midtown. They agreed to split the rent fifty-fifty, as both of them could afford it. Both Celia and Rose planned to attend Juilliard School, as they both considered themselves talented musicians. Celia was a trained pianist, taught by her mother, who was the organ player in the family church in Harlem as well as a teacher to some of the parishioners. Celia wanted to be just like her mother but on a bigger scale. She wanted to be the first black internationally known classical piano player, and when she could not do that anymore, she wanted to teach kids how to play instruments. Rose played the violin. She did not have as much training as Celia; she only began playing the violin in high school. Both of them were waiting to hear whether they would receive scholarships to Juilliard as they both submitted materials to admissions. The competition was incredibly fierce; Juilliard had applicants from all over the world.

Both Celia and Rose came from working-class families. While Rose had two active parents, Celia was raised mostly by her mother. Her father went in and out of her life because her parents divorced and he started a new family when Celia was just five years old. He went on to have four other children, with whom Celia never had much contact. The two mothers did not get along, as her father had had an affair with his new wife while still married to Celia's mother. Her mother, Agnes, found solace in church after the divorce, and some days Celia would go straight to the sanctuary from school. Some of her other local family also attended the same church. She spent a lot of time with church friends and cousins as a child and into her teen-age years. Celia began playing the piano after watching her mother do so and seeing other people enjoy her music. Celia's mother became injured at her day job and had to go on disability months before Celia graduated from high school. Agnes did not stay immobile, but her injury lim-ited her work options. She took a permanent role as church staff but on a part-time basis. The pay was barely above welfare wages. Agnes told Celia, "Do not worry; life is not supposed to be easy. It will challenge you. You can meet a man who you think will be your future, and God will let you know that he has other plans for you, better plans. Don't you worry, child, I'm gonna be fine."

Because Agnes's income was limited, Celia decided to put off college and get a job to help her out until things got better for the both of them. The Playboy Club was not her first choice. Celia worked as a clerk at a steel company be-fore hearing about the openings for the new Playboy Club in Manhattan, which was paying more than she was earning at the time while answering phones. She figured that she was in shape and felt pretty enough to try out. The club hired her on the spot. Celia never told her mother about the job. The family would disapprove. Her mother and family still thought she worked as a secretary at a shipping company and was working toward her degree because that was all the in-formation she gave them.

John frequented the bars and areas around town at night as a way to escape the stress of home life, work, and the struggle to bring in new business and to scout new recruits. He felt he could easily approach the best workers while they were helpless, intoxicated, and out of options. He was not concerned with how long he spent at the bar because he and Edina were fighting again. He was sleeping in his backup apartment away from their marital home. This often happened, as he would make her mad (sometimes on purpose) when she got on his nerves, and she would demand that he leave. Fights are an ongoing cycle between the two, so John became a staple around the city. He had a good rep with bars around most of the city's hotspots because he tipped well. He tipped the bartenders with money; they tipped him with women to take back to his apartment. His favorite bar was a small club called P. J. Clarke's on East Fifty-Fifth. He frequented that bar the most because it had a great atmosphere and a beautiful variety of female customers.

John did not become intoxicated often, but when he did, he always managed to make it home without incident, until that night. While at the bar, John briefly noticed a man staring at him disapprovingly in the back, but he looked away because he did not know the man. He thought nothing of it and continued to socialize. John flirted with the women as usual and attempted to pick up a leggy brunette woman, but she decided not to take him up on his offer. Women did not reject John very often. This night, John struck out and decided to go back to the apartment, as it was close to midnight, and he wanted to get some sleep before the next day. He had plans that he wanted to start back at the office. As he waited outside the bar for a cab, he stood alone. No cabs picked him up although he waited for twenty minutes. Many of them passed him but did not stop. He decided to walk down a few blocks to a busier spot so he could get a ride home. He made it to Sixty-Second Street before he jumped by a man.

"Where's my money, motherfucker?" the person yelled at John while pushing him from behind. John turned around and noticed immediately that this was the same guy from the bar. John had never been good with names, but his photographic memory was immaculate. John had never seen the man except for that brief glance, and he did not know what money the man was demanding. The guy was not one of his clients, but the attacker knew who John was. The assailant told John that his people owed him money, and he wanted his payment immediately. John assured the person that he had no details of the transaction. The attacker was one of those people who dealt with Bernie and Ben directly, and they never discussed him with John or anyone else in the group. He was one of the jurors whom Bernie had promised to pay off to keep Ben out of prison. Bernie kept the identities of top clientele secret from the other men. He did so for their protection because these clients dealt directly with law enforcement, the courts, and specific cases. Bernie would buy out jurors as favors for some of his friends and clients if necessary. He did this for a small fee. Somehow, the client that was involved in Ben's case knew about everyone else at Chimera. Ben was supposed to mail this man a check for his services, but he never got around to doing it. The man had been waiting months for his payment and had begun threatening Chimera about going to the police with the jury tampering, even if it got him in trouble.

The attacker punched John, and John hit him in the back. The attacker picked up a brick that was in the street and hit John in the head with it, knocking him to the ground. When John's intoxication kept him from getting up quickly enough, the attacker began kicking and punching him some more. John had never felt scared before, but he was worried that for the first time, he was losing a fight, and the consequences of this loss would be dangerous for him, he could die right there on the ground. A few people on the street were watching the bout, but they did not stop; they did not want to be involved.

After a busy night at the club, where she had to fight off yet another round of awkward flirting from Dr. Smith and others, Celia decided to walk home with Rose, which was something they often did to look out for each other. On their way home, they both heard a commotion in the street, which was not uncommon at the time. The neighborhood they lived in was not posh but middle class. The area was not immune to some of the street violence that occurred in Manhattan. The girls knew that they were taking risks by walking home at that time of night, and they sometimes took cabs if they were alone, even if it was just a few blocks.

As they walked closer to their front stoop, they stumbled upon two men fighting, with one clearly winning. One of the men was kicking the other one while he was down on the ground. When the kicker noticed Celia and Rose walking close to them, he took off and left the other man lying in the street moaning in agony and covered in blood. Celia wanted to go over to the man to see if he was OK. Rose, who was apprehensive, attempted to discourage Celia from walking too close to him, as they did not know why the men had been fighting. As far as Rose was concerned, they could have been gangbangers or robbers. Rose wanted to go in and call the cops instead. Celia walked over and knelt next to the mysterious bloody man. She told Rose to stop being mean and to get an ambulance to help him. Rose did so but kept an eye on Celia from the window while on the phone.

As Celia knelt over him, the man tilted his head over, looked at Celia, and gave an approving smirk—the same smirk he always gave when he saw an attractive woman. A broken nose, busted lip, bloody face, excruciating pain and some cracked ribs did not stop him from trying to pick up a woman. His never turned off his chick radar. He complimented her beauty, as she still had on her makeup from the club, sans the bunny ears. He could not see the rest of her body because she was wearing a closed trench coat and kitten heels. Because of her positioning under the streetlight, Celia had perfect lighting, making her easier to see with his squinty, injured eyes. Celia reassured the man that help was on the way and that she would be there for him until the paramedics arrived. As he was asking for her name, the sirens blasted loudly and help finally arrived. The police and first responders asked for Celia's identification, and she informed them that she did not know this man, but she stayed to help when she saw him in distress. When the police officer looked at John, he immediately noticed who the man was and told him that everything would be OK; he would take care of everything. The officer thanked her for her help and reassured her that the injuries did not seem life-threatening upon initial inspection. If she called the hospital later on, they would update her on his condition. She never got the mystery man's name, and he never got hers. Once they put him in the ambulance and drove away, Celia walked to her apartment with a sense of accomplishment. She did not check on the man, as she did not know which hospital they sent him. She just hoped for the best and moved on.

A few weeks later, John returned to work after a brief hospital stay and temporarily moved back to the marital home. He needed Edina to take care of him and cook him meals, as he was not able to do so himself while he healed. He could have taken more time off, but he did not want to spend another twenty-four hours straight with his wife, as she was beginning to push him for sex and attention. He was not into it but partook in it to keep the meals coming and to keep some peace in the home until he healed. He did so because he needed a release and it had been some time since he had been with any woman. John was vulnerable, and Edina took full advantage of him. John told her that random thugs robbed him, even though he knew that Bernie and Ben had caused the attack by maintaining poor bookkeeping and defaulting on a payment. Bernie and Ben shared responsibility for the funds in the company. Bernie had the most power in monitoring how funds were distributed. Ben kept the books for tax purposes and made sure that the numbers added up correctly and that people were compensated for their work. He was the pseudo accountant.

John's incident was one of the very few times he found himself in trouble while working for Chimera. Each time something happened, this being the worst, he would take a lesson from it. This quality made him stand out from the rest. John was determined never again to be caught in a compromising manner. This incident would be one of the last times it happened to him. While John was on hiatus, Bernie, Jerome, and Ben had been keeping Chimera afloat. They eventually paid the man who jumped John, but not before Jerome and Ben returned his beating to him twofold. After that, Bernie, Jerome, and Ben kindly asked him to leave the city with his money and life. The man complied. If one of the four cores of Chimera was hurt, they all went in to defend his honor. John was often the one fighting for the others, whom he considered his brothers, even Ben. This time, they stepped in to help John.

Bernie had friends in high places, and that included Hugh Hefner. Mr. Hefner wanted Bernie and his crew to come by and check out the happening Midtown location of his Playboy Club, which had become the spot in the city to be seen if you were a high roller and big name. Bernie had been too distracted with work and the issues with John to take advantage of the offer, but he decided to do so after the management also offered him, John, Jerome, and Ben keys to the club and their bottled table. Bernie felt that a trip and membership to the club would boost morale in the group. Bernie offered John the first key as a reward for his troubles, and John decided to go for a preview before everyone else.

John was ready to find a new bar home. He felt that if something went terribly wrong in his life, he should cut all ties with everything associated with it within reason. He felt that Clarke's was tainted. He did not know whether other bar patrons had it out for him and the group. He was 80 percent healed from his injuries and was ready to get back out there and mingle. He was not prepared to start sleeping with women just yet, but his eyes worked just fine. The Playboy Club appealed to him since it had every type of woman he liked under one roof. The place was full of eye candy, and he could not resist.

After John had checked in, he was seated at a table set aside just for Chimera's arrival. The bunnies added his name to the members-in-attendance wall for the very first time. The wall had each member's name or company engraved on a sliding card, prominently displayed so everyone could view who was in the crowd for the evening. All of the bunnies' colorful suits overwhelmed him, and immediately his spirits rose. The club was buzzing that night, as they had a special musical guest. Tom Jones, a tall, handsome, and young Welsh crooner was at the club, and he agreed to sing one song with his band. The bunnies were excited to see and meet Tom Jones, as many of them were new fans of his. As Hugh Hefner took the stage to announce Tom's performance, the crowd became excited, and the Bunnies and patrons hit the floor to dance. Tom's band started playing the music and singing "Chills and Fever," to the delight of the crowd of bunnies and patrons doing the twist, watusi, and boogaloo.

Instead of getting up, John decided to sit back and enjoy his drink and take in the excitement as he would if he were at his old spot. The Playboy Club was just a short distance away from Clarke's. As Tom Jones crooned, he noticed the face of one of the bunnies that were dancing provocatively with other bunnies on the dance floor. John could not take his eyes off her; as the only brown bunny there that night, she stood out. With his immaculate facial recognition, he remembered her after only a few seconds. The mystery bunny with the lovely face was the same woman who had saved his life on the street just two months before. "Well, I'll be damned; it's her," He smirked his signature expression, in which one side of his smile went up higher than the other. He had used that same smirk when he first saw her, and it returned as he lit up like a lightbulb. His eyes scanned every curve of her body as she danced and shook her ample chest and fluffy tail. For the first time, his heart skipped a beat. He watched her as the song ended and the crowd offered a thunderous applause. She went back over to the bar to pick up drink orders, including his.

When Celia made it to John's table, she greeted him as she would any other keyholder—professionally. She did not recognize him, as his face had mostly healed from his injuries and it was no longer covered in blood. She did make a mental note of how tall and handsome he was. Celia had always had a thing for tall, athletic, full-lipped, tan-colored men. John looked at her with a grin that turned up at the left corner of his mouth. She found him sexy and gorgeous. *He could be one of the New York Knicks*, she thought. She couldn't show him her thoughts. She had to remain professional.

"You're a bunny," he said to her. Celia made note of his accent, which had a drawl to it.

"Yes. What gave it away?" she asked in a sweet but "OK, Captain Obvious" way.

"So you work here, and you save lives. That's impressive," John told her.

Celia did not immediately recognize what he was saying. "Well, yes, I guess you can say that we bring life to people while they are here." John continued smirking and stood up to extend his hand to kiss hers and formally introduce himself. He towered over her, all six feet two inches of him. Celia only stood about five feet five inches in midsize heels. She was a petite but shapely woman. Celia reluctantly extended her hand to him, as touching keyholders were restricted; she hoped that no one noticed the exchange.

"I'm sorry if I seem apprehensive. It's just that it's against the rules to physically touch keyholders. I don't want to get in trouble, and someone is always watching," Celia told John. He understood.

He told her, "I just wanted to extend my gratitude and say thank you for saving my life in the street a while ago." Celia stood there in shock, as she didn't realize that the man at the table was the same guy from the street.

"My goodness, you're OK, and you look different," she told him. "I'm happy that you're OK, and you look well."

"Can we go somewhere and talk?" he asked her.

"I can't. I'm on duty, and you are a keyholder, and if I'm caught, I can get fired. I can't afford to do that."

"I understand," John told her. "How about a round of pool?" he asked while pointing over to an empty pool table.

"OK, that's safe," she told him. Bunnies did not physically touch keyholders but were allowed routine activities such as dancing (with distance) and playing pool.

"My name is John, and yours?" he said.

"I'm Bunny Celia," she replied as she pointed to her ribbon lapel pinned to the upper thigh on her uniform. They went over to play a couple of rounds of pool. John was determined to get to know her better, as he found her innocence exquisite. This situation differed from any other pickup he had with various women, as the circumstances this time were extraordinary. This woman had a naive innocence he was not accustomed to. He felt that encounters like these happened for a reason. He was incredibly sexually attracted to her, but he also loved her spunk and discipline, a quality he had been trained to look for when recruiting for Chimera. After some small talk and a couple of games of pool, during which some others watched them play, they ended their encounter, and she soon returned to the bar to continue serving the other guests.

John took a pen, wrote on the napkin under his drink, and flirtatiously made her promise to call him. He told her that he would patiently wait for her call. He scribbled on the napkin, "You make me smile.—John L." Below that, he wrote his number. She picked up the big, empty wineglass, folded the napkin, and placed it in her bustier. Celia, for the first time, while working at the club, was tempted to break the rules. A man like that did not come along too often.

Chapter 3

Feeling good about himself, John returned to full work at Chimera. He had a new zest in his step while out on the field. He did not seem as aggressive. Like clockwork, John left the marital home again to go back to his apartment. He told Edina that he needed space for the time being. A blow-out between the two usually preceded such revelations. He paid the door attendants at the building to keep a watchful eye and make sure that Edina did not show up uninvited. He considered it his only sanctuary, his man cave, and the one place he could call his own without having to share.

Seeing Celia in the club gave him a spark. For the first time in his life, he had a real crush on a woman. They went on several dates and spent time at his apartment. Celia agreed to meet up with him, but only on the condition that he would keep the meetings discreet. If other bunnies or her shift manager caught her, she could be in a lot of trouble at work. She kept stressing this point. She felt that the risk was worth it, as she was also developing a crush on John. John was breaking his non-attachment rules when it came to Celia. He was different from the rest. Although he was attracted to her, for a number of reasons he did not want to rush into bed with her. Celia and John went out on dates that were either on the outskirts of the city or in the suburbs to keep their relationship quiet. He knew that Celia wanted to see some Broadway shows, and they did watch a couple of them to her delight. They saw the play *The Boys in the Band* because Celia thought it was music related. She appreciated the consideration and care that John paid to her situation. These were qualities that Celia wanted in a man, right along with him being incredibly handsome looking.

The two never had full intercourse while they dated, which was a rarity for John. He was still healing from the attack and did not feel confident in his stamina. He did not want his back or ribs to give out in the middle of the act, as his sexual interactions were a source of pride for him. He wanted to heal fully first, which meant John had to use that time actually to get to know her. This was something he had never considered before, not even with his wife of ten years. His penis needed a time-out, as it had been overworked in the last year, and he did not want to risk embarrassment from a poor performance. When Celia visited his apartment, she observed some of the photographic work he had on the walls. When he was bored, he took photos of landmarks, nature, and sites around the city. He used his walls as his personal art gallery. When Celia came over, he pulled out his camera and had her pose for photos. He looked at her as his muse and told her that she inspired him. He converted a spare bedroom into a darkroom to develop his pictures.

John also had a mini wine rack, in which he kept his most expensive wines. He rarely touched that stand except when he felt truly frustrated and needed to reward himself. The wine rack also attached to an elaborate floor console radio and a record player that he'd had custom built. It was about seven feet wide, and he'd had to install it in pieces. The speakers lit up like equalizers as the music played. He used it to entertain guests, mostly women when they visited. He had an impressive record collection. He would pick songs that set the mood, and when Celia visited, it was no different.

"You are very talented. I would have never guessed. You don't meet a lot of business guys who are good at creating art. They just buy theirs instead. The ones who are cultured are ones you meet at the museums," Celia said to John while browsing his walls.

"Been doing this since I was a kid. I like it," John responded.

"Ever thought of selling any of these pieces?" she asked.

"No. Well, unless I have to. It classes up the place."

"And your taste in music...that's also surprising," she said as she listened to the Jamaican jazz record John put on his system.

"I got it like that. Sit," he responded while directing his hand toward his sofa. Celia and John sat on the couch in front of his television to watch Bonanza, but they did not look at the show. The sound in the background served as mood music. They talked, which was something they ended up doing a lot.

"I play the piano," Celia told him. "My mother played in the church, and I watched her. I looked at her fingers as she played, associated the keys with the sound, and was able to remember it that way. Then she started teaching me the basics. I thought it was just nice to know an instrument because I thought it made me stand out from the other kids."

"Do you still play?" he asked.

"Yes, but on occasion. They have a piano at the club, and on off hours, when it isn't open, I take requests from the girls and play a few songs. It's my way of practicing free. I can say that I am pretty good at it, but I don't brag. I submitted a tape for admission to Juilliard. I'm hoping to get in. Rose, my roommate, also sent in her tape, but she plays something different, the violin. The problem is that I can't pay for it. It's expensive," she said. "Too much of my money is divided into other places. When I can save enough, I will get me one of those new portable piano players so that I can practice at home."

"Will you play for me one day?" John asked.

"I will, I promise," she said.

"The money thing, I understand you on that. I have that problem too," he added.

"I want to be the first black female classical pianist headliner at the new Lincoln Center. That would be big," she added.

"Oh, I get that. I wish you luck," John responded. "Lemme ask you this. Why on earth is a lady like you still single?" he asked her.

"Guys flirt, but I don't respond to them. Most of them are jerks," she said.

"Yeah, a lot of us are." John grinned. "You have never met anyone that you even considered going out with?"

"No," she said. "Well, there was this one guy, a doctor who goes to the club a lot. I don't like him, but he sent me a dozen long-stem roses. I didn't want him to think he had a real chance with me, so I told them to send those roses right back to him."

"Oh, damn, that's brutal," he said. "That's it?"

"Because I work all the time. It's hard to meet people when you have to work all the time. I work at a place that I can't even touch the clientele, not even small talk," she said.

"But you are touching me."

"Well, OK, you got a point. This is different. I didn't meet you in the club. I met you on the street," she responded flirtatiously. "I don't pick up street people, so don't get that idea from me. I like helping others," she added.

John grinned. "I'm your first street person."

Celia inquired about why someone was beating him up in the street. He gave her the same explanation he had given his wife, saying that he had been robbed. He told her that the police caught the man and that everything was taken care of, much to Celia's relief.

"I'm gonna say, I remember you clearly from that night, but man, I saw you in the club and thought you were the finest thing I've ever seen," he told her. "That costume looks beautiful on you. Everybody had the same thing, but you stood out. Can I call you Bunny? You don't mind if I call you Bunny?" Celia asked him why he did not want to call her by her real name. He told her that he liked the endearment. It was the first thing he thought of when he saw her. It made him feel good on the inside. He assured her that he meant no disrespect when he said it.

"That's the sweetest thing. Thank you, and yes, you can call me Bunny. I see you like that," she replied. Celia thought the name was cute. It stuck, so she accepted it, and he called her Bunny from then on. "Now my turn," she said.

"Uh-oh," he replied, anticipating something he was not quite ready for.

"Now, why are you by yourself? Why hasn't a lady tied you down by now?" she asked.

John paused. The silence was on the verge of becoming awkward, but he started talking. "It's complicated. There are a lot of things going on that I can't even explain myself. I don't know why I am even in this situation or how I got here in the first place. I know where I want to go now." John quickly changed the subject and kissed her.

"I have to go to work in the morning, so I can't stay here all night," Bunny told him.

"Why not? I'll make sure you get there," he responded.

"I can't. But you can dream of me," she told him.

"You mean that?" he asked.

"I do," Bunny answered. She got up and dialed a taxi. They both went down to the lobby of his building. When the taxi arrived, she went to give him a peck. "If you do dream of me, remember, I like it rough," she said as she sashayed to the door. She got in the cab, and it drove off. John stood there and stared at her, feeling an intoxicating tactile euphoria in his whole body. His eyes lit up, and the corner of his mouth turned up again. The surprise of little, innocent Bunny having a dirty mouth gave him dirty thoughts.

The next day, John went on about his routine activities in anticipation of his daily phone call from Bunny, among other things. He knew that if she did not call him, he would have the opportunity to see her again at the club, so he never worried. John thanked Bernie for the key to the club. He raved about the atmosphere and recommended highly that the rest of the guys go and visit as soon as possible. Bernie seemed pleased that John had enjoyed the experience, as he had hoped it would boost his spirits. A successful leader was a leader who brought in lots of money. John finished the day at work seemingly pleased with his productivity. When he went back to his apartment for the night, he retired in front of the television. The phone often rang. Most times, on the other line, was Bunny, much to John's delight.

When John felt comfortable enough to start talking, he told Jerome and Ben about the new club and informed them that they now had keys to it. He mentioned that one of the women who worked at the club was the hero who had saved him on the street. He said they had to see her, as she was a beautiful woman. Jerome had never heard John rave on about an encounter with a female, as they both had rules about attachment, especially John, being a married man. The other two guys kept his indiscretions a secret and did not ever rat him out because many men at that time had side encounters with women. Once Jerome and Ben learned about their new status at the club, they were excited to see the girls. Bernie and the crew decided to take their brand-new membership keys for a spin at the Playboy Club as a company and check out the atmosphere that John raved about so much. They were curious about the fuss, and they wanted to get a glimpse of this new girl that John praised.

Once they arrived at the club and were seated by the hostess, good music, good drinks, and beautiful women, were happening. John spotted Bunny and discreetly pointed her out to the other three guys. She was once again in the middle of brushing off Dr. Smith's advances. She broke away and walked over to take drink orders from the guys at Chimera's table. When she came over, John introduced her. Jerome immediately recognized her and exclaimed, "Ce Ce!" Bunny returned the greeting, much to John's confusion.

"You know each other?" John asked in a nervous tone.

"Yeah, this is Ce Ce, my cousin. I didn't know she worked here," Jerome answered as he looked at her. Bunny looked like she had been caught with her hand in the cookie jar.

"So you guys are related. That's cool," John replied in a relaxed tone.

"Her mother is my aunt," Jerome said. He went on to introduce her to Ben and Bernie, and they greeted her.

"Small world, isn't it?" Ben said as he picked up his water and drank some of it. "You are beautiful looking," Ben added, but he did not think much else about it. His eyes focused on the blondes in the room. Bunny went on to take their drink orders before going over to the bar to have them made and picked up. Dr. Smith looked at her as she went but did not say a word to her.

"Hey, man, we need to talk," Jerome told John as they sat at the booth. John did not know for sure what this was about, but he presumed that it was about Bunny and agreed to speak to him. They both went outside to talk. Although Jerome knew of John's extramarital affairs and was nonchalant about them, that instantly changed when he learned that John was dating his little cousin. All of a sudden, this activity was unacceptable to him. "Did you ever tell her that you were married? I mean, I've known her since she was little and just can't see her agreeing to that. She is a respectable young lady, even if she works here," he told John.

John told Jerome the truth: that he had not informed her yet. "No, I haven't. I was going to get around to it."

"When?" Jerome looked at him with a doubtful face. "I know you, man," he said matter-of-factly. Jerome then suggested that John inform her that he was indeed a married man and said he should break things off with Celia, out of respect for her. John did not want to do this, as he was now fully aware that he would lose Bunny if he did so. He reluctantly agreed out of respect for Jerome and her feelings, as he now cared for her.

This development ruined John's evening. He went home right after the conversation, much to Bunny's confusion. She wondered why he did not stick around with his coworkers at the club. She sensed that something was wrong and called him as soon as she made it back home for the evening.

Bunny had the next day off, as one of two floating days she had off during the week. She reserved one of those days for visiting her mother in Harlem, and the other she took off to get errands done, relax, soak her feet in Epsom salt, and elevate them. Working in heels for many hours took a toll on her feet. Bunny and John agreed to meet each other and have a talk, which he initiated. He took her out for a meal, drove her around in his drop-top Chevelle Twin Turbo 540, bought her flowers, and took her to Central Park for a stroll. Today was a good day for them because he enjoyed her company and she loved that a good-looking man was courting her. Their encounters had entered the double digits by now. They sat down on a park bench and started to talk. He reluctantly and slowly began to explain his situation.

"I have something to tell you," John told her. It made him sick to his stomach, as he knew what would happen next. He was not looking forward to her reaction or the fact that she would walk away from him.

"What is it? Are you OK?" Bunny asked as she grabbed his hand to comfort him.

"I'm all right," he replied. "I left out some things that I should have informed you about me. I didn't want to tell you because I did not want you to go."

"OK…" she said worriedly.

"Bunny, I am married," he told her. She let go of his hand. She looked at his left hand, the one she had been holding.

"You don't have a ring; I don't see an imprint anywhere. Are you separated? Are you divorcing?" she asked him.

"Not officially," he replied.

Instantly crushed about this news, she asked him, "What am I supposed to do with this information now?"

"I don't want you to go, but I'm stuck," he replied. Bunny had heard enough at this point.

"John, I am not that woman," she told him. She could not help but think back to her childhood, during which her mother had been the wife whose unfaithful husband cheated on her. She did not want to inflict that kind of pain on someone else. "John, I don't wanna share," she said, as tears welled in her eyes. "I want my own, and I thought you were that person. I can't see you anymore." She stood and walked away from him. He tried to keep her there a bit longer, but she walked to the street and hailed a cab back home. John stood and watched as she got in the cab.

After she had ridden off, he went to sit back down on the bench and rested his head in his hands. Today was the first time that John felt real heartbreak. He found it a strange and ominous feeling. He only knew that he did not like the feeling. Bunny did not contact him for the next week despite his many calls. That was their longest period of separation since being reintroduced to each other. The situation put John in a somber mood for the time being and crushed Celia's hopes of finding a real husband. John became somewhat depressed.

Back at Chimera, things were a bit awkward between Jerome and John. They were not fighting or angry at each other, but Bunny had made things between the two even more personal than before. Jerome was perplexed and bothered by the fact that "Ce Ce," as he called her, had decided to take a job at such a risqué club. Not knowing about her dire financial situation, he had assumed that she was already on her way off to college for music, as she had told many of her relatives. He wanted to help her in the same way that he had been helped out of his dire situation before he landed the job at Chimera. He knew that the company needed help with paperwork and the books. Although no women were working there, he thought that she had the skills necessary to handle the job since she once worked in an office environment. Jerome also trusted her. He put a lot of thought into this scenario because of the situation with John. He knew that bringing her into the equation would be risky. Jerome, however, was sure he had made his expectations clear to John when it came to Celia. Jerome knew that the level of respect between them was still intact, and he decided to bring up the idea to John.

Although John was in an emotional slump, he continued to thrive otherwise at work, and Chimera was having a
great month in gains. Jerome decided to pull John aside to
talk to him about the possibility of bringing Celia in to work
for them as their secretary and bookkeeper. "Hear me out.
I know talking about Celia—uh, Bunny—upsets you, but
what would you think if I brought up the idea of her working
here as our bookkeeper?" he said to John.

Stunned, John said, "Are you fucking serious? I don't get
it. So first you tell me to let her go, and then you are going
to just dangle her in front of me." He added, "No."

Jerome replied, "Like I said, hear me out, bro."

"Go on," John responded while sitting back in his chair.

"Bunny works at that club, and to be honest, I do not
like it one bit. The family if they found out about it wouldn't
like it either. It would be a mess. I am going to present her
an opportunity to get out of that environment. That is if
she considers it. I'm going to need you both to make up, as
friends," he said.

"How the hell am I supposed to make that happen, captain? She won't pick up my calls," John responded.

"We will talk to her together. OK, wait, maybe not a
good idea. I'll speak to her," Jerome answered.

"So she doesn't know," John said.

"No, she does not," Jerome answered.

"Great, so not only will she be pissed at me, but now you
are going to have her torturing me on a daily basis," John said.

"If we get her in agreement, we both present this to Bernie to see what he says about it. We have a good argument. We need the help, and we know who she is. If you want to repay her and if you care about her as you say, you will help get her into a better position," Jerome ended.

John later on gave this some more thought, and he concluded that it might be a good idea after all. It would give him an opportunity to get back into good graces with Bunny and to keep an eye on her on an everyday basis while he got the rest of his life situated.

Celia continued her job at the club. She thought that no one knew the extent of her relationship with John except Rose, who kept their secret. Rose was trustworthy, as she was not a saint herself. Bunny had covered for her numerous times when she broke the rules. When Rose first found out the identity of the bloody man in the street, after Celia told her, she thought it was romantic and felt happy for her friend. To her, it sounded like a storybook with a happy ending. Celia used to go on forever about how sweet and romantic John was to her, but Rose would just tell her that the romantic feeling was nothing new; it was more like common sense leaving her body. When Celia told Rose about John's actual marital status, Rose replied that she'd always thought that John was a derelict and that any guy you pick up in the middle of the street at night cannot be right for you. Rose suggested that Celia find a man who is well adjusted and she did not think that John fit that criteria. Celia finally listened to Rose on that matter and realized that her friend was looking out for her. Perhaps she should have just kept walking that night. It would have saved her some heartache.

The usual things happened at the club; Bunny served, smiled, and fought off advances from keyholders. John decided to pay a visit to the club. This time, he brought his camera, the one he'd used to take photos of her before—the same camera his wife Edina gave him as a trap gift. It was a good-quality Polaroid, and he grew quite fond of it because he got great photographs, and it was easy to carry. He spoke with management about getting some photographs of bunnies in the club, and they granted him permission to do so. The club had a resident photographer, but since John and the rest of Chimera were good friends with management, he was able to do so. They gave him strict notice, however, not to resell the photos, and he agreed. Although he told management that he wanted the photographs of different bunnies, he went there for Celia. He wanted to take pictures of her wearing her uniform. He was borderline obsessed with how she looked in it, and he spent the time they were separated looking at the photos he had already taken and developed of her.

Celia spotted him in the club and tried her best to avoid contact with him, as she was still morose about their situation. Another worker went over to Celia to tell her about John's requests. She could not say no to them, as she did not want to seem suspicious. She went over to him, looked at him blankly, and said, "Hi." He greeted her but noted the blank expression on her face.

She acted as if he were a total stranger to her. That was Celia's way of coping. She put on her best smile; she knew that photographs of bunnies were necessary, and she did not want any bad ones of her floating around. She did her best poses until she thought that he was satisfied with what he had.

At John's request, she posed for one last photo with him, having another bunny take the photograph. John's and Bunny's backs were to a wall. He briefly brushed his hand across her behind right under her tail. She gently pushed it off. She wished John a good evening and walked away. The entire evening seemed tense and maladroit to her. She was still mastering the shift in her emotions, and the visit from John did not help matters.

"Wow, that guy likes you," one bunny mentioned to Celia. "He took all those photos of you and no one else."

The meeting with John was not her only awkward encounter of the evening. She was used to the regulars and their occasional awkward exchanges, especially Dr. Smith. When Dr. Smith spoke to her throughout the week, he was his usual self. However, that day he used a different tone with her. It was no longer the polite, flirty, toothy resonance but more direct. He seemed irritated at times, and Celia took note. She did not know what changed with him or why he seemed mad at her, but she did not care. Dr. Smith made a comment to her as she was walking away from him. "I should have brought a camera with me. That would've gotten your undivided attention."

This was a bad night for her, and she was not in the mood to deal with Dr. Smith or anyone else who gave her a hard time. When she got home, she took the time to clean out her pocketbook. During this moment, she ran across the napkin that John had given her with his number and note on it. She'd held on to it as a good-luck charm before, but now she considered tossing it in the wastebasket. She sat and looked at it for a bit and instead folded it up and put it in her wallet. She put it in one of the hidden compartments that is less frequently used so she would not have to see the paper while casually browsing through the wallet.

Celia was ready for the night. She looked forward to her comfortable bed. It was a small bed, but she felt that she had it broken in. It was the same bed she'd had when growing up. She felt that keeping this piece of furniture made her humble. It was big enough for her, as she was a petite woman. The bed also fit the rest of the charming decor of her bedroom, which was modern for the time. She was nearly asleep when her phone rang. She was reluctant to answer it, but she picked up the receiver. It was Jerome. He wanted to talk to her about an offer. Celia was too tired to talk, but she decided to give Jerome a few minutes of her time since he was family. Jerome wanted to discuss possibly getting Celia into Chimera.

The discussion lasted for about an hour and a half, with Celia expectedly blowing her top at the initial suggestion of working with John, the man who had just broken her heart. Jerome put out some good points for her to consider, which included more money that would eventually allow her to go back to school. She would not have to rely on the hopes of scholarship money, which was Celia's main obstacle. The job would also help her get out of that club. The scholarship letter would be arriving any day now, and she and Rose were anticipating receiving acceptance and some financial assistance. Jerome assured her that John would remain professional, that he trusted her, and that the both of them would behave. That offended Celia but Jerome assured her that he was just joking. He made sure to let her know that he had confidence in her and her abilities. He said that she was better than the Playboy Club. She told Jerome that she would think about it but had no immediate plans to leave the club. He told her that he would run it by the boss and see what he said, but he would need an answer soon, as they would be adding another person to the higher-up team.

Jerome informed John that the conversation went OK. He said that she did not agree, but she did not say no, either. John considered that enough, and they both went into Bernie's office the following Tuesday to ask him to open a bookkeeping position for her. Bernie was apprehensive about this. He did not know Celia; he did not know her skills, and his only introduction to her had been at the Playboy Club. He also noted her age and realized she was about a dozen years younger than the youngest person in their group. He thought John and Jerome were out of their goddamn minds at first. Jerome then argued that having someone else keep a watchful eye over the paperwork and numbers would prevent another incident like what happened to John and ensure that funds were in their proper place.

Bernie and Ben did all of the work themselves, and Bernie felt that the load was starting to overload him. He thought Ben needed a second set of eyes. Bernie was getting up there in age, and he wanted to relax more. This would help everyone, and if they were going to have finally a woman on the team, it might as well be someone they knew and trusted, according to Jerome and John. To them, she had already been vetted. They knew that Bernie was considering hiring another person, and this would save a lot of time. Bernie caved in, but not before he expressed more concerns about the change in environment. He told the two he would consider it and asked them to let him know if she wanted it in a couple of weeks.

Finally, the day arrived when the letters from Juilliard would come for Celia and Rose. Both of them had their attention on the mailbox as they awaited the mail carrier. They were excited because those envelopes contained their futures. Both women opened the envelopes together, and the news was great for one and not so great for the other. Rose got a scholarship and acceptance letter. Celia got an acceptance letter but no financial aid. Celia was happy about the opportunity to get in, and she was also happy for Rose. However, she was crushed internally, as she would have to foot the entire bill for tuition. Rose felt awful because that would mean they would have to separate. Rose would move on from the club to concentrate on studies, and Celia would have to find money, get a new roommate in a short time, or move back home with her ailing mother. Celia kept it together as she congratulated Rose and went into decision mode. She had to make some choices in a hurry.

Celia returned to work at the club with the goal of putting in overtime to bring in more money. That now meant six-day work weeks and sometimes twelve hours a day if they let her, to make up the rent money she would lack once Rose left. This would be a challenge for her, but she was determined not to fail. She did not want to live as the stereotype of an unmarried woman. She knew how to take care of herself and survive, but it was expensive. She was confident in her abilities because she learned these skills from her mother, who'd had to learn to fend for herself with a small child. Trends were changing for women, and she considered herself part of that revolution. Celia put up a flyer in the bunnies' dressing room in hopes of finding a roommate replacement. She walked over to one of her shift managers and requested overtime. Celia had never had issues with bringing in more money from the club, as she was always favored by private parties and extra bunny activities. She went to her immediate shift manager and asked if there were any private events on the horizon. The shift manager looked at her in a way that she never had before and told her that there was nothing for her. Celia interpreted that to mean it was just a slow week and went on to get ready for her night on the floor.

The bunnies were changing and turning in their uniforms for cleaning at the end of the evening while discussing their daily lives in the dressing rooms. One bunny mentioned details about a private party for a celebrity that she was working. She and a few more bunnies were scheduled to be there, and the compensation for that event was more than the regular pay scale. Celia did not say anything, although she knew she was a favorite and thought it was strange that she had not been informed of the event, despite asking her shift manager. She thought that maybe the person running the private event had a specific requirement for the type of bunnies who were to work the event. That was not uncommon, as some clients had their personal favorites and even at times racial preferences. That did not bother her because she knew of the climate in which she worked; not everyone was open to accepting all types of beauty. The other black bunny, whom Celia rarely worked with, was working the club that evening as a fill-in. Phyllis, an attractive darker-toned bunny, had a different build than Celia. She could be a clone of Claudia Lennear. Celia had recruited Phyllis into the club. Celia was always looking out for other bunnies, as the club offered incentives for bringing in quality recruits. She had earned nearly three hundred dollars from the new people she brought into the club. Phyllis worked part-time, and club employees went on a seniority system. She mentioned that she was working the event.

Celia was not a jealous woman by nature, and she always looked at the entire picture before she judged situations. However, she could not help but feel a bit bothered that a spot that would usually be given to her went to a part-time bunny with less seniority and experience without explanation. She did not feel entitled, but she felt as if she had been brushed off. Celia went to Phyllis and asked her for the details. Phyllis told her that their shift manager had pulled her aside and offered her the job. She spoke of how excited she was about working the event. Phyllis noted that she did not know what to do in that environment since it was different from the club setting. Celia looked over at the wall and noticed that someone had removed her roommate flyer while she had been on her shift.

Celia went back to her shift manager and requested a sit-down. The shift manager told her that Bunny Mother Shirley would speak to her very shortly. Celia wanted to make sure that things were OK with her standing at the club. She was desperate for the extra work. She knew that it would be only a matter of weeks before Rose left for the spring semester, and she did not want to have big gaps where the burden of the rent would all rest on her. She could pay it, but she would not eat or have a phone, among other things.

Bunny Mother Shirley came over and sat Celia down. "Look, hun, I don't know what else to say to you. The general manager told me to remove you from the rotation after this week. It was a matter of bunny behavior."

Celia was stunned. "I am not sure what instance of my behavior would be in question," she replied.

"OK, I am going to be upfront with you because I love you dearly, and you have been one of our top girls. We had a person approach management about you. They were told that you might have been carrying on an inappropriate relationship with one of our keyholders, and they saw excessive mingling on the floor, which is the number one rule we have here. It is important to maintain a professional environment," Shirley replied.

"The only floor issues I've had were with Dr. Smith," Celia said. "He flirts with me every night he is here. I have advised him politely on numerous occasions that we were not to date or talk for too long. He is always trying to get excessive small talk from me, get my number..."

Shirley cut her off. "Celia, you are still very young and exquisite and have a great future in front of you, but I am speaking to you now woman to woman. You cannot claim harassment from one man in the same space where you are fooling around with another. We have had girls get themselves in a tizzy because they decided to pursue a wealthy client," Shirley said. Celia sat there in disbelief. This was the worst month for her, and now she would add unemployment to the list of troubles. "You can finish your week, but after that you must turn in your tail, your ears, and your ribbon. You may keep the spare uniform you purchased for yourself, but you must turn in the original two that were issued to you," Bunny Mother Shirley concluded. Celia stood up, gathered her things, and left for the night.

Celia made it home and went to her room. She did not see Rose, and she did not want to interact with anyone for the moment. Celia cried, as she had never been fired from a job before. When necessary, she always aimed to transition from one place to another without ever missing a pay period. Celia suddenly went from having a plan for the future to being out of options in practically an instant. After a couple of drinks and a couple of hours, Celia picked up the phone and called Jerome. When he answered, the first thing she said was, "Is the offer still on the table?"

Chapter 4

A few doors down from the office was a diner that the guys frequented for their sit-down lunches. They discussed important but not overly sensitive matters over plates of food. Anything that went on the record was done within the walls of the office. They used code names in public because there was always a possibility that someone around them was wired. Since they were growing in popularity, they would often walk with security guards when all four of them were in a group together. Bernie felt that it was safer that way. Lose one and the company would still run; lose them all and then Chimera would be no more. He was not ready for that. Bernie knew that the company would not last forever unless they changed focus. He did not know of many gangsters that had pensions, and he would often remind his men that they always had to have a plan B.

These meetings occurred about once a month right around pay time; however, this month would be different. Bernie decided to call a meeting in the office with a smaller security detail, as he had some important things to discuss. He felt that he could not do so in the public space. He had the food delivered to them, as he wanted the guys to be comfortable in familiar surroundings when he made his announcements. Bernie had many things on his plate. He had not divulged details about any of them to the guys before, but he planned to do so that day. He would occasionally spill personal secrets only to Red. That usually happened after they had sex and shared cigarettes or drugs. She did not care much about his problems as long as he took care of her. The issues Bernie was ready to discuss included money, crime-family problems, and new hires. He would first discuss Ambrosino-family problems, and then gambling, and finally new hires.

Not far away, Bunny had spent the morning figuring out what to wear for her first day at her new job. She was to meet her new employer by one, which gave her time to get her things together. The location was convenient, as it did not take longer than a bus ride and a couple of blocks of walking to get there. She was nervous. She had become accustomed to evening hours after working a few years at the club. Instead of fishnet stockings, ears, and a tail, dry-cleaned blouses, and form-fitting skirts became her work attire. The heels remained the same, as she loved them. She knew that she would not have to do as much walking, as she would be returning to an office environment, which is where she got her start in the world of employment. The heels made her frame sexy, although they hurt her feet at times. Her feet were the one sacrifice she was willing to make for beauty. Confident in how she would handle herself this time, she decided to make the best out of her new start, although she was not sure exactly what to expect.

Bernie discussed wanting the men to play bigger roles and enlarge the company. Chimera was very well known and successful within city and suburban limits, but Bernie wanted to expand. Hustling the public for funds was lucrative. Bernie figured he could use his resources, mainly his brain, his friends, his staff, and his girlfriend, who could provide him with firepower if needed. He intended to move more into the legal gambling business and away from the local Ponzi structure. He had a direct connection from Philadelphia, who had already set up shop in Atlantic City. Lucca "Luci" Graziani had been part of the Philadelphia mob, but they exiled him after his behavior became questionable within mob circles. Luci Graziani directly competed with the Ambrosino family from New York City for power in contract negotiations with the steelworkers and concrete unions. He and Bernie struck up a good friendship and agreed to do business. Bernie thought of this as the company's plan B. Bernie understood that this brought his group to a new level—and possibly a new degree of danger. He justified the entire thing by saying they were smart. Egos and poor planning, not smart business decisions, got bosses and associates killed.

Atlantic City, New Jersey, was in the midst of a transition. In the past, it had allowed only two legal forms of gambling: horse racing and social gambling, which consisted of scattered slot machines and bingo games throughout the state. Atlantic City was currently legalizing gambling, and it was in the early planning stages of building its first casinos. Crime families in Philadelphia controlled most of the activities in Atlantic City, and many of the New York City crime families wanted a part. This setup caused some members of various families in New York City to cut deals with families in Philadelphia. Other instances of unauthorized side deals resulted in the murder of one or more members of these families. If Bernie wanted a chance to compete, he had to restructure. They could not build casinos until later on in the next decade, but Bernie felt that since it was early 1971, it was time to look into the future. First, he and Graziani planned to link up with executives that he knew were working on obtaining licenses from the Casino Control Commission. He also wanted to use his connections to see about getting the unions involved in the potential projects. This meant a lot of travel for him. Before this meeting, Bernie gave John a heads-up and informed him that he was making John the leader of New York City and its surrounding areas for the time being. He did not want Ben or Jerome to know the plan, as he did not wish to create conflict within the group. He knew that Ben wanted to advance, but he did not trust his astuteness.

At the meeting, Bernie and the other three discussed their initial course of action for the first hour and felt satisfied with their plans. They went on to the next subject.

"Gentlemen, I've hired a new person. Due to the nature of her job, she will be considered top tier, one of us. Our square is becoming a pentagon. That sounds great, doesn't it?" Bernie said. John and Jerome nodded and did not say anything. Ben looked over at them and back at Bernie.

"So what is this person doing with us? Is she recruiting the homemaker demographic?" Ben asked in a joking yet sarcastic tone.

"She is our new bookkeeper. She will help us with the numbers," Bernie answered. Ben's face changed from amused to concerned.

"But I do the numbers. You and I, we do the numbers. Things are fine the way they are. I don't see any reason we need another body here," Ben said.

Bernie explained that since Benjamin and the others were spending more time out on the field these days, they were no longer watching the books or keeping an eye out as closely as they had been before. Bernie referred to Ben by his full first name, Benjamin, when he became annoyed with him. Bernie added that he needed someone there to pick up phones, take messages, and make sure that everything was in order back at the office. Bernie made a point to note that their paperwork and bookkeeping were a mess. Their office had been bare bones since day one, and he felt that it was time to grow a little. When everyone left, the rooms were locked. That left the place vulnerable to burglary and vandalism. Rivalries were becoming tenser between Chimera and other crime families, Bernie told his crew.

"So we are hiring Batgirl or some shit like that? How is she protecting the office?" Ben asked.

"Benjamin…we will move three of our workers to office security, and they will get training. She will be protected. I would not put a lady in danger," Bernie answered.

"Is she hot? Like, is she a hot blonde?" Ben asked. He looked over at John and Jerome. "You two are too quiet. Usually we can't shut you two up when it comes to chicks."

Bernie interrupted him. "I'm approving the revised budget for this. I think all of our increased productivity supports it."

The door buzzer rang, and they saw that Celia had arrived at Chimera, thirty minutes early. She wanted to make a good impression on her new employers. Jerome got up and checked out the new arrival from the window. He went to bring her in. As he greeted her at the door, he asked her, "Are you ready, family?"

Celia answered, "As ready as I'll ever be." When they both walked in, John said hi to her. Celia looked at him and nodded. Ben turned around and looked at her. He also said hi to her.

"I've seen you before," Ben added. Jerome informed Ben that he had indeed met her before at the Playboy Club. "Oh," Ben said, drawing out the word. He looked over at John. "John's lady friend. Bringing your girlfriend here to visit?"

"Well, no..." Celia attempted to say before Bernie stepped in.

"A formal introduction is due. I know that some of you already know her, but this is Celia Jones, Chimera's newest member. She will be here in the offices every day handling our books and some of the accounting. She is helping take some of the load off of me, which I appreciate very much. She will be a good fit for us. I am confident," he said. Ben looked at her and then back at Bernie before turning to John in an annoyed way.

"Can we go somewhere and speak?" Ben asked Bernie.

"Sure, Benjamin," Bernie answered. "Men, while I am speaking with Benjamin, you two can show her around the place. Security won't start until next week, so I will be generous and pay her in advance for the week until they arrive. She can come in and get things in order before she starts."

When Ben and Bernie went into the other office and closed the door, Ben began to pace and rub his hair back. "Bernie, is this some fucking joke?" he asked. "You hired a waitress to assist me at my job?"

"Benjamin, this has nothing to do with you or your job. You put in great work. I need the help. This is not for you. It's for me," Bernie told him. "I am taking a sabbatical from the paperwork and want to go out there in the field more. I have plans. If both of us are out there, who will watch the fort? We got a girl, some of us know her well, and she worked in an office environment before. She's pleasant."

"So you think John's girlfriend, Jerome's sister, cousin, or whatever, is the person for this job? No disrespect, and I am not questioning your judgment, for the most part, but I just don't think she is a good fit for here. Where would a woman fit in here?" Ben asked. "No one discussed this with me. Don't you think I should have some input on the matter? I'm the one who knows this like the back of my hand. That's not fucking cool…Did they bring her here? You know they are taking over," Ben said in an exasperated tone.

"Who is 'they,' and what exactly are they taking over?" Bernie asked as he leaned forward.

"Nothing. Forget it," Ben answered.

"She will fit just fine, and you will train her," Bernie said sternly. "She is here now, and you will show her what to do. It won't take that much time." Bernie stood up and left the room. Pissed off, Ben kicked one of the cabinets and knocked over the pile of papers that had been sitting on top of it. He left the office for the rest of the day without sitting with Celia.

Bunny walked into the office where Ben usually did the paperwork and bookkeeping. She anticipated him still being there but realized that he had left. She looked around at the unorganized mess. Papers were stacked a foot high in multiple areas of the room, even on top of the cabinet. She noticed some of the papers had fallen from it. She found three-ring binders full of papers with no tabs and no markings to identify what they were. Coffee cups lay everywhere. There was a chalkboard on the back wall behind the desk with various writing on it, and books and more papers were stacked on the built-in bookshelves. Since Ben was nowhere to be seen, Jerome encouraged her to make herself at home and clean up if she must.

She sat down in the chair at the desk after Jerome left the room. The black leather chair had a permanent dent in the seat where Ben usually sat. She made a mental note to order herself a new chair. She opened the drawers and found more junk. She rummaged through the top drawers and found a bag of cannabis and rolling papers. Bunny was not into drugs of any kind, and she only drank alcohol socially. She looked further and found rubbers and cigarettes. She quickly closed the drawer and continued surveying the area. As she was attempting to tidy up the office, John came to the door.

"Welcome. This is where we work. Sorry about the mess. He's a fucking pig," John said.

"Thanks," Bunny replied.

John closed the door so he could talk to her. "Look, I don't want this to be uncomfortable for you, and I want to clear the air. I'm sorry. I never got the chance to say it," he said. "I don't want you to think that what went on between us was a farce. It wasn't. I do care for you, and I don't care about a lot of people."

"It's OK; I'm over it. Things happen for a reason," she responded. "I just want to get started."

"Are we still friends at least?" John asked as he extended his hand to her.

"OK, we are friends. Here's to a brand-new start," she responded. She stood up to shake his hand. Instead of shaking it, he kissed the back of it.

"See, I couldn't do that at your old job," he said and smiled. He walked out of the room. Although she was disappointed in John and the way their relationship had ended, she still found his swagger irresistible. *Control yourself*, she thought.

The next day, Bunny decided to go into the office to finish her initial cleanup. When she arrived, Ben was already there looking around at some of the progress she had made while straightening up the day before. He looked a bit disheveled smelled slightly of alcohol. "This place looks nice," he said to her.

"Thank you. I wanted to wait until you were here, but the guys told me to go ahead and start. You had a lot of things here that seemed out of order," she told him.

"Well, for your information, they were organized. My filing system is different from everyone else's. To you this looks like chaos, but I can find and identify every single piece of paper in here," he said.

"OK, well, we have to make this work since we are sharing this office," she said. "I wanted to clean the drawers, but I saw you had some personal things in there," she added.

"Well, thank you for your consideration," he said with a bit of snark. He walked over by her and sat on top of the desk. "So what is the deal between you and John? Are you two still 'dating'?" he asked while making the quotes sign to her. "Is that how you got this job?"

A bit offended by what he'd just asked, Celia snapped back. "I shouldn't even answer those questions; they're personal. But for your information, we are not a couple. We are just friends."

"Well, yeah, because he has a wife at home, or were you aware of that? Oh, I'm sorry," he said to her.

"I know about that, and once again, we are just friends. Can we discuss work matters now?" she responded.

"OK, fine. Just one more question. Why does he call you Bunny? Your name is Celia, right?" Ben asked.

"Yes, my real name is Celia. He calls me that because he thinks it's nice, as an alias. I'm not offended," she answered.

"Well, I don't want you to take this the wrong way, and excuse my language, but Bunny is the most stupid fucking thing I've heard for a name. I won't call you that. I'll call you by your real name, Celia is it? John must have made that up. He's a prick. He thinks he can run everyone. Celia is a more decent name. I can't have people know that I share an office with a colored girl named Bunny," he said.

Ben's mini rant took Celia aback. It seemed that he had a problem with John, and it dawned on her that he might also have a problem with sharing a position with her. "OK, well, you can call me whatever you like, but please keep it respectful," she said, trying to lighten up the moment. She continued to clean up for the day. She had Ben tell her the basics of what she needed to do with the books and numbers. Despite his uneasiness, he knew that business was the most important thing, and he could not be held responsible for some woman messing it up. She got the gist of what he told her. From then the transition into Chimera became smooth for her.

Over the course of the next few months, the office that had once housed Ben and his hurricane of mess became a neat and organized area, equipped with a brand-new desk and chair for Celia. It even smelled better. The mountains of paperwork now were organized, and each binder labeled according to Ben's and Bernie's specifications. She would need those papers neat and organized because she would be crunching numbers soon. She would view all the mail at the office, but not before her hired security inspected it. They knew of no immediate threats to them, but Bernie, John, and Jerome insisted that she stay safe, just in case someone wanted to send tainted mail to the office.

Many of the envelopes were junk and some contained bills, which she also took charge of overseeing. She became the office management behind the scenes, much to the delight of Bernie, whose focus shifted to making deals with some people in the area. Bernie's initial questions about her turned to adoration as he came to see her as one of his kids, the same way he looked at the guys.

She would get flyers from the Jamaican tourism board, which advertised heavily in the New York area as an alternative to the snowy weather. The headline of the flyers read, "Jamaica's more than a beach, it's a country." Celia had always wanted to travel, and she thought that since she was making decent money at Chimera, someday she would get to go. Celia and Jerome had cousins in Jamaica, and she thought it would be nice to visit them one day. She took the advertisement and pinned it to the wall next to her desk as inspiration. Celia had received her week's advance check when she first started, and it had been more than her weekly check from the Playboy Club plus tips. However, she did not receive another check until a month later. Bernie informed her that he distributed money on a monthly basis, and the amount depended on sales and fluctuation of markets and trends, so she had to budget wisely. This was why they all needed to hustle hard. They had not yet told her about the company's other activities. They felt that for now those were outside of her jurisdiction.

Celia worked so many hours at the office, she had to put her plans for school on hold for the time being. She was not worried; the paycheck after the first month more than made up for it. For the first time in her life, she had received a four-digit paycheck. It would be enough that she would not have to move or even get a roommate once Rose left for good, which would be in a matter of days.

Celia would go out with the guys on the lunch outings. The lunches were different, as the four men decided to maintain the rule of discussing only the nonsensitive items in the public and around her, keeping the big issues to themselves. Although no one on the team was massively overweight, all of the men ate as if they skipped meals for days. Celia was a light and delicate eater. Her diet consisted of lots of fruits and vegetables, with baked chicken for protein. She mostly loved to snack on berries and grapes, a habit that did not go unnoticed by John. She had eaten the same things whenever they dined out while they were dating. He asked her about this out of curiosity. She told him that those berries had vitamins, kept you young, and made sure your body functioned properly. She said they were delicious and suggested he eat some. It was something that the women in her family had taught her. John was not sure what she meant by that. He declined and told her that he only put that stuff on hotcakes.

Celia often found time in the office mundane. She spent most days alone as the guys went out and conducted their daily business. On occasion, she would be stuck with one of them on a slow day. Jerome and Bernie were always out. John and Ben were the two people of whom she spent the most time. Ben had slowly begun to warm up to Celia, occasionally saying something nice. At those times she figured either Ben was having a good day or his other activities had turned his attention elsewhere. She made sure not to make him feel like she was completely taking over, as she had sensed the tension from day one. Working at the Playboy Club had given her an understanding of the male ego, and she knew when it was appropriate to bruise it.

Ben knew that the balance had shifted once Celia arrived. He felt that he had an ally in Bernie as John had an ally in Jerome, so the scales were even. With the edition of Celia, the scales tipped in John and Jerome's favor. He had intended his aggressiveness toward her in the beginning to scare her away from the place. Now, with the increased, complicated workload, he needed her. He would not admit that he liked her personality, as it was not anything he had expected from someone like her. Ben would also not reveal to her that he had displaced some things with the accounting. He had not been completely honest with her the entire time. He'd forgotten over the years how much he had lost track of and why it had happened. If she were as good as they claimed she was, she would figure it out for herself, according to his logic. He was not worried about it, as he felt that she would be bombarded with enough that funds from the past would not be important.

John often kept Bunny company when she was alone. He was glad to have her there, but he still felt uneasy despite having the security detail to watch her. They would talk as the tension between them had subsided over time, and they became friendly. Before that point, they had not spoken about the reasons behind their breakup. Celia did not want details, as she felt a tinge of jealousy that someone else had the man she wanted. She had become fully aware of what kind of person he is. Their time at the office became reminiscent of the time that they were dating. Only the intimate moments were missing. John obsessed with her. He had spent nights after their breakup in his apartment either staring at the photos he took of her or sleeping with random women, occasionally calling Bunny's name as he imagined having sex with her. They had never consummated their relationship while dating. Since their breakup, John had released his frustrations in over a dozen women so far, although never with his wife.

Bunny had learned a lot more things about John since she started working at Chimera. She discovered his sexual prowess with women and his reputation of leaving a trail of sad women behind him. She realized that she had ended up being one of those women. He was known around town as a man whore. Their relationship was able to heal, however; the lack of physical contact saved it.

"OK, I'm up for asking. What is the deal with you and your wife? Why do you not stay faithful?" Bunny asked him. "I just want to know how you men think, for the future."

"I'm not perfect," he answered. "It's complicated."

"You told me it's complicated before, and we ended up here. You can be honest with me now," she said.

"Have you ever felt trapped in your life?" he asked her.

"No. What do you mean by that?" she asked.

"When I married Edina, we were both young. I thought it was something that I was supposed to do. She's a Jew, and her family hated my guts the moment they discovered that I wasn't one of them," he said.

"Well, I know what you are. Jerome knows what you are. Ben and Bernie know what you are, I hope. You are light, but that hair, that walk, and those lips ain't foolin' nobody, at least on this side of the tracks. Passing can only get you so far," she said.

"I don't care about what anybody thinks. I do it because it gets me ahead. It's hard out there. I know what I am, and that's all I care about. I mean, they may look like nice people, they may seem nice and tolerant and understanding of who you are, but when they get angry at you for whatever reason—when she gets mad—her white hood comes out. I left Louisiana to get away from that, and I am still in it. Makes me sick," he said.

Bunny replied, "Oh. That's horrible. Well, there is annulment; you would have been done with it all. You should have left that a long time ago."

"And what, go back to being one of the boys on the street? I was one of the flunkies we hire to do our dirty work. I was the flunky, Bunny. I was what Jerome was when I met him. I helped him like Bernie helped me. We were all discontented and disruptive. This place saved us," he said. Briefly stunned at the revelation, she paused. For the first time since beginning work there, she internally questioned what kind of place she had agreed to work.

John continued his thought. "Her family felt since I slept with her, I was obligated to be with her. She said she was pregnant then lost it, but I never saw any evidence of it. Nothing about the situation is right. I'm not bitter about it; I don't want kids with her. I like them, but not like this."

"Why are you still with her if you feel that way?" Celia asked.

"When you join a place like this, you stay loyal even when at times you don't want to be. I enjoy my position; Bernie is like a father to me. I did not grow up with my dad," he said. "She helped me get here. She knows Bernie from way back. I felt that out of respect for him at least; I had to stay with her, but I didn't want to. I can't get rid of her. I tried. She won't divorce me. She says that it would make her look bad, and she gave up too much to be with me, so I owe her. She would use that when we fought because I guess she thinks she is making me feel guilty or something. She thinks she is punishing me for not being her pet. I do my duties and show up with her in public because it keeps our names respectable. Like I said, I'm stuck. How do I get out now? I'm a slave to her. I want other things."

"What do you want, then?" Bunny asked him.

"I want to be filthy fucking rich. I want my own island, my own wine company. You know I've been trying to find something to launch it. I want my signature flavor. I don't even have a name yet. LeBlanc is too obvious. I'm working on it," he said. John never shared his feelings with anyone when it came to his marriage. Not even his best friend, Jerome. John and Bunny had cultivated a relationship of trust on a foundation of distrust.

"You'll get it. I'm so sorry to hear all of this. I still can't condone cheating. I wouldn't want to be cheated on," Bunny said, and she paused again. "Everything will turn out OK for you. I know it. I have to go. Rose is leaving this evening, and I want to see her off," she added. She stood up, kissed John on his forehead, and left. The scene was similar to the one in the park, but now it was in their workplace.

On her way home from the office, Celia stopped by a Chinese-food store for takeout. She saw Phyllis from the club waiting for her order. She was thrilled to run into one of the other bunnies she had worked with, as she missed them all. No one had contacted her since she left, as everyone was afraid of the consequences of communicating with her. Management did not divulge the details of her dismissal. Celia would only hear updates from Rose. She asked Phyllis, "How are things going at the club?"

Phyllis replied, "We miss you, sister. We didn't know what was happening when they told us that you were not returning. You know people talk and gossip, so there were all kinds of rumors flying around. It was everything from you got another job to you did something inappropriate. Don't worry, girl; I'm not there anymore either."

"Where do you work now?" Celia asked her.

Phyllis told her, "I'm not working at the moment. I met a guy." Phyllis's takeout order was ready, so she hugged Celia and headed out. Phyllis promised to catch up with her later. As Celia watched her walk out, she saw that Phyllis was heading to a Cadillac. In the driver's seat, she saw an unmistakable face. It was Dr. Smith. They caught a brief glance of each other, and he snickered at Celia before driving away.

Chapter 5

Jerome's life consisted of his daily activities at Chimera and his evening life with his girlfriend, Mariana. Mariana was a short, light-brown-skinned, dark-haired Dominican. Her family had recently immigrated here and settled in Queens. He met her during one of his weekly outings at the jump clubs in Harlem. The way she dressed attracted him. They hit it off instantly. Mariana and Jerome would venture out every Friday night because both of them loved having a good time. They were partners in clubbing. They attended his family's church in Harlem, and he had introduced her to his relatives. Mariana and Celia were around the same age. Celia met her when she reconnected with Jerome. The two women would occasionally hang out with each other, and Mariana became the replacement company when Rose moved out of the apartment. Mariana had a day job as a waitress, which meant she could not keep an eye on Jerome twenty-four hours a day. She had to work long hours to earn a decent wage. Jerome occasionally had one-night flings with other women, but he established a full relationship with Mariana. Mariana never found out about his side activities because she was busy with her schedule. They had discussed marrying one day.

John and Edina's marital home was a penthouse located in upper Manhattan. John went there only sparingly, as the couple fought often. He made sure to pick his separate apartment enough distance away from her. Edina never dared to venture over to his place. She did not want to set him off and have a confrontation in public. She figured she could get him to come home if she wanted him to. This had been the longest time away from home since their wedding. She was curious as to why he would want to spend so much time away from her. In Edina's eyes, she was a real catch who had lowered herself to be with him. According to her, he should have been more appreciative. Why wouldn't he want a well-to-do white wife like her? She often thought.

Edina did not work. Her income came from John, and she had her money. John would send money to her to keep her quiet. He had established a marital account and a separate one for himself. The rest of her funds came from her family, who had softened their bitter feelings about her marriage to John. They decided that since she was the only daughter, they should take care of her properly, despite John's income. Her family still loved and cared for her. Edina took care of the home, which Richard Neutra had inspired, and she had total control of the design. She thought that her tastes were more refined than John's, so he had no say in the way the home was furnished. She took the time to design the pristine white walls with wood accents in the living and bedroom areas. The kitchen included yellow walls and brown cabinets with wood accents that matched the living room and the rest of the place. It was fully equipped with the latest state-of-the-art chrome-finished appliances. Edina never prepared food. Instead, she ran out and ate with her girlfriends.

She decided that if John stayed around long enough she would learn how to cook things he liked. She only knew traditional cuisine, which directly clashed with the southern dishes that John had been raised on.

The modern furniture reflected current trends in design, and Edina took pride in showing it off whenever she had guests over. In John's absence, she would tell them about his important job that required him to travel often. The truth was that she had no idea of his whereabouts most times.

Edina's family often spoke with her about moving away from the city into suburban Westchester for safety. They were concerned about the change in climate in New York City. John loved the city and refused to move to an area that he considered the country. He told her that he was built for city life. Edina did not like New York City that much but had to stay if John stayed. It would not look good for her reputation if she lived on her own. She thought that the city was messy and not charming. Violent crime was on the rise, and she did not feel comfortable walking the streets, especially at night. Edina was critical of the new groups of people who were moving into the area, and she wanted to follow the white flight out of the city. Laws in immigration changed, and the city saw an influx of immigrants from places like Asia, the Caribbean, and Puerto Rico. Edina did not have a lot of knowledge or understanding of such people; in her conversations with her friends, the discussions about those groups was often prejudiced in tone. Manufacturing jobs started to diminish, which meant that the blue-collar workers that supported the neighborhoods began to weaken financially, leading to high crime and drug-infested streets. The city was a center of national protests about race and the Vietnam War. Edina thought that, unlike her, the students involved in such protests did not have real direction and should focus their energy and time elsewhere.

In the beginning years of the marriage, Edina explained to her parents why she and John did not try again to produce children. Edina often thought of adopting, but John did not support the idea. She had spent time coming up with scenarios on how to get a baby. She took tests, which revealed that she was the problem. Even if John agreed to the adoption, she learned from agencies that they would have a difficult time finding a convincing mixed-race child to pass as their own. She would never tell her family that the possibility might never happen. Instead, she reassured them every time that she and John had chosen not to have kids. Uttering those words hurt her to the core every time. Edina wanted to be a mother. She was often the only one in her circle without a child, so she would instead spend time with her nieces and nephews from her brother and sister-in-law. At the beginning of her marriage, her family suggested an annulment. She knew her rep had diminished with some in the community because she had married a colored man. No respectable white or Jewish man of means would follow that, according to them.

John's mother and brother were not fond of Edina. Both of them thought that she was a controlling monster who tried to prevent John from associating with his family. John's side of the family did not attend the ceremony in New York. Edina never made a real effort to assimilate herself into John's family. Edina felt that they were uncouth and that John was in a different environment now. His mother often had to bite her tongue during the very few interactions that she had with her. Edina had a way of insulting people with a big smile on her face. His brother, Jimmy, refused to speak to her. John's mother wished for him to move on from Edina but understood the complexity involved in doing so. She often prayed for a change in his situation. John would send his mother jewelry as a token of his appreciation of her and also as a forgive-me gift to her.

Out of embarrassment, Edina never shared her concerns with her friends, and she could not talk to her family. John was the only person she felt that she should express her frustrations to, much to his displeasure. John was never a fan of a difficult person, and if he did not like the individual, his irritability magnified tenfold. This was the source of their fights. She felt that he was not supportive of her feelings, and he felt that she treated him as if she were his superior. They responded to each other with passive-aggressiveness. Edina knew that he was possibly miserable but felt that she could turn things around in her favor if she could just come up with the right plan. Her ways were always the right way to be, according to her, and that pissed him off.

Edina was sexually frustrated because of John's unwillingness to sleep with her. They only made love on an average of once a year at this point. He had no desire to touch her, so he needed to find physical release with outsiders, and often. John became emotionally unattached to her as he became fed up with the situation. He had thought about disappearing altogether to get rid of her, but he decided to stay once he landed the job at Chimera. The lack of affection from John led Edina to have an extramarital affair of her own, which was short lived. The man she dealt with did not want to commit to her, as her personality was too abrasive for him and she was not attractive enough for him to commit, according to him. This led Edina to a minor depression, which made her more aggressive with John. She had a feeling he had numerous trysts with women, but she looked the other way. She owned him. She resented that he was seemingly content with his extra activities.

John and Edina kept up public appearances occasionally for the sake of both their reputations. She considered it important that they make a strong favorable impression and avoid exposing problems at all costs. He fulfilled his holiday obligations and went to social gatherings if they both were invited, weddings, and family funerals. Edina wanted him to convert to Judaism, but he refused. That led to a compromise. She would observe Hanukkah and other Jewish holidays, and he could celebrate Christmas, much to her disdain. The only black Jew John knew was Sammy Davis Jr., and he felt it should remain that way.

———

Ben was feeling left out of the fray as he finally figured out that the primary New York City operations at the offices had been handed to John, without a formal announcement, while Bernie worked in the Atlantic City area. The writing was on the wall. Ben felt that Bernie had let him down. Although they worked side by side as brothers, Ben did not understand why John was a better candidate than he was. He never envisioned a minority running the primary operations. Ben felt that he would look better as the underboss. He thought he did an overall good job and brought decent money into the company. He started to wonder if John and Jerome were teaming up on him. The addition of Celia made the suspicions worse, as he was now outnumbered in representation. He indulged more in drugs as a result. New York

City at the time was a hotspot for illegal drugs because of the changing social and economic times. Ben's drug problem became worse but remained manageable. He was still careful to make sure it did not interfere with his daily duties. He would go from work back to his apartment at night to shoot heroin and snort cocaine to relax his nerves. He never did this at the same time. The women he would invite over also used, so he always had someone there who knew what was happening and partook in the activities with him, just in case he passed out. The expense of his habit was high, as he insisted on only using reputable dealers who had high-quality drugs. This cost him thousands, and often he fell short with money to support his habit and pay his dealers. After a while, he had some of the dealers on loans. He figured since he was the accountant, he could use funds from the company and maybe pay them back later. He did this without the knowledge of Bernie or the others. Ben dipped into the public's money. He was in charge of those books. The mob money was safe, as only Bernie held that information. Since John was unofficially leading, he now had knowledge of that information as well.

Ben felt that if he was to stay afloat in the company, he needed allies. John and Jerome were out of the question, which left Celia. He knew that he had not gotten off to a good start with her and decided to make amends. Ben bought her a bottle of wine as a gift to break the ice. He had apologized for being a dick to her over and over again. He was unaware that she was not a daily drinker, and it was likely that the bottle would go unused. Celia only drank when the situation was appropriate. Alcohol triggered her headaches, and she could not tolerate more than one glass of wine. At the club, the wine glasses were large, and she used those as a measure of her alcohol tolerance. Bunny accepted the gift, as she was relieved that he had decided not to be so rough on her anymore. She did not want any enemies on the job. Ben took the opportunity to get to know her and see what she was about as a person. Ben observed the interactions she had with John and noted how close they were. He wanted to mimic those conversations to get her to trust him. He also wanted some attention. Over the course of the next few months, Ben and Celia became friendly.

After getting to know Celia more by speaking with her, Ben found himself falling for her. He had never been attracted to a black woman before, and he wasn't sure how to process those feelings. He knew that John was still carrying a torch for her and would probably not like the notion that Ben would be encroaching on his territory. Ben felt that he needed a relationship with Celia so he could get ahead and have someone on his side. He was beginning to like her, so this would work in his favor. Ben thought he was better than John, so he felt that this would be a step up for her from what she had been dealing with before.

Celia was OK with being friendly with Ben; however, she still considered professionalism important. She did not want things to get weird at the job. At the advice of Rose, with whom she spoke on the phone often, she began to go out on dates secretly with men on the outside. None of these resulted in intimacy, as she was not ready for that just yet. Those feelings for John still lingered.

The New Year rang in with the beginning of a new decade. The year was 1970. A few months after the New Year, Chimera decided to celebrate their recent successes and their future outlook with a party at the Drake Hotel in the city. They shared the space with other patrons but had one section of the ballroom to themselves. They meant it to be a small affair for them and their guests. John did not bring Edina. Chimera was the one business activity that John had to himself, and he did not feel the need to share it with her. She brought him to her functions enough and made him put on fake smiles. He was real here, and he wanted to keep it that way. Jerome attended with Mariana. Ben came alone, and Bernie introduced Gina to the crew. Celia went alone and was ready to have a good time.

The place was filled with food, drink, and music. Celia, wore high heels and her tight black sparkly dress that fit her nicely in the right places, felt comfortable for the first time in a while. She finally had a decent bank account, and her apartment was secure without the assistance of a roommate. She missed Rose because the woman kept her company and they were like sisters, but her friend was already doing well at Juilliard. Celia had put Juilliard on hold. She had been upset about it at first, but she'd changed her mind because she was doing so well at Chimera. The apartment was quiet without Rose, so she had to get used to the quiet. She considered getting a pet to keep her company. She once told John that she liked cats, but John had discouraged her from getting one, as he did not trust or like them and they did not like him.

Celia decided to get up and dance, something she had not done in a public setting since her nights at the Playboy Club. The disc jockey was playing "Lay a Little Lovin' on Me," by Robin McNamara. She loved the song, and she asked anyone at the table if they wanted to join her. John did not, as he did not dance; none of them did so in public, to each other's knowledge. He was content just watching her as he had before. He was too suave to be seen dancing. Jerome declined, as he was comfortable in his seat with his drink and food next to John and Mariana. Ben took her up on her offer, to everyone's surprise. He got up and joined her. They danced together in the middle of the floor, and both appeared to enjoy themselves. Three more songs played before they stopped and went over to the open bar for drinks.

John and Jerome sat and watched Ben and Celia dance. Ben had a smile on his face, a strange expression for him. Ben always looked serious. He thought people would not take him seriously if he showed his teeth excessively. John stared at them hard, and so did Jerome. The two of them started a conversation at the table, as they both had unspoken feelings about what they were watching. It made John sick to his stomach and Jerome uneasy.

"Do you see that?" John asked Jerome.

"Yeah, I do. Can't say that I like it either," Jerome answered.

"What does he want with her? He doesn't dance. That motherfucker doesn't dance," John said.

"I just don't trust it. He's like our brother and all, but I don't trust him. I don't think a white man has good intentions when he looks at our women," Jerome said. "I can't control her, but I can talk to her about him. It's not right. There are too many brothers out there for her to go to the gutter with him, and I won't allow the disrespect to my family," he added.

"He did not like her. He was an ass to her. Bernie had to check him. I had to check him. Why is he in her face?" John asked.

Jerome and John did not care about the hypocrisy of their concerns. Both men had had relations with numerous white women, and they did not have a problem with doing so, as they felt that they were entitled to the practice. John could not help the feeling of jealousy coming over his body. He felt that she belonged to him and should only have eyes for him, as he still held strong, deep feelings for her. This was the first visual evidence that he may be losing his grip with her. She had begun to seek male attention elsewhere.

Later on that evening, John went home frustrated. He received a phone call from Edina, who was checking up on him. His tone with her was more bitter than usual. He felt that his involvement with her was ruining his life. His tone did not sit well with Edina, as their very brief conversation about money escalated into a shouting match. He hung up the phone after she suggested that he go to their marital home. John had been verbally aggressive with her before, but this time his voice had more anger. Edina was always the one initiating the slam of the phone. The aggressiveness on the other end of the line took her aback. Things were progressively getting worse between them, and she felt that she had to do something soon.

After that phone call, John got up and decided to venture out and pay Bunny a visit at her apartment. It was after one in the morning when he arrived. He buzzed her door, but she was not there. He went over to a pay phone to ring her apartment. No answer. Frustrated, he went to a bar that was still open. He had never been to this place before. He chatted with a leggy brunette who was smoking at the bar. John took her back to his place, and they had sex. He promised to call her back, but by the morning, he didn't even remember her name.

Bernie lived in Greenwich Village on West Tenth Street. The block was full of townhouses whose construction dated back to the 1920s. The area was considered well-to-do, as celebrities and well-known socialites and politicians lived there. The Weathermen Underground Organization's New York sector on West Eleventh Street was a block away. Gina's parents owned the building it occupied but rarely spent much time in it, as they also had property on the West Coast. While they were away, they left Gina in charge of watching the property. Her parents had no idea of the activities that were happening there.

Bernie had first met Gina when she'd passed him on the sidewalk. She was frantically moving along when he stopped her in her tracks. She was exquisite to him and young. Bernie was not into women his age. They reminded him of his pushy grandparents. He had a high-powered, active lifestyle, and he needed someone who was not interested in commitment, who was useful to him, and who could keep up. Gina fit the bill. Bernie was so smitten with her willingness to please him with her skill in fellatio that he nicknamed her Red, because of his view of the top of her head as well as her crotch area. He was also impressed with her connections and her political passions.

He visited her building often to keep up on the Underground's latest plans, lend support, and give them information. He would tell them about the activities of the local police departments, who kept a watchful eye on the collective at the advice of the FBI. Bernie was careful not to be seen going in and out of the premises so that he would not be on anyone's radar. He did not know whether anyone was watching who was entering and leaving the townhouse. Bernie made deals with the people who were posted there. If he needed firearms or bombs, they would make them for him in exchange for financial assistance. This kept the

Weathermen Underground going, and they became a weapons source for Bernie.

Bernie developed feelings for Gina because she was the one who became the most aware of his personal problems, such as his medical issues, which would occasionally show themselves while he was in her company and when they had sex. Bernie had trouble breathing and discomfort at times, which he dismissed because of his age, his present activities with Gina, and his duties at the company. He forgot these issues once he took an aspirin for the pain and it went away. He would often turn his attention to her instead, especially when things became tense in her involvement in the underground.

One evening while they were lying in his bed after sex, they were watching the news. A sound bite of Richard Nixon denouncing the riots and protests flashed across the television. Nixon called the rogue groups thugs and hoodlums. Bernie looked at Gina, who stared at the television with disgust. "What do you think of that?" he asked her.

"We are revolutionaries. We are ready to fight and overthrow anyone in government who continues to oppress those who are not white or male. Everyone built this country," Gina said. "We are organizing white kids to fight with us, fight on the side of the oppressed, or they can continue to be the oppressors. We will go after them too. Revolution is imminent; world revolution is imminent. Fascism needs to end now. We have to accept that the status quo will not remain for much longer."

"Aren't you afraid of what may happen to you? Everyone is on your ass because of the rioting on campuses, and they will have no reservations about taking all of you out to make themselves look good. Did you see what Nixon just called you? They are calling you communists. He is riling the public," Bernie responded.

"Fuck Nixon, fuck pigs and fuck those who are complacent. If you do nothing while all of this injustice is happening, then you are part of the problem. It's a risk I am willing to take," she said.

"I understand your fight, but I worry about you. My concern is you," Bernie said.

"You shouldn't. We're soldiers. I'm a soldier just like you are. You were sent to an unjust war where many innocents lost their lives, just like our brothers are out there fighting an unjust war right now. Our black brothers and sisters are being beat down in streets as we speak. Brother Fred Hampton was gunned down in his bed in Chicago because he wanted equal rights for everyone and they shot him down like a dog. He was only twenty-one years old. That could be any one of us. That could be you just because they don't like how you operate. They hate that we are aligned with the Black Panthers. They don't want unity between races and nations. United States imperialism has to go," she added.

"I support you; I am one of you. All I am saying is to be careful," Bernie told her.

"Like I said, you don't have to worry about me. I'm all right. You're worried about me, and I am worried about you and everyone else. You know what they do to us, people like you and me? They break into our apartments and ransack them. They attack us and attempt to choke us and stuff cloths in our mouths to shut us up. They record our phone calls and take photos of us for simply walking down the street. That is a police state, a state run by pigs. They do that to you; you already know what it is like," Gina said to Bernie.

"If you go to jail, I promise I will bail you out," Bernie responded. "You can jail a revolutionary, but you can't jail a revolution."

On the morning of March 6, it was crisp and cold outside. It began as a typical day in New York and at the Chimera offices. Chimera had a visitor come in. Fred Silver, a member of the Weather Underground, arrived to pick up a cash payment in exchange for some ammunition and the order of a bomb, which Bernie requested as a favor for his Atlantic City connection Luci Graziani. Graziani was having issues with some of the Philadelphia families because of his involvement with the Atlantic City casino developments. They felt that he was side negotiating with the unions. Word had got out that he was working with New York families, but they did not have all of the details as to whom exactly he was working with. This resulted in harassment of Graziani and some threats to his life. Graziani wanted to send a message back to them, and he asked Bernie to provide firepower to him. In exchange for the payment, Bernie arranged for the Underground to have their Philadelphia sector send an explosive message to the Donati Family. Bernie agreed to the deal and had Gina make the arrangements. She would travel to Philadelphia. These monetary exchanges, as well as donations from secret outside sources, enabled the Underground to operate and cover expenses for materials and daily living.

As the deal was being completed in the Chimera offices, the other members of the Underground in the Greenwich building were preparing their packages. They were packing bombs with roofing nails and dynamite. This time they wanted to use explosives that were more powerful and sophisticated than previous ones they had assembled. These new explosives were for a larger bombing campaign on college campuses and government buildings. Before, other members and Gina had been known for their skill in Molotov cocktails, which they used to bomb government buildings and target officials.

Returning from his meeting with Bernie, Fred Silver made it to the front steps of the townhouse just before it suddenly exploded into a wall of fire. Gina and her bomb-making partner were still inside the basement. The four-story building collapsed, and the bricks and rubble crushed Fred Silver to death in an instant. The bodies of Gina and her partner were charred and shredded into hundreds of pieces. Neither Bernie nor anyone else knew that she was in the building until much later when he could not get in contact with her to follow up on the deal for Graziani. She was not supposed to be in town.

Chapter 6

Bernie took some time off to process and mourn the sudden death of Gina as well as to get some needed rest. He became mentally and physically tired. Gina was positively identified weeks later by her fingerprints, which were the only verifiable part of her left at the gory scene. Bernie had witnessed a lot of death in his time, but nothing had ever jolted him like this. He had developed feelings for Gina, and the stress of it took a toll on his health. Time went by, and he began to have more pain and anxiety from the pressure of the situation. Despite the state of affairs, work and life could not stop. He knew he needed to make changes quickly. Her parents did not know of their relationship, but many of her friends knew. He attended her services to pay his respects to her. There was nothing but a very small urn with containing the ash of what was left of her remains and a photo of her, surrounded by flowers. Her parents were devastated to find out the extent of her involvement in the terrorist organization, and they pleaded for the Underground to end their operation so that others would not get hurt.

Gina's death meant that Bernie no longer had a direct connection to a weapons source, and the package for Graziani was never delivered. Bernie had to scramble to find a suitable alternative quickly. This kept the tensions between Graziani and the Philadelphia families from boiling over to his side. The pending projects and rulings on the development of Atlantic City casinos were causing families in both regions to compete fiercely for power over the unions. The conflicts were turning deadly in some cases. Bernie and Graziani had to establish new relationships quickly. It was only a matter of time before their partnership would be exposed. The Ambrosino family was also cutting deals to get in on the action, and suspicions about Bernie began to emerge from them.

In a matter of weeks after the explosion that killed Gina and her friends, President Nixon declared extended bombing from American and Vietnamese in Cambodia. This caused the nation to explode. The Weathermen and their branch groups led the way to nationwide campus strikes, in which students walked out in protest and rioted. Bernie sat and watched the developments and wondered if what they were going through was worth it. Was it worth Gina and others who were in the fight, their lives? Soon after, the protests started again. During the riots at Kent State and Jackson State College, the police began to retaliate and kill students.

—⊷—

It was the sixth of April, Celia's birthday. John, Celia, Ben, and Jerome were looking after the office. John decided a few days before to surprise her with a cake and a gift in the office as a sign of appreciation. He wanted her to feel good and to see him in a good light. It was a way to lift both of their spirits. He had never done anything like this before, not even for Edina. He went out and took the time to pick the right cake and design and the right gift for her, a special item that he thought she would enjoy and that she did not already own, something that would have her think of him every time she looked at it. He saw a mink fur jacket in a store window. He focused on it and thought that she would look beautiful wearing it out. He walked in and bought the jacket. He left the box with a big, red ribbon on her desk to surprise her. When Celia arrived at work and saw the box, she picked it up and shook it. She did not hear any unpleasant noises, and the box was not heavy, so she assumed it was safe. She opened it and gasped. It was beautiful. She took it out of the box and put it on. It fit perfectly. It was the most expensive item she'd ever held in her hands. There was a white card in the box, and she opened it and read it.

Celia walked out of the office with the coat on and a smile on her face. Ben saw her and smiled back. "Good morning. That's a nice coat. Did you just buy it?" he asked her.

"Well, no, I didn't buy it," she answered. John came around the corner and saw Celia in the jacket. She was clearly enjoying it.

"You look beautiful in it. Happy birthday," John said. He walked up in front of Ben and kissed Celia on the cheek. "We are getting ready so you can blow out your candles. Jerome is lighting them up now," he said.

Ben knew when her birthday was, but because he had been so busy, he had forgotten that today was the day. "Happy birthday. I have something for you later," he told her. Celia looked at both men.

"You guys, thank you. Thank you for this. I don't know what else to say," she said.

"Enjoy it. Bernie also left something for you," John told her.

"Well, I don't want to stand over a candle with this on. I may start a fire. I will be back," Celia said. She went back into her office for a moment. John and Ben stood there.

"A fucking fur coat? You have some nerve. What happened to a card, like normal people?" Ben said as he pushed John's shoulder.

"Don't push me. The fuck is your problem? I gave her a card too," John said as he pushed him back.

"My problem is you. You do not know when to quit. She is not yours. Get over it!" Ben said.

"And what, you own her now? She's yours now? I met her first. We're friends. I can buy my friends whatever the hell I want," John responded.

"You don't buy a friend a four-thousand-dollar fucking coat. You are not even supposed to be looking at her now," Ben said.

"What? Are you mad? Are you mad because yours isn't good enough, or did you forget like you always conveniently forget shit?" John demanded. Celia walked back in, and both men immediately quieted down. They escorted her to Bernie's office, where other junior associates were waiting for her.

"We are here to celebrate our lady," John toasted. Celia blew out her candles. The tension between John and Ben was so thick that you could cut it. Jerome noticed it. He did not know what was going on, but he attempted to lighten up the mood by turning on some music and handing Celia a knife to cut the cake.

———

John, Jerome, and Celia went to the New York Knicks NBA Finals championship game seven at Madison Square Garden. Bernie managed to score everyone floor tickets because he was a good friend of head coach Red Holzman. Celia had never been to a live NBA game before. John and Jerome were regulars. Ben did not attend the game because he could not be located. As they sat there, Celia looked at John and said to him, "You could be one of those guys. You are tall enough."

John looked at her and smiled. "You think so?" he asked.

"Why not? Do you know how to play?" she answered.

"I play a bit on my off time," he said.

"Are you any good?" she asked.

He looked at her again. "I'm pretty damn good."

Celia returned the smile. "I bet you are. You can teach me."

"I didn't know you were a fan like that. That would be interesting to see. I'll show you as soon as you teach me how to play the piano like you promised," John responded.

Celia laughed and continued to make small talk. "Thank you again for the coat. It is beautiful," she said.

"It fits you. You should be out here in style, in nice things. Not the subway, but nice dinners, good stuff. You deserve the best. It brings out your skin tone," he said. "Chimera's first lady should look like a regal woman."

"You guys see me that way?" she asked.

"I see you that way. That is all I'm concerned with. I wish circumstances were different," John said. He resisted the urge to put his hand on her thigh.

"Nothing wrong with the way things are right now. We are all happy right now. Look where we are, with all of this excitement. We are living the American dream," she told him.

"I'm almost there. If you really knew what I dream about at night..." he replied.

"You're dirty. I know where your head is all the time," Celia responded, and they both laughed. Celia put her arm around his shoulder and gave him a quick hug and a peck on the head. The Knicks won that game and the NBA championship over the Los Angeles Lakers.

"Wanna meet Walt Frazier?" John asked her.

"Um, yeah. My father would love an autograph."

Celia was making waves with the group. In Bernie's absence, she had progressed at her job so well in such a short time that Bernie felt that she should be rewarded with a small monetary gift. He wanted to thank her for her support of him and the group. He would reward the people he felt were doing a great job for him. Bernie and Celia became close, and he looked at her as a daughter, much as he viewed the guys as his sons. She had gained his respect, which was what she wanted the most. She knew that being the lone female in a male-dominated group was a challenge, and she was determined to prove herself. Celia initiated into the group via ceremony like the men, although her duties were to remain separate from mob activities as per Bernie's orders. He did this so she remained protected. He considered her high-level support staff.

Ben spent less and less time at the office, which led Celia to start looking at the accounting on her own. She wanted to make sure funds were in order just in case of a surprise audit. It took her weeks and long hours at the office to organize the piles of records stored in binders. The results of the findings she would give to Bernie once she completed them. She felt that the reports were overdue, as Ben only did this sparingly.

She viewed personnel records, lease agreements, year-end payroll reports, paid bills, and the general ledger. Celia combed through five years of paperwork and noticed some inconsistencies with the balances that had been noted in the books and the information available in the public accounts. If they were to be audited today, Chimera would be in trouble, she thought. She did not want the company to suffer any difficulties. She checked and double-checked with her calculator and looked at the printed receipts repeatedly. She knew that she was decent with math, but this did not make any sense to her. Celia was concerned as to why the statements were so different. She wanted to ask Ben about the discrepancies, but he was too busy out in the field to have any time to sit down with her. She did not feel right about going over his head, but in order to complete the job, she needed some questions answered. She waited until Bernie returned from his break to discuss the situation.

When Bernie returned to full duty, Celia made sure to sit down with him to chat about her results. Happy to go back to familiar territory, he set aside an afternoon for lunch with her so he could get the updates. She handed him a binder that contained a typed, completed report of her findings, something that Ben had never provided. She informed him about numbers not matching and possibly missing funds that did not have an explanation for their whereabouts. She'd found extra withdrawals from the company's main bank account that were not present in the reports. When she'd acquired receipts from the bank, she'd noticed that Ben had made all the withdrawals. She told Bernie the personnel records were out of order, and she could not account for some of the people who were listed. There were no start dates or any way to track them. Ben's paperwork only listed their names, their jobs, and the amounts they were supposed to be paid. There was no personal information about the people listed, and she was not sure if they even existed.

Bernie was dumbfounded at the findings, but he did not show any emotion to Celia. He did not want to alarm her. Bernie was good at coming up with quick solutions. He told her that most of these issues were fixable, as he knew who worked there and whom the workers hired as subcontractors. He could get that information simply by asking them. As far as the money was concerned, he told Celia that he knew about it, although that was not true. He assured her that he would provide proper documentation and told her not to worry her pretty little head. He would help fix it. He also told her that she need not confront Ben about it. He would talk to Ben.

After their lunch, Bernie retired home for the evening. It thundered outside with heavy downpours. The forecast called for flash flooding in the city that night. Bernie loved rainstorms, as the sounds and fresh breezes that accompanied them relaxed him. He often opened the windows to experience the full effect. Doing so helped him sleep peacefully.

The stench of the destroyed building a block away still lingered in the air, months later. He had taken his break to leave the chaos of news trucks, FBI investigators, onlookers, coroners, firetrucks, and police officers that lingered in the area in the aftermath of the blast.

He poured himself a drink, looked at the report Celia had given him and sat down. The paperwork showed that an extra $450,000 had been withdrawn from the company account without his knowledge. All the signatures belonged to Benjamin, and the withdrawals were listed as petty cash. His mind was going a thousand miles a minute in disbelief, as the thought of one of his sons stealing from him was hard to process. He knew that other families handled betrayals within the ranks with hits, but he did not want to respond in that manner. He did not want to believe it, but the paperwork presented to him told the story. He was not ready for confrontation, as he was still emotionally tired from dealing with the loss of Gina and he knew that his body could not handle the stress. Bernie sat there thinking of possible explanations for this. Why wouldn't Ben come to him if he needed help? Why hide? He thought. The only logical reason that Bernie could think of was that Ben had fallen off the wagon despite his close watch. Bernie knew on the inside that what he thought he had in his circle, the notion of total trust and loyalty turned out not to be. Out of habit, Bernie picked up the phone to call Gina. She had been his ear in time of need. Then he remembered that he could no longer do that. She was gone forever. He slammed the receiver.

Bernie became tired and put the papers aside to lie down. He could not stay still, so he got back up and started pacing the room. He looked down while he was walking and noticed that his left ankle was swollen, and he had minor pain in his arm. This had happened to him before while in the presence of Gina. He figured that his body was experiencing stress and took an aspirin. When he was able to calm himself down, he lay back down on the couch to elevate his leg. He thought to himself, *I will speak to Ben about it in the morning, and everything will be resolved.*

A couple of days went by before Celia finally got a chance to catch up with Ben. She told him things were going well and that she would have the books and paperwork in order with the help of Bernie. Bernie had not been in, but she attributed that to him needing more time to take care of himself. Bernie had assured her that he would return after their meeting.

Ben was pleased to hear that things were progressing well. Feeling good, he decided to take the plunge and finally ask Celia out on an official date. He had become incredibly attracted to her. She knew that dating him would make it a bit uncomfortable in the office. She was reluctant at first, but she changed her mind. This place was different from the club, and the rules were not the same. She had spent the entire time while she was working at Chimera concerned about how John would feel and what he and Jerome would think. Ben did not care what the other two thought of him at this point. He had a plan with Celia, and he would not let them mess this up for him. She realized that she was limiting herself to a married man and selling herself short in the process. Ben could be something good for her. He was certainly different, as she had never dated interracially before. She agreed to a date, and they began making plans for later in the evening.

Celia left work early to get ready for her date with Ben. She had decided to live a little and not be so old fashioned. She had unopened rubbers that Rose had left over at the apartment. Rose dated a lot, and like Celia, she was not virginal. Rose was careful. She did not want to end up at the clinic for a procedure, like other young graduate-aged women she knew. Celia had only had one sexual partner in her life, a boyfriend from high school. They broke up when she began working at the Playboy Club. That relationship had hurt her so badly that she was determined to protect her heart and her vagina from disappointment. She wanted to wait for the right man. But just in case, she put those condoms in her purse. Celia wore a fitting blue wiggle dress. It was long but sophisticated. The dress was one of her favorites, as it displayed her curves correctly.

Ben arrived on time, and they took the train to a restaurant in Chinatown. When they arrived, the streets were crowded with couples, families, and people walking. They entered a restaurant called Chef Ma on Pell Street. Ben knew of her indulgence in Chinese food, so he figured that he could not go wrong with this destination. He also wanted to take her to the Mee Sum Mee Tea House and Pastry. This restaurant was one of Ben's favorite places to get a bite in Chinatown. They talked and laughed all night about their likes and dislikes. The radio began playing "Bring 'Em Home" by Pete Seeger. Celia asked him about his time in Vietnam.

Ben had only served a couple of years before being discharged from the Army. He had been only twenty-two years old when the war began and twenty-seven when he entered. Benjamin decided to join the military because they boasted the benefits of service. He was just fine being a young person trying to find his way in life on his own, but he felt that he did not have enough money to survive. Ben thought that a couple of years enlisted in the army would not be bad; the time would allow him to reap the benefits and cause people to view him as a hero to his country. Before he went, he approached Bernie for possible work, and Bernie put him on as an intern. Bernie accepted him once he explained that he was an enlisting soldier. The war began, and Ben shipped out shortly after he started working. Bernie promised him employment if and when he returned. When he left, Ben's other friends volunteered, believing the military's promises of special training and choice assignments, which never came to fruition. All of them eventually became disenchanted with the war and began to rebel. Instead of fighting, they focused on CYA, which meant Cover Your Ass. Morale was down, and instead of inspirational chants of encouragement, they sang, "You're going home in a body bag, doo dah, doo dah…"

Ben and the other soldiers turned to drugs to take their minds off the situation, and the mental illness Ben had fought to shield from the world was beginning to manifest itself on the field. He used marijuana and morphine to deal with the environmental stress. The soldiers would rig a gun with a smoke pipe and use it as a bong. They would pass it around and inhale the cannabis smoke from the shotgun barrel. They called it riding shotgun. Ben first got his taste for heroin in Vietnam, where the purity was nearly 100 percent. The purity back at home was only about 5 to 10 percent. He started using heroin because his friends were snorting and shooting it and he wanted to blend in. It was also cheap, costing only a couple of dollars for a vial of white powder in Vietnam. At home, the same amount would run about fifty dollars. The residents of Vietnam used it for leisure, and so did Ben. Ben would get sick from viral or mental stress and snort the heroin to feel better, which usually worked for him. Before he knew it, he was sick and addicted. Many of the soldiers contracted hepatitis from dirty needles, and some overdosed. Ben overdosed on heroin. About three months after his first use of heroin, his five-dollar vial purchases turned into hundred-dollar purchases. The Army provided rehabilitation and gave him amnesty for admitting he had a problem. Frustrated by the requirement that he remain at Fire Support Base Aries, which was fifty miles north of Saigon, Ben was one of ten GIs who staged a pray-in for peace. When he declined his squad leader's and officer's requests that he stop praying, they court-martialed him for refusal to follow orders. Bernie's connections to military personnel helped bail Ben out of the situation. Bernie sympathized with Ben because he had also been in trouble while serving. Ben began working for Chimera full time.

Ben did not divulge all of this information to Celia. He did not want to scare her away. He kept the conversation about the war light. Celia wanted to talk about the protests that were happening throughout the country. She told him about the time when she attended the march that went from Central Park to the United Nations building. All sorts of people attended the rally. Martin Luther King walked with them from start to finish. She told them that some people even burned their draft cards. "Would you have burned your card?" Celia asked him.

"I would have. I thought by joining I was doing something honorable. I would have run to Canada with the rest of them if I really knew what I was getting myself into. It changed me forever," he said. "Thank you for marching for us," he added.

Celia reached her hand to touch his. "You're welcome. Most of us think this war is senseless," she said. The date was reminiscent of her times with John, and she had a brief flashback. She quickly cleared her mind and continued on the date. Neither one would ever have thought a meeting like this possible when they first met each other.

Once they left the restaurant, they went to the movies and watched *The Me Nobody Knows*. He thought it was appropriate since the storyline seemed to parallel their lives in New York City. After they had left the theater, they went back to her place to end the night. Ben was impressed with the way she arranged her apartment. Celia had her eight-track player running. She had the bottle of wine that he had gifted her still unopened. He noticed it and suggested that they pop the bottle. Celia went to get the wine glasses. Ben looked around, sneaking a peek into her bedroom. He noticed her bed. It was small. He wanted to ask her about that but decided not to. He then saw a keyboard in the corner of her bedroom. It was a Bontempi electric organ. She had splurged on it as a gift to herself. She did not want to get rusty in her piano playing and thought this would be an excellent way to brush up on her practice, just in case she decided to return to school or play for someone special. He asked her about it.

"I didn't know you played instruments," he said.

"I do. I have been playing since I was a little girl. My mother taught me," she replied.

"Can you play for me?" Ben asked. Celia did not want to do it. She had promised John that if she were to demonstrate her abilities, he would be the first to hear it. She was a woman of her word, and she felt that some things were reserved for special occasions. This was not one of those occasions.

"Not today. Maybe some other time," Celia answered. They both sat down. They were comfortable on her bed as they continued small chatter. He gave her a loving glance. He leaned over to kiss her, and she kissed him back. He unzipped the back of her dress and proceeded to remove it. She paused. For a brief moment, she thought, *It was supposed to be John doing this.* She had to shake him out of her head. She let Ben continue, and they ended up making love on her twin bed.

When they were done, he got up and used her bathroom. While he was there, Celia's telephone rang. It was John, and he just wanted to chat with her. She spoke to him for a few minutes, not mentioning that she had Ben over at her place. While Ben was in the bathroom, he heard Celia talking to someone on the phone. He noted her lowered voice and peeked through the crack of the door.

John wanted to come over, and he said that he missed hanging out with her, but she told him not to come. She said she was on her way out on the town with Rose and some other friends. Ben continued to peek through the crack, and he noticed her face was relaxed with a slight smile on it. He made a noise to distract her. Celia sensed that Ben was finishing in the bathroom, and she told John that her friends were there, and she had to go. Ben returned from washing his face, and Celia ended the call with John. Ben looked at her and then lifted her chin with his finger. He kissed her, and they were ready for another round of lovemaking.

Another day passed with no word from Bernie. Celia was concerned, but the guys were not. They had known Bernie to take days away from the office often. He did not always divulge his whereabouts. He felt that some things needed to remain private. Celia decided to pay a visit to Bernie's townhouse to check on him. She was terribly concerned. She took a cab over to his place. To ease her nerves, she had a conversation with the driver, who was polite. When she arrived, she got out of the cab and made it to the top of the stairs. She rang his doorbell to no answer. Celia had obtained keys to Bernie's place; he had locked spares away in a safe at the office. He kept a backup of important things in his life in that safe just in case he misplaced his first set. He was a big fan of redundancy. She unlocked the door and went upstairs. His front door had several locks for security purposes. She knocked and called his name but received no answer. She figured if he had gone on vacation, everything would be okay and she would inform him of her visit to his place. She knew that he did not have a lady to look after him anymore since the sudden passing of Gina. She was willing to take on the role, as she had been used to visiting her mother to check on her. It took her a while to get all of the locks undone, as she had to figure out which key went to each lock. She finally got them all open and walked in.

She walked through the short hallway, which led to the living room. Both of the windows were open, which she found unusual since it was early April and it had snowed after the rainstorm a few days prior. The temperatures had dipped below freezing. It was freezing in the apartment. She looked over at the couch and found Bernie covered in a blanket. He looked like he was sleeping peacefully. She did not want to scare him with a sudden noise, so she slowly walked over to touch him. He was cold, stiff, and unresponsive. She shook him to no avail. In her heart, she knew what she was seeing. Bernie was gone. She leaned over and hugged him. She thanked him for everything and cried. She went to the telephone to call the police.

When the ambulance arrived, they attempted to revive him to no avail. They announced him deceased at the scene. They inquired of next of kin, and Celia replied, "We are his family." She informed them that she would let the others know. She went back downstairs and stood by the steps to collect her thoughts. She watched them remove his body, which was covered with a white sheet from the apartment. Her mind kept returning to the open windows. She looked up at them from below. When she was younger, her mother had told her that when a person dies, you have to open the window so the soul can go up to heaven. Celia wanted to think that he had known that it was time and had been letting himself go. She took the information she had about where he would be located and returned to the office to find the others and inform them.

When Celia returned to the office, all three guys were there, to her surprise. It was a rare occurrence these days for all three of them to be together with a few subworkers and security. They were having a discussion among themselves when she walked in. They welcomed her back in unison.

Her eyes were red and teary, with smudged mascara, as she had cried in the cab ride back to the office. All three looked at her. They asked her whether anything was wrong with her and asked everyone else to clear the room. They had never seen her in such distress. They wanted to make sure that she was OK.

"He's gone," she said.

"Who's gone?" John asked.

She looked at him. "Bernie's gone," she replied. All of them stood silent. You could hear a feather hit the floor. They were all in shock.

Chapter 7

The first two weeks after Bernie's sudden passing went by in a blur for everyone at the company. It was the first time in Chimera's existence that they had no leader. Productivity completely halted for a week before Celia and John agreed to reopen the offices so they could move on and heal. John was a mess, and Celia thought that he should get out of the apartment. Jerome was stressed and sad. He had his parents, but Bernie was the second father to him and a person whom he felt understood him and his ambitions the most. Ben handled the situation the best way he knew how, by disappearing and indulging in mind-numbing narcotics.

People from all over the city came together for Bernie's funeral. The church pews filled. Mourners included some of Bernie's distant relatives who had not spoken to him for years. Some of them still held a grudge about the way he'd handled his grandparents' store. Chimera's security was heavily present because John wanted everything to go off without incident. The services made the local papers and evening news. Despite some questionable activities at times, Bernie had a stellar reputation in New York City. At the funeral, Edina and Celia finally came face to face. John was forced to introduce them. Edina had no clue about Celia besides her being a person who worked with John. Celia was uncomfortable, to say the least. She did not want to talk more with Edina than she had to. Both were seemingly too distraught to socialize. John looked like he just wanted to leave the area entirely.

John became the boss of Chimera by default and presumed the leadership role. Bernie had left him in charge of most of the activities in the company, excluding his plans for Atlantic City. John met with Luci Graziani briefly after the burial to discuss what would be next for them. Graziani was still interested in working with them. John wanted to avoid a hostile takeover, a possibility since the other families knew of Bernie's passing and were ready to seize everything Chimera had built in the past decade. John was determined not to let that happen, as Bernie's legacy was important to him and everyone who was still there.

Ben began to slide backward. Celia had ended her outside contact with Ben altogether. There would be no more dates. She just did not feel right about the entire situation. The one-time sex with him had fulfilled a physical need, she realized. Ben wanted to see her more often, as a support crutch and a girlfriend, but she declined. Ben would not admit it, but his feelings were a bit hurt by the distance. Much like John, Ben used his time at work to be close to her. His productivity slowed, and he did not want to take orders from John. He was too busy snorting coke on his off time to deal with his grief about the breakup. It had become so bad that he was now experiencing nosebleeds. Ben did not want Celia to see this, as he knew it would scare her away for good. He needed her because now she was his only ally at Chimera. Celia had become the neutral point in the group as well as the unofficial number four in the company, even if she did not participate in the initiation ceremony. Her role was now more important than ever. Ben was bitter overall, and he thought that he had to make moves soon or else he would fade away from all the work he had put in over the years. He had helped build Chimera, and he felt unappreciated. He began to use his time with Celia as a way to get at John, even mentioning to John that they went out, which made tensions worse between the two. John knew that Ben was no good for Celia but understood that he had no real power to control her. He had no choice but to sit back and hope their relationship would implode.

Jerome sought comfort in his girlfriend. The shock of Bernie's death prompted him to propose to Mariana on a whim. She accepted. He felt good about his decision to finally settle down. Nightlife was becoming mundane to him, and he needed a higher purpose to justify some of the things he did on a daily basis. The entire death situation had Jerome questioning life. He felt that he should do the things he had always wanted to do before it was too late. Jerome and Mariana had discussed marriage before, and he felt that now was the time to take the plunge. They planned to walk down the aisle soon, as Mariana did not want to wait too long. Her family wanted her married sooner rather than later, but first Jerome had to get a few things in order at Chimera before he could settle down.

———

Since Bernie was no longer there, Edina knew that John was not handling things well. Instead of using the combative tone he typically employed when they argued, he now sounded defeated. He was too occupied to hate her. Edina was aware of the father-and-son-like relationship between John and Bernie. John had not spoken to her much since the funeral, and he had increased his drinking. John's workload increased, and he split his time in too many places. Edina felt that this was a prime opportunity for her to step in, provide the comfort that he needed, and help him. Besides, she and John had been there since the beginning with Bernie; therefore, she and John should be the ones who kept things afloat. Before she could plan, she had to do some investigating. She needed to know the details of his other residence and find out why he wanted to spend so much time there instead of at home with her.

Edina made the trip over to John's apartment. It was situated in a luxury high-rise. She had called his place earlier in the day to make sure that he would not be home. John was traveling out of town for the day, which gave her plenty of time to take a cab over, get in, survey the place, and get back. When she arrived at the building, the door attendant stopped her. He did not know who she was. He was usually the night-shift door attendant, but he had agreed to fill in for the day-shift attendant, who was sick. John had only tipped off the day-shift door attendant about the chance of his wife showing up unexpectedly. There were also different people working the concierge desk that day. The replacement staff were not fully aware of John's security protocols. Many who worked at the tower often saw John bring numerous women back to his place. For privacy reasons, they never divulged details about that to anyone.

Edina asked to speak to management to see if she could gain access to the apartment. She identified herself as John's wife and said that there should not be any problems. She claimed that he forgot to leave her the keys, and she had to get something important out of the apartment. They knew she was his wife. The woman at the desk was aware of John's extracurricular activities. She felt sad for his wife. The manager woman agreed to let her in for a time. They led her upstairs and into the apartment.

Edina looked around and was surprised by how clean the place looked. She had expected a pigsty. The decor was decent, but not as good as what she would do. To her, it was enough to be passable. She thought the light fixture on the ceiling was gaudy. It looked like a lunatic had designed it. Black-and-white framed photographs covered the light-gray walls. The sofa was a dark gray with black pillows, and the

carpet had a strange pattern on it. He had a large floor television against the wall. She thought the entire setup was a
bit drab and sad. The city views were excellent, as the windows in the living room were nice and large. She saw clear
evidence that another woman had been in the apartment at
some point, as she found an earring on the kitchen counter.
His refrigerator had minimal food in it. Just some opened
wine, TV dinners, and what looked like an old carton of
eggs. Edina quickly closed it. She looked over and saw the
wine rack and record console with his collection on the side.
She knew he liked to drink, but she had not been aware of
his fondness for music. She felt like she was learning about
a brand-new person and not the man she had been with for
a decade. She peeked into his bedroom and saw that his bal-
cony was attached from there. She found the bed unmade
and saw some clothes lying on the floor and the chair. His
dresser held his comb, brush, cufflinks, and deodorant. She
could smell the scent of his favorite cologne. She looked
in his closet, through his drawers, and under his bed. She
saw nothing out of the ordinary, except the numerous unopened packets of condoms, one recently used condom, and
women's underwear that was not hers under the bed. He
must not have realized those items were under there. She
was disgusted.

Another door in his bedroom led to a small, attached
room—his darkroom. She peeked in. The first things she
noticed were hanging photographs. A couple of them were
drying, and she was careful not to ruin them by turning on
the light. The natural sunlight coming from the bedroom

was enough for her to see by. She looked over and noticed the camera she had bought him. It made her happy that he was actually enjoying something she had given him. She looked up to get a glance at the photographs he had taken with the camera. Many of them depicted architecture. She noticed that these were the same photos he had hanging on his walls. She made mental note of his talent. Other photos were of women. She took one down and attempted to look at it carefully. She wanted a clearer view of the picture, so she went back out to the bedroom toward the window to look. It was a photograph of Celia in her bunny suit at the club. She recognized Celia's face immediately from their meeting at the funeral. She went back into the room to look at the other photographs. One by one, she discovered that each of the photos were of Celia. John had taken some at the club, and others appeared to be at an eatery and at the office. There were two pictures of the four men of Chimera and one of all five of them together. John did not have a single photograph of Edina in his darkroom.

The discovery surprised her. She had been under the impression that John was into blondes like her, despite her being bleached. She had not thought that he would find any colored girls more suitable than her. Edina associated with colored women when she went out on social events, but they were never close to her. Edina became angry. Her competition was at his place of work. No wonder he loved spending time there, she thought. Edina knew more than ever that in order to fix things, she would have to get to the source. It was time to make her presence known at Chimera. She had nothing else to do besides be a professional socialite.

———

Jerome headed to Atlantic City to meet with Luci Graziani. After Graziani and John's discussion at Bernie's funeral, they had decided to pull their resources together. Jerome met with Graziani on a Sunday at the Little Belmont Club on Kentucky Avenue. Besides talk, they wanted to catch a breakfast show. Jerome had heard about this club because of its rich history. It was frequented by the likes of Louis Armstrong, Ella Fitzgerald, Nat King Cole, Cab Calloway, and Frank Sinatra. During their conversation, Graziani suggested that since Chimera was currently short staffed, they should team up with the Jet Mafia family in Philadelphia. Many of the helpers that the four guys in Chimera had hired left when Bernie passed away.

The Jet Mafia was an all-black crime family on the rise in the city. They were known to have a tight grip on the drug trade. Graziani insisted that he was in good standing with Jet and that they were willing to work with Chimera because of the group's connections in New York City. The Jet family wanted to expand, so this was a partnership of convenience. Graziani would tip them off to crime families and their shell businesses, and the Jets would rob those businesses for a small cut. The Jet Mafia were very violent and had a reputation for extortion, murder of rival dealers, and the dismantling of other criminal businesses.

They were planning a hit on one of the businesses, disguised as an antiques shop, that the Donati family, a top crime family in Philadelphia, owned.

Graziani thought that all of them together would make a strong enough group to rival the other New York and Philadelphia families, as he felt that they were just as deserving of the piece of the Atlantic City pie as the rest of them. Jet had the funds and the firepower; Chimera and Graziani had the connections and brains. The planning was successful, and Jerome returned to New York to update John. They decided to continue to head into the Atlantic City gambling race with Graziani as their anchor.

Edina suspected that John was involved in illegal activities. She had heard whispers about his activities when she attended social events. All types of moneyed people in the city, including those who had ties to the mob, attended the same events. She only had faint information about the Ambrosino family, but she ran across a few of the wives at the same functions. The women never discussed tensions between the families, but they were nice in general. They had no idea who Edina was or how she was connected to Chimera. She decided to see what she could do to put Chimera in a better position. She knew that John and the others were having a difficult adjustment period, and she wanted to see if she could help save the situation and become the hero.

At one of the lunch social functions, Edina pulled aside Roma Ambrosino, Dante Ambrosino's wife. Roma was a delicate-looking woman. She was tall and waifish, and her brunette hairdo consisted of a French roll on top, fringe, and an upward flip at the bottom half of her hair. Edina had always thought that this woman had too much going on with hair, and her furs were too big, but she found her to be pleasant. Edina spoke to Roma, bringing up the idea that their families could work together. She figured that if they merged, they could become powerful together. Edina wanted to meet with the bosses on her own because she knew that John would never go for it. Edina had to get into the offices of Chimera to see how the whole thing operated so she could report back. When she came up with a solid plan, she would present it to John. She figured that he could not refuse such an idea. It would be too profitable to turn down. It would be the most peaceful solution for both parties.

Things moved quickly, and Roma took Dante aside that same night and told him what she had talked about with Edina. Dante thought about this and figured it could work, although he did not like Chimera. They could buy out the competition, dismantle them, and possibly take out any Philadelphia speedbumps, mainly the Jet family.

The day after their meeting, Edina showed up at the Chimera offices for only the second time in their entire existence. John was out when she arrived, and she met Ben first. Ben had never been introduced to her formally, and he made sure to mention that John never talked about her either.

Then she met Jerome. John always said he had a best friend named Jerome, and she finally put a face to the description. She had seen him briefly at the funeral but didn't think much of it. Edina thought Jerome was OK, but he seemed common to her. In the back office sat Celia. Edina walked right into Celia's office as if she were cool with the place and the person in it. Celia was surprised to see her.

"Hello," Celia said.

"Hi," Edina responded curtly. "I'm here looking around. I am John's wife. We've met before, at the funeral."

"I do remember. Nice to see you," Celia responded. Edina eyeballed the office.

"OK, you can get back to what you were doing," Edina said. Celia sat there dumbfounded. It sounded as if Edina was ordering her around.

Jerome contacted John and informed him that Edina was in the office. John flipped out on the phone. He did not know why she was there. She had never warned him about her arrival and told him her reasons for showing up. Before John arrived, Edina walked in and looked around his office. John had taken over Bernie's space, but he had only commingled necessary items from his old desk to Bernie's. He thought it was important to keep everything Bernie had intact. She looked at the photos in the room, which Bernie had left. He had a copy of the group photo with all five of them framed on his desk. There was also a picture of Bernie and Gina together. She continued to look around to see if John had put photos of Celia in there too. Edina did not find any.

When John walked in, Edina was sitting in his chair and leaning back on it with her feet propped on top of the desk. He hated body parts on the desks unless Celia was sitting her butt on it. He did not mind that. "Why are you here? Why are you sitting in my chair?" He asked her.

"I'm your wife. I can't come and visit you?" she responded in a cutesy way.

"Well, no, you can't," he responded.

"What?" she said.

"You can't just be showing up here," he said. The conversation was just loud enough for everyone to hear. Jerome and Ben watched as John closed the office door behind him.

"The hell is going on here?" Jerome asked Ben. Ben responded with a shrug.

Celia came out of the office, walked over to Jerome and Ben, and said lightly, "She burst into my room and was just, I don't know."

Jerome responded, "Something is going on."

"Do you want something?" John asked Edina.

"I want my husband's company," Edina said.

"I am OK; I'm not lonely here," John responded.

"Oh, I bet you aren't," Edina replied.

"What is that supposed to mean?" he asked her.

"Oh, nothing," she said. "I am here because I know you need help, and I am here to help."

"We are not hiring," John said.

"I am not asking for payment. John you are so funny sometimes. I have ideas that will help the company. You are running it now, and I feel that my input would help us make this place great," Edina said.

"Us?" John interrupted.

"Yes, us. We are a union. Or have you forgotten that?" Edina said to him in a cross tone.

"Look, if you want to help, you can get lunch for everybody. Did you at least bring food with you?" John asked her.

"You can eat me," she said in a sexy tone as she opened her legs slightly.

Blank-faced and repelled, John responded, "Well if you are not going to get any food, I still have time to get to the diner down the street before it gets crowded."

———

Shortly after the New Year, the Jet Mafia, assisted by information from Luci Graziani, conducted a hit on the Smith Antique store in Philadelphia. The Donati crime family owned the store. The Donati family had attempted to kill Graziani before for his dealings with New York crime families. The scene at the antique shop was so violent and gory that it made national news. The employees in the store had been stripped of their garments, hog-tied, forced to lie down, and whipped with a pistol and rope. After they had cleared the safe of thousands of dollars, the Jet Mafia burned the place down with everyone in it. The Donati family in mourning declared an all-out war on anyone who may have been involved.

Months passed after the hit from the Jet Mafia. Graziani was at Club Harlem, a nightclub in Atlantic City, having appetizers with his date and enjoying the entertainment. A gunman entered, took aim, and shot Graziani in the head at point-blank range. The bullet went through his head and hit a shot glass on the table next to them. Security fired back, and the gunman continued to shoot, killing Graziani's date and wounding the security guard. The gunman was also shot to death. The rest of the patrons ran out of the club. Upon learning of Graziani's sudden death ordered by the Donati family, the Jet Mafia family and Chimera quickly became full partners, sharing resources among New York, Philadelphia, and parts of Atlantic City. John felt that the manpower from the Jet Mafia would help Chimera tremendously.

Graziani was out of the picture, which left the Jet Mafia and Chimera on the radar of the Donati and Ambrosino families, who were working together. They had a deal to work together in Atlantic City. The hit on Graziani simply eliminated competition. Graziani was the common denominator.

Soon after the hit, John and Ben began to get harassing phone calls at the office. Ben was not sure who had it out for him. He assumed that it was one of his dealers, whom he owed money. Ben had been dipping into the company funds to pay them, but it had become increasingly difficult to do so. Celia was now in charge of finances, and despite Bernie's reassurance, she remained suspicious of the past activity that she had tracked from Ben. She was strict with funds and access to checks. John's calls came directly into his office. He suspected that they were being recorded because he could hear a light clicking sound as he went back and forth with the caller.

"So why are you calling me and hanging up? Are you recording this shit?" John would ask.

The unidentified caller would occasionally respond, "Why are you worried? Gangsters don't worry, right? You guys do the threatening. Is that what you people like to say?"

John would get irritated. "Now it's you that's threatening me."

Jerome received harassing phone calls at his residence. The calls frightened Celia so much that she opted to work from home on some days until she thought it was safe to return to the office full-time. John had a few members from the Jet Mafia come to New York to work security for them and to protect her. The Jet Mafia family had about thirty members, so John enlisted ten of them to come to New York.

Edina often returned to the office, much to the dismay of John, who could not do much to stop her from showing up periodically. He locked his office door to keep her out of it, so Edina would linger around various sections of the building not doing much. They had a couch for visitors, so she would sometimes sit there until John arrived. Other times she would have conversations with Ben. When John came, he would acknowledge her presence and then retreat to his office, closing the door on her. Celia attempted to strike a friendly conversation with Edina a couple of times to break the ice. These did not end well. She felt that Edina was sizing her up, and a couple of comments Edina did say to her were patronizing and bordering on disrespectful.

After a few such conversations, Celia decided to pull Edina aside and talk to her woman to woman. Edina was always reluctant to speak with Celia. "Did I do something to you?" Celia asked.

"You can't do anything for me, sweetie," Edina responded snidely. "Look, I know that your people are fighting for their rights and access to everything; that's wonderful. I support it, I do, but that does not mean you can infringe on others' territory."

"Woah, wait a minute," Celia said.

Edina cut her off. "No, you hold on a minute, sweetie. I only tolerate you because everybody else likes you here," she said. "You are screwing my husband. Here is not your place. John and I have been here from the beginning, and I just don't think it's appropriate for you to be even here."

Jerome overheard the two women in a heated discussion and decided to interrupt them. The tone Edina used did not sit well with him. Edina snapped back at Jerome, "I don't need your assistance. Don't you have something to do?" Jerome looked at her in disbelief; she had some nerve to talk down to him.

"It's OK, Jerome," Celia assured him to get him out of the way.

"I know you guys stick together," Edina said to Celia.

"OK, look, I've never slept with him. I don't know what your problem is, and for your information, we do stick together. Jerome is my family. He is a good guy, and he doesn't like disrespect. Plus you need to be reminded that you are married to one of us! I don't get that," Celia snapped back. Edina knew she was married to a man who had black heritage, but she did not see him as one of the "others," as she called them.

John walked in and heard the commotion. "What the fuck?" he yelled. "Edina, go home. You can't be here anymore. You can't linger here all day; do something."

"I can't be here? I am your wife. How are you going to kick me out?" Edina yelled back at him.

"This is a place of business, and you cannot be bothering him or her," he said.

"Who are they? Why aren't you defending me?" Edina asked. "You and I were here first! If anyone doesn't belong here, it's her," Edina said as she pointed to Celia. This made John angry.

"Go, Edina!" he said after a deep breath.

"No, you let her go. Fire her now," Edina said. Celia looked at John, and he looked back at her.

"Fire her for what? I'm not doing that."

Edina looked from Celia to John and Jerome, and then she walked out. Fed up with the situation, Edina made it back to her residence and dialed Roma Ambrosino. She wanted to discuss a deal with them.

Before they could deal with Edina's appearances, Chimera had to solve the issue of the harassing phone calls. Jerome thought that the Ambrosino family was behind them. Ambrosino had been their chief adversary. The harassing phone calls to Jerome's home had increased. The calls were used to taunt them. Mariana would pick them up, and the caller would insult her. She expressed concern to Jerome about the situation, as she had recently discovered that they were with child and did not want anything to happen to them. Sometimes the caller would refer to Jerome as a monkey and warn that he and the rest of their monkey family had better watch out if Chimera did not back down. This call was no different. Mariana called Jerome over to the line to help this time. Jerome took the phone from her.

"Luci was a waste. I never really saw the appeal of dealing with niggers," the caller said and hung up. From that statement, Jerome knew whom he was dealing with. It was Dante Ambrosino. Dante had been the main voice of opposition to Chimera and their attempts to expand. He would often taunt Chimera as he felt that a group like them did not fit into the culture that the families had cultivated in New York City. He felt that the Cosa Nostra had no place for a mongrel group. The Ambrosino family did not want to take Chimera seriously, and they figured that the group would be easy to diminish. Jerome did not take kindly to threats to his family. He felt the obligation to protect them at all costs. He called John, and they got together, but not before Jerome had Mariana removed from the residence into a safer place.

A few days after the phone calls and the incident at the office, things returned to normal at Chimera. Edina's visits had made everyone uneasy. They were smiling again now. Edina was only friendly to Ben and John. She was offhand to Jerome and Celia. Edina saw those two as a threat to her and John's future. John had finally decided to make up his mind and begin the process of divorcing Edina. He was fed up with her. Bernie was no longer with them, and the lingering obligation to him regarding Edina no longer played a factor in the situation. John felt that he finally had an out. He knew that he would lose out big in a divorce financially. Edina had different plans. She thought if they had any chance to make it at all, Celia and Jerome would have to go, and she was determined to see that materialize. Roma Ambrosino put Edina in contact with the chief Ambrosino-family boss, Enzo Ambrosino, and they had a lengthy conversation.

John and Jerome decided to pay a visit to Dante Ambrosino themselves. They knew that his wife and children were out of town visiting another family. Edina leaked that info to John to make small talk with him and to ease him into what she was planning to do. John had never been interested in hearing what she had to say or learning about any of the Ambrosino activities until now. It was 10:10 p.m. later that evening. It was pitch black outside, so it was hard to spot them. The neighborhood was in a rural area in Westchester that did not have a lot of street lighting. John and Jerome staked out on Dante's property, hiding in the shrubbery and massive snow piles that were left on the lawn. Both were dressed in all black from head to toe. They wore black face paint and ski caps to make sure they exposed no identifying characteristics. John then went and disabled the power on the generator outside. They knew Dante was in there alone. His wife had revealed to Edina that her husband liked to sit and drink alone in front of the fireplace at night.

Before they entered the house, John looked at Jerome. "You ready?" he asked.

"Yep," Jerome said.

"Let's go and light his ass up," John responded.

John and Jerome entered the house through an unlocked side window. They were surprised how easy it was to get in. That meant they did not have to leave any visible signs of a break-in. The window was located away from the room where Dante was sitting and drinking while reading the paper. Dante did not immediately notice that the generator was off, as he only had the fireplace and moonlight for light. John and Jerome made it in without tipping off any alarms. Dante did not have dogs, as Roma had an allergy to them and did not like them around the children. The Ambrosino family felt that no one had the balls to touch them in their homes, so they did not worry about security in the area. John and Jerome quietly walked through the house until they reached the room where Dante was sitting. He had nodded off. As they inched closer, John quietly cut every phone cord he passed. They walked up to Dante. John stood behind the chair, and Jerome stood before it. Dante suddenly woke up and saw the unidentified person standing in front of him. Dante asked him to identify himself.

"It's Monkey Man, motherfucker," Jerome answered, and both he and John attacked the man, placing a chloroform-soaked cloth over his face until he passed out. Once he was out, they took part of the newspaper, lit it from the fireplace, and began burning things to make it look like an accidental fire. They burned his clothes and chair while he sat unconscious. The fire spread quickly, as many of the materials in the home were flammable. Jerome picked up the cloth they had used, and they headed out and left the area quickly. They burned the cloth when they returned to the city.

Chapter 8

After the hit on Dante Ambrosino, the calls stopped. The Ambrosino family was preoccupied with the death, which the investigators ruled an accident. The house burned quickly, and the top of Dante's body burned beyond recognition. He was positively identified by a tattoo on his foot. The coroner found no signs of other trauma on his body. They established that there had been no foul play, as they could not detect an accelerant or any sign of illegal entry. The investigators concluded that a spark from the fireplace might have started the blaze, as Dante had used unsuitable wood that produced flying embers that spread into the room. John and Jerome had a clean hit. They could have had the Jet family come and do the job, but this was personal to both of them. They intended to send a hard message about the years of taunting and threats. Chimera was not to be fucked with. This counted as a needed hit in the way that Bernie had taught them. When your life or your family's lives are in danger, you take the necessary steps to ensure their safety.

———

Edina completed the secret deal with Enzo Ambrosino the night of Dante's death. She was excited about the agreement and the future of the group, as well as her and John's livelihoods. She had her entire plan to present to John, but she knew she would have some resistance. She called the office again, but this time asked to speak to Ben. She needed a pathway to John. Celia and Jerome were out of the question. Ben agreed to meet with her. She had not told him what the extent of the conversation would be.

Ben and Edina met at a diner in Staten Island. Both of them thought that the place was off the radar and somewhere that John, Jerome, and Celia would not venture to. They began their conversation over a pasta dinner. Ben was still unsure about the meeting since their encounters had only been brief. Edina decided to break the ice and ask him about his life. He told her just the basics about himself, as he did not fully trust her with all of his information because of her connection with John. Edina then questioned him about Celia.

"What do you know?" Edina asked him.

"I work with her," he answered.

"That's it?" Edina said.

"No, but why is this important?" Ben responded.

"OK, I will tell you what's happening. I think they are having an affair," Edina told him. Ben's suspicions about the meeting waned. He was more than willing to spill what he knew about John. He started providing more information.

"Well, I can tell you that nothing is happening now with them. They used to date, but I don't know how far that went," he told her.

"Oh, but how are they now?" Edina probed.

"I'm with her now," Ben said to her. Celia had subsided contact with him, but Ben was in denial. Edina was slightly relieved to hear this. "But he keeps interfering. It bothers me, and she has now started to brush me off," he added. Edina's relief turned to discontent. "Look, I don't know if he has feelings for her or what, and excuse me for my language, but I've wanted to punch him in the fucking mouth for a year now," he added before putting a fork full of pasta in his mouth.

Edina sat silent. Ben had just confirmed her worst suspicions about John and Celia. Edina knew that John slept with women, but she had always dismissed that as something physical only. He didn't love those girls. John was emotionally vested in Celia. This was worse. Bernie had kept him obligated, and now that he was no longer there, she knew John had no one else to answer to. She realized that if she wanted a chance in hell to save their marriage, she would have to get Celia out of his mind. Edina cut to the chase.

"Ben, I brought you here to sit you down and give you some important information. There have been things going on behind the scenes, a project that we've been working on," she said.

"Go on," Ben said.

"To put this simply, we're merging," Edina said.

"What? Merging with whom?" Ben asked her.

"Merging with Enzo Ambrosino," she replied. Ben coughed as if he were choking.

"Merging with Ambrosino? That makes no sense. They hate us," Ben said.

"No, it's not like that. I've met with them. They are OK. They are investing in us," Edina replied.

"So, John is OK with this? Who else knows about this?" Ben questioned.

"No, John does not know yet. Nobody knows. You are the first person who knows as of now," she said.

"If John wasn't there, then who did the deal?" he asked.

"I did," she answered. Ben sat silent for ten seconds.

"So you're running things now?" he said sarcastically.

"Ben, no, this was on the side. You know, and I know, and everybody else knows that since Bernie died, the group has been in a terrible position, and I know that you all are still trying to adjust. John needs the help. I used my connections and expertise to give you and him a life raft," Edina said. "They were willing to bury the hatchet if we joined forces. It's better for everybody. This move will make both groups stronger. I'm part of this as John's wife. I knew

Bernard before everyone else. I wanted you to know first because I need you as an anchor to John. He is going to resist this," she said.

"And rightfully fucking so. This is unbelievable," he said. "This is disrespectful to Bernie. He put his life into us. What's in the company—the money, the property, the clients, the history—it belongs to all of us."

Edina sensed that Ben was not thrilled about the news. She needed his cooperation. She decided to use Celia as a draw, and if that failed, she would put the moves on Ben herself. "Ben there is something else I have to tell you. The way the Ambrosino family works, there will be no purpose for Celia or Jerome, so we will have to let them go. You stay with us, and you will have a bigger role. You are one of them, I mean the Italians. They will relate to you the most," she said.

Ben sat there again in a ten-second pause. Despite their differences, dumping Jerome did not totally sit well with him. His only personal issue with Jerome was his cliquish relationship with John and the fact that Jerome has passed him in the ranks. He took an oath not to burn his brothers, even when at times he disliked them.

"Think of it like this: we let Celia go, and you can have her to yourself or whatever. She will not be around John anymore, so there will not be any barriers between you two. I sense that you care for her," Edina said. Ben did not want to admit it, but he had fallen for Celia hard; however, his ego would never let him show that to her or anyone else. "We will buy them both out. It will be generous, I promise. I know it is not what you want to hear, but it is necessary, and it's final. It's already a done deal," she said. "Just tell me that you are in. I promise you that you will be better off in this new system. Just give me your word," she concluded.

Ben sat there for the longest quiet period since they arrived at the restaurant. Edina put her hand on top of his and rubbed it gently. She looked at him seductively. She wanted to make sure she pulled all the stops. Ben knew what she was trying to do and pulled his hand away. He felt bad, but then again, Edina sold him an excellent opportunity. This would remove Jerome and force John to share the wealth. Ben was at a point of desperation. "OK," he told her. "OK, I'm in. What do you need me to do? And when does this take place?"

Ben's decision thrilled Edina. "All I need you to do is keep quiet right now. I want to break the news to Celia myself, you know, have a powwow with her. I think this is something that another woman will have to discuss with her. We understand our wants and needs better than a man would. Just sit tight. I have taken care of everything. If I need your help with John, I will bring you into it. We help each other," she said. Edina extended her hand to him, and he shook it. She gave him her number and address and told him to contact her when he needed to.

Pleased with herself, Edina went back to her residence. There she had money paid as a binder from the Ambrosino family. She had accepted a down payment of four million dollars for the company and would receive another two million once everything merged. Edina felt that this was a great deal for all involved. She thought that she and John could branch off into something of their own and Ben would move up the ranks in the new family. She spent the rest of the evening calculating how much she should compensate Jerome and Celia for their time so that she could be rid of the both of them once and for all.

———

Back at the offices, everything seemed normal until Edina paid another unannounced visit to Chimera. She went there to see if Celia and Jerome were present so she could give them the news. Celia was there alone with her security detail. She had many invoices and payroll issues to address, so she was very busy. John and Jerome were out on the field with members of the Jet family. Ben's whereabouts were unknown. Edina thought that this was even better. Remove Celia without an audience. Edina walked into Celia's office once again unannounced and sat down in a chair that Celia kept in front of her desk.

"May I help you?" Celia asked tersely.

Edina took a deep breath. "I'm here to speak with you. It's important, and I need your undivided attention," she said.

Celia returned a deep breath. "I'm listening," she said.

"We got off to a bad start, and I would like to acknowledge how unfortunate that was," Edina said. "I came here to give you news of changes in the company. We are growing! We are merging with a bigger group, and that will begin shortly. That's exciting!" Edina said. With each word, her voice went a little higher. Celia continued to sit silently. "That means we had to do some trimming, as they did not need all of us. We do not need your position anymore. They have their people," Edina added.

Celia cleared her throat, as she thought that Edina was testing her again. "So what you are trying to say is that I am supposedly fired again," she said.

"No, we are eliminating your position. But I know how much the guys care about you, so here. This will make the transition go more smoothly for you," Edina told her, handing her a check for two hundred thousand dollars. Celia looked at the check to see if it was legit. It was from John and Edina LeBlanc. Celia sat there in shock.

Celia rebutted. "Why isn't John telling me this? He is whom I work for, not you."

"John and I are a union. I know you have never been married before, but when that happens—if that happens—decisions are made as a couple. I do not always have to ask John permission about decisions regarding our family. I am sure you will experience that one day, sweetie. He's busy right now and doesn't have time to hurt your little feelings. There's no need to talk to him. Take the check, start over, and live your life away from here. Two hundred grand is a lot of money, and you can do so much with it," Edina said. "I will leave that here for you. I wanted to talk with your cousin too, but I see that he is not here. You two are closer, and I think you would be a better candidate to inform him of our decisions. There is a nice send-off gift for him too and a letter in this envelope. Make sure he gets that. You can collect your things anytime today when you're ready." Edina stood up to leave.

"I'm not collecting anything," Celia shot back at her.

"Well, you do not have a choice. It's a done deal," Edina said as she walked away. She paused and turned back toward Celia. "I do not know what it is with you people. You do not know how to be appreciative when someone helps you," she said and walked away.

"I used to feel sorry for you. You are what he says about you!" Celia yelled as Edina was walking out. Edina took a cab back home feeling self-assured about what had just happened.

Panicked, Celia went to one of the guards and asked if he could locate John. She needed to speak with him urgently, as this could not wait. Her heart was in a panic. She could fight words, but she could not deny a check with both of their names on it. That was as legal as it got. She sat there a few minutes while tears rolled down her face. She had not felt this uneasy since she was fired from the Playboy Club. The similarities between the two situations could not escape her. *How could I have been so stupid?* She thought.

After an uncomfortable hour, John made it back to the office to see what was wrong with Celia. If she were ever in a panic, John would always rush right over to her. Celia told him to come into her office and close the door. He had the security stand outside of it. "John what is this?" she asked, handing him the check Edina had given her.

John took the check from her and looked at it. "It's a check," he said. He examined it further and realized that this was a personal check taken from his joint marital account. It had Edina's handwriting, and he noted the amount. On the *notes* line, it said *severance*. "Bunny, I don't know what this is. I did not write it." He crumbled it slightly and tossed it in the wastebasket.

"She told me that we were merging and that that eliminated my position. She fired Jerome," Celia said.

"What are you talking about?" John asked her. "I don't know anything about this, and I didn't let anyone go. We are not merging. I don't know anything about this."

Celia became frustrated. "Who do I work for?" she asked. "She's always here now. She's insolent. I can't fight her."

"I'm sorry. It won't happen again. She will never be here anymore," John said to reassure her.

"But you said that before, and she keeps showing up. John, do you know how hard it was for me to come here, to give up my pride because I needed to work? I had to look at a man who I thought I had but who belonged to someone else, and to now have her come here and taunt me…And all I keep thinking is that there is nothing you can do about it; you're stuck!" she said.

"You are not the only one who is being tortured around here. You think I like hearing about you and Ben? How does that make me feel, Bunny? Do you like spreading yourself among the group?" John said.

Celia was stunned. "John, there is a difference. I am not even with him now. That was one time. That was nothing. Not only do you have a wife, but you sleep with everybody. You can't put me in the same category as you. I have never thrown that in your face," she interjected. "The threatening calls here from them. Everything makes sense now." She added, "I have to go. I am not feeling well." She started picking up papers and removing others from her board. One of those papers included the Jamaica advert that she pinned up the very first week she started working there. She bent over to pick up the check.

"Bunny, wait," he said while trying to stop her. She left the envelope for Jerome on the desk. "Bunny, I'm sorry, I did not mean that."

She replied, "I have to go home." Bunny left John in the office. The scene reminded him of when she had left him in the park.

———

An enraged John told a Jet guard to find Jerome and Ben and make sure they got back to the office immediately. John unlocked his office and went straight to his phone. He went to dial Edina, but the phone rang before he picked it up. It was Enzo Ambrosino.

"Hello, Mr. LeBlanc. I like how you are running things without Papa Bernard. Wise choice. I look forward to doing business with you. You have a lovely wife there," Enzo said.

John replied to him, "Fuck you, fuck her, fuck your family. We are not doing business. Oh, and enjoy your charbroiled brother!" John slammed the phone. He quickly dialed out to their marital residence. Edina picked up. "What the fuck is wrong with you!" he screamed into the phone.

"John, lower your voice," Edina responded.

"What the hell is going on? What the fuck did you do?" he asked her.

"John, this was necessary. Calm down," she said to him.

"Do you realize what you've just done? Ambrosino does not want to do business with us. How fucking stupid can you be?" he yelled.

"We are now bigger than ever. Thank me, John," Edina said.

"No, fuck you, Edina. They do not like us. They are our enemies. They want our business, our money, our people. They want what we have, and you sold it all. You sold our legacy! You just had them pay us to kill us all off one by one! We're screwed!"

Edina was quiet for a moment, and then she responded. "John, I did this for us," she cooed.

"No. You did this for you! When you go behind my back and change shit, disregard any authority I have, like you always do, that's not for me. You're trying to hurt me. That's sabotage. You've been undermining me since day one," John told her.

"Really? And who told you this? The trollop you work with?" Edina responded.

"Don't interrupt me while I am talking. It never fails. You really are a disrespectful piece of trash," John said to her.

"I can't believe you just called me trash. You were a lout when I met you. You had nothing. You don't listen, and you are a cheater," Edina said.

"Well, I guess it takes one to know one, doesn't it? Did your fiancé feel that way about you before? How about your old boyfriend? Even he didn't want to be bothered with you," John said.

"Fuck you, John," Edina yelled.

"And that's why you are here, isn't it?" he responded.

"Fucking blue gum," Edina said. This put John over his limits.

Jerome came in with a guard to see what was going on. He overheard John yelling on the phone.

"Enough of this. We're done! I don't give a shit if I lose everything; we're done. I'm done with you. I'm done with this farce. I regret ever meeting you!" he screamed. "This is your problem. I am not doing shit with them. You fix it!" he said and slammed the phone. He kicked the chair. John had turned red from all the yelling. He saw Jerome.

"What's wrong in here?" Jerome asked, looking at John.

"We have to get everybody here from Jet. We've got to clear the safe, and we have to move these papers out of Bunny's office and mine now. Burn them, move them, or whatever. Swap them out for blanks. We've got to move before they get here," John said in a panic.

"Who?" Jerome asked.

"Ambrosino," he responded.

"Shit! Wait, why are they coming here?" Jerome asked.

"She fucked us all," John said.

"Who?" Jerome said.

"Edina. The biggest mistake of my life." Jerome shook his head. The guards, John, and Jerome, proceeded to clear the office of all paperwork containing company info, contacts, addresses, phone numbers, bank account information, and more. "Where in the fuck is Ben? Can't ever find his ass," John said.

Ben was in the South Bronx. This was not his normal work area. Even though he had agreed to participate in the merger, the conversation with Edina had stressed him, and he had retreated to his dealer's basement apartment. It was located in a brownstone on East 172nd Street. The streets that once were filled with lively culture and pride had morphed into a run-down depressed shell of themselves. The place resembled a war zone. Violent death was frequent among the youth in the community, and parents taught their kids survival early. The heroes were those in the gangs. There were abandoned buildings everywhere, garbage on the street, and plenty of burned-out skeletons of structures due to the many fires that occurred. Block after block was filled with storefronts that converted into churches and liquor stores. There were plenty of empty lots full of trash and abandoned stripped cars. Numerous homeless people stood around at night keeping their hands warm with fire-lit garbage cans. Graffiti covered walls everywhere, and scores of sneakers and sometimes baby dolls with no clothes hung from various power cables and poles. When you saw a sneaker hanging, it was a sign that a drug dealer had marked the spot. The drug problems manifested the most here. Kids outside played on a dirty, shredded mattress, and addicts walked the street. Ben used to think that he was better than these people, but when it came to dependency, he knew he was no different from any of them.

He had gone from snorting cocaine to shooting heroin. He was beginning to feel guilty, like a complete failure. He knew that he should have done more when he had the opportunity to stop Edina or do something, say something. That had been his time to shine, but he had let his jealousy of John get to him. He felt that he was letting down Bernie, the only person ever patient enough to deal with his shenanigans. Chimera as they all knew it was over, and they had to regroup. Ben did not know what else to do but run away. He knew that his chances with Celia were dwindling by the second and that she may resent him if she found out that he was in on the deal. The only plus that he saw was that he felt he should get a cut of the money Edina made out of the deal. He could pay off his dealers once and for all. Ben was stressed. He took a syringe, injected himself, and passed out. He woke up later.

Edina held herself in her marital home. She had not turned on the news or read the papers in hours. When she did, the reports focused on the beginnings of Watergate, in which she had no interest. She spent the time staring at what was left of the four million in cash. She had paid Celia and cut Jerome a check. She needed to put the rest into the bank, but she knew that she could not handle all of that money at one time by herself. It would tip off the Internal Revenue Service. John was good at hiding money. She had thought he would assist her. They both had the love of money in common, if not anything else. Her mind was racing about what to do next. She was scared that John was not going to go through with the deal, and she could not locate Ben anywhere. The whole thing was falling apart quickly.

She could not believe that John had told her the marriage was over. They had their difficulties, but she knew that he would eventually want to settle down and come home to her. She turned on the floor television in the dayroom and watched the news. They began discussing the fire at the Ambrosino Westchester Mansion. She gasped. She had no idea this was happening, as she had barricaded herself in the apartment to protect the money.

———

John, Jerome, and the Jet guards cleared out all essential paperwork and items from the Chimera offices in what seemed like record time. They finished the entire operation in five hours. They had guards posted outside to protect them. Jerome had sent a guard to collect Mariana and place her in a safe house in Yonkers. John took everything that was important to him and Bernie—photographs, keepsakes, personal papers, etc.—and left the office. He had Jet security pick him and Jerome up from the premises. Later on that evening, both Jerome and John continually tried to contact Celia to no avail. Celia was not on the radar, and John did not know how much information Edina had given to the Ambrosino family. He needed to get to Celia. Once John cleared his apartment of the items he wanted out, which included money, jewelry, and some of his favorite photos of the crew and Celia, he went to his safe house to drop them off. He left the camera that Edina had bought him in the apartment. He threw it across the room and broke it. He attempted to contact Celia again to no avail. Frustrated, he and Jerome got back into the car with security and went over to her apartment. By this time, it was early the next morning.

John and Jerome knocked on Celia's door. They did not care that they were loud enough to wake neighbors, although Jerome suggested that they quiet down so the neighbors would not alert the authorities. Instead, he said they could pick the door. After ten minutes, they got in. Celia was not there. John and Jerome called for her. No answer. They realized that some things were missing that had been there before, like clothes, personal artifacts, photos, and her prized electronic organ. John went into her bedroom and looked in her closet. It was half-empty. Her drawers were mostly empty. They found no sign of a wallet or keys left behind. They were worried. They hoped she went to a friend's house.

Her phone book was still there. They took it and returned to their safe house. Once John and Jerome arrived, they began calling people. Most of them were relatives, and a few were friends from the Playboy Club that she kept in contact with over the years. They phoned almost everyone. Rose's number was no longer working. Jerome called Agnes to check on her and see if Celia was with her. Not wanting to alarm Celia's mother, Jerome only told her that he needed to ask her something. Agnes had not talked to her in two days, and she told Jerome that she'd had no indication that anything was wrong. The night ended, and they were no closer to figuring out where she was so they could talk to her. John and Jerome were becoming more anxious by the minute.

Edina's doorbell rang. She was not expecting any company. She was uncharacteristically disheveled, as she had not bathed in nearly a day. What if it was John? She thought. She quickly straightened herself out and peeked through the peephole. It was Ben, and he was not looking clean himself. She let him in. "They're looking for you," Edina said to him. "What happened? Where were you? I've been calling everywhere."

"You should have told me this was going down now. I need money," he said. "What the hell am I supposed to do now?"

"You were supposed to talk to John. I'm dealing with this by myself. That was our agreement," Edina answered.

"I'll do that, but I need money, and I know they gave you money," he said.

"How much do you need? A few hundred?" she asked as she went to the stashed money.

"A million," he said.

"A million? Are you out of your goddamn mind?" Edina asked. "This is my family's money. I never agreed to give you a cut. I decided to leave you in the group," she said loudly.

"Fuck!" Ben rubbed his hair back, but since he had not washed it in days, it was greasy. "Your fucking husband and the rest of them have been shortchanging me for years. I've dealt with dis-re-fucking-spect for eight years! I am not going to deal with it from you either. Give me my fucking cut, or I'll kill you right here," he said. Ben's voice had turned borderline demonic. His eyes were bloodshot, and Edina knew that he was angry enough to do it. Ben walked over and saw a cardboard box of hundred-dollar bills in stacks sitting on the floor of an open closet. It was one of two boxes of money she had in the apartment from the payment. She separated the money just to keep it neat. He picked it up and proceeded to walk out of the apartment with it.

Before Ben left, he gave Edina some advice. "You're not one of us. Stick with what you know." He walked away. That box had over nine hundred thousand dollars in it. Scared out of her mind, Edina had a breakdown right in the middle of her living room floor.

Edina collected herself the next morning. She was scared about everything. She got up, took a bath, dressed, fixed her hair, and gathered what she needed for a trip to the bank with what was left of the money. Between the checks she cut and the box of money Ben took from the residence, the four million dollars had been reduced by almost half in about forty-eight hours. She had to do something before the Ambrosino family began calling her—or even worse, paying her a visit.

She hailed a cab over to the bank in Midtown. She arrived at the teller and handed her the box of money and a deposit slip. Bewildered at the amount of cash, the teller had to call a manager over to help her. The bank was familiar with Edina and knew that she was well off. They were pleased that she was depositing money. They did not question why she was carrying around a large sum of money, but they did speak to her about their concerns in a couple of days prior. Both Celia and Jerome had cashed their checks. John had emptied out the remainder of his personal bank account and the joint marital account. After the withdrawals and before this deposit, John, Jerome, and Celia had left Edina with eighty-three dollars to her name. Edina was offended and angry with John for betraying and abandoning her after everything she had done for him.

She knew she could not do very much about the withdrawn money since she had written the checks to Celia and Jerome. John also owned those accounts and had a right to access them. Once she deposited all of the remaining cash, which was slightly over two million, Edina headed back to her apartment. On the cab ride back, she began thinking about whether she or anyone else in her family knew of any prominent divorce lawyers whom she could contact. When she made it in, she went straight to her phone. First, she called the police. "Hello. I've been robbed."

Chapter 9

The Ambrosino family sent people to the Chimera offices with chain cutters and tools to pick locks if necessary. They went to see about their investment. They attempted to contact Edina to no avail, and no one answered their calls to the office after the conversation between John and Enzo. When they broke in, they discovered the place nearly empty, and no one was there. They went into each office, ransacking whatever was left. When they went to Celia's room, they discovered that many of the papers had been replaced with blanks and others had had acid poured on them to dissolve the paper or compromise the ink, making them unreadable. Bernie and John's old office had been cleared of all photos, documents, contacts, and any items of monetary or sentimental value. The Ambrosino family got nothing from the search. John saw Chimera the same way that he viewed religion. He felt that Chimera was a group, not a building. They could have the building, but they could not have its soul. They reported their findings back to Enzo Ambrosino, and he flew into a rage. He felt that he had just been duped into giving up millions, and he wanted his money back immediately. The deal was off. He ordered his associates to find Edina and bring her to him. He needed to have a word with her.

Edina spoke to the authorities and reported that a large sum of money had been taken out of her apartment. She said she knew who the person was. She gave the police a description of Ben and threw on an account of a couple of members of the Ambrosino family. She did this just in case they were after her. She wanted the police to keep an eye out for them. She needed to do this for her survival. She had no one else to go to for protection. She contemplated going to her parents' house upstate, but she was afraid to involve them in her situation. Edina was not sure if she was more afraid for her safety or of hearing the constant nag of her parents telling her that they told her so. She packed the basics, took enough cash to get by, and went to the Drake Hotel in Manhattan. She planned to remain incognito there until she could fly out of the area.

John and Jerome stayed at the safe house with some members of the Jet Mafia and Mariana. Mariana cooked for them to make sure that they kept up their energy, as their spirits were down. John's mind had been in a blur for the past week as he struggled with the possible demise of Chimera and Celia's unknown location. Jerome was still trying not only to track her down but to locate Ben. It appeared that Ben had fallen completely off the radar, but they knew he had the ability to fend for himself. It was not like Celia to disappear and not inform anyone, even her family, of her whereabouts. John kept thinking about the last words he spoke to her. He had not meant to insult her; the words had come out of a place of frustration and pain. His mind was full of regrets. He knew he should have addressed all of the issues with Edina and their marriage, and he was mad at himself for using Bernie as an excuse for being indolent.

John grew up in a family that went to church, but he never considered himself a religious person. After he left home, he only ever stepped foot in a church to attend someone's funeral. He thought that religion was for sheep and for those who did not have the ability to make choices for themselves. John needed hard-core technical facts in front of him to believe that something was true. He would hear stories from the Bible as a kid and would question them to his mother, which would get him into a lot of troubles. John would think, why would a man sacrifice his son to turn him into a goat, just because he heard voices in his head? That's stupid. John looked for proof of whether one could split water or turn it into wine. He did not live his life on faith. He thought that faith left you vulnerable, and he did not like being vulnerable to the unknown.

John had taken a couple of bottles of his favorite wine with him when he cleared his apartment. He opened one and began drinking it. He finished the entire bottle in ten minutes, guzzling glass after glass. He leaned back on the bed and stared at the ceiling. He contemplated praying, but he knew he had done a lot of things in his lifetime that religions considered wrong, and he thought God would pay him with dust. He felt he had no other options at that moment. The situation was out of his control. For the first time since he had been required to pray as a kid, he asked God to help him find Bunny and to do whatever it took to have her return safely and to make things right again.

—⁂—

Edina spent the evening at the Drake Hotel planning her escape from New York. She decided to go to the West Coast, where she could start over and get away from anything associated with the mob. She figured she could complete a divorce there and move on with her life while she still had a few her looks left. Edina made travel arrangements with Pan American Airways, where she had connections. Edina retired for the night after she laid out her outfit for the early morning departure and arranged for a car service to pick her up.

Edina was four hours into her sleep when a noise suddenly awakened her. Before she could react, someone covered her mouth to muzzle any screaming. She did not have a visual to tell her who was in the room. It was completely dark, with only the light from outside peeking through the curtains. Three men tied her hands and feet together and picked her up from the bed. Other men looked around the hotel room to see if they could find anything of value. The found her Chanel tote with cash, identification, and a plane ticket for a morning departure. They took the purse. They proceeded to take her down the hall and into the back stairway. Edina attempted to wiggle out of their grip, but one of the men dropped her tied legs. Angry with her, another man dragged her by her arms down eight flights of stairs. Her bound feet dragged and hit each step on the way down until they got to the waiting car outside and threw her in.

Edina and the men arrived at a location she did not recognize. They threw ice water on her to wake her up. She had passed out on the ride over due to shock. She could not identify the place. It looked like an empty room in someone's home, just without windows. She was lying on a cot. Her wrists and ankles were still tied together. She looked down and noticed that her ankles were swollen and sore; therefore, she could not attempt to stand. She could hardly bend her knees. As three men stood by her, Enzo Ambrosino walked in. What Edina did not know was that the Ambrosino family had connections at the Drake Hotel. In fact, they had connections in hotels all over the city, as well as in Atlantic City and Philadelphia. One of those connections spotted her and alerted the associates.

Enzo wanted his money back in full, and he intended to use her as an incentive to dangle over John and the rest of them to get them to cooperate. Enzo did not know the extent of her relationship to any of them. If he did not have his four million returned to him very soon, she and the others would learn the consequences. He had the men remove the tape from her mouth. Enzo knelt down to her.

"You are a delicate woman, I can tell, but not very smart," he said. She stared at him with frightened eyes. "Where's my money, dear?" he asked her.

"I have some of it. Just take it," she said with a shaken voice.

"I did not give you some of what you asked for. In my estimate, if this had worked out, it would have been a good deal for me. You'd save me tens of millions. But now, it will be free. Every cent comes back to me. Until then, you lay here," he said. "Where are the rest of them?" he asked.

"I don't know," she answered. "If you let me go, I can help you find them. We can work together."

"I don't work with people who steal from me, I demolish them," He said. He motioned for the men to cover her mouth again.

Enzo sent his associates over to the Chimera offices in the middle of the night. They tossed multiple Molotov cocktails into the building, causing it to go up in flames. The fire was extensive, so hot that the Chimera symbol that hung out front, the steel sign that Bernie had taken so much pride in creating and displaying, melted. The building was gutted, and everything left inside was destroyed.

Ben and the money he took from Edina ended up back in the Bronx. He had abandoned the thought of hooking up with John and Jerome. He had also paid a visit to Celia's, but he could not locate her either. He wanted to take the money and run away with her, to no avail. He and his dealer, Jose Jimenez, split the cash. They considered it payback for all the drug debts Ben owed to dealers in the area. Ben suggested to Jose that they join forces. Ben would share his contacts from working at Chimera, and they could expand beyond the Bronx and Harlem. Ben knew that some of the high-powered clients they had also used drugs on the low. Those users included homemakers and, shockingly, those who worked in religious sectors. He knew many of their secrets, and he told Jose he could use that information against them if they ever got out of line. Inexpensive heroin had a large addict chunk in the city courtesy of Italians and the mob, and Ben had many connections. Many of them had served in Vietnam, from where the CIA, through Air America, had heroin smuggled back in body bags.

Smugglers would hide heroin in cars being shipped into the United States, stashing it in every crevice of the vehicle. They did this through their connections to the warlords in

Thailand, who were American allies. Heroin entered New York City directly through the Port Authority, which made it the main destination for narcotic-bureau investigators who worked with customs agents. Getting the narcotics in this way made the selling price on the street much greater because the odds of it being redirected and destroyed were much higher. Despite efforts to curtail heroin's use and sale, two tons made it to the United States every year.

—◦—

Jose was open to the idea as long as Ben did not smoke or shoot up the entire inventory, he joked. Ben did not find that funny. They combined their resources and began setting up a heroin and marijuana factory and farm in one of Jose's relatives' buildings in the South Bronx. Ben had some experience in cutting heroin. He would get the supply and blend it with milk sugar in the kitchen. It resembled baking flour. Cutting it made the heroin weaker. He and others who were working with them would sell each small packet for five dollars in the neighborhoods. An original bag of opium that they purchased from farmers and delivered here for three hundred and fifty dollars would net them half a million dollars on New York City streets.

Ben and Jose would have competition. Many gangs in the city also had their hands in the heroin trade. The Black Panthers who were tired of the destruction caused by the distribution of heroin would dump it into the sewers or destroy it by other means. They would never report their findings to the law-enforcement agencies. They knew that law enforcement would confiscate the paraphernalia and resell it to the dealers for a profit. Sometimes the police would forego an arrest altogether if the dealer handed over the drugs. The majority of the hard-core addicts resided in the ghettos and slums; the Bronx and Harlem held half of the nation's users. Some corrupt law enforcement saw this opportunity as too lucrative not to have a hand in it. The NYPD filled the jails with drug abusers, whom they booked on possession alone, causing a case overload in the system. Many of these addicts could not afford money for proper legal aid.

Jose Jimenez was a third-generation Bronx-born Puerto Rican. Jose was eating at the Horn and Hardart Automat Café with a young female companion when he met Ben in Manhattan. Ben bought drugs from Jose and realized that the narcotics were good quality. Ben decided to keep in touch with him and make Jose his connection. When other clients wanted to buy good-quality drugs, Ben would call Jose to get the supply. Jose was part of the Ghetto Brothers, a mostly black and Puerto Rican gang based in the South Bronx. They were part tough, part political, and part social. The group considered Jose one of its heads. He was well respected in the community as a whole, and he loved to talk to people. Some community members felt that the Ghetto

Brothers did a lot for them, such as cleaning the streets and helping children, despite some members being involved in high crime. Jose was one of the most lightweight members who were in the process of converting to Islam. He knew he was one of the few Islamic Puerto Ricans in the area, but Jose was not perfect. Before he fully changed, he continued to sell drugs to make ends meet. He was not employed by traditional means, and many of the residents of the Bronx shared his predicament. Half of the residents depended on public assistance because of the economic downturn, which affected poor blacks and Hispanics the most in the city. Jobs were scarce. Jose was not violent, and he vowed to deal only as a temporary means until he could become settled financially. He was sensitive to the excessive amount of homicides in the community. Any time one of his colleagues was hurt or killed; he provided counseling and comfort to the group. The group trusted him because he kept his street sense.

Jose knew that the conditions were causing many Bronx natives to flee the borough, and the population was dropping dramatically. Many of the buildings had been abandoned by not only the residents but also the owners. These empty places became money traps for the owners, so they would pay dealers to burn them down for the insurance money. Other abandoned buildings became refuges for the homeless or drug deals and crime. Some of the people involved had been found tossed out some of the windows after being beaten up or murdered. He knew that his heroin trade was the leading cause of death among young people in the borough and the surrounding area, and heroin deaths were unusually high for his people. Jose planned to move on soon, but he still had some more business to build before quitting for good.

In order to fit into the neighborhood, Ben had to include himself in one of the groups to survive. He decided to join Jose and become one of the Ghetto Brothers, which made him one of two Italian natives in the entire gang. Ben did not go through the same initiation as others because some saw no value in jumping him in. He was too connected, and he made them money. The Ghetto Brothers were inclusive, as they took in people from the area. Despite their different ethnicities, they considered themselves a family, much like Chimera considered themselves a family, except in a more organized fashion. It took Ben a little time before they trusted him. The group did not want any law enforcement infiltrating them, and they had to make sure to vet him before giving him his jacket. They liked Ben because of his connections to Manhattan; the Ghetto Brothers were successful in the Bronx and Harlem, but they looked to branch out.

Edina's parents became worried. Her connection at Pan American Airways contacted them, concerned about her whereabouts. The person informed them that she had missed a flight to Los Angeles and the airline could not reach either she or her husband at their residence. They wanted to check and see if Edina or John was there with the family. Edina's family told them no. She never told them that she was taking a trip, but they said they would update the airline when they had more information.

Edina's brother and father went to her residence and found that the door showed evidence of tampering. Edina was particular about how she kept things, so this seemed unusual to them. They walked in. Nothing looked out of the ordinary in the immediate living area. Edina kept her place impeccably. They continued to look around and found nothing out of order. Edina's brother looked into her bedroom. A large box sat in the middle of the bed, and it was wet on the bottom. A printed note taped to the top of the box read, To Mother and Father. Her brother opened it, looked in, and gagged. It was Edina, in pieces.

Chapter 10

The day is bright, beautiful and the weather was just right. Everyone in view is in good spirits. Guests were settling and relishing in the drinks by the bar. Others were walking about, enjoying the music and atmosphere as the palm trees swayed in the wind. In the <u>cool</u> breeze by the blue waters, Celia laid her tanned body under a blue beach umbrella. Her giant straw fedora covered her face from the sun. She had her fruit bowl full of berries, her sangria, and her book by her side. She was indulging in a hardback copy of *Our Bodies, Ourselves*. Relaxed, she exhaled, closed her eyes, and began to nap. She let her mind wander off to the sounds of…gunfire. Celia quickly sat up, removed her sunglasses, and looked around, as did the other tourists, to see where it was coming from. She grabbed her towel, book, and bag and ran back to the hotel with other guests hoping not to be struck by crossfire. The sound reminded her of the place she was hoping to forget until she figured out what she wanted to do with the rest of her life. Once the staff and local law enforcement calmed the guests, she decided to return to her hotel room. She was staying in a medium-sized suite with ocean views. The room was not the best the hotel offered, but it compared to what she had at home, except without the traffic, smog, noisy people, blowing horns, and snow. She did not want to blow all of her money, as it had to go a long way until she could find other employment. When she woke up in the morning, she saw ocean views, breathed fresh air, and felt cool breezes.

Jamaica in the 1970s was a political hotbed. The tourists' areas were supposed to be safe havens from the turbulences in the mainland. Opposition to certain policies by the recently elected prime minister spilled over to areas where holidaymakers frequented, scaring them off. The unrest did not bother Celia, as the violence was comparable to what she left in New York City. She rented a hotel room at the Playboy Resort in Ocho Rios for the month. In her eyes, once a bunny, always a bunny, and she felt comfortable in the familiar territory. Celia liked that the bunnies who worked there looked more like her and that the brown ones made up half the staff. She intended to plan the next few years of her life. After the argument with John back home, she did not think twice about cashing that check. If it had only been John in the picture, she would have reconsidered, but she felt that she could no longer emotionally ignore John and Edina's union. She thought the best way to move on was to get away completely. The money gave Celia options. She would be able to return to school to pursue her music and teaching aspirations. It also made her wealthy where she was now. Two hundred thousand US dollars went a long way in Jamaica. The money would firmly place her in the upper classes in the region if she decided to stay. Celia and Jerome had relatives who had married into the wealthy community there so she would not have a problem integrating into the culture if she chose.

Before leaving New York for Jamaica with an advert in hand, Celia visited Rose. Rose was adjusting well at Juilliard. She had her own place, where she practiced her violin, much to the dismay of her neighbors. Unlike Celia, Rose was not a natural player; she required a lot of practice. Celia dropped off some items she wanted to keep at Rose's apartment. She would send for them later. Celia did not trust leaving them at her apartment for fear that whoever was after the group would come to her eventually. Among those items, she included the spare bunny uniforms that she bought herself and the coat John bought her. She wanted to keep the outfits as mementos, and the fur coat from John was too beautiful to let go. Celia made Rose swear to keep her whereabouts secret for the time being; she did not want people to know what was happening until she had a plan. Bernie had taught her the importance of having a plan B. After seeing Rose, Celia then visited her mother to assure her that everything was fine and that she would call. She left without telling her mother that she was leaving the country.

Once the coast was clear and Celia had on her touring outfit, which consisted of a sweater, sunhat, sunglasses, and miniskirt, she headed out to sightsee. Celia slicked her hair back in a low bun, which was a departure from the perfectly coiffed roller-set hair that she took time every day to fix. She thought her former style was no longer practical because of the hot weather. She began her venture out into the mainland. She went to Kingston on the suggestion of one of the waiters who worked in the restaurant at the hotel. She wanted to see if it lived up to the stories she had heard from family members. Celia arranged for a trusted cab to chauffer her around for the day and went on a visual tour. Her driver introduced himself as Karlus; it sounded like he said Carlos, and Celia pronounced it that way. He told her that he didn't mind; everyone did that. On their way to the city, she noted some of the graffiti written on the walls, buildings, and concrete barriers. Most of it comprised colorful drawings and writings. Others were political: *Judas Manley, Liverance Now! Manley is a Traitor! JLP Yes, Cuba No!* Celia asked Karlus what it meant. He explained everything to her.

The political unrest in the area resulted from Prime Minister Michael Manley's collectivist policies, which mirrored the communist policies that Fidel Castro had enacted in Cuba. Manley and Castro were good friends. Manley wanted a socialist nation that was rooted in black pride and African heritage. He gave land to farmers and created jobs for the poor and women. He desired free education for every child and wanted Jamaica to be in charge of its own destiny, an ideology that mirrored Cuba's. This was decidedly different from the philosophy of the United States, and it angered local businesses as well as officials from Washington, who were already having trouble with Cuba and Fidel Castro due to their policies. Celia thought the idea was refreshing. She knew that the economic downturn occurring in the New York area meant that many families had to suffer and that those who were already wealthy would make more attempts to separate themselves. Celia also knew that any effort to put poorer minority groups on equal footing made rich and some middle-class people nervous. She witnessed many people she knew fleeing from New York City to the surrounding suburban areas and taking all of their resources with them. She did not understand why people would be angry at Manley's plans as it helped everyone.

As he drove through the main avenues and the narrow neighborhood streets, the driver pointed out prominent places in the area that she should visit. Many of the houses resembled shacks, but the residents took pride in their homes. The driver recommended that she try a beef patty as well as some jerk chicken and insisted that she would enjoy these better than the fried chicken, Chinese food, and burgers she was used to having back at home. He also suggested the curry goat. Celia promptly told him no, as she could not stomach the thought of eating one of the goats they passed along the way. Goat was not one of the meats that she was used to eating. They did not eat goats in Manhattan. Karlus laughed.

On their way, they passed law enforcement keeping the peace in their navy and light-blue uniforms, which resembled the air force uniforms worn in the United States. Groups of schoolchildren walked to and from school. The girls wore navy uniform dresses and white shirts. The boys had khaki tops and bottoms. Some of them were eating icy cones, and others were riding their bikes in the street. Young people in scooters intertwined with the traffic. All of the children seemed happy. Celia thought they were neat, and the mood was a departure from the doldrums and despair of Harlem.

Once Celia and her driver arrived in Kingston, which took about two hours, she sought to stop by the St. Joseph Teacher's College Education Programme. She wanted to see what they offered and review their teaching platform. If she liked it and decided to stay, the program would help her. Despite the unrest and harsh economic climate, Celia wanted to make Jamaica a real option for her education. She took a tour of the college and met some of the administrators. She loved it and promised to let them know of her decision to return.

Celia and Karlus headed back after a meal of jerk chicken, plantains, and vegetables. She took a few patties with her to bring back to the hotel. The driver told her that they were also building more schools in the area with the help of the Cubans. He thought that maybe she could consider helping with those once they opened. This made her excited. Celia would love to run a music program one day. They headed back along the scenic route filled with mountains, lush greenery, and exotic flowers. Throughout the ride, the cab driver flirted with her and complimented her on her beauty. She thought he was very sweet and somewhat handsome. He had a beautiful and even skin tone, which highlighted his bright smile. Karlus differed from the men she normally found attractive, but she thought that he would make a great friend and a connection for her to the mainland. He offered to help her the next time she needed something, and they exchanged contact information.

Celia asked him what else he did for a living. Karlus told her that driving a taxi was his day job, and he was a minister at night. He headed a small church locally. The taxi job helped pay for daily expenses for his family. Karlus invited Celia to his church and gave her the address. She told him that she would visit soon. Karlus asked her why she was still single. Celia was embarrassed to answer at first, but she told him that she had bad luck. Karlus responded, "There is no such thing as bad luck. God has a plan, and everything that is happening now is part of his plan." He told her to be patient. Celia thanked him and tipped him handsomely. She returned to her room.

Celia sat down on her bed and turned on the radio. Her mind wandered back to the situation at home. Not only did the disagreement with John bother her, but thoughts about Bernie's death haunted her. All she could think was that right before he died; they had talked about money and that

Ben may have mismanaged it. She thought that Bernie had just been too calm about it as if he'd had to fix Ben's errors before. Since Bernie knew that she and Ben were friendly, he may have been trying to protect her feelings. Celia's gut had told her that things did not add up with Ben, and when she'd realized this, she had decided to dial back her physical contact with him outside of work. The little trust she did have in him had diminished as doubts about his character arose in her mind. Celia was lying there mentally beating herself up with guilt over her self-inflicted stupidity regarding Ben and John. She had ignored all the signs of who they were. She realized that she had indeed worked for the mob. She questioned her motivations for staying there once she understood the setup. A good paycheck had taken precedence over common sense. Celia sat up and decided to order room service, but first she removed her velvet shawl and clothes, took a bath, and changed into her nightclothes.

While in her bubble bath, Celia could not help but think back to the cab ride over to Bernie's home before she found him. She'd had a conversation with the driver. He'd told her about how much he loved his job and how, on occasion, he got the opportunity to drive pretty girls like her. He also met all sorts of people, like politicians and entertainers. He said that the delinquents caused trouble with his job. He had been robbed three times that year already, but he stayed because that was where the money was. Sometimes you had to do things that you questioned because the money was good.

As long as you had to make a living, you had to stay at your job unless something better came along.

—⊶—

John, Jerome, and Mariana had been holed up at the Yonkers safe house for some time. Mariana was getting restless. Her belly was expanding and becoming uncomfortable. She wanted to venture out to see her family and friends and she complained to Jerome about being stuck in the house all day. She did not like Yonkers very much. They began to have heated arguments, but they were never loud enough to blow their cover. Both of them were still mindful of their impending birth, and they did not want to elevate Mariana's blood pressure. Mariana warned Jerome that she would walk out if things did not change soon. She could not have a baby under these circumstances. Jerome understood her stance and promised her that things would be better for them. He just needed her patience.

John, who had a separate room in the house, would hear the two of them talk and argue. It reminded him at times of the conversations that he and Bunny had had when they were on good terms. John missed that companionship and tried not to stress himself in worry thinking about it. He would just sleep through his troubles. He had begun losing his hair at the crown, and his hairline was slowly inching back. He did not know whether it was from genetics, years of wearing pie hats, or stress. It did not take away from his looks, as his face remained handsome. He decided to shave his hair down to camouflage the loss. Doing this made John look more mature. He had gained ten pounds from drinking and eating Mariana's cooking, and the extra weight was noticeable around his waistline. He made a decision to straighten up, as he never knew who might turn up, and he did not want to be out there not looking like himself. John still took great pride in his appearance and reputation.

One morning, Jerome woke John up to show him the front page of the *New York Post*. "Socialite in a Box," the headline said. The subtitle added insult to injury. "Parts of socialite gift wrapped to family," it read. John had the newspapers open and television on, staring at the headlines in shock. Flashing across channel four, the screen said, "Manhattan socialite found dismembered in the Drake Hotel." Followed by that headline were Edina LeBlanc's name and a photo of her and him together, smiling.

Things had taken a turn for the worse, and for the first time, John came to the realization that he may be in trouble. He knew he had to call his law-enforcement connections, which meant he had to get out of hiding and tell them that he and Edina were not together at the time of her murder. He was not ready to publicize this, but he had no other choice. Seeing the headlines upset him. He and Edina did not get along, but he never wanted to see her physically hurt. He was not mourning, but he did feel responsible for not having the situation under control. He knew her parents had to be devastated and felt that he had to call them and put on a show. Bernie would never have let things get this bad or proceeded without a strategy. John had managed to flub both of these matters, and he felt that he failed the entire operation and everyone involved.

The sadness turned to worry, as neither he nor anyone else they knew on a personal level had heard from Celia or Ben. John wondered whether Celia had met a similar fate. The very thought of that happening broke his heart. He would go off the deep end if something ever happened to her. John was not terribly concerned about Ben, as he was a man and could take care of himself. John put on his clothing, told Jerome and Mariana that he had to go, and went to the precinct where he knew the officials. He made sure to tell the two of them that he would return as he knew his presence in the city right now was not in his best interest. He wanted to make sure he was not implicated in Edina's murder and to put out an official missing person's APB on Celia.

Law enforcement informed John that Edina had filed a police report a few days before she was found. She told them that she had been robbed and alerted them that members of the Ambrosino family were harassing her over money. John told them that the Ambrosino family had been giving them issues and had been at it for some time. The detective told John that the Ambrosino family was already under investigation because of the recently enacted laws against organized crime, as were a few others who may have been involved in mob activity. The Ambrosino family, especially Enzo and the late Dante, were high on their list of people to prosecute, but they needed evidence to build a case. This made John a little uncomfortable, but he knew that since Bernie was no longer there and Chimera had left no trail of their activities, neither he nor Jerome had anything to worry about unless Ben snitched.

The detective told John that they had discovered fingerprints on the box Edina was found in and shoe prints in the carpet. They were currently trying to match those. They had already interviewed workers at the hotel she was staying in and the complex where their marital home was located. He also informed John that Edina had specifically named Ben in her robbery and said he had stolen almost a million dollars from her. They were still trying to locate him.

"That son of a bitch. Fuck that motherfucker," John cursed. The detective asked John if he thought that Celia would be with Ben. "I hope not. She doesn't have anything to do with any of this. She's a smart girl, a good woman," John answered. The detective suggested that if they found one, perhaps that might lead them to the other. He hoped that the outcome would be different this time.

"Why would he steal money from Edina? He wasn't around," John said.

"Maybe he was in on whatever transpired," the detective answered.

"He disappeared. They could have him, too. We could not find him," John said. He was careful not to say too much to the detective, although he had his own reservations about Ben. Despite the tension between Ben and him, John always stayed true to the code of Omertà, which they all swore to uphold when they joined. The code said that an associate should never go to government authorities to seek justice for a crime and never cooperate with authorities to investigate wrongdoing against an associate. If the government questioned you, you were clueless about the details.

John became heated at the thought of a possible betrayal by Ben, but he did not have enough information to connect the dots. Why would Ben kill Edina for money and take Bunny? John figured killing Edina would be Ben's way of getting back at him. He was not sure because that would not make sense either. Ben knew that Edina and John were not close. Their continued relationship would have left him open to pursue Bunny. John realized that Ben was a degenerate and a druggie, but he had known Ben long enough to know that he would not kill without a reason. To him, Ben was a crook, perhaps, but not a killer. It did not make sense to him.

John voluntarily left his fingerprints and any other information that the authorities felt they needed from him and proceeded to go to Edina's parents' home in Westchester. The police had already informed them of the progress in the investigation. For the first time since John and Edina were married, the family embraced him in the midst of their mourning. He and her parents put their differences aside and jointly planned her service at the synagogue and burial in Jewish tradition. Both occurred within twenty-four hours, and John attended and participated. He was not sure whether the truce was genuine, but he accepted it and decided to close this chapter of his life once everything was over.

Word of Edina's sudden and shocking demise spread around New York City and the other boroughs. Jose spotted the *New York Post* and handed Ben the paper. Edina's story made the front page of all local newspapers and headed the local news broadcast for the next four days because of the gruesome details.

"Hey, check this out. Did you hear about that lady who got chopped up? She must have pissed somebody off. Don't nobody do that unless they really mad? You can just shoot 'em and get dat shit out of the way, but chopping them up takes work. I wouldn't take time and do that shit," Jose said to Ben.

"No. What lady?" Ben asked.

"Look." Jose handed him the paper, and Ben stared at the front page for thirty seconds. "Da fuck, you look like you saw a ghost or something. You know her?" Jose said.

"No. No, I don't. It's just fascinating to me," Ben answered. He sat down on the sofa, lit a cigarette, and continued to read the story on the inside of the paper. The story mentioned that before she was murdered, she reported a robbery to the police. They already had a description of the suspect, and they were trying to locate him.

"You've been looking at that too long. Don't get any ideas; I'll fuck you up. Ain't nobody cutting me," Jose said. Ben looked at him, grinned, and shook his head. Jose went out for the day, leaving Ben in the apartment by himself. He continued to read the story.

Twenty minutes after Jose left, someone began knocking on the door. When Ben asked who it was, a female answered. He got up, opened the door, and saw this petite young brown girl with deep, wavy hair tied back into a bun. She had on a scarf, a tight V-neck T-shirt that showed her ample chest, and flared jeans. She asked for Jose. Ben told her that she had just missed him. She insisted on coming in and waiting for him to return. She identified herself as Brenda, Jose's girlfriend. Ben remembered seeing her briefly when he first met Jose. She had looked a bit younger then, and Ben had not realized they were dating. Brenda remembered Ben's face, and once she learned that he had moved in with Jose, she decided to pay a visit to check him out. Brenda recalled that he had dressed well and worn expensive jewelry during the brief moment she saw him. He had looked like a high-powered executive back then.

Brenda walked past Ben and sat down on the couch. Ben closed the door behind her and walked to the kitchen with the newspaper in his hand. Brenda commented on how disorderly the apartment was. Ben suggested that she could clean it herself if she were not satisfied. "How long have you known Jose?" Ben asked her.

"Long enough," Brenda answered.

"You look young," Ben said.

"I'm legal. That's what's important," she said.

"Not sure if I believe you," he replied.

Before Ben moved in, Brenda had become accustomed to showing up at the apartment anytime she wanted. She was seventeen years old and barely out of high school. She would turn eighteen soon, and she had no plans to attend college. She could not afford tuition. She lived with her mother and four siblings. The family survived on welfare. She felt that she did not have a place in the small apartment that was filled with her full family, so she sought validation from the outside. Brenda met Jose when she was in her third year of high school. Brenda saw him on the street one afternoon on her way home from school. She noticed that he was part of a crew. She knew that if she became the girlfriend of a leader, it would make her part of the crew by default, and he would take care of her. Brenda attached herself to any man she thought had money. Many girls were part of the Ghetto Brothers, but they had their separate name and their own jackets. The Wildflowers, they called themselves. They became her surrogate family.

Brenda was a flirty girl. Just because she was dating Jose, it did not mean that she had stopped looking for what else was out there. "You got money, white boy? You look like you do," Brenda asked Ben as she sat on the couch.

"What would make you think that? Look where I live. I live in a basement in the South Bronx. Moneyed people don't live here on purpose," he answered.

"You look clean. You could be one of those people who come here to hide out. A lot of you move here after you fuck up somewhere else. They don't look for the white boys in the hood, not here at least. The cops too busy beating our ass to notice y'all," Brenda said. Ben looked at her. "Nah." She got up and went to the kitchen, where Ben was fixing himself a sandwich while still reading the paper. "You don't look like you are from around here. The guys from here are rough. You are sexy. You smell good," she said while checking him out.

"Thanks. I don't look like I used to," Ben said.

"I see that. Skinnier, but I like that shit," she said. Ben had a feeling that Brenda was putting the moves on him. He resisted because she was Jose's girl and he had no reason to disrespect him.

"I don't know when he's coming back," Ben said. He wanted to encourage her to go, but it seemed like she had no plans to leave.

Brenda reminded him of Celia in her height and shape. She had a delicate way about her like Celia, but Brenda was more aggressive, urbaner, and not as refined. "Do you act this way toward everyone you meet?" Ben asked her.

"Nope. Just sexy motherfuckers." Brenda walked closer to Ben, put her hand on his crotch, and began to rub it. "Oh, you are not like other white boys," she said. He moved her hand away. Her actions made him nervous, but he had not touched a woman since Celia.

"I don't think this is OK. Jose may come back at any minute," Ben said to her.

"He won't know unless you tell him," Brenda said.

"What do you want? Money?" Ben asked.

"I didn't ask for any, but if you are offering, I am not gonna say no," Brenda replied. She unzipped his pants, knelt down, and began to suck him off. Brenda put in the work, and both were into it so much that they had sex on the kitchen floor with no rubber. When they finished, Brenda put on her clothes. Ben watched her as she went into his wallet and pulled out the cash. She promised to come back. She kissed him, got up, and vacated the apartment, leaving Ben on the kitchen floor with no pants or underwear on.

Ben lay there in utter confusion. *What just happened?* He thought. For a brief moment, he felt as if he had been taken advantage of, but he did not know how to mentally process the feeling. He was used to making the moves, being the aggressor of women. Ben collected his thoughts, and soon after, he had to get to work. If Brenda could smell him out, who knew who else could find him?

Ben realized it was time to change his look. In a short amount of time, he dropped thirty pounds and became gaunt. He had replaced proper meals with weed, alcohol, and heroin. His looks were fading away fast. He was paler than before. His teeth were not as pristine as they had been. Also, he smoked a pack of cigarettes a day. The nicotine began to stain his teeth, and his voice became raspy. His skin, which had once been smooth despite the scar, became blotchy. He had not decided whether to grow his neatly cropped hair into a long bob or to get rid of it altogether. He thought growing it out would take too long.

Ben got up, went to the bathroom, and began shaving his head, light beard, sideburns, and mustache with an electric razor. He also reshaped his eyebrows and cut lines in them. He now resembled a skinhead. Ben felt that this would help him blend in with the Puerto Ricans in the neighborhood so he would not be a target. He left the apartment and went to a tattoo parlor to get a couple of the images on his neck, just to throw off anyone who could identify him on the street. His old clothes had become too large for him because of the weight loss. He tossed the sharp suits and sweaters that he used to wear at Chimera in a bag and opted for articles of clothing that blended in with the area. His new clothes consisted of a skull cap, gang leather jacket, and sunglasses instead. He purchased Dr. Marten boots and T-shirts and jeans. He put the bag of clothes on the street in hopes that one of the homeless would find the bag and make use of them. Since it was winter, the weather was still cool, so he was able to go out and about and continue his drug deals undisturbed for the time being.

After some time in Jamaica, Celia called her mother. She had wired home some money, and she wanted to see if it had arrived. Agnes was angry with her. By then several people had already contacted Agnes regarding her daughter's whereabouts, and she had no answer to give them. This was an irresponsible move by Celia, according to her, and she demanded an explanation for her behavior. "Where are you?" Agnes asked.

"I'm in Jamaica, Momma. I needed a break," Celia answered.

"You're all the way in Jamaica? You could not tell me this? People are calling here asking for you, and here I am thinking everything is normal and you are at home working. Someone called your father looking for you. He called me back asking where you were. Do you know how embarrassing it was for me to tell him that I didn't know? It makes me look like a bad parent," Agnes said.

"I'm so sorry. A lot is going on. I can't explain it all right now, but I needed to get away. Please don't make yourself sick with worry. I'm OK. I'm better than ever, actually," Celia said.

"When are you coming home?" Agnes asked.

"It won't be for a while. I have some things to figure out," Celia said.

"A while? You're on vacation? How are you paying for this with so much time away from work?" her mother asked.

"I made good money. I am not with them anymore," Celia answered.

"You were fired? Again?" her mother asked.

"No, I quit this time. Wait, what do you mean 'fired again'?" Celia said.

"This is your mother you are talking to. I know more than you think I know. People talk around here. I knew you were in that club with the ears, the skimpy outfits, and the tail. I was disappointed at first, but then I stopped worrying about it. You're a grown woman. It was an honest living. I was more worried about your safety. There are crazy people out there who go to places like that and prey on the girls. I didn't want you hurt. No matter how old you get, you're still my child. I was glad when you changed jobs again," Agnes said. "What are you going to do now?" she asked.

"I might stay here. We have relatives here, and they are very nice. I like the atmosphere," Celia said.

"I don't know, little girl. On the news, they are saying that Jamaica and Cuba are allies, and that is not good. Castro is no good. I see the violence. It's not safe there," Agnes told her.

"Mom, there's violence at home. You live right in the middle of it. As far as socialism is concerned, it is not good according to the news because it doesn't serve the best interest of America. America can't make money off of the new system here. It's not like other places, where their people would be slaves or depressed. Jamaica wants to be an independent country. Their structure doesn't exclude poor people. No one has to suffer. Look at the Bronx. Look at Harlem. The children there are in bad shape with low-quality education and resources. Do you think the way things are being run there are any better? It favors the wealthy. At least here I will be given the tools to help people. Manley doesn't want his residents to go without food or proper education. He's going to change all of that. Back home you can get those things only if you are well off. Jamaica is going to be the model for the future. Once I get my degree, I may teach at one of the new schools they are building. It is going to take some time, and that is why I am here. I want to fight the good fight with them. I feel like a different and better person now. When everything is settled, I will bring you here too," Celia told her mother.

"I am fine where I am. I don't know about this. I feel you are rushing things. Think about it. I hope you are making proper decisions," Agnes told her.

"Momma, you worked so hard your whole life. You worked for the church; you worked as a maid. Don't you want to go to a paradise where you can retire and relax? I am looking for a home, and we can share it," Celia said.

"I am OK where I am. I've been here my whole life, and this is what I know," Agnes answered, before quickly changing the subject. "Did you meet any guys yet? You're aging."

"Mom...I met a lot of men here, and I am not rushing," Celia answered.

"Good. I'm glad you are finally growing up. You were never good with your decision making when it comes to men. Don't get into bed with them so soon. Go for the guy who waits for you," Agnes told her.

"OK," Celia answered.

"Hurry up and return home so these people can stop calling me asking for you. Either that or you tell them yourself. Do you want me to tell them?" Agnes asked.

"No, Mom! Don't do it. Rose also knows where I am. Don't tell them anything. Not even Jerome. Please promise me that you won't do it?" Celia said.

"Oh, so you tell your friends where you are before your mother, and you want me to lie to your friends? Fine. I won't tell them, but I deserve updates. You owe me at least that, young lady. Have some respect," Agnes told her.

"OK, Momma, I'm sorry," Celia answered.

"Jerome's baby is coming soon; you know," Agnes said.

"A baby, wow. I did not know. I guess he's doing OK. I am happy for him. He deserves it," Celia said.

"Shame. Your other guy friend's wife died. It was all over the news," Agnes told her. Celia remained on the line, quiet. "Are you still there?" Agnes asked.

"Yes, ma'am. What happened?" Celia asked her.

"I don't know much, but they found her in a box, and she wasn't all together. They cut her up and put her in her house that way," Agnes said. Celia gasped. "The husband looks OK," Agnes told her. Celia exhaled in relief. "I think you should call them, Celia," Agnes said.

"I will soon, Mom when I am ready," she answered.

Celia gave her mother all of her contact information in Jamaica and promised to call every other day from now on. After the call had ended, Celia sat back and thought about John. He must have felt some stress when he found Edina. Despite the issues between the two of them, Celia would never want to see anyone hurt in that manner, and she had an urge to contact John to comfort him. She stopped herself. Her feelings were still raw.

Chapter 11

Mariana was heavily pregnant and about to give birth at any moment. She had been patient with Jerome and all of the changes he and John had been experiencing in the past year. John had almost become part of the extended family. Jerome felt more comfortable stepping out into the area. John kept members of the Jet family paid as security for all of them. It had been almost a year since he saw Celia, and the lack of word from her had John fearing the worst at times. Mariana would tell him to have faith and that Celia would come back to him one day, at the right moment and not a second before. Her words brought him little solace. John had lost the desire to sleep around, despite the temptation around him. Before, he had used sex as an outlet for his frustration, but he had become tired of the chase. He didn't remember 90 percent of the women he had bedded.

Edina, the cause of his frustration, was no longer a factor, and he had to face his emotions and reality for the first time in years. He found comfort in alcohol. His mind was too occupied, and he wanted to rebuild Chimera. Despite everything that Edina had ruined, he did not want to give up on the group. He wanted to start over again, and Jerome supported the idea. Both felt that Celia should be there with them to make it happen; they did not wish to start until they found out about her fate.

Jerome wanted some stability and decided that he and Mariana should go on and tie the knot. She was due to give birth at any moment, and he did not want his first child to be born out of wedlock. He and Mariana decided to have a small family ceremony the next weekend with John as the best man. Mariana informed her family of their decision, and they planned a quick wedding at Mariana's family church in the Bronx. Jerome told his parents, and they were delighted. They had liked Mariana the few times they met her. They felt that she was honest and hardworking, and she obviously truly loved their son. Secretly, they would have preferred that he marry a black woman. Tensions between some black and Hispanic groups were high, and Jerome's family had not met anyone from Mariana's side of the family. They were not sure how things would turn out between families of different cultures.

Both Mariana's and Jerome's families cooked traditional Spanish and Southern dishes. John provided the drinks and cigars for the celebration. Mariana had to borrow a full-figured friend's white dress. It was the only one she could find that fit her on such a short notice. Her little cousins wore their lacy communion dresses and black patent-leather shoes as her bridesmaids. They bought flowers from the local florist, and the church pastor of Jerome's family church, who was available on short notice, married them.

During the ceremony, John performed his duties as best man. His mind kept wandering back to the day that he married Edina and his internal misery. He had not felt the same elation as Jerome did at this moment. There was no one looking at them with disapproving eyes, no one wanting to kill Jerome on his wedding day. Jerome was in charge of his fate, and his new bride had a real baby in her. John thought to himself; this is how a wedding should feel. Jerome had everything now. John was envious of the activities. He wished he had met Bunny before Edina; maybe things would have been different. His mind wandered again, and he imagined that it was he and Bunny up there. She should be here with us, he thought. He became sadder.

After they had finished their vows, Jerome was permitted to kiss the bride. He kissed her, and it was official. Jerome was a married man. Everyone cheered, and they all proceeded to the reception area of the church, where they celebrated. Some of the guests who recognized John from the news gave their condolences to him for losing his wife. He had to pretend that he was devastated. They all attempted to comfort him by offering him food. He did not turn any of it down, and he enjoyed every bit. He did take note, however, that he wasn't as svelte as he once was. The stress and drinking were causing his midsection to expand. Mariana would joke with him at times, asking John if he was competing with her. Jerome and Mariana made their honeymoon local. Local meant that John had to go somewhere else for the week while they had the apartment to themselves.

A few days into their honeymoon, Mariana went into labor. Jerome was nervous and did not know what to do. He called his family and hers. For support, he called John. John did not know why Jerome called him, but Jerome felt there were so many females around that he needed some male support. Jerome would joke to John that he would have uncle duties, like changing diapers, which made John nervous. What on earth would he do with a baby? How would he hold one of those things? Jerome would joke that both of them needed the practice and that maybe one day John could use those skills on one of his own.

Mariana spent two days in labor. Jerome was not in the room with her for most of the time. Her mother and sisters occupied it. He loved her family, but at times they could be overwhelming. Jerome spent the majority of the time in the waiting room with John for the company. They discussed their futures while eating the finest of cuisine from the vending machines. They would go home when Mariana managed to sleep or if they needed to freshen up. John revealed to

Jerome that Edina once told him that she was pregnant, but in his heart, he never believed it. That baby probably belonged to the guy she cheated on to be with him, for all he knew. He thought she was loose when he met her. He told Jerome that Edina kept trying to convince him to have children, but he was against it. John admitted that he longed to be a father but did not want it in that manner. He said he admired Jerome for not settling until he found the woman he wanted. Jerome was flattered, but he felt sorry for John. For the first time in their friendship, Jerome had a full understanding of John's behavior when it came to his relationship with his ex-wife. Nothing bonded John and Edina. A baby would have made things more toxic, and it would have involved an innocent person. Jerome understood at that moment how blessed he was, and he hoped that raising his new baby as a productive member of society would absolve him for the wrongs that he had done.

A couple of hours later, it was time for Mariana to deliver. She had a baby boy. The entire family was delighted. Once everyone in the family met Jerome Dexter Jr., he was introduced to John. John looked at the baby and said, "He's cute, but why does he look like an alien?" Jerome laughed but assured him that the baby did not resemble an alien; he looked like his mother. Jerome told John that he would be one of the baby's godparents. John did not know how to take the news, but he was honored. Jerome let John hold the baby but had to instruct his friend on how to hold him properly. John found the feeling strange. Afraid that he was going to drop him, he quickly handed the baby back to his father.

A word about the change in ownership in Chimera spread among some of the clients who had money invested in the company. Many of them were not pleased with the rapid exchange, and they demanded their money back. Since Bernie was no longer alive and Enzo Ambrosino owned what he could get his hands on, the clients went to him directly. To keep some of them quiet, he had to pay them off. This upset the entire Ambrosino family, who felt that the deal was a bust and the losses justified how they had handled Edina. To them, it was just business. They had not known her well enough for it to be personal, although Enzo had not liked her flip mouth. Burning Chimera's home base had been a way to collect on insurance so that they could pay some of the people.

Several of the clients needed the funds because the economy took a sharp downturn. The previous year, President Nixon had announced a freeze on all prices and wages in the United States because inflation had skyrocketed. Many of Chimera's investors worked at factories that were highly dependent on steel and oil. Others were farmers based upstate who sold the bulk of their inventory to city vendors. When production of petroleum and steel slowed due to trouble with Egypt and their rationing of oil exports, and the United States' support of Israel, companies began laying many of the workers off. The factory where Celia began her work career also closed. The unavailability of steel meant that they could not drill for oil on the mainland. Shortages of all products began to surface because companies could not increase supply. The farmers upstate had been affected by the economic downturn, and they could not nourish some of their livestock when the price of feed rose. They could not afford to fatten the animals. This affected the price of poultry the most, causing it to skyrocket. The situation for them became so dire that they resorted to killing the baby chicks by drowning them.

These conditions had people reevaluating how they spent their money. Organized crime also took a hit. Many people were not participating in illegal gambling or other leisure activities. Instead, they were saving for gas, which was cheap but hardly available because of shortages. Long lines formed for blocks as many people waited for new shipments of gas at the stations. Debts piled up quickly. More people depended on welfare, and to deal with their dire situations, many of them turned to illegal substances, which were most prominent in the poorest areas of the city, the South Bronx and Harlem. When all the clients finished collecting on initial investments in Chimera, the Ambrosino family ended up losing millions, which added fuel to their fire when it came to seeking revenge on the remainder of the group.

Ben decided to take a chance and venture back into Manhattan. It was still cold out, so he used that excuse to keep his face and head covered and avoid recognition. A friend of his reached out to him at his old address, and the message made it back to Ben when he sent someone to pick up his mail. The letter said that he wanted to meet up with Ben. The person was his closest friend from Vietnam. Ben contacted him over the phone and talked to him for hours to catch up on some things. His friend told him that the other guys were meeting up and that they could all catch up at the bar with a few drinks. A couple of soldiers from Fire Support Base Aries, who had served with him in Vietnam, made it back safely. Other fellow soldiers he served with did not make it back home, or they were severely injured when they returned.

Ben sat in front of the television with his friends, watched MASH, and had beers. It was his favorite show because it reminded him of his time in battle. A special report appeared announcing that President Nixon would address the nation shortly. Nixon announced that Kissinger and the Democratic Republic of Vietnam had reached an internationally supervised ceasefire agreement to end the war. This would begin the restoration of peace in Vietnam, and the agreement would be finalized within the week. Troops would withdraw within sixty days, all prisoners of war would be released, and January 27 would mark the official end of the draft.

All the men sat there quietly. They could not believe that it was really the end. One of the men turned to Ben and asked, "If they are not done, why are we leaving now? Why did we even go there in the first place?" Ben did not say anything. He did not know if he had to answer this or if it was a rhetorical question. He only responded with a shrug. All of them had struggled with the deployment, and most of them had left with a lingering drug problem hanging over their heads. Some of them hid it better than others, and Ben thought he was one of those men. He was for a while, until he let the drugs be his anchor.

Everyone in the group was unemployed. Many of the soldiers who returned from the war could not find jobs, and that contributed to the high unemployment numbers. Most of them were either on welfare or living with the help of their family members because they were injured or mentally impaired. Out of that group of friends, only Ben was dealing narcotics as a source of income. He had cash on him but nothing else, just like John and Jerome. Ben proposed a toast to all of their brethren who fought, won, and lost the war. Each one of them picked up a beer or shot glass and gave a celebratory toast.

Chapter 12

Jerome decided to visit the South Bronx to pick up some things from Mariana's grandmother. He had never visited this neighborhood before. He did not want to have the Jet Mafia doing security detail for him. He felt that they would scare her grandmother, because they were big, buff, black, and intimidating. Mariana's grandmother lived in the middle of gang territory, and the men of Jet Mafia looked like they belonged to an outside group. This made them bait for the gangs in the area. Such a situation could escalate quickly. Jerome also did not want to make residents suspicious of his identity. He sent the two Jet guards off for the afternoon. He would take a car service back to Yonkers. Jerome left the bodyguards at East 170th Street, right at Mariana's grand-mother's building. When Jerome arrived, he picked up a box of hand-me-down baby clothes. Jerome had plenty of means, but Mariana considered it important to take her family's offerings, as some of the items were family heirlooms passed on from generation to generation. He did not want Mariana traveling with the baby in this area. He felt that it was not safe.

Ben went out for the day on the corner of East 172nd Street and Hoe Avenue. This location was the most lucrative for him. Others included sections in Mott Haven, Morris Heights, and Hunts Point, as one of the clerks in the corner grocery store brought customers in for Ben in return for a recruiting fee. Before he arrived, he needed a pick-me-up. In preparation for marathon drug pushes, Ben would sometimes smoke crack or get a shot of heroin in his left foot. His foot had so many needle pricks that he had to switch feet. He felt that the drugs gave him an advantage, the ability to leave his conscious at home. A bag would give him about four hours of obliviousness. Ben would stand there, make a sale, and hit on the women who passed him throughout the day.

Jerome took the box of baby clothes and began to walk down the street so he could catch a cab home. While walking, he thought he saw Ben but did not know for sure if it was him. Ben's looks had changed dramatically, and Jerome could not get over his shock. Ben's once model looks had all but disappeared, and his disposition was shambolic. Ben had turned into one of the dealers on the street corner. Jerome walked over to get a closer look. Ben noticed Jerome immediately. He wanted to walk away but could not. On the one hand, he was embarrassed about his current state; on the contrary, he was relieved to see a familiar face.

"Hey. I saw you coming," Ben said as Jerome walked closer to him. Jerome used to shake Ben's hand when they greeted, but some of Ben's nails were so long and filthy that he did not want to touch them. He held onto the box instead.

"What happened to you? Why do you look like that?" Jerome asked him.

Ben took a hard sniffle. "I'm good. I live here now. This is my home. This is my job," he answered.

"What is that on your face? Is it dirt?" Jerome asked.

"It's a tattoo, something different," Ben said. He looked down to see what Jerome had in the box. He noticed the wedding band. "I see your ring. Newlywed? Congratulations." Ben pulled out a cigarette, lit it, and began smoking.

"Thanks. I was just here picking up baby clothes from family," Jerome told him.

"So I'm going to be an uncle," Ben said.

Jerome winced. "The baby is already here..." he said and quickly changed the subject. "We were looking for you, like really looking for you. I just did not expect to see you like this."

"I think I look fine," Ben answered.

"Look, we are in trouble. All of us are in trouble," Jerome said.

"I know; I read. Shame what happened to her," Ben answered.

Jerome stared at Ben for a second. "Where's Celia?" he asked sternly.

Ben shrugged. "I don't know where she is. Isn't she laid up under John or something?"

Jerome shook his head. "No, she isn't. We can't find her either. We were hoping that you knew." Jerome paused.

"Well, if she were smart, she would have gotten the fuck out of here by now," Ben answered.

Jerome began to pace a bit. "They trashed everything and burned us down. We're still a team, though. I've heard some things about you, and we need to talk, now," Jerome told him.

"Yeah, we do," Ben said. He had Jerome follow him to the basement apartment that he shared with his roommate, Jose.

When Jerome arrived at Ben's apartment, he saw a couch, a loveseat, two mattresses, and a table full of drug paraphernalia and cups. Jerome had not suspected such a scene, and nothing resembled the lifestyle that Ben once led. Trash and piles of clothes lay in the corners. There was a pair of women's panties balled up between the sofa cushions. Large rocks from outside sat on top of newspapers and magazines. None of the articles of clothing strewn about resembled the style and polish that Ben once wore proudly. The apartment had a strong smell of marijuana. The couch was dirty, and Jerome chose to sit on the arm instead so as not to ruin his suit. He put his box to the side.

"Brother, we can't keep saving you. You got to keep it together," Jerome told him sternly.

"I don't need fucking saving. I am just fine here. I'm not John. I am with people who get me, who appreciate my work. I'm a Ghetto Brother now," Ben told him.

Jerome laughed. "There's nothing ghetto about you. You are a wannabe. You are one of us. Once a rude boy, always a rude boy."

"That's over. I am getting a real chance now to show my skills, and if that stupid bitch didn't fuck up, everyone could have seen what I was capable of doing," Ben said.

"Wait, wait. You knew what was going on? You were in on this, you and Edina?" Jerome asked him.

"I knew she was selling. She told me she was selling the group to Ambrosino. Oh, well," Ben said.

"Shit, Ben! And you did nothing to stop her? Did you tell no one? None of us? You disappeared like you always do. You mean to tell me that something about that plan did not click on your head, that perhaps just maybe this wasn't right? You owed us that!" Jerome yelled at Ben.

"For your information, I did. Yep, I did. Then I got the fuck over it. It wasn't Bernie's company anymore. I had no power," Ben said as he threw his hands up. "For all I know, she and John probably put this together. I never trusted him. It don't matter anyway. Bernie gave it to John, his prodigal fucking son, his favorite, and I'm gonna tell you, I was not taking orders from him. John is not my boss. You, he, or she was not going to be my bosses. I owed you nothing. She cut you a nice check," Ben told him.

"Bernie gave you many chances. You kept fucking up! Don't blame that on us. Bullshit, man! Fuck that!" Jerome said, and then he paused. "Did you take the money from Edina?" Jerome asked him.

"I don't have to answer that," Ben responded.

"Did you kill her?" Jerome asked.

"No," Ben answered, and he walked closer to Jerome. "I'm not the killer in this group. I served in a war where I had the opportunity to shoot children in the face, like the others, and I didn't. Don't ever accuse me of being a murderer." Ben stared into Jerome's eyes and pointed at him. "You of all people do not have any grounds to judge me," he said.

"I should never have let you within two feet of Celia," Jerome said.

"What's the problem? Celia is a modern lady; she can make her own choices," Ben said snidely.

"She didn't know about you," Jerome snapped.

"Oh, and what were you going to do about it, run and tell John? You were always John's bitch! Yep, the John, and Jerome show. You two always conspired against me. You two made decisions with Bernie without including me! I put in just as much as anyone else there, more than you! You were never supposed to be that high! Ah, Celia, flower, I miss her. The inside of her felt so good," Ben said.

"You fucking druggie!" Jerome stood up and punched Ben. He let no one disrespect his family. Ben hit him back, and they began to wrestle on the floor, on the dirty carpet and trash. They continued to fight until Ben became enraged in a heroin-induced schizophrenic episode. A small amount of foam began to form in the corner of his mouth, and his neck started to bulge with purple veins. He started choking Jerome until Jerome managed to hit him in the face to get Ben off him. While Jerome sat up and attempted to catch his breath, Ben picked up one of the large rocks he had placed on top of the papers and hit Jerome in the head, cracking his skull. Jerome hit the floor backward as blood splattered on the carpet, couch, and walls. He did not move anymore.

Ben stood above him in shock. He saw that Jerome was not moving. Ben knelt down and tried to shake him, getting blood on his hands and pants. The blood reminded Ben of the time he accidentally cut his face when he was young and of all the blood he saw in the war. The bleeding freaked him out. *Maybe he is just unconscious,* Ben thought. He continued to shake Jerome to wake him, but no success. Jerome was not breathing anymore, and Ben got scared. He backed all the way into one of the corners in the room. He slid down onto the pile of clothes and stared at Jerome, lying lifeless and bleeding on the carpet. Ben began to sweat and shake back and forth while continuing to look at Jerome. The room started to spin. It all happened so fast, he thought. In Ben's drug-induced state, he had a brief moment of clarity. "What the fuck just happened?" he kept repeating until he lay down in the pile of clothes in the fetal position. Ben blacked out.

Hours later, Jose returned to the apartment to find Jerome stiff and lifeless in the middle of the floor, and Ben still crouched in the corner. Jose went to get a cup of water to throw on Ben to wake him up. When Jose poured it on him, Ben sat up.

"Get up, fuckface!" Jose yelled at him. "Why is there a dead guy in the living room?" Ben looked over, saw Jerome, and instantly felt regret and sadness. He faintly remembered the occurrences of hours before, because he was so high. "Get him out of here before he starts to smell, and you clean that shit up," Jose said, pointing to the blood splatter.

"Help me," Ben said to Jose.

"Help you with what? Why is he in here? Why is he bleeding on the carpet?" Jose asked.

"I didn't mean it. I got upset. Just help me pick him up. I have to put him someplace," Ben answered.

"You know this guy, or is he a client?" Jose asked.

"He's a friend of ours."

Jose looked at him in repugnance and shook his head. "Ben, you need to straighten up your act. I will help you, but you can't be involving me in this kind of a mess. We can't have cops here. I don't have a record; you do," he said.

Ben and Jose picked Jerome up and wrapped him in a bedsheet. Ben took the rock he had used to hit him out of the apartment with them. When the coast was clear, they moved Jerome's body into Jose's car. They drove to one of the many abandoned lots in the Bronx and placed him there. They put him in a spot where they knew he would be found quickly. Ben removed Jerome's wallet, keys, chain, and gold wedding band so it would look like a robbery. They unwrapped him, leaving him exposed to the elements. Before they left, Ben looked at him and said, "I'm so sorry, brother." When Ben and Jose left the lot, they drove the rock over to the Hudson River and tossed it. It sank to the bottom.

When they went back to the apartment, Ben looked around. He grabbed the bleach and a washcloth and began cleaning the walls and carpet of Jerome's blood. He looked over and saw the box that Jerome had brought in with him. He opened it and saw the baby clothes for a boy. He had a son, Ben thought. He closed it, pushed it to one of the other corners, and continued to clean up the scene. Each scrub brought more regret. He took all of his anger toward his life situation and jealousy of John out on Jerome. He broke his vow never to harm any of his brothers. There was no returning for him.

As the afternoon went on, kids started getting out of school. The neighborhood did not offer many after school activities, so many of them would go to the abandoned lots and scavenge to keep busy until it was time to return home. Two kids, one nine and the other ten years old, went to a lot that they had not visited before. They stumbled onto the well-dressed body of a black man, missing his expensive shoes. They figured a homeless person had removed them. His other clothing would have been stripped off if it wasn't already bloodstained. That man was Jerome. The two kids went to get other children to show them the dead body. Other kids went to get help for the bleeding man. Not too long after the discovery, ambulances and law enforcement arrived. They conducted an investigation, and when they were done, they removed Jerome's body to the coroner for identification.

Jerome had been missing for almost twenty-four hours when Mariana became worried. She was concerned that he had not called and checked in on her and the baby. This was unlike him. John sent out some of the Jet Mafia to trace Jerome's tracks. He became angry when one of them informed him that they left him in the Bronx at his request. "You are never to do that. I pay you enough money. We are still targets," John exclaimed.

"Hey, he said he knew these people," one of the guards told him. John and Mariana began calling people they knew. Mariana contacted her grandmother to see if he made it to her place. Her grandmother informed her that he came and left with the box, but she had not heard from him since. Mariana began calling hospitals, and John contacted his connections in the forty-second precinct. One of the officers there told John that they had found a male that fit Jerome's description and that they were frantically trying to identify the remains because there was no wallet on him.

John knew that crime was common in that area and that the body the officer was describing was probably not Jerome. For all he knew, it could have been a gang member or another homeless person. He told the police that he would be down there later on. John continued to call other people to locate him, including Jerome's parents. After hours of unsuccessful looking, John went to the precinct, and from there they directed him to the coroner's office, where he met with the chief medical examiner. They took John into the freezer where the bodies were held to see if he could identify the body. When the examiner opened the freezer drawer, John immediately noticed the bloodied suit jacket. Jerome's head was swollen and unrecognizable, and he was pale. John felt light-headed and sick to his stomach, and he immediately vomited on the floor. He crouched down.

"Are you OK?" the examiner asked him. John shook his head. "Is this Jerome Dexter?" John nodded.

The coroner told John that they suspected robbery but required further investigation. It looked as though he had been killed and dumped there. John dreaded making the phone call to Jerome's family and his wife. After sitting down for forty minutes preparing himself while dealing with his own grief, he picked up the phone to call Mariana first. When she answered, he told her with a shaky voice that the police had located Jerome, and he explained his friend's fate. Mariana let out a bloodcurdling scream on the other end. She nearly dropped the baby, which made him cry and scream. Her mother ran into the room to see what the commotion was about. Mariana cried to her mother that someone had robbed Jerome and he was dead. Her mother attempted to comfort her but could not contain her own emotions. They both wailed in unison. John then called Jerome's parents, and his mother did the same. The sounds made John break down in the office.

Celia by this time had begun looking for housing in Kingston. She settled for a colorful little house for sale on Old Hope

Road, the same street where Bob Marley and other musicians lived. Celia wanted to be a part of the musical community and knew this would be a great place to settle and find inspiration. She had just completed the closing process and was ready to move in. Celia was very proud when she held the keys for the first time. She did not have any furniture yet, but she was willing to sleep on a cot until she got everything settled. She had filed her paperwork to start a teaching program in the fall and had been brushing up on her piano skills. She had also decided to apply for a part-time job to keep her busy in the meantime. She was ready to get out of the hotel and on her own property. She had all of her affairs in order, and she had informed her mother that she would make Kingston her permanent home.

Celia returned to the Playboy Hotel to gather her things and give them notice that she would finally vacate the room. The front-desk concierge handed her a note from her mother instructing her to call home immediately. Not thinking much about it, she went to her room to begin packing her things. She had enlisted Karlus to help her with the move by offering generous pay. She sat down on the bed and called back home to her mother.

Her mother told her about what had happened to Jerome in the Bronx. Celia began crying hysterically and told her that she would be home shortly. While in tears, Celia continued packing and had all of her things moved to her home. She booked a flight to Miami and a connecting flight back to New York. Before she left, Karlus suggested that she stop by his church to say some prayers for Jerome's soul. She took him up on his offer.

—∞—

Many people in the community attended Jerome's viewing. John waited until most of the crowds had passed and the chapel was nearly empty. He spent most of the early day with Mariana and her family. He wanted to mourn alone. When the coast was clear, he walked up to the casket and knelt down. He apologized to Jerome for failing to protect him and for letting his family down. It had been John's job. John wept as he had for the entire week since Jerome's body was discovered.

As he knelt in front of Jerome's casket, John felt the lowest he ever had, even worse than when Bernie passed away. He saw no other way out. He had no one to turn to. John took the gun barrel and put it to his head. He wanted to pull the trigger. He felt he had no one left. Everyone close to him was gone.

"Go ahead and pull it. Do us all a favor and off yourself," a voice behind him said. Startled, John paused, put the gun down, and turned around. It was Ben. John had not seen Ben since the day he found out about Edina's sale of the company. It took about ten seconds for John to recognize Ben since he looked dramatically different. Ben had on a skullcap and his Ghetto Brothers leather jacket. John looked at him in bewilderment. "Go ahead and do it. You like showing off. Just don't get your blood all over me when you do it," Ben added.

John stood up to Ben. "I ought to punch you in your goddamn face."

"For what? Taking your wife's money? I bet you were devastated when you found out what happened to her, weren't you?" Ben said to him snidely. "Or are you pissed about something else? What is it really?" Ben asked while he folded his arms.

"You're nothing but shit," John said to him. Ben looked at the gun in John's hand.

"Yet you are here, ready to blow your own brains out. See, I know you; you won't do it. You were hoping someone would come here and stop you. Too bad you got me, and if you want to kill yourself, well, I agree with you; I think you should," Ben added.

John became heated. "You left your post! You abandoned your family!" he yelled.

"No! I left a shit show. In twelve months' time, you turned what took Bernie and us ten years to build into a trash operation. You let your whore wife sell us down the river for pennies on the dollar because you were not paying fucking attention. You lost a girl. We have no clients; the fucking building burned down, and now you are in front of Jerome's casket with a gun to your head. You failed, and you don't want to man up to it."

John shook his head. "No…no…I am not taking the entire fall for this. I bet you knew. You knew, and you did nothing, like you always do. That's why you ran away. You are a thief, you are a fiend, you're entitled, and you will never be anything more than that. Bernie never trusted you, because you are a big fuckup!" he yelled.

"Right, because you are the golden child, the prodigal son, the chosen one! LeBlanc can do no wrong. That should be you there in his place. You had him as your fucking gofer," Ben said while pointing to Jerome's casket. John took a step back, raised his gun, and pointed it at Ben's head. Ben raised both hands. "Go ahead and pull it; you will be no different than me…brother," Ben said.

"Oh my God!" Celia expressed in the background. Both men turned and saw her standing in the back of the chapel with one of the workers at the funeral home. "Don't do this, John. He's not worth it," she said. It was the first time the four of them had been in the same room in a year, even if one of them was in a casket.

"Oh, welcome back, darling," Ben said to her sarcastically. He looked over at John. "Hey, why aren't you yelling at her for abandoning her post? Where the fuck was she for a year?" he asked.

"She didn't take a vow not to abandon or dishonor your brother," John said as he looked at Ben angrily.

"John, listen to me, please. Put the gun down. Don't do this. Enough of the killing. Just stop," Celia said. "Not here," she added while looking at him. She walked closer and separated them, not caring that there was a loaded gun with two angry men around it. "Ben, just go...Leave," she told him.

"Celia, you will be nowhere with this guy," Ben told her.

"Really, asshole?" John said to him. Celia looked at Ben and tried her best to get him to leave. Not only was she attempting to defuse a potentially tragic situation with John, but also she was trying to save Ben's life. She knew John; he could shoot someone when he was in this state.

"Celia, please come home with me," Ben said to her.

"Go..." she responded.

Ben looked at her, and then he looked at John and her again. Ben stormed off angrily. It was quiet for a moment.

"Can't lose you too. Put that away," Celia said sternly, referring to John's gun. "It's one thing to die from a broken heart like Bernie or for someone else to take your life like Jerome, but don't do it yourself. It's wrong, and I would never forgive you." John took a deep breath and put the gun back in his pocket. They stood there and hugged in front of Jerome's casket. John buried his face in her hair.

"Nice tan. Where did you go?" John asked.

"I went to find myself," Celia answered.

"Well, did you?" John asked.

"Yes," Celia answered.

"I'm sorry for everything," he said to her.

"I've already forgiven you. I needed this for me," she said.

"I'm glad you came back. I waited for you," he cooed.

"I am too," Celia replied.

The burial took place the next day. John had ensured that everything would be handled correctly. Jerome's grieving parents, wife, and baby left after the preacher had said a few words and they lowered the casket. John and Celia stayed and were the last to go. When the gravediggers began throwing dirt on top of the casket, John stopped them. He wanted to do something before they continued. He asked them to lift the casket back up. Despite their reservations, they did so. John took out a pocketknife and began to scratch words on the side of the wood casket: "Once a rude boy, always a rude boy." This was Jerome's favorite pep chant for the group. Celia did not know what was happening, and she thought that John was having a breakdown.

"John, stop! Why are you doing this?" she asked him frantically.

John looked up at her and said, "Sometimes, funeral places, they bury you, and when they think the family is gone, they come back and dig you up. They take you out of the casket, dump you in the hole, and resell the casket. I won't let them do that to him. I won't let him be dumped again." He handed Celia the pocketknife. She wiped the tear from her eye and took it from him. She knelt and began to scrape a heart in the casket. She wrote *Chimera* in the heart. When they were done, John motioned the gravediggers to lower him into the ground. John and Celia stood next to each other and held hands. "What now?" he said.

Mariana returned to her parents' home in Harlem with the baby, and John took Celia with him to the safe house in Yonkers. During the week leading to Jerome's funeral, John promised that he would help financially take care of Mariana and Jerome Jr. as long as they needed. He felt this was his duty as godfather, and he gave her a generous sum of money to help her get on her feet. Celia also offered to help. She apologized for not keeping in touch and for missing everything. Celia and Mariana patched things up; they were still family.

Celia moved from the hotel to stay with John for the time being while she took care of affairs locally. He did not think that a hotel would be safe for her, so he had her check out to go with him instead. He also did not want her to lead a trail to her mother's apartment. John did not know how volatile the situation remained, and he wanted to keep her close to him. John and Celia struggled with guilt together. Celia had not spoken to Jerome since she left, and she had regrets about not keeping in touch. The stress of the situation had got to her. John took to heart some of what Ben had said to him and knew that the threat of total failure was looming over him. If Celia had not shown up, John would not have been here either. He thought back to what Mariana had told him—that Celia would be here and right on time. When they made it to the house, they settled in the living room. Both of them sat down after Celia turned on the television.

"It's just us," John said as he looked at her. "I messed it up. I messed it all up." He began to cry. Celia held him. He put his arms around her as they both sat. She placed his head on her chest as he cried. "Bernie picked me, Jerome trusted me, and I let them down. I let us all down. I am not good at this. This is new to me," he added.

"You tried," Celia said. "You had no time to mourn like the rest of us. It wasn't fair to you," she added as she rubbed his back. "I should not have left for so long. I needed a break because I was angry. I should have come back sooner. I should have been here for all of us," she said. "We are not perfect, and I've made some mistakes too, but I am here now, and we will fix this. We will make it." The two of them sat quietly for a moment. Celia felt the need to reveal something. "I was feeling guilty," she said.

"Guilty about what?" John asked.

"Before Bernie passed, I was going over the accounting and paperwork. We had a sit-down meeting, and I told him that during my audits, I found things that were wrong. All of the numbers were wrong. Money was missing, and I could not account for any of it. The paperwork was a mess; everything was wrong," she said.

John sat up. "How much?" he asked her.

"Almost five hundred thousand. Ben wrote all of the checks to himself, John," she said. "I don't think Bernie realized what was happening until I told him, and he covered for him. I sat there and watched Bernie cover for him. It had to be hard to save face, even in front of me."

"Fuck. Bernie always saved his ass, and this is how he repays him," John replied. "That wasn't your fault; you did your job."

"I hated him after that, and I hated myself for letting him get close to me," Bunny said.

"I didn't like him touching you at all. He was not fit to breathe the same air as you." John paused. "Why didn't you let me shoot him?" he asked her.

"He is as good as done already. No need to throw away your life shooting at a dead horse," Bunny answered. "He didn't want to stay; let him go his way." They continued to talk.

"We were here the whole time. Me, Jerome, and Mariana. I felt like the third wheel, but they were patient with me the whole time. They made me feel like part of the family. All we had left was lots of money. I never thought I would say that. I could have left, but I didn't know where you were, and I didn't want to leave you here. I thought you were hurt or dead. We were mourning," John said. Bunny began to tear up. "When I was young, all I wanted to do was grow up and be rich, because my brother and I had nothing and my mother worked like a dog to support us. All I could think of then was if I were rich, I would be happy," he said. "I wanted to come here and make money, and I did. Why didn't it make me happy?" he asked her.

Bunny wiped her eye. "I don't know. The money will buy you things; that's it. That's what it is supposed to do. You cannot buy emotions. Those are things you feel on the inside. You do not buy happy; you feel happy. You have to find yourself to be happy," Bunny said.

"Is that what you did when you were gone?" he asked her.

"Yeah, it is. I know exactly how you feel," she said.

John was quiet for ten seconds. "Bunny, I don't want you to leave me again," he said. "I love you, and I won't mess up anymore, I promise."

"That's not realistic, John. I know you are not perfect, and I am not expecting that from you. I realize that you just may be an ass. I accept that. I can handle it. I'm even turned on sometimes. I just want you to respect me as a woman. Right now, I am your equal and not just a trophy to be won. Times are different. I am different, and I think I have earned the right. I won't emasculate you in any way, but I need you to do the same for me. I need to see it," she said.

"I understand, and you will. I am not the same person you left before," John said.

"If I stay, it's my choice to do so and not because you asked. That doesn't mean that you can do whatever you want to me. No more hiding, no more dishonesty. No more chauvinistic stuff. I know that's what you guys do. All of you do it," Bunny said, and she paused for a second. "Oh, and I don't live in New York anymore. I have a home in Jamaica."

"You live here, too," John said.

"I am just visiting here. In Kingston, there is a lot of work to do. This is a time when people are fleeing, and I want to be one of those who build there. I feel there is a future. I have a place now, and I can make a difference there. I am returning to school; I'll have a job. I'm settled. Here, it's hopeless. Look what 'here' did to Jerome; he's lying in a box. Look at Ben. He's a shell of himself. Why in the hell does he look like that? Look what 'here' has done to you.

Something in you is missing. I never thought I would ever see you in that state," she said.

"I had no one. I thought I lost you forever. I miss them, Bunny. This is new for me," John responded, referring to Jerome and Bernie.

"I know you do. I need you to go back to the fiery John that I knew. That is the John I fell for...I'm visiting here because I need to make sure that you are OK. Sometimes, I wish I did not love you. I could make a clean break," Bunny said.

John stayed quiet for a couple of moments. "Can I go to your place in Jamaica with you? I've never been there before," he asked.

"Are you serious?" Celia and John laughed. It was the first time she had smiled since she came back to New York. "Fine, if you behave. You haven't changed all that much; you know that, right?"

John was taken aback but refreshed by her newfound confidence. They were tired from the day, as it had been emotionally draining. They fell asleep the way they were, sitting up with their arms wrapped around each other.

The next day, John woke up early. He started thinking about the future. Bunny was with him, and he felt that if they were going to make it as a couple or have any future, he had to start planning their comeback. He could not remain in hiding forever. Too much had happened. Chimera as a company was gone, but the name was more important to John. Chimera was Bernie's legacy, and he felt the least he could do would be to take the name and rebuild it into something better, something legit. John felt that he owed it to him. Bernie had taught him always to have a plan B.

John knew that to get the name back, he would have to face finally the Ambrosino family. It had been a year since Edina's death, and he hoped that cooler heads had prevailed. He figured that they would be busy worrying about other things. Congress had passed a new law, the Racketeer Influenced and Corrupt Organizations Act, intended to combat organized crime and its leaders. The Ambrosino family's ownership of the company relieved John from any association and criminal charges, as he was no longer a leader. That position now belonged to Enzo Ambrosino. John's tenure and the passing of Jerome meant that his trail remained clean. John was going to buy the name back from them, and he was willing to return their four million dollars for the rights.

John ran this by Celia, who did not agree. She had a fit when he told her. "What if they hurt you? You've been away all this time, and now you want to see them. Let the name go. No one will hate you," she said.

"I think I can make this work. The one thing that I know about these people, like all of us in the game, is that it is just business. I give them their money back; they give me the name, and we break ties. There is nothing else for them to do but take the cash. It's all good for them. It's necessary. They got their revenge already. Killing me will gain them nothing," John told her, referring to the death of Edina. The one positive twist to Edina selling them out was that in the end, it had protected them from future prosecution.

"John, I'm scared, and I don't agree. They just may kill you. They are sickos. They are not going to play nice and just let you go. That's not fair to me. You just made me promise not to leave, and you do this. I cannot continue to run in these circles. No more death. I can't take it," Celia said in a panic as a tear rolled down.

"Trust me. We will win; together; this will work. If I don't come back, then I want you to know I did this for us," he said as he put his hands on her cheeks, leaned in, and kissed her.

Chapter 13

Ben returned home to the South Bronx. He put his issues about John on the backburner and decided to let his feelings for Celia go. He knew that she would not go for him, not now. He had changed dramatically since the last time she had seen him, and he still had to compete for her attention with John. He was a mess emotionally, and his drug habit was spinning out of control. He finally let his past with Chimera go. He thought that it would be easy to do this, but it upset him. He felt the loss of the group just as much as John, Jerome, and Celia did, but his pride would never let him show this. If Bernie were still alive, things would be much different right now, he thought.

Brenda continued to visit Ben behind Jose's back. All they did was have sex, and he would pay her from his wallet. Ben would also pay her in weed. The visits became frequent, and Ben became concerned that Brenda was developing feelings for him. Brenda had become so comfortable that she would walk around the place naked to entice him, and it would usually work. She would make herself available when he made batches of heroin in the kitchen. She made sure that she asked how he created his batches and how the game worked. Ben was high much of the time and did not think to keep some things to himself.

Brenda was there to fish for information, so she could get herself into the drug game. She knew Jose's schedule, and when he was on his way home, she would dress and tell Jose that Ben was looking after her, and he would believe it. Jose was street smart, but when it came to relationships and women, he was gullible. Brenda would also have sex with him. Ben saw the triangle as a distraction from everything else. It was risky but worth it. Sometimes he would feel sorry about it, but the sex was too good, and she had a way of getting into his head.

Ben knew it was time for him to move on with his life. He returned to the streets to continue his hustle. Sales of heroin in the South Bronx were higher than ever, and he wanted to take advantage of the boom while he could. While he was out, a commotion between two rival gangs, the Dark Hearts and the Seven Immortals, was taking place within one of the neighborhood parks. The small fight turned into a melee when other members from both gangs joined, and a few members of a third group arrived. The fight began when one gang member demanded the jacket of the rival gang member, and he refused to give it up. If you walked into rival communities, the unwritten rule was that you were to remove and hand over your colors to the rival gang. If you did not, it was considered the ultimate disrespect to their community, and you were asking for a war.

Word of the melee spread quickly in the area, and kids, residents, and members of the gangs involved, as well as other rivals, assembled at the park to watch the commotion. Members of the Ghetto Brothers arrived to see what was going on and to put an end to the fighting. Jose stepped up in between two of the fighting gang members to ask for peace. The members of the groups involved told him to eat shit and began to attack him. Soon after, one of the gang members picked up a pipe and started swinging. Soon after, all the groups in attendance were fighting each other. They were beating each other to a pulp with bats, sticks, chains, and whatever object they had on their person.

Ben heard about the situation and ran from his post. He joined in the melee, beating and hitting rival gang members with his fists and objects from the ground. He was desperately trying to defend his group. Someone began beating Jose to the point where he became unconscious. After Jose was down, they continued to kick him. Authorities soon arrived after one of the residents called the police. They were ready to arrest the participants for unlawful assembly. Gang members scattered while those injured remained on the ground. Their brothers were assisting them until ambulances arrived.

Other members started throwing rocks and other objects at the police officers.

An hour after Jose arrived at the hospital, he passed away from injuries he sustained during the beating. This angered Ben, and he went out immediately to seek revenge. He left the hospital and began walking home. Since Ben had already had a taste of what it was like to take a life, his conscience no longer processed the consequences of his actions. He did not care anymore. When he passed the block where the fight occurred, it had already returned to normal, as if nothing had ever happened. Little girls were back outside playing double Dutch, older men sat at makeshift tables playing dominoes, and kids were throwing a football.

Ben spotted a member of the Seven Immortals walking down the street. He knew that the man had been one of the gang members in the melee. Ben yelled at him, saying that he was walking into the wrong territory. The man stopped, turned around, and told him, "Shut the fuck up, white boy! I'll fuck you up too."

Enraged, Ben reached into one of the pockets of his jacket and pulled out a gun. This was his James Bond moment; he thought to himself. He could hear the theme music playing in his head. He began to march to the gang member, who started to run up the center of the street. Ben yelled back, "I'm gonna give you hell, baby!" and chased him. He started shooting at the guy as they both ran down the middle of the block. The girls who were skipping rope stopped, the men stopped their game of dominoes, and the kids stopped throwing their football back and forth to watch what was going on. None of them ran. Everyone paused to see what the outcome of the street shooting would be.

Ben used all of his bullets but did not hit the man once because he managed to run off. He succeeded in hitting cars, the sides of buildings, and a storefront window, and he narrowly missing one of the children in the street. That kid ran home to tell his parents what had just happened. After the shooting was over, everyone in the neighborhood turned around and resumed their activities, as if this had been just another episode of a show. Ben headed toward his apartment.

Word on the street of Jose's death and the shooting afterward spread quickly. Members of the Ghetto Brothers wanted to put an end to the fighting. They were all mourning Jose's sudden death. Instead of continuing the cycle of attacks and retaliation, they decided to call a truce. Not all of the members were on board, but enough of them agreed to participate. Jose's death affected many people throughout the community because heads of rival gangs had respected him. Some of the lower members did not share the same regard for the Ghetto Brothers or Jose, but the leaders knew what he was about and appreciated him because he represented peace.

Ben sat on his dirty couch and stared at the wall. The apartment was quiet, and he knew it would remain that way because Jose was not coming back. Some parts of the wall and carpet were pristine white; other parts of it had faded to a light-brown eggshell color due to time and dirt. The white parts were the areas he had scrubbed with bleach to get Jerome's blood spatter off the walls. For the first time in a while, he sat there and did not pick up a needle to mask his emotions. He wept without the help of narcotics. Instead, he wondered what had become of his life and how he had ended up here. He felt like the failure that he had accused John of being. Ben continued to cry until he fell asleep.

Bangs on the door suddenly woke him up. Ben asked who was there as he picked up his pistol. "Police!" the voices shouted, and they knocked down the door. Ben had nowhere to go. The only ways out of the basement were the front and back doors, and police had both surrounded. The cops told him to drop the weapon. Ben complied and put his hands up. He begged the police officer to shoot him. The police rushed over to him, knocked him down to the floor, and cuffed his hands behind his back. The detective announced that he was under arrest for some charges, which included possession of an illegal weapon, destruction of property, assault with a deadly weapon, and the robbery of money from Edina's apartment.

The parents of the child who ran home after the street shooting had called the authorities and that kid had led them right to Ben. People knew that Ben and Jose were roommates. After the police had read Ben his rights, they proceeded to take Ben to the county lockup. Brenda was on her way to the apartment to see him after leaving the hospital. She walked up as they were taking him away. She began to scream at the police. "Where are you taking him? Put him back, you fuckin pigs! That's my baby's father!" she said.

"Be quiet before we take you in," the officer said to her. Ben looked over at her as they were pushing him toward the vehicle.

They pushed Ben's head into the police car and shoved the rest of him onto the back seat. He and Brenda looked at each other through the window as the police drove away with him. She attempted to go into the apartment, but the police would not let her in, as they were conducting an investigation. On the way to the holding facility, Ben knew what was ahead for him, and he did not care anymore. He just wanted to get away from life. He knew he would fail every ballistics test they took; however; he would not confess to anything—not to taking Edina's money, not to drugs, not even to Jerome's murder—unless they could prove 100 percent that he was responsible. He knew how the system worked.

After he had arrived at the precinct, they photographed and fingerprinted him. Central booking staff interviewed him for more information. They asked him why he had Jerome's personal belongings in his possession. He refused to expound. They then escorted him to the court building and spoke to the assistant district attorney, who told them that this case was going to the courts and filed a formal complaint against him in criminal court on the behalf of the people of the state of New York. He was arraigned before a judge and appointed counsel. They informed him that they were charging him with assault, robbery, drug possession, drug distribution, and illegal use of a weapon. More charges were possible pending the results of an investigation. He pleaded guilty. He knew that if he went to trial, it would guarantee that he would be put away for life. The judge decided to hold Ben without bail, as he was a flight risk. The judge ordered him confined in custody pending a grand jury action.

Ben was taken back to holding, stripped of his clothing, and given prison garb and a roll of tissue. Because of overcrowding due to a large number of arrests in the city, and because he was not likely to receive bail, they transferred him from the precinct holding cell to the central jail until his next court hearing.

Investigators continued to look around the apartment after police took Ben away. One of the detectives noticed what looked like dried blood on the couch and a few spots left on the carpet and the walls. Ben must have missed them while cleaning up the scene. They sorted through the other piles of miscellaneous items strewn about the apartment and found various drug paraphernalia, suitcases of cash (mostly hundred-dollar bills in stacks), and Jerome's wallet, wedding ring, and chain in a purple Crown Royal bag. The box of baby clothes that Jerome had brought into the apartment with him lay closed in the same spot next to the couch. The police were aware that all of these items were missing. They had a forensics crew come in and take samples of the spots to see if they were indeed blood splatter. They wanted to check and see if this was Edina's blood.

Twelve hours after placement in the tank, Ben began to have withdrawals from the heroin. He began to sweat profusely and to experience stomach cramps and muscle aches. He asked the deputies for help. They ignored him. After a couple of hours, they gave him a garbage bag and told him to vomit in it. The cops said that the drugs needed to leave his system. The officers would take him to the hospital if his symptoms became worse. They had seen many like him go through there before, and they thought he was a little dramatic. They handed Ben a cup of water and suggested that he sit in the corner and wait it out. This was different from when he had overdosed in Vietnam. There, they had been more willing to treat him. The local law enforcement did not care.

Brenda returned to her family's place. She was worried. Ben was in jail, and it did not look like he would be getting out anytime soon. She was pregnant. She was almost sure it was Ben's child. She was not planning to terminate the pregnancy. Having a white baby was seen as a novelty in that area. She and Ben had never used protection, and Jose always used rubbers, sometimes more than one at the same time because he did not trust her. During her visits to the apartment,

Brenda had discovered cash hidden in furniture and holes that they had cut in the walls and the couch. When Jose and Ben were not looking, she would take a stack. She figured that they would not miss it. Over time, she had stolen eleven stacks, which totaled about eight thousand dollars. She hid the money in a hole that she cut in her mattress so her brothers and sisters would not find it. Brenda planned to use it to take care of herself and her baby. She had started spending some of the money before she learned of her condition. Until she could find some financial support for herself, she decided to go to Jose's family and friends and pass the baby off as his until Ben got out of jail, if he got out. She knew that the Ghetto Brothers would make sure that she was taken care of in the meantime.

After Jose's funeral, which many of the gang leaders in the area attended, the co-leader of the Ghetto Brothers decided to call all of the leaders of the other gang families to have a peace summit. The head of each sector attended as the voice of the eleven thousand members they represented in the Bronx. After hours of arguments and tough talk about reality, they all agreed to a resolution of peace and decided to make an attempt as a whole unit to better their neighborhoods instead of tearing them apart. They concluded that the enemy was not each other but the status quo that held them all down as a community.

Chapter 14

John and a few people from the Jet Mafia met with Enzo Ambrosino. Their numbers were even. Five from each side were in attendance in the room, drawn along racial lines. John was ready to negotiate with them in exchange for the rights to the Chimera name. Both sides were armed, as this meeting could end in a number of ways. If John's years of experience paid off, he would leave this meeting a victor, just as Bernie had done many times before when John accompanied him to meetings with other families. Enzo Ambrosino agreed to meet with John but warned him not to get out of line, or else he would end up like his wife. John enticed him with not only money but also the promise not to testify against him if anything went down with the feds. John felt that he was negotiating with the devil and had to agree to do things that he considered wrong to get things done. Enzo Ambrosino did not care about the Chimera name, as it meant nothing to him. He only wanted the money-making potential that came with it. He did not gain much from the company when it was all said and done. They barely made anything more than their initial investment, despite the company being worth millions more. Chimera's assets had mostly been in cash, which John had removed before the Ambrosino family raided the office and accounts. John had kept that money hidden away the whole time, using it to support himself, Jerome, and Mariana as well as to pay for the security for all of them. That totaled tens of millions. Four million was not much for him to give back to the Ambrosinos.

The thrill of taking down Chimera was already gone for Ambrosino. Enzo compared the takeover of Chimera to shooting down an animal as a hunter. He and Bernie never got along, and this had been an ego boost for him and the family. Edina's death had been his trophy, and he could have hung her head on the wall if he had wanted to. John knew that the Ambrosino family was responsible for Edina's death, and he added that as a negotiation tool. Enzo stared at John for a second.

"An eye for an eye. Your wife was an eye for my eye, my son, my everything, Sammy. You know of him?" Enzo said.

John stared back. "No, I don't know anything about that."

Enzo frowned. "Being only a witness and complacent to an action does not free you from guilt. My son, he was only nineteen years old. He had his entire future in front of him. Losing a child is a pain that no parent should feel. How would your mother feel if she lost you before she died?" he said.

John shrugged. "Oh, it's me, of course she would be devastated. I don't get what my mother has to do with anything going on here. Whatever this is about, I'm sorry for your loss," he said.

Enzo continued. "Imagine his mother's devastation at the thought that some trash put a bag over his head and that he slowly suffocated and the extra step they took to humiliate him. The devastating thought of him grasping for his last air sent his mother and me into a breakdown."

John responded. "One, if you are implying that I put a bag over your kid's head. It wasn't me. Two, perhaps your kid should have been doing other things besides activities that put him in that compromising position. Most sons are loyal, and they do their father's dirty work if instructed. Some even do the dirty work of their fake partners. That's something to think about isn't it?"

Clearly irritated, Enzo responded to John, "Well, I guess our losses match up, don't they?"

On John's stealth instruction, the guys from Jet Mafia decided to distract Ambrosino's security. Anytime one of the Jet Mafia moved an inch, Ambrosino's security moved to attack by pulling out their guns. This also sidetracked Enzo's attention. Enzo would get up to get in John's face. While the guards were distracted, one of the Jet men took out a syringe and quickly squirted the contents in Enzo's drink. The act took no longer than three seconds. When John noticed that it had been done, he urged everyone to calm down. The syringe contained thallium.

Hours had gone by since John left, and he had not called back to check in as he had promised. Celia began to get worried. She started looking around and noticed some old papers from Chimera—the company stationery. She looked at it and began to reminisce about the good ole days when they were all happy. She began drawing on it to see what it would look like if it were updated. She did this to keep herself busy until John made it back. He'd had the security stay with her to keep her safe. When she finished doodling, she had nothing else to do. She was becoming restless and frustrated. The worst began to invade her thoughts. If something bad happened to John, she would never be the same.

Celia decided to calm herself and sit down. She turned on the television. CBS News broke into programming to air a special report. It was about Watergate. The televised testimony about the scandal had already begun in the Senate. An informant had indicated that President Nixon had recorded incriminating conversations and that the investigation was widening. The president reassured the questioning public and Congress that he was no crook.

Celia had been so inundated with her issues that she had tuned out of what was going on around her. Back in Jamaica, the people had been fighting for economic freedom and against Kissinger for opposing their policies, but at home, the country was falling apart, with Kissinger being a participant. She wanted to leave and go back to warmth and paradise, but she knew that she needed to be here with John and her family at this time, at least until things were settled.

John had plans, but she wanted to pack everyone up and take them back to Kingston with her. Frustrated with the news, Celia fell asleep for the night with no word on John's return.

Celia awakened the next morning. She looked next to her, and John was not there. She panicked as she got up and looked around the house and did not see him. She wanted to pick up the phone to call out, but whom would she call? She sat down on the bed. She looked over at the clock and knew that something had to have gone wrong. She put her head in her hands and covered her face. Celia felt weak and defeated. She did not know what else to do except call the police. As she sat there, something touched her shoulder. She jumped and looked up. It was John, unscathed. Relieved, she stood up and kissed him, which put a smile on his face. Then she slapped him, which confused him. "You didn't call home. I thought you were dead," she said.

"Bunny, I didn't want to wake you. I sent the security home for today. We did it!" he said.

"What does this mean now?" Bunny asked.

"It means that we can move on," he said.

"What's next?" she asked.

"I have ideas, but we should talk about it together," John responded.

"When I was here waiting for you to show up, I was thinking about what you said. I was looking at an old letterhead with the symbol on it. I think we should redesign it. Not change it too much, but make it represent something new," she said. Bunny suggested that he keep the symbol but put fire around it.

"Why fire?" John asked.

"Well, I know a little about the symbol. I looked it up in the library when I first started. The sign is associated with burning rock. It's solid, and if you burn it, the fire never goes out. You can burn it, and it stays alive," she said.

"Wow. You're so smart. I thought it was just some weird shit Bernie made up. The way you were explaining it, I was thinking it had something to do with the place burning down," he said. "Fire it will be." John paused and looked at Bunny. "I had a rough night, and I would feel better if you hugged me," he added.

Bunny laughed. "You are such an ass," she said. She put her arms around John, and he picked her up.

John put her on the bed and began to kiss her. He removed her clothes and took his off. He began to kiss her all over, from the top of her to her bottom, where he began to please her orally. Bunny moaned, and John kept going. As he was pleasuring Bunny, he tasted her, and the feeling lit him up on the inside. He loved it. Something popped into his head. This was it. Not only was this the moment he had been waiting for and dreaming about for years, but they would finally consummate their relationship. John and Bunny made love all day.

John went out to meet with the new partners he had recruited to help rebuild Chimera. He needed some gum and had no time to stop by a store before going to the meeting. Bunny told him that she had some in her wallet. It was smashed but still fresh. He went into her checkbook wallet, looked, and found it. He also found an old, folded napkin that was practically flat. It was from the Playboy Club. He opened it and saw that it had writing on it. He read it and realized it was the same napkin he had given her with his old phone number on it. She had kept that paper all of this time. He could not believe it. He put it back the way he had found it and returned her wallet to her purse.

Celia finally made it back to Harlem to visit her mother for the first time in a year. The reunion was great, and they were happy to see each other. Celia felt sorry for leaving her for so long but promised to make it up to her. Celia made plans for her mother to leave finally the wasteland of Harlem and live in Jamaica with her after much convincing. Celia promised her that she would enjoy it and that she could retire in peace and the sun. They went out for lunch in Manhattan, where they sat and talked to each other for hours. They discussed Jerome and the conditions in Harlem. She informed her mother that she had promised Mariana that she would remain in their lives in some capacity. Celia felt that was the least she could do. While they were enjoying lunch, she saw a newspaper that someone had left on another table at the café. She went over and grabbed it to look at the headline. On the front page, she saw a photo of Enzo Ambrosino with a headline announcing his death. She took the paper and set it aside. She decided to pass it along to John when she went back to the house. Celia and her mother finished their lunch and returned to Harlem to start packing. Before they left, she informed her mother that she wanted to introduce her to her old, new boyfriend, John, and invite her to his first wine tasting.

"You like torturing yourself, young lady, don't you?" her mother said.

Bunny returned to Yonkers later on in the evening and examined the headline and story further. The article stated that Ambrosino suddenly fell ill with strange symptoms and died at Bellevue Hospital. John made it back home for the day and was glad to see her as usual. Bunny walked up to kiss him. Then she handed him the newspaper. "John, did you see the paper today?" she asked him.

"I did," he responded.

"So, you have anything to tell me?" she asked in a sweet, flirtatious tone.

"No, I don't," he responded in the same way. "Just because I go and see him and he dies a few days later does not mean that I had anything to do with it. He was decrepit. I had nothing to do with that. I have excellent negotiating skills," he said.

"Uh-huh," Bunny responded.

"Uh-huh, nothing. I have a surprise for you, but you will see that at the get-together." John pulled her closer to kiss her.

Ben remained in jail as he waited for his trial. The news that Brenda had blurted out to him sat in his head while he recovered from heroin withdrawals. He applied for treatment and rehabilitation, but in the meantime, he had to continue to wait. He did not want to be a father, but he had no choice. His mind kept going back to the box of baby clothes that Jerome had left there. He felt guilty. He would be responsible for yet another kid growing up without a father. What kind of father could he be in prison? How do you raise a child from behind bars? Would his child end up like him? Would he ever see Brenda and the baby? Was it even his baby?

Ben's cellmate was another man being held for drug possession. His name was Patrick. Patrick had been jailed for unlawful possession of needles and illegal possession of heroin. He also was charged with selling to a minor. He faced up to a forty-year prison sentence with no probation or parole if he was convicted. He had been convicted before for lesser drug crimes, and recent changes in the law made the penalties tougher for repeat offenders. Patrick was an older white male who had a long grayish beard and sparse long hair. He had tattoos on his face and arms, from what Ben could see. He looked like a mix of scary, intimidating, and old hippie. He had served in the Korean War. He did not say much. He had a pocket Bible that he would take out and read occasionally. As he read it, he would make cheering gestures. Ben did not know what to think of him, but he decided to break the ice. The awkward silence bothered him. For all he knew, this person could be one of those who would shank you while you slept. "What are you in for?" Ben asked him.

"I sell drugs, and I smoke them too," Patrick said while he laughed. His sparse, brown teeth became more noticeable. "I know what you are in for; it's in the news, and everybody is talking about it. I'm Pat," he said while extending his hand so that Ben could shake it.

"I'm Ben."

"You read the Bible? It's some good shit in here. There's killing, some weird shit like parting water, and locusts. Lots of locusts. There's drinking blood; there's sacrificing animals, and shit. It's better than a movie. You have to read this," Pat said.

"No, thanks," Ben said.

"No, actually, I see why people go to church and talk about it. It's entertaining. There is one story where Adam and Eve, they were naked; they had kids, the kids were jealous of each other, and one killed the other. The guy murdered his brother because he had the better girl. Can you believe that? It's just like one of those soaps the women watch. There were only two of them, so the one that was left had to sleep with all the women so they could make more people. Cain and Abel, it was," Pat said.

"Are you some preacher?" Ben asked him.

"No, man. I'm just here spreading the good message. That will be my next career. People pay good money to have some guy tell them what they can read for free. I can sell them some dreams," Pat said and chuckled.

The explanation about Cain and Abel intrigued Ben. He took Pat up on his offer to read the book. He thought it could take his mind off other things until he went to court. Before he began reading, he asked Pat about his tattoos. Pat went down both arms and legs, explaining what each symbol represented. When he got to his face, he pointed out a small one under his eye. It was a teardrop. Pat told him that it was a symbol of the old fraternity. The old fraternity referred to the Cain and Abel story. It symbolized the killing of your brother. "If you ever kill your brother, you get one. Everyone will know what you are capable of doing, and they won't mess with ya. I haven't killed anybody yet, but it's good to have," Pat told him while laughing. Ben thought that people avoided Pat because he was crazy, but the idea made sense. Ben inquired about getting a teardrop tattoo. "Have you ever killed your brother?" Pat asked.

"Do I have to answer that?" Ben replied.

Pat leaned back and looked at him. "Well…I have a stick pin and some ink from this pen here. I'll do this, but no screaming," he said. Ben lay down and let Patrick do a quick inking of a teardrop. It was nothing dramatic but enough for a first-time jail tattoo. Once the tattoo was complete, both of them turned in for the night. The next day, Patrick was led out of the cell. While he was being escorted out, he turned back to Ben and said, "Let the good book guide you." They took him away, and Ben never heard from him again. Ben stayed in the cell for the next day by himself with nothing to do but read the Bible, looking for the stories that Patrick had mentioned.

The next day, Ben was awakened from his sleep, handcuffed, escorted by guards, and moved to another room. In the room his lawyer, Mark Sullivan, and the court-appointed mental health professional waited to ask him some questions. Sullivan informed him that the grand jury had voted to indict him and that he was requesting a motion to look for more information about his case. He was going to use most of the forty-five-day timeframe to do so. In the meantime, they wanted to do a test on him. Ben did not know what that entailed. Sullivan explained to him that he wanted Ben to be forthright with his answers so he could help in the best way possible. Sullivan then questioned Ben. "What happened under your eye?"

Ben had to come up with something quick. He knew that what he said in this room could mean the difference between life in prison or prison with parole. "It's a tear because I am sad. I'm sad in the world; it makes me cry like sadness makes Jesus cry," he said. "What you find on me is the work of the Lord, and I do as he instructed me to do. I hear a voice from him telling me to do something, and I do it. I'm a good servant." Ben proceeded to pull up his sleeves and show his lawyer the needle marks and bruises. "You see those? They are marked by God. I fought the enemy, and it left scars. I fought the enemy in the war. We were all soldiers for God. 'Kill a gook for God' was our motto. Look at my feet, scarred like Jesus was scarred when he carried the cross. This city is my cross," he added.

Sullivan had paused before he proceeded to ask, "Did you understand that what you were doing was wrong?"

Ben responded, "I'm doing the Lord's work. The Bible. It's all in there, and you should read it. The drugs help people to escape the pain. Ask them; they will tell you." He pulled out the Bible that Patrick had lent to him and slid it across the table. Sullivan and the doctor looked at it.

"We know what this is, Benjamin," Sullivan said. "Do you understand that some of your actions broke the law?" he asked.

"The law made by man is not God's law," Ben said. "I am only required to follow the law of God. You take from the rich and give to the poor; you help them numb their pains; you take out criminals who harm the communities. That's God's work. He instructs us to do so. I can't control that. I can't stop God. He uses my body as a vessel. God is telling me now to silence that woman, but I can't because you have me tied," he said as he looked at the mental health examiner with them.

Sullivan sat back in his chair in disbelief. The mental-health examiner fiercely wrote in her notebook as Ben spoke. "Are you still using?" Sullivan asked him.

"The drugs, you mean? They give me superpowers. If I had some now, I could get out of this chair, these cuffs," Ben said. Sullivan and the mental-health examiner motioned to the officers that they were done.

"OK, well, I will see what I can do," Sullivan said as he motioned for the guards to let him and the doctor leave the area. They were escorted out, and Ben was sent back to his cell. Watching Patrick in the cell had given Ben a map on how to communicate with people and appear insane. He only had to mock Patrick's mannerisms and actions. Ben hoped he had played well enough for his lawyer to have any statement he said to police suppressed on grounds of mental incompetence.

When it came time for Ben to face the charges, a true bill for an indictment was issued, and Ben went in front of a judge for a bench trial. The judge had ordered a presentencing investigation and report to make sure that the decision they came to was thoroughly examined and complete. His lawyer withdrew Ben's guilty plea and entered a not-guilty plea. He bargained for lesser charges due to insanity, using the "M'Naghten Rule" as a partial defense. He presented the findings of the mental health professional stating that Ben was mentally ill. He recommended that Ben be placed in an institution for long-term treatment, as he had been treated before for substance abuse in the military. Sullivan claimed that his client was mentally deficient but that long-standing drug abuse and trauma from the war had caused this state. Sullivan said that substantial long-term treatment could cure him.

The investigators could not find a weapon that would have caused the blood spatter in the apartment, nor could they prove that he had committed the crime since he shared the apartment with a roommate who was now deceased. They only had hard evidence of his weapons and drug distribution, as well as the robbery charge. Prosecutors argued that the evidence they had against him was strong enough to put him away. They said that made him ineligible for release, although they were satisfied with the mental-health examiner's findings. Ben had been convicted before during his court-martial in the US Army, and that fell under the ten-year predicate violation law.

Ben made a statement that his lawyer had informed him of the physical evidence and had to convince him that he had committed these actions that broke the law. The judge determined that a costly trial was likely to produce the same outcome with an insanity ruling. The prosecutors noted that the people were satisfied that the affirmative defense of lack of criminal responsibility by reason of mental disease or defect would likely be proven by the defendant at a trial by a preponderance of the evidence. The judge determined that he be committed to a state psychiatric facility for ten years.

A mental-health professional showed up to escort Ben to an inpatient mental-health facility at Bellevue Hospital. He would finally receive an opportunity to deal appropriately with the trauma of war and years of heavy narcotic use. Ben was placed in an antiviolence program. Part of his rehabilitation program would include retraining for society. The program taught participants that people who lost their bond with society caused delinquency, and the program retrained them to assimilate.

Chapter 15

With a clear head, John went to work. After making love to Bunny and informing her that she would not be able ever to get rid of him now, he had to draw out what he wanted for the future of the company. He was going to turn Chimera into a multifaceted corporation, but he knew that he needed to make his first venture a hit before he could think about expanding. The focus of the company would first center on his winery. He finally understood why Bunny ate so many fruits and berries. It made her juices sweeter. She tasted so good to him, and he wanted to make that his signature flavor. He had to find a way to duplicate her body juices without tipping her off. That meant that he had to make love to her repeatedly until he nailed it, which was something that John did not mind doing and Bunny did not mind receiving. They were finally in love with each other with no interferences.

The despair of the South Bronx and Harlem had spread into New York City. In less than ten short years, New York City had transformed from a once promising metropolitan municipality that benefited from the positive economic growth of the past thirty years into a fiscal hell. Incidences of murders and snatchings of personal property, such as chains and handbags, were at a record high. Joblessness went through the roof, and morale plummeted. Drug culture ruled the atmosphere. Disgruntled citizens had come to a point where they discouraged tourists from coming to New York because conditions were so bad. Union officials distributed flyers around the city that warned people not to go outside after six o'clock, not to walk anywhere, to take cabs, to stay off public transportation, and not to venture past Midtown Manhattan. The unions used these leaflets to protest looming layoffs and the dismissal of four thousand officers. Some argued that these layoffs would make the city more unsafe than it already was.

John knew that the conditions in the city were not ripe to start a new business. He suggested to Bunny that they relocate to her new place in Jamaica, where they would find fertile lands, warm weather, and better business-growing conditions. He wanted to buy land there to start the winery. The prime minister's socialist-leaning policies were beginning to fail, and the tide had returned to the favor of economic growth and development. Many of the protests there mirrored those in the States when it came to dissatisfaction with the government. John felt that this would be a good time to get out of New York City, start over there, and take advantage of what Jamaica had to offer. Bunny agreed to it, but she was adamant that he would have to find a place on his own. She had made it clear that she was taking her mother and moving away for the time being. She was not interested in housing extra bodies that did not belong to relatives, and that included boyfriends. They were a couple now, but she did not believe in shacking up before marriage.

John knew this about her already. Once he realized that she would stay with him, he made sure after the meeting with Enzo Ambrosino to stop off in the diamond district in Manhattan to pick up a ring so he could propose to her. He did not intend to let Bunny walk away from his life for the third time. Before he knelt down, he wanted to get everything in order so there would be no delays at the beginning of their new life.

John contacted a wine distributor that he knew in New York City. He suggested a meeting with him and his wine-making team to help him create the right flavor, blend, aroma, and texture. The winemaker asked about John's inspiration for the flavor. John explained only that the taste came from a particular woman. "Did she create the flavor?" The winemaker did not know what he meant.

"Not quite, but it tastes like her," John answered.

"Tastes like her? You aren't a cannibal or something?" the winemaker joked.

"No, but her juices are sweet," John said.

The guy stared at him for a second before he got it. "Oh. OK, just a quick question: Do you want strangers to know what your lady's—um, what should I say?—lady parts taste like?" he asked.

"I won't tell them the specifics, no. I have not decided if I will tell her either. She may kill me. She'll figure it out one day," John said.

"Wow, well, this is a first." The winemaker chuckled.

"It is. That's the point. There is a goldmine between those thighs. Good stuff in there," John said.

"Well, let's get to work then," the winemaker chimed back. They proceeded to make wine magic in the studio.

John knew exactly what he wanted, and after a couple of hours of mixing flavors, they came up with the perfect taste. He asked a designer to create a label for him and ordered to have some bottles made. John brought in a photo he had taken of Bunny while she was still working at the club. He hired an artist to draw her silhouette as the logo. BunnyWine was officially born. He wanted to introduce the new wine to friends and Bunny at a get-together before they left the city. After John had told him about his plans, the distributor put him in contact with a landowner in Jamaica who had a winery there. The process took months, as they needed time for the wine to ferment, clear, and age.

⎯⎯⎯

The night of the wine-tasting party finally arrived. He had not told anyone about the name or flavor of the wine, as he wanted to reveal everything to everyone all at once. Everyone was dressed to the nines. Bunny wore a red wrap dress that highlighted her curves perfectly. Red had always been Bunny's best color, as it made her skin tone glow. John wore his best suit and loafers, remaining faithful to his Rude Boy roots. John's and Bunny's friends attended. Some of her old coworkers from the Playboy Club were also there. John invited all the new business associates he had brought in as partners for the New Chimera Group. These new allies consisted of Wall Street investment bankers, lawyers, risk arbitragers, and those who were involved in corporate raiding. John had officially exited the Mafia game for now.

He held the get-together at his old stomping grounds at P. J. Clarke's. The bar was still as he remembered it. Had it not been for this place and his poor drunken unawareness, he would never have met Bunny. His corporate partners had powerful connections, including Jacqueline Kennedy Onassis, who would bring John Jr. and Caroline for lunch on Saturdays. She also attended the get-together. Attendants dressed all in white were serving the guests, and hired orchestra players entertained in the background.

Everyone eagerly awaited the reveal. When they pulled the curtain, two giant six-by-four-foot cardboard posters with the silhouette logo stood beside a beautiful display table full of dark wine bottles, elegant table napkins, and ornate large wine glasses. A backdrop that displayed the full logo,

"BunnyWine, An Intoxicating Concoction by Chimera," stood behind it all. The bottles were black with a sparkly fourteen-karat-gold wrapping at the top. The label was also black, but Bunny's silhouette was outlined in fourteen-karat gold, as was the writing on the label.

Everyone commented on how beautiful the entire set-up was. Bunny was surprised and happy. She'd had no idea that John had been working on this for all of this time. John turned to her and said, "I wanted to get this right. You inspired all of it," he said.

"Is that me?" Bunny asked as she looked over at the poster.

"Yes, it is," he answered.

"I'm all flustered. Thank you." Bunny smiled and kissed him.

The guests began drinking the wine, and it was an instant hit. They had never tasted anything like it before. It was fruity and spicy at the same time. John reveled in the positive feedback from the crowd. Many of them inquired about buying crates and barrels of this from him. Bunny took a sip and asked John how he came up with it. She thought it was great and familiar, but she could not put her finger on it. John began to blush a little. He did not want to tell her then. He told her that he would explain it when they returned home. She pressed on about it in a playful way. He finally told her, "Now I understand your obsession with consuming fruit, and I enjoy drinking you."

It took her a few seconds to derive a conclusion. Bunny's mouth fell open, and she turned red, almost the same color as her dress. She was tasting herself, and so was everyone in the room. She did a once-over glance around the room and saw everyone drinking glass after glass. She looked at her flute and thought, *I am drinking my own orgasm.* He leaned down and kissed her. He walked away and went about chatting with the other guests. She stood there, took a deep breath, and thought to herself, *Damn, I'm fantastic. I had no idea.* She shrugged and continued to drink up.

When Bunny and John made it home after the successful evening, John wanted to lie down and talk with her. They sat in the bedroom together and relaxed. He had some things to say to her. He told her that this was one of the best days of his life and that none of it would have happened without her being there and saving his life in the beginning. The only thing that would make him happier right now was if she would accept his ring. John pulled from his pocket a box that he had been carrying around with him for the entire time since he bought it. He had thought to propose to her many times before, but he wanted everything to be right and for both of them to be in a good mood when he did it. Bunny wanted to cry. This brought her back to when they first started dating, and she dreamed of his proposal. She said yes. Both of them called their parents.

Getting everything ready for the move and setting up the plans for the winery took almost a year. During that time, John and Bunny remained in Yonkers. Bunny was not familiar with Yonkers, but she had some knowledge about the public housing there. She knew they had all the black residents segregated in a small section of Runyon Heights. Their house stood at the edge of the Homefield neighborhood. Bernie had owned this home but rarely used it. He'd bought it as a safe house just in case he needed to leave the city or had business in Westchester. When he died, he left it to John. John never told the neighbors that he now owned the property; he just said he was housesitting for the time being. The Homefield Neighborhood Association did not care for black residents in their part of town. They maintained a four-foot strip of land as a barrier between the streets of the two sections. They used this to make clear to the minorities in the area that they should not cross into the neighborhood. Celia could not wait to get out of there.

John organized several meetings with his partners in the New Chimera Group in Midtown to discuss business development plans in Jamaica and Los Angeles, and those were successful. Once he completed those meetings, he decided to forego the cab or car service and walk around for lunch, since the day was beautiful. It had been a while since John was able to walk up and down the streets without fearing for his life. He revisited the café he and the guys used to frequent, which brought back memories. For a brief moment, he became nostalgic and thought about how things would be now if Bernie had not passed away. Would everything be the same? John ordered lunch to bring back home for him and Bunny.

While he was waiting, a woman walked up to John. "Remember me?" she asked with a big smile. "I waited for you to call, but you didn't." She hugged him and kissed him on the cheek. John looked at her in utter confusion. Was she a client? Was she a plant? How did she know him? He could not place her. "You look different with the shorter hair, but you are still handsome," she told him. "I had a great time. Maybe we can go out again." She grabbed John's hand.

John was uneasy; he did not want to be seen holding another woman's hand. In his mind, you never knew who was looking. Bunny had taught him this. He felt guilty about not remembering who she is. He had to get more information from this woman. His photographic memory was failing him for the first time. He started fishing for information. He did not want to seem like a jerk and outright tell her that he did not know her. He remained polite. "Refresh my memory. I am having an off day," he said to her.

"The bar, your place, we had a good time," she said while smiling. "I'm Jeanie." John stood there and just nodded.

They'd had contact before. She and John met during one of his trips to the many bars in New York City. They had sex the same night they met. He showed her a good time and promised to keep in contact with her, but he never did. He had forgotten about the encounter by the next morning. "It's good that I saw you here. I've been working down the street at the department store for a while. I'm on lunch break," she told him.

John finally decided to answer her. "That's great. Your name is Jeanie."

With more excitement, Jeanie told him, "I have the same number, but if you lost it, here it is. Call me tonight. I will be home." She took a pen and a piece of paper from her pocketbook and wrote her number on it. She handed it to him and kissed him again on the cheek. "I have to go," she said, and she walked off, leaving John standing there.

He looked at the paper. He balled it up and tossed it in the wastebasket near the street. He took off his blazer, rolled one of the sleeves inside out, and wiped his face with it to make sure she had not left any lipstick on his face. He looked at it afterward and tossed the blazer in the wastebasket too. He walked off. When it came to business, John was sharp. When it came to women, they were a blur. How many more blurs were out there? It was only a matter of time before this happened again. How would he explain a random woman's approach to Bunny if they were out? Too much of his past was still there, lingering and trying to catch up with him.

In the meantime, he and Bunny made several trips to and from Jamaica to get their affairs in order. She introduced him to her extended family, and John fell in love with the area. She decided once she settled there she would continue her education in music, and she had donated money to one of the schools. She hoped to become a music teacher and start a family once she finished her studies. John planned to open a winery there and become the business contact for the changing economy in Jamaica. The members of the New Chimera Group were spread in New York, Los Angeles, Chicago, Miami, and Jamaica. He wanted to woo businesses back into Jamaica so that the country could build wealth again. John and Bunny celebrated their first Thanksgiving and Christmas as a real couple, as well as their birthdays and all events in between. Everything remained quiet, but by the end of August 1974, New York and the rest of the country were changing for the worse, and both of them felt it was time to leave.

John contracted the Jet Mafia to remain as security for him and Bunny until they officially left for Jamaica. John passed them all of his contacts from his dealings in Chimera's old days. This enabled them to grow in areas such as the Bronx, Harlem, and Brooklyn. Many of the Jet Mafia were affiliated with the Black Panthers, and their growing influence in these areas helped them build wealth due to the booming drug trade. The Jet Mafia was able to succeed because law enforcement had a tough time finding people who would testify against them or report their illegal activities.

This was John's thank-you for their service. The Jet Mafia's influence in Atlantic City and Philadelphia had dwindled somewhat because of the increased pressure from the FBI, due to their hits on rivals and their involvement in the drug trade. They were also misusing government grants that were meant to rebuild their communities. Some of them had already branched out in New York City and parts of Delaware thanks to John, and they began dealing with other crime families. They had virtually moved into the Mafia ranks in New York City.

John and Celia were ready to head out of New York City for the last time. They had a late-night flight to Miami for the connecting flight to Jamaica in the morning. They decided to sell the house in Yonkers. The day was warm and beautiful, but the atmosphere in the city and the country was tense. Celia was packing her things and going through the clothes that she wanted to keep. She had retrieved the remainder of her items from Rose's apartment. While packing, she located her suits from the Playboy Club. She had not worn them since she left, and her curiosity got to her. The launch of BunnyWine inspired her, and she decided to see if she could still fit in them. She took out the black suit and put it on. She added the ears, tail, collar, bow tie, and heels. She located the ribbon with her name on it and pinned it on. She looked in the mirror and said to herself, *I still got it.* Celia did not know that John was standing in the doorway watching her check herself out. She had a smile on her face. Seeing Bunny in her suit for the first time in years, outside of photographs, made him happy. John made a slight noise, and Bunny looked over to him. She smiled back.

"Bunny..." he said. She walked over to him and asked if he wanted her to bring him a drink. She went and poured both of them drinks in a couple of glasses they had not packed yet. She brought over the drinks and stood next to him. "Are you allowed to do this? I mean, I don't want you to get in trouble," he asked her with a grin.

Bunny laughed. "No one's looking," she said. He put his hand on her butt, right under her tail. This time, she did not move it away. He leaned over to kiss her. They kissed each other with the wine glasses in their hands. He unzipped the back of the costume.

Later on, by the time they made it to the airport to catch their flight, the rumors were flying from earlier in the day that Richard Nixon had decided to resign his position as president of the United States. They sat in Kennedy Airport following the news like everyone else. An air of uncertainty lingered in the atmosphere as many people around them had conversations about what was going to happen to the country. John and Bunny felt good about their decision to leave and start a new life. For a moment, she was sad that she was leaving home for good. She was going to take everything she had learned from growing up as a native New Yorker and apply it to the rest of her life in Jamaica.

⸺

Celia had her hair pinned up with a white flower in the back. She wore an airy white slip dress, as the weather outside that evening was warm but breezy. There was not a cloud in the sky. John had on a white shirt and tan pants with sandals. Celia's mother was dressed in her church whites. John's mother and brother, along with his brother's wife and kids, were there. They had never had the opportunity to travel outside the Gulf area before. Mariana and the baby also joined them. Both John and Bunny wanted her to be there. Rose came in from New York, as Bunny's maid of honor.

Rose was happy that Celia was happy, but on the inside she felt that her friend was making a mistake. Rose didn't think that John was marriage material. She felt that he was poison to Celia, a bad influence. Rose would never tell Celia this, but she vowed to continue to support her friend in case she was needed.

Bunny's father and her half siblings also joined her. John and Bunny's father, Arthur Jones, appeared to be getting along just fine. Arthur walked her down the aisle. John's associates came down from New York and Los Angeles. John paid everyone's expenses to fly out and join them for the wedding. Bunny's local Jamaican relatives attended.

That day was special. They were back at the Playboy Hotel in Ocho Rios. They rented the entire eight-hundred-foot beachfront for themselves and had the family celebration fully catered. This was their wedding day, and no one from either family wanted to miss it. Bunny found Karlus when she returned, and he agreed to officiate their ceremony. They wanted the traditional vows because their parents were in attendance. They had not known how the relatives would react to each other since this was the first time the entire family was getting together.

Agnes looked at John while the couple stood there in front of Karlus. She had not had the opportunity to spend a lot of time with him. Agnes only knew what Celia had told her and what she had read about him in the papers or heard in the general gossip on the street. Some of the talks were not favorable; it mentioned his promiscuity. John reminded her of her ex-husband. Both were broad, handsome, fiery, arrogant, and full of swagger. Agnes thought to herself, *My God, she is marrying her father.*

Karlus read a Bible verse. He then blessed the rings, and the couple exchanged them. They said their traditional vows, and then Karlus read another prayer and they lit a unity candle. Once they finished, the officiant announced them, man and wife. He permitted John to kiss the bride. For the first time in his life, John felt sure of everything and knew that everything would be okay. He had lifted her veil before he kissed her. Everyone cheered and celebrated for the rest of the evening, and they all enjoyed the sunset.

John and Bunny broke away from the festivities. They had one more important part of the night to complete. They had another ceremony, just him, her, and a witness. The witness was his business partner from Chicago. John and Bunny pricked each other's finger with a pin and held a picture at both ends with their pricked fingers. Blood from both of them spotted the edges of the photo. The snap was one of the pictures of the both of them taken with his old camera when she worked at the Playboy Club. The witness lit the picture with one of the candles on the side, and both of them held it as it burned.

John and Bunny spoke together. "If I betray you, may I burn as I do in the photo. If we betray each other, we will both perish." They grasped the picture until they could not hold it anymore. The picture dropped to the ground between them, and they watched it burn in a small fire until it curled and then turned into ash.

John said to Bunny, "At ease, rude girl." He kissed her as the smoke from the paper seeped up between them.

AUTHOR BIOGRAPHY

Writer Victoria Bolton lives in New York. A graduate of the College of Westchester, she works as a computer technician in schools and as a part-time actress. Bolton previously released the book *Looking for Mr. Potential* under the pen name La'Ketta T. Bolton in 2000.

27356644R00174

Made in the USA
San Bernardino, CA
11 December 2015

Emily Andrews lives in Seattle, Washington. Her poetry has been published in the *International Library of Poetry* and Poetry. com, and featured on one of their spoken albums. Her interests include indie, punk rock and industrial music, journaling and old horror movies.

The Finer Points of Becoming Machine

EMILY ANDREWS

SADDLEBACK
EDUCATIONAL PUBLISHING

CUTTING EDGE

Breaking Dawn
DONNA SHELTON

The Finer Points of Becoming Machine
EMILY ANDREWS

Marty's Diary
FRANCES CROSS

The Only Brother
CAIAS WARD

The Questions Within
TERESA SCHAEFFER

Seeing Red
PETER LANCETT

© Ransom Publishing Ltd. 2008

This edition is published by arrangement with Ransom Publishing Ltd.

SADDLEBACK
EDUCATIONAL PUBLISHING
www.sdlback.com

ISBN-13: 978-1-61651-761-8
ISBN-10: 1-61651-761-1

Printed in Guangzhou, China
0512/CA21200795

16 15 14 13 12   2 3 4 5 6 7

Firstly, I'd like to thank my friends and family for their love and support during the creation of this book, especially Victoria Lane, who introduced me to Peter Lancett.

Special thanks to: my mother, Kyle, Jenna, my fathers, and my husband, who have in some way or another walked through each step of hell with me. Thank you for loving me, despite the fact that I am a complete mess.

A special thank you to Peter Lancett for his patience, knowledge, skill, and never ending support. You are an amazing writer and editor, and I am truly humbled as well as incredibly grateful to call you now my friend.

Lastly, I would like to dedicate this book to each and every person who has lived, died, or survived a life of abuse.

CHAPTER 1

"Can you feel, now?"

"Call 911. I did something really stupid," are the last words I remember saying clearly. Whatever pills I had swallowed had begun to make me loopy, or maybe it was the bottle of Puerto Rican rum I had washed them down with, or hell, maybe it was from the blood loss as my arms streamed ribbons of ruby red. Either way though, the night takes on a nightmarish quality that leaves all but the major details hazy to me.

The day had started out normal enough. I woke up, and sighed in exhaustion at still breathing. I had gotten dressed in my usual outfit, black combat boots, black pants, black shirt, black sweater, heavy eyeliner. The vacant look in my eyes comes naturally now; I don't have to put that on anymore. I am sixteen years old. I am that weird kid in your class you whisper about and make fun of because she dresses in black and the few friends that she does have also dress in black and listen to depressing music while smoking cigarettes in the bathroom at lunchtime.

My name is Emma, but that isn't important. This could be your story, the kid down the street's story, and in a way I wish it was; but it's not. It's mine, and mine alone to tell.

It was a fairly noneventful day. Get on bus. Go to school. Ditch most of my classes. Smoke cigarettes. Get on bus, go back home. December 16th. The only reason I remember the day is because this is the day that the shit hit the fan and I was forced to start dealing with all the crap in my head—or spend more time in a padded room than anyone should ever have to.

I had an older boyfriend named Donnie.

He was a 21-year-old musician with bleached blond hair and beautiful features and looked *just* like the lead singer of my favorite band, which is probably the entire reason I loved him in the first place.

Anyways, school ends and he doesn't meet me like he was supposed to. A phone call a few hours later manages to tear my heart in two. "You've got too many problems, Emma. I'm sorry, I think we shouldn't be together anymore."

Looking back, it wasn't so much him that broke me. It was the fact that I poured what was left of my love and humanity into him and he, like everyone else in my life, hurt me. When I called my mom for condolence, she simply said, "I'm sorry you're hurting," but her voice told me the exact opposite. She didn't care either. Something bad and dark inside me clicks.

You see, I am the product of an abusive home, where violence, guilt, and lies are a way of life. I grew up watching my mother get beaten black and blue, and eventually that happened to me as well. But I'll get to that a little later.

Anyways, after years of stuffing it in, hiding it, drowning myself in booze and drugs and sex in the vain attempt to forget the past, I had finally reached a breaking point. I was going to kill myself.

I put my favorite song on repeat, grabbed a butcher knife, emptied the medicine cabinet and crawled into the bathtub with a bottle of rum. "One way or another, this is going to end," I had told myself. I had scrawled the requisite suicide note but I couldn't think of anything to say, so all I said was that I was sorry.

I steel myself for this. Take a deep breath. Go. Slice ruby lines into porcelain skin. Swallow this bottle of pills. Chase it with rum. Repeat until finished. I don't know what made me get out of the tub and tell my grandma and little sister to call 911. But I did. And everything gets hazy after that.

Flashing lights and sirens. Emergency medical team working on me. And I was laughing, can you imagine? Laughing at the whole situation. It wasn't anywhere *near* funny, but somehow, it was all I could do.

Fade out.

Fade in to an ambulance and being strapped to a stretcher. I can feel my mascara running down my face. I think I am afraid, but I'm not entirely sure I can feel anymore. My body is bones and skin and blood right now. I am wet and cold. I try to hold on to this paramedic's clothing, to feel something so I know that I am still here.

Fade out.

Fade in to intravenous lines and tubes being pushed down my throat, and that's when I black out, hoping oblivion has finally agreed to take me.

I wake up and have no goddamned clue where I am. The lights are too bright, the walls were obviously once painted white, but time and dirt have turned them dingy and sallow looking. I try to sit up and realize that I am strapped to a stretcher. A slow moan comes out of my throat when it dawns on me that I am not dreaming. Things start to flash back to me, the phone call with Donnie and then my mother, the pills, the knife, the bath, the ambulance ride.

I notice a fat, middle-aged man dressed in a black uniform. He's not paying attention to me, though it's my guess that he's supposed to. I twist my arms, even though the leather straps dig into my cuts and reopen them, until I get a hand free. I am beyond feeling pain now. I undo the buckles quietly, slowly. He's chattering away with some pretty female nurse who couldn't care less about him but is trying not to be rude and tell him straight out to piss off.

I am in the emergency room of a hospital and look for signs to the waiting room. My feet hit the floor, and Jesus, could it have *been* any colder in there? It's the dead of winter and it doesn't feel like the heat is on in this dirty, overcrowded hospital building.

I make my way to the entrance of the waiting room. I look through the bulletproof glass in the door and see my mother. I try to open it, but the door is locked. She is crying and hunched over, my stepfather is holding her as her body is wracked with sobs. I put my bloody and bandaged hand on the glass. She looks up and sees me and runs to the glass, slipping from my stepfather's embrace. About this time I hear the fat security guard asking people "Where is that girl who was just in this bed?" and I figure I have about five seconds when I hear the footsteps coming behind me. I do not look behind me, I know what is coming and I just want to be near my mom, even if she hates me after what I've done tonight. I start to cry when she starts to cry and she puts her hand to the glass too.

She says one word in the form of a question, and if I could have felt anything at that moment, it would have broken my heart. "Why?" I cannot hear her, maybe

I didn't want to or maybe it was the bulletproof glass and the locked door, and all I can say is that I'm sorry before security guards drag me away.

I am held down by a combination of nurses and security guards and strapped down to this bed again, in this alien room, cold and praying that this is all some horrible nightmare, just like the rest of my life has been.

A nurse comes and sticks a needle hard into my damaged arms. I remember thinking to myself "She didn't have to be so damned rough. I mean shit, obviously I am *not* having a good day,..." but the thought disappears. I am fading into black, and the last thought in my head before the dark claims me are the words "Can you feel, now?"

CHAPTER 2

A rude awakening

Cold, sharp metal pierces my skin again and I wake up. Sort of. Whatever the nurses gave me has put me into a complacent haze and my limbs move wherever they decide to push them into place. Which happens to be in front of me, as more cold metal touches my body. This time, it's handcuffs. I look down in an amazed stupor and then look up again. The police are arresting me for trying to kill myself? How screwed up is this?

But they aren't arresting me; they are transporting me to a mental hospital. I am placed in the back of a police van and I slip back into sleep until the door is slammed open and I am ordered out of the van.

The Finer Points of Becoming...

I am escorted into the county mental hospital. I am guessing it's around 3 a.m. Red night-lights illuminate the hallways and I cannot help but think that some extremely screwed up individual planned that. Wails of inmates, prisoners, patients—whatever the insane are called in a place like this— greet me, and chills go up my spine. I am half convinced that I am actually dead and I am in the waiting room of hell.

The policeman handcuffs me to a cold, fake-leather bench while he goes to talk to the night orderly. I can hear them arguing. I can hear a female voice telling him "there just simply isn't any room, you know how busy it gets in here around Christmastime..." and I silently say a prayer of gratitude. The nurse brings me a blanket and I curl up as best as I can on this cold bench, that one wrist is still handcuffed to. I fall asleep.

"Emma... wake up Emma..." my mother's voice whispers to me. I jerk awake and look around. She is not there, just some strange nurse and the policeman from before. "Wake up Emma. We're moving you."

Once again, I am loaded into the police van and I am checked into a new hospital, where I am handed a blanket, a pillow and a sheet and shown into a room with two beds. "Keep quiet, you have a roommate; don't wake her."

Great.

I am convinced that my roommate is the type of inmate that eats flies and spiders while thinking that she's Santa Claus. I am mildly concerned that there is going to be some horrible incident in the middle of the night with her. Sleep claims me quickly though, and she doesn't bother me.

I am woken up again, after what feels like just a few minutes, by more needles in my arm. I don't even care at this point. I cannot feel the cold anymore or the pain in my arms and the ache in my heart. I fall back asleep.

Nurses pound on the door, announcing their unwanted and uncaring presence before entering. I am given a pair of pajama-style pants, a hospital gown, and a pair of socks. I am told to shower, where I am watched by a nurse who is there to make sure I somehow don't injure myself bathing.

This creeps me out, and I am irritated because the water doesn't seem to get above 78 degrees. Shivering, I put on the crappy, ill-fitting, nearly paper-thin hospital clothes that hang off my broken and emaciated body. The nurse leaves.

I sit on the edge of my bed and notice, now that it is daylight, that there are old bloodstains on it. But I am too exhausted to be as grossed out as I should be. I notice my roommate and she is younger than I am, cute and bouncy and chipper. This annoys the shit out of me. Who the hell is happy in a place like this?

Her name is Cindy, and I don't get to find out why she is here before we are told to go to the dining room for breakfast.

I follow everyone else, seeing as how I don't know where I am going. I look around at the other patients here and I notice that they're all minors. Some of them are zombies, shuffling toward breakfast. I try not to dwell on this thought too long because if I do, fear will kick in that "they" will turn me into one of those drooling, shuffling patients.

We are served cold, nearly inedible cafeteria food with plastic spoons that are counted up at the end of the meal. I am not hungry and let the other inmates pick from my tray.

Next, we're all herded into a room with half-inch thick windows, scuffs and stains on the cheap linoleum floor, and couches that were most likely brand new about twenty years ago. A doctor comes into the room and all the giggling and talking comes to a stop.

Dr. X is a fairly young and not unpleasant looking brown-haired, blue-eyed male doctor, wearing glasses and a white coat. "Good morning everyone. Please get out your journals."

I don't have a journal and somehow, I feel instantly ashamed.

He looks at me and says, "Emma, I understand you got here late last night. We will provide one for you during this session. You are expected to write in it at the appropriate times. Failure to do so will result in loss of privileges." I don't say anything at all, I just simply stare and finally nod my head when I feel the rest of the room staring at me.

Dr. X continues with the bored monotone of someone who does this every single day. "Since we have someone new here, let's all introduce ourselves and say why we're here."

Oh Lord. I roll my eyes as I get flashes of an Alcoholics Anonymous meeting. Everyone goes in turn, announcing their name and why they're here. Some of the patients are so out of it they have no idea what the hell their names are, and say them slowly; like it's a new word they're trying out, off the cover of their journal.

When it is my turn, I stand up and I say "Hi. My name is Emma. I'm an alcoholic."

Nobody gets the joke, or if they do they don't appreciate it.

Dr. X scolds me and says, "I don't find that very appropriate, Emma."

Chastised, I blush and manage to sputter out "Uh, I tried to kill myself." The words sound strange to me, and again I am awash in the feeling that this can't really be happening.

During this group therapy session, people talk about their feelings. I scoff, and sit there silently judging them. Some of them have no reason to be here from what I can tell, other than that they wanted attention. I hate them. They make me sick. I feel superior to them in my pain, in my suffering. My walls go up. "You will not reach me," I scrawl on the inside cover of the journal that was passed to me.

I have a private meeting with Dr. X right after therapy where he asks me a series of what I imagine to be typical questions for this type of in-patient setting. I lie to nearly all of them and answer flawlessly until he comes to one question that throws me for a loop. "Are you now, or have you ever been, beaten or been witness to a parent or guardian being beaten?" I pause. I want to say yes, some small part of me wants to say yes and wants help, but I push that weak voice back down and I say "No" instead. Dr. X notices the pause and he looks at me hard. "Are you sure?" I cross my arms and repeat my answer.

Dr. X looks at me until I feel like he can see through me. I fidget. Finally, he breaks the silence and says "You are here for a mandatory three days Emma. You can use this time to begin to deal with whatever drove you to try to kill yourself, or not. At the end of three days, however, if I decide you aren't making enough progress, I can keep you here as long as I see fit. Do you understand?"

I swallow hard. My tongue feels like it's made of wood, and it refuses to move at all. I simply nod at him. "I read the reports of the police and the emergency medical team. I am prescribing some medications that I think will help you. You may go now."

I pick up the stupid journal and I leave the room. I am ushered back into the group area, where the group has "free time." Some pretty Asian girl comes up to me and grabs my arm. "Did you do this to yourself?"

"Uh, yeah." I stutter. This idiot acts like I just told her that I was a movie star and gets all kind of excited and gushy on me.

"Oh my God, I wish I could do that to myself! How does it feel?"

I jerk my arm away from her as she's trying to stick her wretched fingers into the rips of skin. I am at a loss for words. I hate her. She is a vile creature and I wish she would just disappear. She does not notice my contempt of her and continues.

"This is my seventh suicide attempt. I swallowed a bottle of aspirin."

Without any further comment, I walk away. Unlike her, I am not proud of these cuts on my arm, not proud of the fact that I am in here. I sit in a chair as far away from her as possible and begin to brood.

A dorky, tall, white, pimply-faced boy introduces himself as Ricky to me. He begins to explain how this place works; what we are allowed to do and when we're supposed to do it.

When the nurses come in with trays of pills and water, we line up and take whatever is in the cup. I have a little blue pill and a slightly larger white pill in my paper cup.

"What is this?" I ask the nurse.

She curtly responds to me. "Your medicine."

"Yeah, I got that. What kind?"

This stocky, ruddy, un-pretty middle-aged nurse who is giving out Prozac and lithium likes it's candy looks up at me. Like I am deaf or stupid, she repeats herself. "YOUR MEDICINE."

Ricky is behind me and whispers to me quickly. "Just take it, or she'll call a code on you, and you don't want that."

I take his advice, and swallow the medication with the tepid cup of what tastes like toilet water. I stick my tongue out and they check to make sure I took them.

An orderly comes in and unlocks a big plastic bin and passes out coloring books and crayons. I scoff. I color the angel picture they gave me to color in with the darkest crayons in the box. I color her wings black. Then I draw blood dripping down them, just to upset people. "How the HELL is this supposed to make me better?" I think to myself.

A bell rings and we put the books and crayons away. We go to lunch. We are supposed to write in our journals before evening therapy but I don't do it. I think it's stupid. Not as stupid as the crappy coloring books and the cheap, shitty crayons they gave us to color the pictures with, but still completely retarded and pointless. Besides, where would I even begin?

CHAPTER 3

My first journal

December ??

I know it's December, but I don't know what day it is. How can I know when there are no calendars around the place? Perhaps they think that if we never know what the date is we won't excite ourselves by looking forward to things like birthdays or holidays. This place is stupid and lame. I really don't know how this godforsaken journal is supposed to do anything, and I really don't know what the hell you expect me to write. Your food sucks ass, it's too damned cold in here, and it would be nice if I had a mattress that wasn't blood-covered. Also, perhaps you're not aware of this, but these clothes don't fit me and it would be nice if I had some that did. All in all, I'm having a miserable time. Screw you.

Dr. X looks at me with a frozen stare that leaves me genuinely afraid. There is an uncomfortable silence. I wish he'd just yell at me or something, not just stare at me. The haughty demeanour I walked in with fades under his icy gaze.

"Perhaps you didn't understand the directions Emma." I pick at nothing on my pants.

"You said to write about my feelings. So that's what I did."

"The directions were to write about your feelings, yes. These are complaints. Secondly, you are supposed to write at least a page a day, half a page in the morning and the evening at the minimum."

Dr. X drops the journal on the desk in front of him and distastefully pushes it back toward me. "You're not trying Emma. I suggest you start."

His words thinly conceal an open-ended threat that I might find myself having to stay in this shit hole. I pick up the journal and leave. I go and sit back in the main room and listen to all the other patients talk about nothing important at all. I am growing more and more irritated. I've focused in on the sound and it grows louder in my head, like the buzzing of bees.

I am afraid I'm going to do something horrible, I can see myself screaming at all of them about their stupid, meaningless lives and I feel like I can't breathe. I'm gasping for air when finally group therapy is called and everyone shuts the hell up. The buzzing stops. I can breathe again.

I cross my arms and scowl at every single person while they talk. I make goals for myself in here to keep myself entertained. Today I have decided to practice staring at people until they feel uncomfortable.

My game is interrupted by Dr. X's voice. "Is there a problem Emma?"

I flinch at the sound. Everyone stares at me. Now I feel uncomfortable. "No."

He waits for a minute and then looks at the pretty Asian girl who accosted me when I first arrived here with her idiocy and her fingers. Apparently Lucy is her name, and she goes back to talking about how she lives a life of luxury and her parents don't pay attention to her, or something else retarded like that. Everyone nods and mutters words of encouragement. I roll my eyes.

It finally gets to be my turn to talk. "I don't have anything to say," I state flatly.

Everyone stares at me again. I ignore their zombie eyes by concentrating on my fingernails. Dr. X is staring at me too; I know it. I am frustrated. I really *don't* know what to say.

Dr. X speaks. "Okay Emma, let's talk about anything you want. Anything at all."

I start to cry, I am so damned frustrated, and my showing of emotion upsets me more.

I bite the inside of my mouth until I taste blood.

"I don't know what to say. I really don't. I'm frustrated because I don't know what to say."

As if God somehow hears my thoughts, a bell sounds and Dr. X sighs. Therapy is over. I say a silent prayer of gratitude.

Pills. Food. Coloring. I am irritated, and it's swelling inside my chest and I can't control it. The same rotten nurse who spoke to me like I was an idiot when I asked her what medication she was giving me, curtly tells me to clean up the crayons as I am putting them away in the plastic baby wipe box they are contained in.

"I *am* putting them away." I respond angrily to her demand.

"*What* was that?" she snaps at me.

I don't back down, not to this wretched, hateful woman. "I SAID, I AM PUTTING

THEM AWAY." I cross my arms.

"Put the damned crayons away, you psycho little bitch."

I lose it. I pick up the fake plastic Christmas tree that has long since seen better days and throw it at her. "Shove it!" I yell.

Her face turns beet red and the room goes silent. She walks out of the door quickly and about three seconds later I hear a code being called.

"God *damn* it," I say and drop the box of crayons on the table when I see four male orderlies who look like they double as linebackers for a football team head toward me. I put my hands up slightly and out to my sides as the nurse stands behind them, smirking.

They grab my arms and legs even though I am not resisting and they carry me toward a room. I remember Ricky once telling me that this is the isolation room. This idea does not appeal to me and I begin trying to wiggle my way out of these ungentle hands that are holding me. It's no use though, and I am put face down on this table while hands quickly begin to strap me down.

One of the orderlies is trying to rip off the hemp bracelet that I have on my right wrist. It was Donnie's. "No. NO! I will take it off, don't rip it!"

For some reason he listens and I take it off and hand it to him right before they grab my hands and strap those down too. A shot goes into my ass, and off to dreamland I go.

I am young here; I don't know how old, maybe four. I am in the first house I remember living in, the one that was painted yellow on the outside and I swore there were ghosts in there. I see my father's tan brown recliner facing the old television we used to have, the one that still had knobs on it and rabbit ears. There is a lace tablecloth, yellowed with age on the scuffed dining table. I am in my room that does not have a door, because it got broken by my father's fists during one of my parents' fights. A sheet with faded cartoon characters is nailed to the top of the door jamb, but it does not block the sound of my parents fighting. I hear the sharp slap of what I already know is the sound of an open palm striking someone's face; my mother's face, and she wails. I clutch Tabitha, my little blonde Cabbage Patch doll tightly. I start to cry. I hear glass break. I am afraid.

"Goddamit Teresa..." I hear my father say and then stop. I hear my mother sniffling. "See what you did?" he yells and I hear him slap her again. "You woke up Emma!"

My mother comes into the room, her eyes red-rimmed and with darker red spots on her face where my father's hand had struck her. She hugs me and tells me to hush and go back to sleep.

"Mommy..." I start crying but she slips from my fingers and goes back out into the living room to keep receiving whatever punishment my father had decided she *deserved. I huddle under the blanket, clutching Tabitha, and cry.*

I open my eyes. They feel like they weigh a thousand pounds each, and it takes me a few tries to get them all the way open.

I am surprised to find that tears have collected in a tiny pool under my face on the plastic table. I am groggy and thirsty. My lips are like sand; they're so dry they've cracked and I lick them in a vain attempt to moisten them, but my tongue is like sandpaper and I give up.

I begin the task of trying to get out of the leather straps on the table. I get my right hand free and about sixty seconds later I have gotten all of my bonds loose. I pick a corner where I can see everything in the room and huddle up in it.

A sob threatens to break out of my chest. "No, you do not cry, you are metal; machines don't cry," I chant to myself over and over, rocking back and forth. The sob is still there and it is spilling into my chant and pissing me off so I say the chant louder until I am practically screaming at myself.

A heavy metal clunking sound comes from the door and I look up as it opens. Dr. X is in the doorway. He sighs when he sees me. "How did you get off the table Emma?"

I look at him with hurt in my eyes. I don't answer. I am clutching myself and rocking, staring at him. He walks into the room and an orderly begins to follow him. He turns and stops the orderly and whispers something to him. The orderly looks at me and then steps back outside. I go back to staring at the floor.

Dr. X is standing above me. "What happened, Emma?"

Years of lying, of not telling people anything about my life or what was going on in it kick in, and I refuse to tell him that the nurse egged me on. He squats down in front of me when I don't answer.

"Emma…"

I look up at him and I can't help myself; tears are spilling onto my white cheeks. "I am a machine. Machines don't cry."

His brow furrows slightly and he tilts his head. "You're not a machine Emma. And you're not violent. Angry yes, but you're not violent. What happened?"

I repeat myself as I stare at the floor, rocking back and forth.

He sighs.

"Emma… I have to keep you here longer now. You know that, right?"

I know. But I don't respond. I just keep rocking.

Dr. X pulls a tissue out of his pocket and hands it to me. He walks over to the door and talks to the orderly standing guard outside, and a few moments later, he hands me a cup of water.

I guzzle it, my hands shaking and clutching the paper cup.

Dr. X goes to the door. "Take a few minutes and compose yourself Emma. When you're done, you can come out. It's almost dinner time."

He walks out of the door and I feel sad that he's gone.

I wipe my cheeks and run my fingers through my choppy black hair. I steel myself, everyone is going to look at me like I'm a psycho when I leave this room, but it's better than being in here. I walk past the tear-stained plastic table and ignore it. I squint at the light in the doorway, and I walk through it.

Pills. Food. Coloring. I pick up my journal. I begin to write.

CHAPTER 4

Machine or ghost?

December ??

Oh God just look at me now... one night opens words and utters pain... I cannot begin to explain to you... this... I am not here. This is not happening. Oh wait, it is isn't it?

You've forced my hand to paper, and now the words don't come, a million things are locked inside my goddamned head. And I still can't breathe, long after you've taken me out of the straps... should I count my words here? Do I need to have it exactly one page or is it okay if it's a few words less?

You want to know how I feel? I feel dead and hollow and I wish I hadn't called the paramedics. That's how I feel. Ghost.

I am a ghost. I am not here, not really. You see skin and cuts and frailty... these are symptoms, you know, of a ghost. An unclear image with unclear thoughts whispering vague things...

If I told you what was really in my head, you'd never let me leave this place. And I have no desire to spend time in hell while I'm still, in theory, alive.

I bite the insides of my cheek until I taste blood as Dr. X reads my evening journal entry.

This is what being honest feels like... goes through my head. I wait for him to finish reading.

That's it, he's going to label you crazy and you're never getting out of here, I tell myself silently and sigh. I don't care right now though; either I'm so damned raw that I have gone numb, or I'm still sedated, or maybe it's both. I just simply don't care.

Dr. X looks up at me and I am startled by the expression on his face. He's not angry with me. In fact, he almost looks sad.

So the bastard does *feel something,* I tell myself again.

He looks down once more, at tear and blood stained admissions of being completely lost, hidden within sentences that don't quite make sense. We lock eyes. For once, for the first time, I am not the first one to drop my gaze. He does.

"No, Emma. You don't have to write exactly a full page anymore," he says softly. "You may go now."

I freeze. Normally I bolt out of this session, which feels like a trial without a jury where I've already been declared guilty. But I feel nothing. He says nothing.

I move in near slow motion, expecting this to be some sort of trick. Like he's going to reveal himself to be the unfeeling sadist that I have been imagining he really is; laughing at me while condemning me to a life sentence in this place. Condemning me to being a zombie.

Dr. X notices my hesitation. "I'm not going to punish you, Emma."

I am confused and just a little bit uncomfortable, but I take his words at face value and leave anyway.

Ricky is outside talking to Lucy. I silently wish her a more successful suicide attempt and walk on by. Ricky quickly ends his conversation with Lucy and comes to sit next to the chair furthest from everyone else in the room, which is where I've made my home.

"Hi Emma," he says. It takes me a minute to look up at him. They've prescribed me about three more medications since *The Incident* and my brain feels like it consists of nothing but fog anymore. I look up at him blankly.

"The meds are hitting ya pretty hard aren't they? What are they giving you?" he asks me.

I try to think. I can't remember the long foreign machine names of all the *dones* and *zones* and *iums* they've prescribed me.

"I... uh... don't know."

My mouth is unbearably dry. I feel like I've sunk into this chair though, and I can't move. My stitches itch in my arms. I look down and realize that half the cuts don't have stitches, and the thought mildly creeps me out before I look back up at Ricky.

"Well..." he looks around to make sure nobody is close by before he continues. "There is kind of a *black market* around here so to speak, and whatever you're on must be good. So if you can find a way not to swallow it, ya know, you could probably trade it for other stuff if you wanted to."

"People want to buy something I've had to hide *in my mouth* for at least two minutes and then let dry out before I *sell* it to them?" I ask incredulously.

"Yeah. Like Lucy over there, *major* pill head. And I don't know if you've met Frank yet, the little quiet skinny black kid. Him too."

I stare at Ricky, inadvertently making him feel uncomfortable. My eyes have become razorblades without me even knowing it.

"Hey, Emma, look, I'm just trying to help, okay?" he offers. "I mean, you haven't really gone out of your way to make friends around here, and I just figured, ya know, you might want to know stuff around here. Stuff that the staff don't tell you."

I soften a bit at his awkward demeanour and his attempts to help me. I've been nothing but rude to everyone, he's right. Maybe I misjudged him by lumping him into the same category as the worthless zombies that roam the halls.

"Thank you Ricky. I'll just... uh... keep that in mind."

Ricky visibly relaxes. He smiles an awkward, unsure, too-kind smile.

I look down at the doodles in my journal. I want to be alone. He doesn't pick up on this. Or maybe he does and ignores it, refusing to let me be alone for whatever reason.

"I just... ya know... want you to know you have someone to talk to that isn't a *narc* or a doctor, Emma. I feel kind of bad for you..." he looks down and fidgets with his hands before he continues.

"...You're obviously hurting. Not like some of the *other* people in here," he says and looks distastefully at Lucy.

I smile. He smiles. I actually start to laugh at our mutual hatred of the *poseur* Lucy. Our short-lived laughter dies down. Silence.

"What put you in here Ricky?" I ask him, my voice as soft as falling snow. I am again reminded that I am a ghost. I don't seem to talk very loud anymore.

He looks down and sighs before starting. I wait with the patience of Buddha.

"My dad was a real jerk. Ya know, he hit my mom all the time. Then, when she finally left, he started hitting *me*. And I wasn't big enough to fight him off, so it just kept going on, ya know? One day I'll be big enough."

He nods, more to himself than to me, assuring himself that one day it will stop. I feel sick.

"So, I tried to kill myself. I uh, tried to hang myself but my dad walked in. And uh, now I'm in here."

I notice faint scars that crisscross his face, among the pockmarks from the bad acne. I don't know why, but I put my hand on his. He grasps my tiny white hand tightly in his big ruddy one. We look at each other and say nothing. I feel uncomfortable with human touch though, and I let go.

"Me too," I whisper. The words start to come as if I'm possessed.

"My parents fought all the time until the divorce. They dragged that out for years. *Years*. Can you imagine that? Telling your kids over and over you're getting a divorce and then not? It was pretty screwed up."

I'm looking down at my fingers, not at him. But I find myself wanting to say more.

"Except my dad didn't just hit her, it was *all* of us. I used to be daddy's little girl. Then I started to look like my mom when I started to grow up and it seemed, after that, that he hated me. He wouldn't hug me anymore. In fact, I remember trying to hug him once in a restaurant and him pushing me off in embarrassment, telling me that *"People are going to think something is wrong."*

I shudder briefly at this memory, but I continue to describe it.

"When I looked at him in shock, that was the beginning of the end with us. Like

I said, things had been bad with him and Mom for years."

I pause. I lick my lips, trying to get some damned moisture on them since they won't give us ChapStick here. I am on autopilot, talking and not really talking; some part of my mind is still not here, not associating these words with real events, with real people. I sigh, a sigh of exhaustion; it's all I can do to get enough air to continue to whisper.

"I used to pray you know, pray to God that He would somehow stop it. All the nights of listening to my mother scream and things breaking. Of holding my brother and sister and listening to them cry and begging me to stop it."

My voice is slow and steady like a freight train at night.

"I was too young, and we were always told that they'd put us in foster homes where people would rape us if we ever said anything. So we explained away the bruises, and my mom wore big sunglasses whenever she left the house. And we invented car accidents if the bruising was too bad to cover with makeup."

Ricky just listens. He isn't shocked. He isn't surprised. He listens to me because he knows. He knows the shame and the guilt and the sorrow and the rage. And he does not judge me. He just listens.

"I know his childhood was bad, my father's. I mean, he has said bits and pieces... his father left him and like, two of his siblings died... and the man his mother remarried was an abusive prick."

I've always tried to justify my father. Because when he wasn't angry and hurting us, he was the most wonderful man in the world to me. He was strong and handsome with beautiful blue eyes and an easy laugh. I smile a little as I bring to mind a good memory of my father, and feel it's not fair if I don't tell it. I've told bad stories, and now I feel like I have to defend him. Ricky waits for me to finish or continue. Just waits. He isn't impatient at my pauses, or horrified at my story. He just sits and waits and listens. I am comforted by this, and continue.

"I remember one time, he found a little lizard on a glue trap, still alive. He sat at the kitchen table with a jar of flour for five hours, ever so gently prying this creature's tiny little claws and body from the trap before letting him go. He wasn't all bad. But when he *was* bad..."

I trail off and finally stop. I see no reason to keep talking. Ricky waits for a minute and gently touches my hand again, just briefly. He walks away. Moments later he brings me a glass of water, and I am stunned by this act of kindness.

"Thank you, Ricky."

"You're welcome, Emma."

He says nothing more.

Suddenly, he's not awkward and he gracefully bows out, leaving me alone to contemplate the past. I look around and notice that the Christmas tree has been taken out of the room. Torn Christmas decorations are still hanging though, faded and God only knows how old.

It's starting to look like I am going to spend my Christmas in this dingy, dirty, tomb.

The nurses come in with trays. It's medication time. One by one, we file in line and we accept whatever is given to us. The snotty, wretched nurse is replaced by a thin, anemic-looking one who is quiet and not completely bitchy. She even smiles at some of the patients who have been here longer, ones she recognizes.

I don't fight it anymore. I don't have the strength to. I swallow the pills and silently walk back to my seat at the edge of the room to wait for the next wave of comfortable numbness to set in.

My journal sits loosely on my lap. All I can do is stare at the wall.

CHAPTER 5

"A dream is a wish your heart makes..."

December ??

I'm tired and jittery from all the medication they're giving me. I don't know what the date is anymore. I feel sick to my stomach all the time, but they expect me to eat anyway. Have you ever taken this shit they're giving me? Have you? It's like taking a fucking speedball and it's scaring the crap out of me. I'm exhausted but you won't let me sleep, the meds won't let me eat without throwing up for half an hour after dinner, and I'm stuck in my head.

It's late at night and I am writing this by the creeping yellow light coming through the broken plastic blinds that cover the clouded-with-dirt window. I just kind of scribbled nonsense tonight in my journal so I wouldn't get in trouble for not writing anything. But something is inside me, trying to claw its way out of my chest and onto this paper.

I'm afraid to write though. I know about child protection laws and I'm afraid of my parents. And what happens if I tell the truth and nobody believes me? Then my parents will beat me when I get home for *almost getting them in trouble*.

I close my eyes against an unwelcome thought; my father. *He's angry at me for being awake. He thinks hitting me will somehow lull me to sleep. I'm crying and he starts screaming at me to shut up and go to sleep.*

I'm what... twelve here? I could never sleep very well. I've always had insomnia. When I was very little, the doctors my parents took me to, after nights of listening to me scream in my sleep, said it was night terrors. They said to let me keep the light on if it helped. They still didn't let me keep the goddamned night-light on though. Bastards.

Anyway, I'm not sure I had night terrors. I think I was probably traumatized from listening to my parents fight all the damned time. I think that it really did a number on my brain, so that even in sleep the fear and the bad thoughts wouldn't go away.

To be quite honest with you, talking to Ricky earlier really kind of messed me up some, and for what reason I'm not sure.

I've heard my friends, other kids, talk about getting knocked around by their parents. Hell, half of my friends had similar situations as mine to endure—parents who should never have got married and sure as hell should never have had us. And who fought all the time, fists and all, leaving us wrecked, sad, depressed, and way too old for how young we are. I'm sixteen and feel ancient. Thoughts and memories race through my brain now, that I don't want to remember. And, since I'm falling apart, my little mantras don't work anymore.

Let's say, theoretically, (and the reason I say this is because if it wasn't theoretical, you could call the police, and then you could take me away from my family, and I wouldn't want that anymore than I like being in this hell hole...) that I have a friend. She's grown up in an abusive home. Her earliest memories are of listening to her parents scream and yell at each other. She's watched her father slam her mother's head into a metal filing cabinet at some age too young to recall. She's watched her mom put on layers of make-up until it just looks like she has permanent dark circles under her eyes. You know, like those older ladies you find at the drugstore buying concealer makeup in the attempt to hide those dark circles...

And she hates herself for it. You see, this girl blames herself for it. Partly because she thinks it wouldn't have happened if she wasn't born. That's what her father says anyway. And partly because she didn't put a stop to it. She never was strong enough or could get out of the house fast enough to stop any of it, and she is so sick with guilt that... let's say that maybe she's even tried to kill herself, that's *how sick it makes her. And now she's sitting in some dirty mental hospital, scribbling pathetically in some journal trying to sort out all the mess in her head...*

I have to stop writing. I re-read what I've just written, and even though I haven't said my own name and even though I put *theoretically* on paper, I wonder—can they still call the police? Can they still put me in some foster home? And if they did, would it be worse?

I chew on my pencil, deep in thought. I ponder this very seriously, but at a distance, like it's some mathematical puzzle that I need to solve rather than it being, well, you know, my life.

I come to a decision. I nod to myself, thoughtfully. Yes. It *would* be worse to be in a foster home. I mean, my parents are divorced, have been for about a year or however long it's been, right? So what the hell is my problem? Why does this still upset me so much? Shouldn't I feel better now? Shouldn't the sounds of fists meeting flesh have started to fade?

WHAT THE HELL IS WRONG WITH ME? I press so hard with my pencil as I write this that I rip through part of the paper. Great, I think to myself frowning. Even when I am trying to get everything out, something falls apart. Like paper.

I'm having an internal debate about whether I should turn this journal paper in or not when another unpleasant thought assaults me.

I drop the pencil and cover my ears and curl up into a tiny ball to protect myself.

I'm sitting in the living room, watching some stupid cartoon about some girl who has a terrible life with horrible stepsisters and an evil stepmother who make her clean all the time. The mice are singing some song about how a dream is a wish your heart makes, or something like that. And then my parents come home. They're drunk. My mother looks slightly panicky. They hand the babysitter too much money and shoo her out of the door quickly. They immediately go to their bedroom, and the door slams shut.

I hear arguing. I sigh—I think I'm eight or so here. I turn the television up, trying to ignore them. They get louder. I turn the television up some more. This is never going to stop. I remember thinking how I may as well get used to it. I am trying to focus on these little mice and the blonde girl and how she wants to go to a ball, whatever that is. I think it's where people dress up and dance funny.

My dad comes out and is too nice, and tells me to go to bed. "But Dad..." I start, and stop just as quickly when his face turns cruel and mean. I can hear my mother crying in the other room as I walk by.

"But I have to say good night to Mommy..." I start again.

"She'll come in later and tuck you in. Get your ass in bed. NOW!"

I run off to bed. He turns off the lights, ALL of them, and closes the door.

The way this house is set up is that my room is adjoining my parents' room. And cheap tract housing doesn't tend to have thick walls, so I end up hearing way more than I ever want to hear from that cursed room.

The sounds are getting louder, the screaming is louder, and Jesus, my mother's screams are always the worst part. It's like hearing a dog being beaten and not being able to do anything but feel sad when you hear the pathetic yelp, and hating the bastard who is doing it.

My mother sounds more terrified than usual. Something, this time, is very, very wrong. I can't remember being more afraid, a vice has gripped me and I can't move, only listen as the sounds grow louder and more grotesque. *Things are breaking, and my father is screaming like he is someone else. I hold my little brother and sister as they beg me to do something, to stop it.*

"If we pray hard enough God will listen and He'll stop him, and Daddy won't kill her."

I keep trying to sneak out of my window to get help. This one is bad and I am afraid. Really afraid. But the son of a bitch keeps coming and checking on us and I am too terrified to do anything but pretend to sleep. Once he almost catches me, but he is too coked-out to notice that I am in a different bed than before.

I keep at the window, but it is childproof and I can't get it unlocked. My tiny fingers cannot twist the metal tab hard enough to get the window open. Even if I could, he'd definitely hear me before I made it through to the backyard, over the six-foot tall fence and to the neighbor's house on the other side.

So we pray in vain. We pray and we cry ourselves to sleep to the sounds of things breaking, our father yelling, our mother's sobbing pleas.

Next day we wake up and all stand in a line at the door and kiss our father good-bye as he goes to work...

No. No, I'm not going to remember this... *NO NO NO NO NO!* I start saying to myself, softly at first, but growing louder.

My roommate stirs. Oh Jesus, I'm about to get a code called... why won't *this* particular memory go away? Why this one, of *all* of them?

I start repeating. "No, this isn't happening, this did NOT HAPPEN TO YOU, THIS DID NOT HAPPEN TO YOU..." over and over again.

If I tell myself this enough, it usually goes away. They are mantras that protect me.

I tear up the cursed pieces of paper that

I now blame for stirring up these thoughts, rip them into teeny tiny shreds, hoping to rip the thoughts up too. It's not working.

Good goddamned job Emma, you started writing and now look what it did to you, now you're sitting here crying and sobbing all over again, and where have all your tears got you?

"*SHUT UP!*" I scream at myself. My roommate wakes up.

"EMMA!" she yell-whispers at me, her hair tousled by sleep and her voice low and hoarse. "Shut the hell up before the nurses wake up or the orderlies in the hall on the rounds hear you. It's late and I'm tired, and to be honest, I really don't care what the hell you're saying! Just shut up and go back to sleep!"

In a final fit of drama, she throws herself back down on the bed and covers her head with her pillow.

I am still curled up in a ball, shreds of paper lying around me. I'm not quiet, like she wants, but at least I'm whispering, and she doesn't say anything else.

I repeat one of my mantras. "This is not happening. This is not real. This did not happen to you. That was someone else."

Normally, like I said, this set of phrases I can repeat *ad nauseam* until the thoughts fade back to black, back to the dark part of my brain where I keep these horrors, and I try very, very hard not to think about them.

Tonight this memory is not going away though. Tonight, just like I did those years ago, I end up crying myself to sleep, praying for the thoughts to go away.

CHAPTER 6
Visitors

Sleep didn't claim me until I saw the gentle changing of the night sky to early morning, and only then did the demons of the night release their hold on me as they faded into the night. I closed my eyes, and it seemed like just a few minutes later it was time to wake up.

Exhausted, I half-heartedly combed my hair and brushed my teeth. My roommate glared at me, obviously still irritated from the night before. I sighed and wished I could have cared more, but it would have taken energy I simply didn't have.

As I walked down the hallway, I heard a

noise I hadn't heard before and it took me a few steps to realize that I had begun to do what I called the zombie shuffle. Horrified, I made an extra effort to pick my feet up when I walked, and straightened my bony shoulders, determined to cling to whatever shreds of dignity I had left.

When we finally entered the main room, I shuddered. Someone had turned on the heat either too late or not high enough, and it was freezing cold. The cheap slippers did nothing to block the icy chill from the floor. And as I settled into the uncomfortable plastic chair to await the crappy food we were here to eat, I awkwardly picked up my legs and crossed them, balancing precariously on the chair, hoping to warm my feet by tucking them into the crooks of my legs.

Bored and tired orderlies brought the food into the room, long since gone cold and never really edible in the first place. I'm not hungry, but I've learned that if you don't eat, you get in trouble. As I'm already underweight, I have to choke down at least part of the rubber eggs and congealed oatmeal, since I've been threatened with intravenous feedings if I keep skipping meals, and I'd rather choke down a few bites of this crap than to have yet another needle stuck into my painfully sore arms.

I don't remember feeling pain like this in quite some time, and I'm not sure it's quite like anything I've ever felt—the feeling of holes in your veins and so many cuts in your arms they outnumber the skin there. It's a different kind of pain from the type of pain that beatings deliver, and I'm not used to it.

I find myself staring at my arms often; like a train wreck I find it impossible not to stare at the mess that's laid out before me, even though it's sad and tragic and disgusting.

The meds come. The evil nurse is gone, the one from the day before is still here and I am relieved by her semi-friendly presence. When I take the paper cup of water, I am surprised by its coldness. I look up at her and she smiles. She had apparently gone to the effort of filling the water pitcher with filtered, cold tap water. When the cold water hit my dry mouth, I breathed a silent prayer of gratitude. This kindly nurse patted me on the shoulder and I actually smiled at her gratefully, before I walked off and got into my chair for morning group therapy.

I'm having a hard time staying awake during this session. A box of tissue is being passed around like a cookie plate. I pass. I don't have the energy or the tears to cry after last night's painful ordeal of remembering the past.

When it gets to my turn, Dr. X looks at me and gives me the *it's-your-turn* look. I clear my throat and fidget with my pants, and I begin to talk about my parents' divorce. It's as close to the truth as I can get without revealing too much about what's really going on.

"My parents began their divorce when I was twelve years old," I begin.

Dr. X interrupts me. "And how old are you now?" he asks.

"I'm sixteen." I respond flatly. He looks slightly confused.

"Their divorce lasted... for four years?" Dr. X asks me.

"No, for about three years."

Dr. X shakes his head slightly. "Continue, Emma."

"My parents didn't have a good marriage. They fought all the time. And I mean, really fought. You know, threw things, screaming and yelling all the time." Ricky nods understanding. I continue.

"Finally, after years of dealing with them fighting, they decided to get a divorce. But you know, every month they'd stop the divorce and try to work things out. A month later they were back to square one, and they'd start the divorce all over again."

I carefully measure my thoughts, my words. The wrong slip of the tongue could land me in foster care.

"And how did that contribute to your being here today, Emma?" Dr. X asks me.

I pause and think of how to answer his question. "It led me here because... I was depressed about the divorce and their fighting I guess. But I didn't really realize it, you know? I was the oldest child and I was so busy taking care of everyone, my mom, my siblings, that I forgot I had feelings too. And one day I just snapped and couldn't deal with it anymore, and that's how I ended up here."

Dr. X nods his approval at my co-operation in this session. I yawn tiredly. I'm so tired my eyes are tearing up, and I wrap my arms around myself to keep warm.

The session ends. We color. We go to education and I practice math problems that I remember from the fifth grade—or it might have been the year after that, when I was eleven. Whatever... I stare at the sheet of paper for a very long time, not so much because I can't do the problems, but because I'm having a hard time seeing.

The pills have kicked in, and brought with them a wave of almost comfortable numbness, or at least apathy, and that's fine with me at this point. Free time comes and everyone is doing something but me. I'm sitting in my chair, at the end of the room, with my notebook, when a nurse comes in and tells me that I have a visitor.

I blink. "Who is it?" I ask, a sinking feeling in my stomach.

"Your mother," she replies.

I am torn between excitement and self-disgust. I am escorted into the visiting area, and I sit nervously while I wait for my mom to enter.

The door opens. My mother walks in, shoulders back, makeup obviously just redone to hide the fact that she was crying. Maybe nobody else knows or notices, but I know. I've seen her cry my whole life, and I know how she looks when she tries to hide it.

My mom and I stand there, face to face. Finally, we hug. She hugs me tightly, forgetting her composure, and her touch feels protective and warm at first, and then it's like she switches off, and then I'm hugging a statue. Awkwardly, we let go of each other and when I look at her face, she has the mask back on, and then she's not really my mom anymore, not the mom I know, soft and loving and pretty.

We sit down. Small talk ensues. How are you doing in here? Are they treating you well? How is the food? How are your arms doing? Is the doctor nice? And then, the question that I was half expecting but still wasn't prepared for.

"What are you talking to them about, Emma?" I stare at my pajamas under my mom's scrutiny. "Uh, nothing really. Just ya know, how I'm feeling, and how the medications are, and stuff like that."

She nods, not really believing me. "I heard you attacked a nurse, Emmy. Why did you do that?" she asks sadly.

I can't tell her. I don't know why. Maybe I'm afraid she won't believe me, but I don't say a word.

My mom is fidgeting with her bag and finally gets so frustrated she explodes. "What is WRONG with you, Emma? You were supposed to get better when I got away from your father. And now this? You're COMPLETELY embarrassing us Emma. Do you know how that feels? How that makes me look?"

I grit my teeth and, for once, I stand up for myself.

"No, Mom, I don't know how that makes you feel. And for once, I don't give a shit."

My mother gasps at my language. I've

never talked to her like this. On cue, she starts to cry.

"Oh *stop* it already." I continue. "It was always about you, and always about dad. It was never about us, about us kids. We couldn't feel anything, we couldn't have friends, we had to be your perfect little children to show off to your friends and now, *now*, you find out that things weren't so perfect, but you refuse to take ANY blame for it."

My mother starts to cry. "Oh, my God, you hate me, I'm such a bad mother..." she starts before I interrupt.

"STOP IT! Not *everything* is about you, okay? This is about me. *This is about me*, do you understand? I couldn't be everything you wanted. You wanted to pretend that Dad never happened, that the years of fighting and all the horrible things we saw and heard and covered up because you *asked* us to, never happened. And maybe *you* were able to, but I wasn't. And neither were Paul or Rosemary. And I tell you what, you'd better watch *them* close, or they'll end up in here just like me."

My mother stares at her purse, clutched tightly in her lap. My words have struck her to the core and she can't even look at me right now. Finally, she remembers she has a voice.

"Is that really why you're in here, Emma? I thought it was because your boyfriend…"

I see the pain in her face and I can't help but feel like an asshole for what I've just said. But I can't lie anymore either.

"Mommy, it wasn't him. It's everything. It's everything I saw and everything I hid and the fact that when you got remarried, you forgot about me. I was your little helper, but not your daughter. It's about losing my brother. It's about things I can't tell you in here right now, but if it makes you feel better, you can blame it on my boyfriend."

My mom looks at me and calmly says, "I've called your father."

My blood runs cold. "Why... would you do that?"

"Because you're his daughter, and I think that he should know what happened. He says he's got some appointments and trips he needs to cancel, but he's worried about you and wants to come and see you."

I never really thought about punching my mother before, but the thought crosses my mind. I grit my teeth and cross my arms.

"You don't want to see him?" my mom asks me, surprised.

I stare at her as if she just told me that she's convinced the earth is flat. "Mom, what do you think? I mean, really? With everything that's happened, what do you think?"

She stammers. "I just thought, you could... you know, use your family right now."

I'm furious. I don't remember being this mad at her, this frail, beautiful, fragile, kind human being before. But now, I want to choke her.

"MOM. I... really... REALLY... wish you hadn't done that."

"But why?" she asks me, like she's confused.

I stare straight into her beautiful hazel eyes and steel myself.

"Because, Mother... because of big sunglasses and lying to schoolteachers and inventing car accidents to cover up your black eyes and broken ribs. Because we sat there and starved when *he* wouldn't pay child support. Because I sat at the goddamned door with a baseball bat and a telephone in case his threats against you rang true and he did come to do what he threatened to do. *That's* why."

My mother's mouth drops. "Emmy... don't say those things, Emmy. Remember, we don't talk about those things."

"Yes, Mom. I remember. That's why I'm in here, looking like this."

An orderly knocks on the door and announces that visiting time is over.

My mother and I look at each other awkwardly, and hug.

"I love you," she says.

"I love you too, Mom."

"You aren't telling them too much are you?" she asks, afraid.

I sigh. "No, Mommy. I'm not."

She's visibly relieved. She leaves the room.

The orderly comes and escorts me back into the main room.

I just sit and laugh to myself.

CHAPTER 7
Dinner

I walk around for the rest of the day in a coma. My head is spinning from lack of sleep, pills, and the visit with my mother. Is it really possible that she has no damned clue why I am in here? Did she really think that the memories would just go away when the ink dried on the divorce papers? Was I too hard on her?

I remember her eyes, and how many times they'd cried, and I think that maybe I was. I am stricken with guilt and catch myself on the verge of tears all day. *I* am a bad daughter, I tell myself. Is it so wrong to want someone to understand what the hell I'm going through though?

"EMMA!" I snap out of my thoughts to the unpleasant sound of someone yelling at me. I look and realize that it's dinner time and I'm still slumped in my chair, not at the table like I am supposed to be.

I'm a child again, hearing my father's voice yell at me to come for dinner. Mom runs into my bedroom wide-eyed and grabs my arm, practically dragging me out of my room and out of my little fantasy world of dolls and houses, to sit at the dinner table and listen to them fight some more.

"Emmy, what's wrong with you?" my mother asks me. "Didn't you hear me? Now you've upset your father..."

And the familiar feeling of knots return to my stomach as we walk down the hallway to the dining room.

My father's steel-gray eyes, eyes that match mine, shoot razors at me from his seat at the head of the table. I start to shake.

My mother sits me down at the table, at my father's left side. I attempt a smile, a shy, unsure, crooked hint of a smile, and I say "Hi Daddy." No smile meets mine, just eyes that cut through me and leave me feeling smaller than I am.

"EMMA!" I hear the voice again and realize that I have been standing, paralyzed, in the middle of the room. Everyone turns to stare at me. Just like my mother had done, a nurse comes and grabs me by the arm and half drags me to sit at a table for a dinner that I don't want to eat. She sits me down next to Ricky, who moves his chair over to make room for me.

I feel everyone staring at me and unconsciously smile the same shy, awkward, hint of a grin I did that day back at the dinner table. My eyes blur when I see nobody smiling back at me and I am ashamed of myself for being so afraid of them that I am ready to cry.

I clear my throat and I stare at the tray intently. I think it's meatloaf. I make a face when I notice the unnatural ketchup-red color that it is on top, and the burned, crusty black it is on one side. I pick at the meal with my spoon, the only utensil I've been allowed to eat with since I threw the Christmas tree at the nurse.

After what seems like forever at this uncomfortable table, I pick up my tray and go to place it back in the steel carts they came in. The same nurse who dragged me to my seat eyes the barely touched food and looks at me. "Sit back down and finish eating."

"Sit down and finish eating, Emma. That's good food you're letting go to waste," my father tells me as he eats another forkful of his own. I freeze and stare at my plate in a panic. I can't finish eating this plate of food, it's too much and I'm so afraid of being here that I can hardly swallow for the lump in my throat that threatens to break into a sob.

I stare down at my tray and tell myself that just a few more bites will do it, just do what they say so you don't get into any more trouble. I sit back down. Ricky looks at me. He leans over and whispers, "You okay, Emmy?"

Paul's fork freezes in mid-air and he kicks me under the table to get my attention. "You okay, Emmy?"

My father stares at my mother, as if this is somehow her fault.

The color drains from her face and she forces a smile. "Emmy, finish your dinner," she says, trying to be gentle, her voice starting to crack.

I'm aware that something bad is going to happen to her if I don't finish eating this mound of food on my plate. I begin to take bites, tiny bites of food as my family stares at me. Time seems to stand still as I scoop up the food, put it into my mouth and swallow.

Ricky nudges me in the ribs. "Emma..." he starts and I am again here in the hospital. I begin to take bites of food once again. The same knots are in my stomach, and I feel like throwing up.

"What the hell is wrong with her, Teresa?" my father snaps at my mother. My father turns to nobody and starts yelling, "I work twelve hours a day to make sure we have food on the table and you ungrateful brats won't even eat it! Well fine, nobody is leaving the table until Emma is done with dinner." My father crosses his arms and stares at me. They all stare at me, the rest of them pleadingly.

My mother is trying not to cry. "Emmy, you're being selfish..." and my father grabs the fork out of my hand, scoops too much food on it for a little girl and forces it into my hand. My cheeks burn red and I give up. I start shovelling food into my mouth, barely chewing now, just to get it down.

I stare at a smudge on the wall across the room, and begin to shovel food into my mouth until I can't eat any more, until I'm sure I'll throw up if I take one more bite. I blindly stand up, choking on the world's shittiest meatloaf and a head of bad memories and put the tray back into the metal thing. The nurse nods her approval and I think to myself that *she* could probably stand to eat *less* dinner. I sit down for a few minutes before I realize that dinner is going to come back up.

After I've finally finished eating, and the kitchen is cleaned up, my parents begin to argue about something miniscule, something I don't remember, and I feel bile burn the back of my throat.

I run into the bathroom and don't quite make it before the vomit begins to pour out of my stomach, my hand clamped over my mouth to keep it in so I can get the bathroom door shut and nobody will hear me.

I throw up dinner, every last bit of it. My body heaves, over and over again, to get that poisoned dinner out of me, and tears run down the side of my face...

I stand up very fast and begin to walk quickly to my room. When I hit the end of the hallway, I burst into a dead sprint and make it into my room in just enough time to feel the dinner coming up.

I hit my knees too hard on the bathroom floor and throw up hard in the toilet. Tears run down my face and blur my eyes.

I throw up until there is nothing left. I feel only slightly better, and I rinse out my mouth and take a swig of the neon-green mint mouthwash that burns my mouth every time I use it. I splash water on my face and sneak out of the bathroom quietly.

Shaking from the effort, I am finally done throwing up and I flush the toilet and quickly rinse my mouth out. I brush my teeth in record time and walk back into the main room.

I breathe a sigh of relief when I realize that everyone is engrossed in a movie that has apparently just been put on, and that my absence has gone unnoticed. I sneak into a chair and a few minutes later some kid I don't know the name of hands me a folded slip of paper. I stare at it, puzzled, when the kid sighs and shoves it into my hand.

I unfold the tiny piece of paper and peer at it intently in the dim glow of the television set, to read the scrawled words.

I sigh. Well, my absence had *almost* gone unnoticed. Ricky had noticed, and had written me a note. "Are you okay?—Ricky" is all it says.

Are you okay? I read the words at least ten times before they sink into my brain. I stifle a laugh that I know will turn into a hysterical crying fest should it crack my lips.

A crayon is passed back to me covertly. I hold the green stub in my hand and look around to make sure nobody sees me writing. I write my response and refold the paper. I bother the kid in front of me again and whisper to him to pass the note and crayon stub back to Ricky.

I roll my eyes at the movie choice. It's some stupid Christmas movie about a kid who wants a bow and arrow set for Christmas, or something like that. I feel staring eyes, and I look up. It's Ricky. He frowns at me as he shrugs and lifts his hands up slightly in a *what the hell?* kind of gesture.

I had been too tired and my head too full to deal with his well-meaning but unwanted question, and I had written a single word in reply—*yes*. Obviously he doesn't believe me.

I ignore him and focus on the movie, half asleep, half awake, lulled to a not-quite-awake state by the dim lights and the fact the heater has finally kicked in after a whole day of having my ass frozen off.

I focus in on the sound of the television and drift off, my mind imagining some other family, some other Christmas I did not experience. I hear everyone laugh through my haze. I chuckle with them softly, though I don't really hear what they're laughing at. It is a nice feeling to laugh at something, even if it isn't real.

I hear whispering become a dull roar and a nurse comes in and yells at everyone to be quiet or she'll turn the movie off. Everyone quiets down, and again I am left alone to dream of cookies and trees and presents wrapped under the tree, and—most importantly— nobody fighting.

I let the feeling enfold me, and picture my family at Christmas, Paul and Rosemary and Mom and my father all laughing and giving each other presents like the family on television. I remember my dogs, the ones that Rosemary and I had to leave behind when we moved into the only apartment my mother could afford after the divorce, running through the house excitedly among the friendly commotion.

I swear I can smell gingerbread when the lights are turned back on.

"Awww..." everyone complains in unison. My eyes strain to open and I begin to breathe too fast when I realize where I am. I am not part of the quaint family movie we'd just been watching after all.

Everyone begins packing up the main room as the nurse rewinds the movie on the tired VCR player. Everything in this damned place is tired and broken. I am no exception.

As I shuffle off to my room, my roommate bouncing annoyingly cheerfully ahead of me, I am tired and disappointed with myself for getting lost in some picture-perfect fantasy of a happy family.

It's not that I don't love my stepdad, and it isn't that I'm not glad as hell that my parents have finally divorced and I don't have to watch their hellish fights anymore. No, I just wish that it had never been that way at all; that my life wasn't so miserable that I had to pretend that I was someone and somewhere else to feel comforted.

I don't even feel the cold water on my face as I get ready for bed. I am still thinking of my mother and feeling torn about our meeting today, part of me feeling guilty and part of me feeling justified in standing up for myself the way I did.

"Lights out!" I hear someone say, and wearily I walk to my bed. By the time my head hits the pillow, I have already fallen asleep.

CHAPTER 8

Interlude

I open my eyes to the smell of homemade cinnamon buns and hot coffee wafting through the house. I'm warm, snuggled in my quilt, next to Paul and Rosemary, who aren't awake yet, but will be as soon as they feel me stir next to them. I try to stay very still and enjoy the quiet. I look at the window and it's frosted over on the outside, but the coming sun has started to melt it and tiny drops of water run and crisscross the frost, erasing it. Everything is calm and beautiful.

We're all asleep in our new pajamas, a tradition that happens every Christmas Eve so we'll look nice in the pictures my parents take, pictures that when they get downloaded *three months later, will be critiqued and criticized. Only the best ones will make it into the photo album. I don't like pictures, and they make me nervous. I never seem to look quite right in pictures, always like a deer in headlights or not smiling right.*

My thoughts are interrupted by noise. I hear my parents talking. I frown and try to make out what they're saying. Paul stirs next to me. Rosemary has the unfortunate habit of sleeping slanted and taking up the whole damned bed, and the lower half of her body is crushing my legs and I fight the urge to kick her.

I become still again so I don't wake Paul and Rosemary yet. They'll immediately start talking, and then I won't be able to hear anything, and then my parents will know I'm awake and the rest of the day won't be this still, quiet peace that is rapidly drifting away from me.

I roll my eyes when I hear my parents arguing and I bite down on my lower lip, hard. I am so frustrated with them that whatever happiness I had knowing today was Christmas has left, along with the melting frost, all but gone from the window now.

I hear another noise, and then I hear the dogs whining and shaking their collars, and I realize my parents have let them into the house. I look down and Paul is opening his eyes. Damn. My peaceful little place is gone now. Paul feels Rosemary's legs on his too and he kicks her legs off him.

Rosemary wakes up and instantly starts to whine. Immediately I interrupt them both. "It's Christmas you guys!"

They stop whining. The child-like look of wonder is quickly replaced by doubt as Paul looks at me and asks me, "Are Mom and Dad awake? Can we get out of bed yet?" Before I can answer him, the bedroom door opens and our dogs run into the room, followed by Mom, smiling.

The dogs jump on the bed and roll all over us before jumping back down to the floor and running all over the house. Paul and Rosemary jump out of bed, both of them managing to elbow and knee me in their excitement.

Paul runs past Mom while Rosemary clings to her. I carefully examine Mom's face; no bruises, no tears. Apparently, whatever they were arguing about a few moments earlier wasn't very important, and I am relieved.

Mom ushers us into the bathroom where we brush our teeth and comb our hair. Now that we look acceptable, we can go into the living room where the presents and the Christmas tree are. We hug our father who is half awake, hair mussed up, a cup of coffee in his hand and his favorite green robe on.

"Oh no, breakfast first!" my father says as we run up to him to give him a hug. He's not really angry right now though, just half asleep. We sit at the table and even though Mom's cinnamon buns are amazing, we eat them at lightning speed so that we can go back into the living room. I mean, really, what kid wants to eat first thing on Christmas Day?

We sit and fidget at the table until my dad is done eating. Halfway through his cinnamon bun, he looks up, sighs, picks up his plate and walks back into the living room, muttering to himself.

My father never looks quite right in pictures either. He never really smiles in them. It's a trained smile he gives for the camera, and it looks alien and uncomfortable on him.

Mom shoos us from the table, and Paul and Rosemary giggle and chase after my dad. I walk around the table and I kiss Mom on the cheek. "Best cinnamon buns ever, Mom." She smiles gratefully at me.

"You guys are holding up Christmas!" my dad yells. Mom and I head into the living room. Mom scolds Rosemary and Paul for being too hyper and tells them to sit quietly on the couch while she hands everyone one present at a time. We open them neatly and slowly, in turn, so my parents can take pictures.

Rosemary usually gets to open a present first because she's the youngest, and she's whiny and fidgety sometimes, and my parents expect my brother and me to behave better than that. Today is no exception, and she's busy unwrapping a present while everyone else sits still and watches.

You have to act excited when you're opening presents. If you don't act excited enough, you could get yelled at. When you're done unwrapping your present, you can stare at it in awe for a few seconds before you have to hold it up for the rest of the family to see and take pictures while you smile. You can never not like a present, even if it's a hideous sweater two sizes too small that you will never ever wear.

Christmas is always like this for us. The day becoming ever more excruciating until Dad decides to take a nap and Mom starts cooking dinner. Then, and only sometimes, we stop acting like Stepford children and act like normal kids who squeal and rip through presents excitedly in a colorful tornado. For now the lie continues.

I look over at my dad and he's petting Noodles and talking to her softly. Noodles is wagging her curly little tail and sniffing his face. He scratches behind her velvet ears, ears that have been rubbed so much because of their softness that they're starting to go bald in spots.

I walk over, with the big brown blanket that I was wrapped in, and curl up next to my dad, who gives the dog a final pet and then wraps his arm around me. All is well right now, and I couldn't care less about the presents.

Rosemary squeals and holds up a doll. Mom takes pictures. Rosemary runs up to Mom and kisses her on the cheek and throws her little arms around Mom's neck. Mom whispers in her ear to hug her dad first next time she opens a present.

Rosemary seems to baffle my father, and he is always slightly aloof with her. She's much more like a normal kid than my brother and me; she cries and whines and pretends, and gets my brother and me into trouble all the time. Her childlike nature confuses my dad, I think, and he doesn't know how to deal with her. She was a fussy baby who only wanted Mom to hold her, and cried whenever anyone else tried to pick her up, including my dad, who was so confused as to why his own child didn't want her dad to hold her that he finally quit trying.

Rosemary runs and quickly hugs my dad and thanks him. Dad pats her on the back and Rosemary runs to sit on the floor and play with her new doll. Mom picks out a present for Paul. Paul opens the present, which is some army action figure, and says "Wow, cool!" before posing for his picture. He runs over to my dad. Paul throws his arms around my dad who lets go of me and they start play wrestling.

My dad was always trying to toughen Paul up, even though he wasn't into sports or anything else considered manly. So when he showed an interest in action figures, my dad had no problem encouraging this new interest.

I sigh, jealous. I am a tomboy; I like sports and the outdoors and wrestling around and bows and arrows and guns. But I am not a boy, and though my dad will get frustrated with Paul and eventually start to play with me, he always wants to play with my brother first.

"Emmy, it's your turn."

I look over at Mom, who has seen me being slighted by my father and calls me over to her. I open the small present, certain that it is a book. It is one from my favorite series, a science fiction book for adults. I never read children's books; I'm not allowed to. They are too retarded for me, my parents say. I am too smart to act like a child, they say. But they encourage my love of books, and Mom has gone through my bookshelf and found out which book I don't have, and has picked out the latest one.

I smile for my picture and hold my book up, and then hug Mom. Nobody is watching me. Rosemary is playing with her doll and Paul is still wrestling and laughing with my dad.

Mom and I sit on the floor, united in our sudden invisibility to the rest of the family. "You picked the one I wanted, Mommy. Thank you."

Mom smiled, a soft sad smile. "I know things aren't always easy for you and I uh..." she stopped and suddenly remembered how things had to be. "...I just wanted to get you the right one, Emmy. Now go hug your dad."

I walk up to my dad and hug him from behind. He looks slightly startled.

"Hey kid, what'd ya get?"

I show Dad the book.

"A book huh? Is it a good one?"

"Yeah Dad, it is."

My dad stares at the book for a second. I have never seen my dad read a book. "Well, good for you," he finally says, and his eyes dart past me, past my book, and to Mom.

He stands up and goes to the tree and rummages around for a box wrapped in the comics section of the newspaper. He hands it to Mom, who smiles, kisses him and opens it. It is a cranberry-colored sweater dress.

"I uh, ya know, thought that'd look good on you Teresa," he says, suddenly unsure of himself.

I feel bad for my dad, who in the midst of his family, and this holiday, had felt... what? Ashamed that he hadn't wrapped the present as well as Mom had wrapped the others?

Suddenly he is a tired-looking man, beginning to look older than he should, unsure of himself among his own family. He's confused by books that his daughter reads—that I will later come to suspect he couldn't—confused by his son's femininity and his youngest daughter's apparent dislike of him, confused as to why his wife flinches every time he goes near her.

My father sits back down quickly and busies himself with drinking the last of his coffee. His vulnerability has disappeared and is replaced by his gray, distant stare, a faraway look that sometimes comes to his eyes and leaves you wondering where he wishes he would rather be.

Slowly, the rest of the presents are passed out, books and dolls and action figures, socks and sweaters and odd gifts, like a gallon of cheap drugstore bubble bath that Paul had saved his allowance for, so that he could give it to Mom for Christmas. Like any mother though, she loved it and hugged Paul, whose hazel eyes matched hers, and promised to use it that night.

That afternoon, after my dad lies down to sleep and while Paul and Rosemary are busy playing with their toys, I go into the kitchen with Mom to help her with dinner.

She brews another cup of coffee and pours me a half-cup for helping her. We sit and peel potatoes and carrots together, whispering and laughing quietly, sometimes so much that we have to cover our faces with dish towels so we won't be too loud and possibly *wake my father. Mom puts the towel in her lap and wipes a tear of laughter away. She hugs me and smiles.*

"Oh, Emmy. You're my best friend, Emmy."

I smile back at her. "You're mine too, Mom."

CHAPTER 9

Paying attention

I'm sitting in Dr. X's office, waiting. I yawn and look around his office, bored and tired. His desk is piled high with papers and patient folders, which surprises me somewhat. Every other time I've been in this office it's been neat and tidy.

When he finally comes into the office, he looks flustered and tired. "Good morning, Emma. I'm sorry I'm late, but we had some patients come in early this morning..."

He trails off and sits down behind his desk, trying to organize the paperwork there. He settles for putting it all in a pile on the right side of his desk.

I wait. He looks at me. My hands are neatly crossed in my lap, not over my chest like they usually are. He doesn't seem to notice.

"So Emma, how are you? No, wait. I need to get your file; just a moment…"

He begins to sift through the stack of folders and papers on his desk. His brow furrows and he mutters to himself until he finds it. He wipes it off, opens it up, and starts glancing over it. He nods to himself and looks back up at me.

"I hear you had a hard time at dinner last night, Emma. Is there a reason why?" He picks up his pen, waiting for my response.

I'm slightly surprised by his question. "Uh, what do you mean?" I ask.

"Well, according to the evening nurse, you didn't want to eat dinner last night. She made a note of it. Now again, is there a reason you didn't want to eat last night, Emma?"

"Um, well kind of. The food was gross, and I didn't like it."

Dr. X looks at me suspiciously.

"I'm serious." I tell him. He continues to look at me without speaking. "I mean, the food was cold *and* burned at the same time, and I'm not a big fan of meatloaf. I just didn't like dinner."

"So it was a food preference issue, and not anything else?" he asks me.

"Yup." I nod. "That's it. Nothing else."

Dr. X looks at me, and I'm not quite sure he believes me, but he accepts my response.

"Well Emma, I must remind you that you're very thin, and that with the different medications you're on..."

I zone out. I don't really mean to, but I just click into autopilot, nodding my head as he continues talking about needing to eat and how if I don't, it affects how the medications get into my system or something like that. I'm busy staring at a picture of Dr. X with a beautiful, well-dressed blonde woman, holding an infant.

"What did I just say Emma?" Dr. X asks me.

"Uh..." I stammer. "You said it's important to follow the rules because if I don't, it affects my treatment." I tell him.

I wasn't paying attention, and I'm not entirely sure that's what he was talking about, but that's become my stock answer any time someone starts talking about something that I'm not interested in hearing, and usually it works out. Today, it doesn't.

"Yes, and then I said that a third leg was growing out of your stomach, to see if you were paying attention. And then you nodded and agreed with me." Dr. X tells me.

Damn. I'm caught. I look down and snicker in spite of myself. Dr. X seems offended by my snickering. "*What* are you laughing about, Emma?" He's irritated now.

"I'm sorry. The third leg thing was funny," I say sheepishly. The humor of his comment seems to escape him until I point it out and despite himself, he cracks a smile briefly before clearing his throat and resuming his usual clinical demeanor.

"Yes well, never mind. How are you feeling today?" Now he picks up his pen to take notes.

I think for a minute. Really, I'm trying to figure out what I'm going to say, so that I'm not telling him too much but not being so vague as to let him know that I'm evading his questions.

"Um, ya know, trying to get used to the medication and stuff..." and I continue to talk about how I'm trying to deal with my parents' divorce and how it upset me, when Dr. X's beeper goes off. He frowns and takes it off his belt, looking at the number before he sighs and interrupts me.

"I'm sorry Emma, we're going to have to continue this later. I hate to interrupt you, but I have to go. Uh, just keep writing in your journal and following your uh, treatment plan."

He grabs a stack of folders and rushes to the door before he turns and looks at me. "I'm really sorry, Emma," he says.

I realize he feels bad and I smile to make him feel better. "It's cool, Doc," I tell him. He shakes his head and rushes out the door.

I pick up my journal and follow him out of the office to join everyone else in the common room. It's visiting time. Cindy walks out of the visiting room laughing and giggling, her parents are behind her. They tearfully hug, and Cindy waves to her parents as they leave.

I glare at Cindy and start drawing little spiral designs on the cover of my journal, irritated with her for being happier than I am. I open my journal and I read what I'd written in it; *You will not reach me.*

I frown and start chewing on my fingernails as I re-read those words over and over again. I had decided when I got to this hell hole of group therapy, bad food, and dingy walls, that I didn't need help.

I look down at my arms and back at the words. I tap my pencil on my journal, deep in thought. I finally stop tapping and start to write.

December ??

I wrote the words "You will not reach me" on the inside of my journal when I got here. Why? What point was I trying to prove, and to whom? That I'm okay, that I don't need anybody? I think maybe I was wrong.

I look at the journal entry and try to decide just where I'm going with this. A thought is starting to dawn on me, that I'm not exactly doing okay. How do I fix it though? I put the pencil back to the paper and continue writing.

I'm not sure what exactly it is that I'm trying to say, other than that I was wrong about not needing help. I still think everyone here is retarded, and Dr. X is too busy to help me the way I probably need to be helped, but now I realize that everything that happened with my parents really did affect me more than I thought it did, and I need to do something about it.

My pencil snaps. "Dammit!" I glare at the offending pencil. I sigh and pick up my journal in irritation, clutching it tightly to my chest as I walk over to the main desk where the nurses and orderlies are busy discussing the events of some television show that I have never watched and don't care about.

"Hey, can I have another pencil?" I ask, and show the pencil to the group. Without really paying any attention to me, an orderly puts a pencil on the counter and continues talking to the rest of the group. "Oh I know! I can't believe that happened on the show! I was like, oh, no way…"

I roll my eyes, pick up the pencil and walk off, muttering to myself as I walk back to my chair. "Stupid people and their stupid fake lives and stupid TV shows..."

I start tapping on my paper with the new pencil and I try to remember what I was writing about. I'm having a hard time remembering, the meds are clouding my brain and making it hard to hold onto a thought.

"Hey Emma! What's going on?" Ricky's voice interrupts me again and I drop the pencil onto the journal. I furrow my brow and I begin to rub the bridge of my nose as I close my eyes.

"Hi Ricky. I'm kind of um, ya know, thinking about stuff."

Ricky looks like I just told him that I hated him.

"Oh. Okay. Well, I just, ya know, wanted to see if you were doing okay. You seemed kind of out of it yesterday." Ricky toes the ground dejectedly.

I feel bad. I don't want to tell Ricky to go away, but it seems like he has the absolute *worst* timing ever. I decide to compromise.

"Oh yeah. Hey Ricky, that was really nice of you to check on me last night. I really appreciate it."

Ricky smiles. "Uh, no problem Emma. It's cool. I think you're really nice and I was worried, so I wanted to make sure that you know that you can talk to me any time." He laughs nervously and toes the ground again, and I inwardly groan as I start to get the disturbing feeling that Ricky has a crush on me.

"Uh yeah. I got it. Thanks Ricky. I'm gonna go back to writing now, okay? Dr. X wants me to uh, ya know, write more and all, so I don't want to get into trouble or anything."

"Uh, okay Emma. See ya later." Ricky walks away. I wrinkle my nose at him before I go to my journal.

Where was I? I tap the pencil thoughtfully on my lower lip. Thoughts are swirling like fog, and I can't seem to latch onto any one of them now. My concentration is broken again, as laughter from the main desk seeps into my ears.

"Goddamned normal people and their stupid conversations..." I start muttering to myself and a thought begins to solidify in my head, a conversation with myself.

Are you mad at them for watching television, or are you mad at them because they're laughing? That's it, isn't it? You're mad at them because they're not like you. They're not in here because they can't live with the darkness in their heads, it's a job to them. They haven't lived your life, and you hate them for having something you didn't have; a seemingly normal life with a normal job and normal friends. You're bitter, and that's just sad, hating other people because you're jealous. And that's what you boil down to, isn't it? A bitter, sad, unhappy, not-quite-little anymore girl. If you don't cut the crap Emma, and

*start dealing with what's really making
you unhappy...*

What's really making me unhappy?
I sigh and write down the answer to this
painful question.

I am unhappy because of my parents.

The words are simple, but they say so
much more than that to me. I read them
and realize that I'm beginning to come face
to face with the years of abuse I watched
and grew up with. I don't know how to fix
what's wrong with me, but as I look around
this room, I know that I don't want to be in
this place anymore. Not just in this room,
but in this place inside myself, this place of
fear and guilt for things in the past that I
couldn't control.

*I could not control what happened to me.
It was not my fault.*

My eyes blur as I read what I've just
written. I've been blaming myself for what
my mom went through, for not being able

to protect her from my father; for Paul and Rosemary growing up watching the same abuse that I was watching, and being unable to do anything about it. I've always thought that it was my fault, that if I had been stronger or older, I could have stopped what was going on around me.

I have turned all my fear and disgust into guilt, and it's been twisting inside of me until I can't even breathe. I'm starting to realize that the night I ended up in the hospital wasn't really about Donnie breaking up with me.

Sure it hurt, losing Donnie. We had a lot of fun together, and he was hot. Plus, it was nice having a boyfriend who could buy booze. But when he broke up with me, all I wanted was for my mom to show me that she cared, and she couldn't, or wouldn't, do it. All I had really wanted was someone to love me.

I sit in the chair, trying to decide what I am going to do with all these new thoughts and realizations that are coming to me.

I've spent years telling myself that I am a machine, that I can't feel, just to let me cope with the horrors happening around me.

"Emma." A voice startles me.

"Huh?"

Ricky is standing next to me. Before I have the chance to bitch him out for interrupting my newborn thoughts, he says "Emma, they want you at the front desk."

"For what?" I complain.

"I don't know. They've been calling you." Ricky shrugs and walks off.

"Goddamned lazy stupid nurses..." I start bitching and angrily snatch up my journal and pencil and storm to the desk. The nurses and orderlies are still busy having some painfully normal conversation about whatever it is normal people talk about.

"Uh, someone was calling for me?" I ask when I get to the front desk.

A chunky, bald, twenty-something male orderly looks up at me. "What do ya want?" he says, smacking the gum in his mouth loudly.

I frown. "I don't know. Someone up here was calling me."

"And who are you?"

"Emma. Emma Banks."

His expression turns to one of recognition. "Oh yeah, got a visitor here for you."

I hope it's Mom. "Who is it?" I ask.

The orderly looks down at the sign-in sheet, still smacking the gum around in his mouth.

"Uhhhh..." he says as he reads down the list.

I tap my foot impatiently.

"Banks, Emma... uhh..."

"Yes. Emma Banks," I snap at him.

"Banks... Banks... Sorry about that. Uh yeah, it looks like your father is here to see you."

"My stepdad?" I ask him, confused. The orderly checks the list again.

"Uh, his name is Austin Banks." The orderly reads the name from the sheet. "Just wait here and someone will escort you into the visiting room in just a sec."

He sits down and rejoins the conversation, leaving me standing, speechless.

The blood drains from my face and my feet feel cemented to the ground. My head starts to spin.

"Oh shit." I whisper to myself, and suddenly I'm shaking and can't seem to stop.

Austin Banks is my father.

CHAPTER 10

The family legend and the rise of the machine

As I sit in the hallway, I start chewing nervously on my nails. I'm waiting to be escorted into the visiting room where my father sits, also waiting.

Why has he come here? Is he here to yell at me? To criticize me? Can I refuse his visit? Do I *want* to?

No. If he is here to talk to me, then I'll try to see him and find out just what *has* brought him here. I wonder if I'll always suspect his motives now. Possibly. Probably.

In my mind I see his face, and though I recognize the features, they are cold and lifeless and waxy, like an exhibit in a museum. When I think of him like this, I don't think of him as Dad, or even my father at all; I think of him as Austin, someone remote from me, someone I don't have to care about who doesn't have to care about me. But Austin really is my father's name.

I know very little about my father's life before he met my mother. From the bits and pieces I've been able to gather together over the years, I know that he grew up on a farm in a small town, and spent more time working on the farm than going to school. He had several siblings, all of whom died very young in slightly suspicious accidents, such as drowning in the bathtub, or falling into a washing machine. Leaves you thinking that Austin was lucky to survive whatever was happening with that family of his. His own father left Austin and his mother while Austin was young. His mother got married again, to a rigid, abusive, and uncaring man. This is how the family legend goes...

The clock seems to have slowed down so much as to be standing still. I'm still here, waiting to see the man who had helped create me, for better or for worse. A curious mix of fear, love, and curiosity overtakes me. I am not totally comfortable. Then the meds just happen to kick in. For the first time I am grateful for them, knowing that they'll keep me calm so that I won't freak out in the visiting room. And now, alongside the waxy head of Austin, I'm seeing in my thoughts the waxy, emotionless stare of Teresa. Teresa, my mother.

Austin graduated high school and moved to the city, where he met Teresa. This much I've been told—over and over it seems. More of the family legend. Teresa had lived through problems of her own, and at the tender age of eighteen had already spent most of her adolescent and young adult life working multiple jobs. She'd had to support herself and her own mother—an alcoholic, manic depressive, abusive mess...

At last, the same bald orderly who had told me that my father was here to see me gets up from the desk. He grabs the keys and escorts me to the visiting room.

I take a deep breath and walk into the room. My dad—*Austin*—is sitting there, looking through a Bible. He looks up at me and stands and I can't feel my legs holding me upright, even though they are.

"Hi Emmy," he finally says.

"Hi Dad," I answer. It's all I *can* say right now.

The door shuts behind us.

Austin was in his early twenties when he met Teresa at the diner where she worked her night job. She was charmed by his accent and quick wit; he loved her hard-working attitude and shyness.

They were married six weeks later in a tiny chapel, with only a handful of guests.

Three months into their marriage, Teresa became pregnant with her first child. I was born seven months later, a tiny, pale, sickly baby. Austin got a job in a factory and worked long hours to provide for his new family.

I've seen pictures of me and Dad when I was a baby, and I can tell by the way he held me that I was a precious, fragile, breakable thing to him, and that he loved me dearly...

We sit in uncomfortable silence for what seems like forever, but in reality is probably only a minute or so. My father speaks first. He sees my arms and he stares, hard, before his eyes meet mine.

"Oh Emma, what the hell did you do to yourself kid?" he asks me, and his voice seems sad. And there's still so much running through my head.

Most of the fights in the beginning were caused by the stress any young married couple feels when the money is too low and the bills are too high. Teresa took on sewing jobs from a local tailor shop to help bring money in.

Teresa became pregnant again, and two years after I was born, Paul came into the world.

I've been told that the fighting got worse around this time. The family legend. But Mom was young, she had no money, and there was nowhere to go with two children aged two and under, even if she had wanted to leave. She stayed, and five months after Paul was born, she became pregnant with Rosemary.

Sitting opposite him, I am surprised by my dad's tone. I am so used to hearing him angry or upset with me that he completely catches me off guard. My eyes well up with tears. I try to fumble for an explanation.

"I, uh, hurt myself Dad," is all I can manage to get out.

"Emma, honey... why?" he asks. Again he surprises me with the concern in his voice.

What can I say? How can I explain to him, especially with him acting so nice with me right now, that it is partially his fault that I am here in the first place? How can I tell him that the years of fighting and abuse has festered inside my head until it has become an infection, one that is killing me? I can't, so I sit and suffer in silence. This is something I've done often enough. We all have. Me and Paul and Rosemary.

I don't remember Paul—or even Rosemary—being born. But I can remember bits and pieces of things shortly after that.

No longer just family legend; I know this for real.

I remember one time, my dad had an old motorcycle that he spent a lot of time fixing up, polishing and working on. One day he and Mom were fighting over God knows what, and he looked at me, picked me up, and we went out to the garage. He sat on the motorcycle and sat me behind him, using a belt to secure me to his back.

We rode and rode until we were in a forest somewhere. He stopped the bike, and we got off and walked into a tiny log-cabin convenience store at the base of a trail. My dad bought me apple juice in a little glass bottle that was shaped like an apple, and we bought beef jerky.

We followed the trail until we came to a little stream, with stepping stones placed so you could get to the other side. When we were walking across, I remember slipping and I fell in. My dad turned around and started laughing as he picked me up, all cold and wet and startled. I started to laugh too, and he kissed me on the head and said "Emma, don't you know how to walk?"

He carried me the rest of the way back to the motorcycle, wrapping me up in his sweatshirt. We rode home to where Mom was waiting, none too happy to see me disheveled and sopping wet. They immediately got into an argument over how long my father had been gone, and what in the hell was he doing with a child that young on the back of a motorcycle anyway?

My father sits in silence, like he's unsure of what to say next. I've always felt that he is made out of stone, a living, breathing statue. His sudden concern for me is shaking me to the core. I'm scared because I feel I'm starting to doubt everything that I've ever thought about him over the years. Then he finds his voice again.

"I brought you this Emma," he says, and hands me the Bible in his hands. It is burgundy, leather bound, and in the bottom right hand corner he's had my name imprinted on it. I am touched, even if right now I have a hard time even believing that God exists, much less that He cares about me.

"I don't understand what's going on Emma, but I, uh, thought this might help you."

"Thanks Dad," is all I can say. I place the Bible gingerly in my lap, not sure what else to do with it. More awkward silence.

My dad was impulsive. One day, he came home with a cream-colored, wrinkled dog that we named Noodles. He showed us the dog first, so Mom couldn't make him take it back when she saw how much we wanted to keep it. Mom resented the dog at first, but she grew to love the protective and ever so patient, wrinkly, smelly little thing.

I think that I remember the fights getting worse around that time too, or maybe I just started to see what was really happening around me.

At first they always fought when we were in the other room, but gradually they started to fight in front of us. And that's when the fear started creeping into me and wouldn't let go.

I had nightmares, constantly. Until I was nearly ten years old, I begged to sleep in my parents' room every night. When they finally wouldn't let me sleep with them anymore, I begged for a night-light.

The effect my parents' fighting had on us kids began to show in other ways too. Paul was having a hard time potty training, and would often wet the bed in his sleep. Mom and I tried to hide it from Dad. But he found out anyway, and hit Paul to teach him not to be lazy, and to go to the bathroom at night.

As for Rosemary, she had the annoying habit of crying constantly and throwing fits. She also had a very vivid imagination. Cute in a child, it developed to become uncontrollable lying.

In addition to not being able to sleep, I began to have problems eating. My stomach was constantly in knots, and I remained pale and thin. And I would cry at the worst possible times, like in front of my classmates if I got an answer wrong at school...

I've been lost in these thoughts in the cold silence of the visitor room. My dad, speaking, brings me back.

"Emma... Why did you do this to yourself? Why didn't you call me?"

Ugh. The question I've been dreading. If I want to answer honestly, I'll say something like "...Because I'm so afraid of you that I couldn't tell you that anything was wrong. And because Mom didn't want you to try to take me away from her..." But of course, those words aren't going to come out of my mouth, so I settle for a half-truth.

"Because Dad, um, you know, we haven't got along real well for the past few years, and I didn't think you'd want to hear from me."

My dad looks surprised at first, then shakes his head.

"Kid, I know we haven't always got along, but I never wanted anything bad to happen to you. You're my little girl. Do you know how upset everyone is that you're in here right now?"

"Yes Dad, I know," I reply, dropping my head. Even in his concern, he is still making me feel bad. Like I have just been selfish in trying to kill myself.

...Through all the troubles my father began to work more and more, and eventually got promoted in his job. But even though he was making more money, his family was falling apart. And he began to fall apart with the pressure of everything. So he clamped down on us, thinking that a tighter grip would fix everything. We, at least, should be something that he could control. Then when he finally realized that that wasn't working, he just blamed Mom.

It became a fact of daily life, just like waking up and brushing your teeth, that my parents would fight, that my mom would cry and that my dad would hit her. And sometimes he'd hit us. But it didn't necessarily happen in that order.

I'm thinking, remembering, but I'm on full alert just sitting there, ready to listen when I have to.

My dad continues, unaware that anything is running through my head. "Do you have any idea what it was like for me to get a phone call saying that you were in this..." he looks around distastefully "...place?"

Again, I feel ashamed at being here. I don't say anything. And then I feel his eyes staring at me. He is expecting a response.

"No Dad. I don't know what it was like for you. I'm sorry."

Our relationship is always going to be like this, I think to myself. I am never going to be good enough, smart enough, pretty enough, or well behaved enough to make him proud of me.

At school I was the weird kid, and since I had no friends and my home life was miserable, I began to escape into books. I was fascinated with a character in one of my science fiction books. An android. I loved how he didn't feel anything, how he was so human but didn't have the same pesky emotions that I couldn't seem to control within myself.

I decided that I wanted to be an android. Whenever I got upset, I would repeat certain phrases to myself, over and over and over again, like a mechanical thing, until I felt calm and emotionless and in control once more.

And if I couldn't control my home life, I could control other things; like whether I ate or not, or even whether I wanted to have feelings for anything at all.

The worse the fighting got, the less I ate and the less I allowed myself to feel. In exasperation one day, my mom finally started screaming at me and crying, "What is wrong with you Emma? You're like a machine; you don't eat, you don't feel, you don't smile. What is wrong?"

My dad runs his hands through his hair and sighs deeply. I wonder if maybe he knows that I hadn't been thinking of what kind of phone call he'd get when I was admitted to this place. I don't want to dwell on that though. Thankfully, he changes the subject.

"Jesus Emma, you look like hell. They have you all doped up, don't they? What do they have you on?"

I try to remember the names of the medications, but my mind is swirling from the meds and from sitting in this room with him. I just can't remember. I begin to panic when I realize that I am unable to answer his question, and I start to hyperventilate.

Back to my memories, back to my memories, back to my memories. They finally tired of fighting all the time and I started to see the change in my mother. Despite the bruises, she had reached the point where either *she* was going to die, or *he* was.

When I was thirteen, they sat us down at the table and told us that they couldn't get along anymore, and that they thought it was best for everyone if they got a divorce. They said something about how they had agreed *to* disagree *and told us that everything was going to be fine. Just words, telling us that they'd take care of us and not put us in the middle, and that it wasn't our fault. I actually thanked God when they told me the news. At least I had the hope that something was going to change.*

And oh, change did happen. My father threw my mother out of the house with nothing more than the clothes on her back. We didn't see her except on the weekends, and more often than not, my father would make one of us stay behind to keep him company.

My parents kept fighting though, and it became scary. One minute my father was drunk and screaming death threats at my mother, the next day they had decided to call off the divorce and pretend like we were suddenly going to become some perfect family. It never lasted. It would all fall apart a few weeks later in some new violent and dramatic argument. Repeat ad nauseam.

It came to the point where they hated each other so much that they tried to push their hatred of each other on us. I never bought it though, which pissed them both off. I couldn't understand why they, as adults, couldn't understand that I loved both of them.

I became more and more isolated from them, and they both began to treat me more as a problem—and occasionally, as a weapon—than their child...

I'm still hyperventilating a little, and my dad is grabbing my shoulder and making me look at him.

"Emma, calm down. Breathe. I'll ask the nurses about the medication, it's not a big deal, okay?"

But it *is* a big deal; he just doesn't know it. He's never taken a long look at himself. Before the divorce, when we all lived together, you had to answer every question with quick, concise answers. You got into trouble if you didn't.

As I grew older, I began to drink and date older guys. Looking back on my behavior now, I'm sure that I was seeking the love that my father wouldn't or couldn't give me, from older men. And I was in so much pain—despite all my best efforts to be a machine—that I needed to numb myself. So I chose to do that through drinking.

My father began drinking heavily round about this time too. He was drunk constantly, and would see-saw emotionally. He would go from being depressed at losing his family, to angry, to hitting the bars and bringing home random women. Just so that he wouldn't be lonely. We began to fight even more as his behavior became more and more intolerable. He refused to pay a penny of child support, so my mom, my sister, and I were practically starving in our apartment. Just the three of us at this time; Paul stayed with his father...

I start to slow my breathing down and clutch the Bible in my lap with an iron grip, in an effort to hide my shaking hands from my dad.

He starts to talk again, like he thinks that the sound of his voice will make things better. At least he talks about something different.

"How are they treating you, kid? Do you have enough to eat?"

"Yes Dad."

"Is the food okay?"

Apparently I make a face, and he cracks a smile, the first smile I've seen on his face since I walked into this tomb-like room.

"Apparently, that's a no then," he says.

"Uh, yeah. The food sucks."

My dad frowns at my use of the word *sucks*. Again, fear washes over me as I wait to get backhanded for saying a *bad* word. But no backhand comes.

The separation was hard on everybody, and it just got harder. My dreams of some peace once my parents finally divorced were shattered when my father, in a drunken rage, threatened to kill a pet rabbit that belonged to Rosemary. Now fifteen years old, and aged beyond my years, I jumped between him and my sister and told him to go to bed and sober up. He looked at me in absolute shock for about three seconds before he started screaming at me at the top of his lungs, about two inches from my face.

"DON'T TELL ME HOW TO RAISE MY KIDS!" he screamed.

"Then raise them so I don't HAVE to."

When he hit me, I hit him back. Rosemary was bawling and hyperventilating behind me, huddled in a corner of the kitchen. I picked her up and went to the phone and called my mom. She came right away and picked us up. We didn't see much more of him after that...

It's strange to see my father sitting across the room from me now. He looks completely baffled, so that I almost think he's noticed how scared I've become.

"Emma, why are you so jumpy?"

It dawns on me that he is completely unaware of the effect his presence has on me. Jesus, he really has no clue as to what all the years of fighting and yelling did to us—Mom, Paul, Rosemary, and me.

Again I'm asking myself; "Do I tell him the truth, or do I just try to get through this meeting with as much grace as I can muster?"

I settle for the latter. "Uh, it's the meds I think, Dad. I'm not used to taking them and I'm a little jumpy because of it." I can lie to him without even thinking.

My father remarried a year later. She was a nice blonde woman who had a son of her own. He moved away with her to a city a few hours away from where we lived. Paul went with them.

Mom also remarried. Daniel was a kindly man she met at work. Rosemary and I fell in love with him instantly. He had big arms that made you feel safe when he hugged you, and a laugh that was warm and friendly. Best of all, he loved and took care of my mom. That was all I wanted.

I thought things would be better after that, but I still couldn't get past the things going on in my head, residue from all the fighting and fear that just wouldn't go away.

I started to cut myself and my mom found out. She took me to a psychologist who prescribed pills for me and wanted to talk about the divorce. I didn't want to talk about the divorce, so my mom told the psychologist about my father when I wouldn't answer his questions...

My dad stares at me, hard. That stare cuts through me, and I can swear that he knows that I am lying, telling him about the pills making me jumpy. But if he does know, he's not saying anything. For now.

"So, uh…" he begins. He's searching for words to connect us, but not finding any beyond those. Neither of us knows what to say.

Not wanting to sit in yet more awkward silence, I jump in and ask him questions. I'm hoping to move the spotlight away from me in this way too.

"How is your wife, uh, Julie, doing?" I ask.

"She's fine. But she's worried about you. I wish you'd give her a chance, kiddo. She's a real nice lady."

"Uh, yeah. She seems nice."

The truth of the matter is, Julie *is* a nice woman. My resentment toward her comes from the fact that my dad seems to treat her so much better than he treated Mom. Because of that, I've wanted nothing to do with Julie. I am bitter and jealous, resentful of his love and concern for her. I am polite with her, but that is it.

...Mom, Rosemary, and me, we all moved up to Daniel's house after he and Mom got married. I should have been happy but it was never that simple. It still isn't. I met Donnie at a football game that I'd attended solely to get out of the house. Anything would do, just to be able to get drunk and smoke pot without my parents knowing. From that point it was mostly drink and drugs and Donnie that I cared about. The break up with Donnie was, of course, like the straw that broke my back. It's why I'm here. In this place. Sitting across from my father...

"Julie wanted to come see you, but she didn't think that you wanted to see her," my dad says pointedly. He has no way of knowing what I've been thinking about. All the same, I'd better pay attention. I still don't know if I can trust him.

"Uh, sorry Dad. I just... I'm not real proud that I'm in here, and um, don't want anyone to see me like this. I don't want to embarrass you."

"Well, that's understandable, I suppose," he finally concedes. "It'd be nice if you'd come to visit us more. After you get out of here I mean, Emma. I'm your dad, and I miss you."

I am suspicious of his motives for wanting me to come visit. I am sure that he wants to show me off to Julie; show her how well behaved and intelligent and adult-like I am. God knows why he'd think I would be. But I just agree with him anyway.

"Okay Dad. I'll come visit more."

I really have no intention of visiting him more, though, and if I tell my mom I don't want to go, most likely she won't make me. I am lying again, but it's best this way. We'll just end up in an argument, and that is the last thing that I want. What I really *do* want is for this awkward visit to end. Even though my dad is being nice, I'm not over the years when he *wasn't* nice. I'm not over the bruises and the hurtful words, and the lying and covering up his abusive nature to the outside world. I can't stop being suspicious.

My dad starts talking about work, about Julie, about his step-son Russ, and how ill-behaved Russ is. That most likely means that Russ is just a *normal* kid. I know how that would infuriate my father.

I figure that we are just about winding down the visit when my dad hits me with a whammy.

"So, I heard about your incident with the nurse, Emma."

I wince. Here it comes, I think. He's going to yell at me and make me feel worthless. I brace myself and stare at the floor.

"I'm not really sure what the hell has got into you Emma, but you need to get your shit together, kid."

I nod in agreement with him, which is what I know he wants. "Yes Dad. I'm trying."

"It's almost Christmas, Emma," he says, changing the subject again.

"Yeah, I know Dad." I bite my lower lip to keep myself from crying.

"You don't want to be in here for Christmas, do you Emma?"

"No Dad, I don't."

"We're going to have a big celebration at the house. We got you some presents, and I've already talked to your mom. She says you can come by for part of the day. *If* you get out of here in time."

I look up, confused. My dad continues.

"What I'm saying, Emma..." he leans closer toward me "...is that you tell these damned doctors whatever it is that they want to hear, just so you can get out of this place. Got it? Just agree with them, so that we can take you home."

I blink. My dad isn't concerned so much with me getting out of here and *being well*; he is just concerned with me getting *out*. As far as he is concerned—or so it seems—

there is nothing wrong with me. There's no reason for me to be in this place. And the embarrassment he feels is oh-so real.

I finally nod my head. "Okay Dad."

My dad nods too, and leans back in his chair. Suddenly, he looks at his watch and I know that he has other, more important places to be. He's ready to leave now.

"I gotta get going kid. Just remember this little talk, okay? I love you, Emma."

"I love you too, Dad."

And that is it. He stands up, gives me a quick hug, and he walks out the door. I'm left sitting in stunned silence.

I whisper softly to myself. "Okay Emma. You heard him. Time to get out."

The family legend is not pretty. But legends mean nothing to a machine.

CHAPTER 11

Time to get out of here

As I sit at the lunch table, my mind is preoccupied with thoughts of the meeting with my father. I'm not sure whether I should consider it a dismal failure or not. I hadn't said much of anything; what I had said was so edited before I spoke, that it felt like I had sat there and lied to him the entire time.

He had confused me, that's for sure. Instead of yelling at me, which I was sure he was going to do, he had appeared concerned for me. Questions still lingered in my head though. Was he really concerned about me, or was he concerned with the family image?

My mom had already told me that I had embarrassed the entire family by putting myself in here. And she had made sure to ask me not to say too much to anyone about the past.

How am I supposed to get better if I don't confront the past though? Does my trying to get better even matter to any of them anymore?

Maybe it's just me. I absent-mindedly push the semi-frozen peas around on my plate, thinking—not for the first time—that maybe I should just get over it.

Everyone else seems to be doing fine since the divorce. Both of my parents have remarried. Paul is on the track team at his school, and Rosemary has joined the cheerleading squad. Their grades are improving, and they seem happy. Unlike me, still tormented with horrible memories of the past.

So why can't I be happy? Why am I busy drinking, smoking, starving myself? Why am I still up almost all night, every night, unable to sleep? Why do I refuse to appear to be even *close* to normal?

While everyone else in my family is thriving like flowers after a heavy rain, I am drowning. Still. The divorce has simply removed me from the situation; it has done nothing to remove the hurt, the way I thought it would.

I suddenly feel stupid and selfish. Once again, I feel like I am back at square one, trying to figure out what the hell is wrong with me. And trying to figure out why I can't get over something that everyone else in my family seems to have put behind them. At the very least, they seem able to pretend that the horrible past had never happened in the first place.

I am an embarrassment to my family. I know by now that everyone at school will know what has happened to me. When (if) I return, I won't be able to walk down the hallway without more whispers behind my back. I can see it now: "Did you hear what

Emma did to herself?" they'll say. And the story would evolve and grow until it's nowhere near the truth. No matter—I can never tell them the truth anyway.

I sigh heavily. The meeting with my father is still confusing me, to put it mildly. Maybe he has changed. Maybe he and Mom just weren't meant to be together, and now that he's with this new, nice woman everything is okay. I suddenly feel like a jerk for not wanting to visit him and his new wife.

Regardless of my confusion about my father and his motives for visiting me, he had at least said something that I agree with. "...Get out of here."

I am tired of being in this shitty place, with its shitty food and fucked-up people. I begin to focus on the idea of getting out of here.

Get out. What is it going to take to prove that I can leave this place? I've already caused a scene, and the hospital is keeping me here until I show "substantial progress." So what exactly do they mean by "substantial progress?"

I am going to have to lie my ass off to get out of here. Lying to the other patients, the nurses and the orderlies shouldn't be too hard. But I am worried about Dr. X.

Dr. X has already shown me that he will not buy most of the half-truths and lies that I tell everyone else. So if I do just all of a sudden start to act like everything is okay, he'll definitely grow suspicious of me. And keep me here even longer.

Dr. X presents a problem, one that I'm not quite sure how to deal with just yet.

I finish eating and put my tray away. I chew on my fingernails, deep in thought. Suddenly, an idea comes to me. Dr. X had been so flustered during the past few days that our meetings have seemed to run on autopilot. He has appeared tired and overworked. I wonder if I can use that to my advantage...

The reality is, I am in a county mental hospital that is overcrowded and understaffed, and needs the space for a seemingly constant stream of new arrivals. Surely I can work that, along with Dr. X's tiredness, to my advantage. A few days of tearing up at group therapy and pretending to confess my deepest hurts and thoughts just might help persuade them that I am ready to change, that I am becoming what they want me to be.

I frown. I feel like I am going to be selling out. I am completely against the idea of acting like every other person in here. Half of them are in here seeking attention, and I hate them with every fiber of my being. The other half consists of genuine whack-jobs who have been in here for weeks.

I finally decide that it isn't selling out, just saying whatever I need to say to get myself out of here. I tell myself that it is a mission, and no different than lying to my teachers at school about why I'd missed class. Or lying to my mom, so she won't find out that I *have* missed class.

This is going to be trickier than just lying to a few teachers though. A plan is slowly forming in my head. The first thing I'll need to do is to quit playing little *games*, like the one where I stare at people until they feel uncomfortable. This thought depresses me. I am bored and lonely in here and my games are keeping me entertained. But then again, maybe they're helping keep me stuck in this place.

I'll have to stop coloring and painting pictures with black and red on everything. I'll have to participate more in the group sessions. I roll my eyes at the thought. Instantly I chastise myself for it. How am I supposed to get out of here if I can't even control my thoughts when nobody is looking?

I'll have to quit ignoring the schoolwork they assign us. I'll have to stop sulking in the back of the classroom, and pay attention. I'll have to stop rolling my eyes and saying as little as is humanly possible in the group therapy sessions. In short, I'll have to start acting like a normal kid who really wants to get better. And I'll have to keep it up until they think I actually *am* doing better. I'll have to start following the joke of a treatment plan that I've never really bothered to read.

I go to my room and dig the treatment plan out from a stack of other papers that I also haven't bothered to read. Dr. X has given me pamphlets on depression, on rebuilding your life after a suicide attempt, and various other lame subjects.

I look at the treatment plan and figure that it is most likely a generic form, handed out to everybody. It has been photocopied so many times that there are black dots on the paper and the writing has become difficult to make out. With some effort, I begin to read what is written on the crumpled paper. There is a laundry list of generic things to do to help with depression and/or suicidal tendencies.

"Journal... yeah, I got that..." I read aloud to myself. "Develop a hobby that will help you deal with stress in a constructive way, such as painting or gardening…" I scoff. Gardening. Who the hell does gardening anyway?

After some thought, I decide that it doesn't really matter; all I have to say is that when I get out of here, I *plan* to have a hobby. Fine. I'll tell them that I am going to continue drawing, since I have a mild interest in it anyway.

I continue reading the treatment plan. "Make a list of trusted friends or family members that you can talk to openly and honestly." I start to laugh. I can't talk openly and honestly to *anyone* in my family. Either they pretend that nothing is wrong, or they really *believe* that nothing is wrong. And the few times I have tried to talk about the way I grew up, my mother either gets upset and defensive or she changes the subject. I finally grew tired of making her cry, so I quit talking about my childhood to her altogether. That leaves me with friends, then. But when I think about my friends, I am stuck there, too.

The circle of friends I have consists of punk rockers, stoners, and other social misfits. They will discuss with a passion why a band sucks or not, but rarely discuss feelings. Unless the discussion involves a general discontent with being in high school and having a curfew.

Once again though, it doesn't really matter if I have friends and family I can talk to. To get out of here, I have to pretend that I have people I can talk to.

I think back to when my mom took me to therapy, and instantly I become irritated. Even in the therapist's office, I wasn't allowed to say what was really on my mind. My mom would interrupt and correct me, or hush me if she thought I was going to start talking about something she didn't want anyone to know about.

In her mind, she was protecting me. She was trying to make sure that nobody would take me away from her. But really, thinking about it, all she was doing was wasting her money, taking me to a therapist and then telling me to lie when I got there.

As I sit here, developing this grand scheme to get myself out of this hospital, I become saddened by what I am doing. Until my father's visit, when he told me to "get out of here," I have been busy sitting and writing in my journal. I've been slowly coming to the realization that the abuse I'd grown up watching wasn't my fault at all. Now, before I can even wrap my mind around the idea and begin to really explore it, my father has come along and basically told me to "get out of here," regardless of whether I am better or not. Once again, my family is too busy being concerned about appearances, and again, I am going to suffer for it. Some things just don't change.

For a second I regret having called the ambulance, but instantly chase the thought from my mind with a firm shake of my head.

"No." I say out loud. "I don't want to die. I just want to feel better."

It is obvious though, that I am going to have to do this on my own. The staff here can't or won't help me; my parents can't or won't help me, and neither can my friends.

I know that I can't stay in the hospital forever, but I had hoped to stay in for a week or two more, simply because, despite the cold and the dirty walls and the crappy food, I am fairly safe here. I am being encouraged to get better. I am not told what to say, or told to hide my feelings. I have started to become human here. That's a heck of a realization.

Now, I am going to have to become my machine-self again. I am going to have to lie, exaggerate, and not feel, while pretending I *do* feel, in order to get out of here. I am going to have to become a *cookie-cutter person*, which is what I call normal average everyday people.

The thought makes me queasy. I feel that all I have left is my individuality, and no amount of abuse or torment or mockery has taken that away from me. If anything, I have used the horrible circumstances of my family life to build the shield that protects me from the outside world. I am machine, something that cannot feel and cannot be hurt. Not like a *cookie-cutter person*. At least that's what I'd thought.

I remain largely unconcerned with things that most *normal* girls my age are concerned with: makeup, labels, and taking stupid quizzes out of teenage magazines to figure out if I am a good kisser or not. I feel superior to girls whose day is ruined if they get a zit on their usually flawless skin. Or if their hair doesn't turn out right any given day.

I am still busy throwing all of this around in my mind when I hear someone call for afternoon therapy.

"Okay Emma," I tell myself. "Time to get out of here." I smooth my hair, throw my shoulders back, and grab my journal. With a new sense of purpose, I walk down the hall, ready for therapy.

CHAPTER 12

Try to be convincing

I take my seat in group therapy, telling myself that all I have to do is act normal and nice, and after a few days, everything will be okay. If I can just figure out what *normal* is...

Instead of Dr. X walking in though, another man in a white coat comes in and introduces himself as Dr. Murphy. I frown. Dr. X is who I need to convince to let me out of the hospital, not this other mystery doctor. I tap my fingers anxiously on my knees as I wait for everyone to finish shuffling papers and changing seats, so they can sit by their *friends* in here. I shake my head. Even in a mental hospital, it's still like high school. I don't even fit in with the *crazy* people.

The session starts. It takes a great deal more effort than I initially thought it would to try to keep my usual, disdainful expression from my face. It's particularly difficult when I have to listen to things I don't consider important. For example, almost anything to do with anyone else my age.

I remind myself of my newfound goal though, and I try hard to listen to everyone else as they talk, and keep my attention from turning inward.

It gets to be my turn in this circle-jerk pity party, and I begin a semi-rehearsed diatribe of woe-is-me teenage angst over my parents' divorce. Even though I didn't care about it much in the first place, and I certainly don't care about it now. I need *something* to talk about, because I just want to get the hell out of this place.

I don't even really listen to what I'm saying, I'm just copying a lot of what the other patients were saying—how I want to live, how I am just depressed about my family and I don't know how to deal with it, blah blah blah. Everyone seems to buy it, and Dr. Murphy makes notes and approving grunts. Thankfully, my turn passes and I breathe an inward sigh of relief. One down, eight more of these to go, I tell myself. I'm planning on it taking about seventy-two hours to undo the damage I had done initially when I got here, with that whole tree-throwing incident.

I catch myself crossing my arms and scowling midway through one girl's speech about her third suicide attempt. It's unbearable when she starts to talk about how she didn't have any friends at school, and how that was her major depressive trigger. And then she starts sobbing, can you believe it? She's sobbing because she's not popular. Give me strength!

Remembering my plan, I change my expression to one of *faux* concern and uncross my arms, despite the fact I think she's a shallow moron. I'm unsure what to do with my arms, so I end up just folding my hands neatly in my lap. My toes trace circles on the floor with nervous energy.

Dr. Murphy asks everyone to brainstorm *constructive ideas on dealing with stress* in response to this girl's question on how to deal with stress.

Almost everyone volunteers a thought, most of them taken from the generic list of ideas on our nearly identical treatment plans—you know, the pieces of paper that say dumb shit about gardening and calling your friends if you're feeling upset or stressed out or suicidal that day.

I panic when I realize I can't think of something that someone hasn't already said, and it's my turn to give a suggestion. And since I'm not in a waking coma, or too drugged out to answer, Dr. Murphy expects a contribution from me.

Think Emma, think... What do normal people do? *Cookie-cutter people.*

"Uh, play with your dog," I finally blurt out.

A snicker escapes Ricky's lips and he

quickly tries to hide it as a cough when Dr. Murphy's head snaps toward him, glaring at him for laughing at me. Ricky continues to pretend-cough, and even starts to pat his chest until Dr. Murphy seems satisfied that he is not laughing at me.

The predictably lame group session ends. I'm sweating. Is it really *that* hard for me to act like a normal person? Then I notice that everyone else is pushing up their sleeves and fanning themselves with their journals. I gather that for once, instead of it being freezing cold in here, the heater must be working. I am relieved to discover that I haven't looked weird or awkward to everyone else.

Ricky comes and sits next to me. "Play with puppies?" he asks, and laughs at me.

I scowl at him, not appreciating his sense of humor and cross my arms. "No. I *said* play with your *dog*."

"Oh come on Emma. What was that all about?"

"Uh, well, I decided after talking to my father today that I should, um, start trying to get better."

Ricky's eyes widen. "Dude, your *dad* came here?"

Aw crap, I think to myself when I realize that he's going to keep asking questions. The only reason I'm letting this conversation even start is in the hope that the staff will notice I'm conversing with other patients and write it up in their notes.

"Yes Ricky, he came by," I say, already bored.

"Well? How'd it go?" he asks, settling into his chair like he's hoping for the lengthy explanation that I just won't give him.

"It went fine. We uh, ya know, hashed some stuff out and everything is okay."

Ricky eyes me suspiciously. "And that's it?"

"Yup. That's it," I answer, nodding for greater effect.

Ricky decides to test my story. "Okay, well, what did you guys talk about?"

"Stuff," I tell him. We glare at each other like gunfighters from the old West, and I realize that now we're in some sort of stupid staring contest. Perhaps Ricky imagines that somehow he is going to be able to make me tell him the truth. I smirk.

Ricky is not going to win this; I've perfected the art of the staring contest. In life, most people don't actually look you in the eye, and it makes them uncomfortable when someone does it to them.

Ricky finally concedes, as I knew he would. "Fine then. Don't tell me," he says, and storms off.

Left blissfully alone, my thoughts switch from getting out of the hospital, to my mom and stepdad. What have they told my friends about me?

I think back to the night I tried to kill myself. I remember very vaguely the fire trucks with their flashing sirens, and the ambulances, and the swarm of people who descended upon the house, intent on saving me from myself.

I live in a small town, on a small street, and news tends to travel fast in places like that. I know that everyone who knows me, knows my family, and hell, even those who didn't know *any* of us, will have heard hints, rumors, and allegations.

I feel suddenly bad. What kind of hell is Mom going through? No wonder she's embarrassed by me. She has tried so hard after the divorce to appear normal to everyone, and here I am, a daughter who refuses to conform, who is depressed all the time, and finally tries... to kill herself.

Is everyone looking at them like they are bad parents? Have they gone back to work? I suddenly see Mom, hopelessly crying on the couch, unable to go back to her job out of sorrow and sheer embarrassment.

What about my stepdad, a man who married a woman with two kids, so poor they could barely feed themselves? He has never complained about inheriting kids with some severe emotional issues. He has really tried hard to be understanding, even though he can never grasp what we've been through. And this is how I am repaying him?

Another thought hits me. I am worried that the insurance won't pay for this, and somehow my parents will have to come up with thousands of dollars to cover my selfish stint in this hospital.

I can't blame everything on my parents. I am old enough to reason, to drive a car, to make choices for myself. I *chose* to try to end my life, because I chose *not* to confront my problems and get beyond them. I'm not sure how exactly I was supposed to deal with my problems. Nobody in my family had wanted to admit that there ever *was* a problem.

I am starting to get very nervous about leaving this place. Do my parents still love me? What kind of restrictions are going to be placed on me when I get out of here?

I sigh to myself when I realize that my panicked, worried parents are going to put me under a very close watch. I can pretty much rule out any sort of social life whatsoever, for God only knows how long. And then there is my father...

Will he want to be an active part of my life, now that I have threatened to take it? Is he guilt-stricken the way Mom most likely is? Does the thought even cross his mind that he had anything to do with this? Does he ever actually feel anything at all? *Ever*?

Now I feel irritated with myself; instead of focusing on *my* feelings, and how the events of the past were poisoning *me*, I am more concerned with how everyone else is.

Slowly but surely I am starting to see past the years of brainwashing that goes on when you grow up in an abusive home. And one of the biggest games that had been played with my mind was to have me grow up thinking that everything was my fault.

I was told, over and over, that if I was only smarter, faster, prettier, better behaved, less selfish, that my mom wouldn't get hit. And that I wouldn't *deserve* to be hit.

I can see so clearly right now; no child ever deserves to go through all that. Something has clicked inside me, and I can feel a sense of righteous anger building up in me.

Okay, fine. I am going to get out of here, because this place is a goddamned joke. I am already at the point where I know what is going to be said in this group therapy session or that one, and in the counseling sessions. I have nothing more to learn from these people.

I'm not bitter. Everyone here means well. This place has been like a safety net for me. It has allowed me time to explore my inner feelings, and Dr. X has encouraged me—you could say he's forced me—to deal with the past. And these are all great things, really, so I'm grateful in a way.

But the biggest issue for me to confront is something that no group therapy session will ever help with. I am going to have to be honest with my parents.

So I have made a decision. I am not going to let myself be manipulated anymore. No one will make me blame myself for what my mom went through, or for whatever caused my father to become abusive in the first place.

I have also made a decision. When I get out of here, after my parents are done screaming, yelling, crying, or grounding me (or maybe even all of those things), I am going to sit them down. I am finally going to be honest with them and tell them exactly what caused me to feel like I had to end my life. If I have to face the past, then they are going to have to, too.

CHAPTER 13

The wrong doctor

I sit in Dr. X's office, waiting for him to show up for our appointment. As I wait, I draw intricate spirals on a blank page in my journal.

At last the door opens. To my surprise Dr. Murphy hurries in. I am shocked and disappointed, and I don't try to hide the fact.

Dr. Murphy walks around to Dr. X's desk and sits in his chair. I am irritated by his assumption of that chair; the one that belongs to *my* doctor, not to him.

Dr. Murphy has my file, and begins to explain that Dr. X isn't here today because of a family emergency. I start to tune him out, but doing that isn't going to help my case. I take a deep breath and calm myself.

Dr. Murphy goes through a series of questions, checking them off as he asks them. He writes short notes underneath the questions, to give to Dr. X, later.

I can reply to most of the questions with short answers. Are you feeling suicidal today? No. How are you sleeping? Fine. Are you having any problems with your medications? No. Are you following your treatment plan? Yes. Do you have any questions about your treatment plan? No.

After about ten minutes, without even looking at me, Dr. Murphy ends the session. I walk out of the office confused, and to be honest, kind of hurt. I watch a string of patients go in and out of that door the way I did. I feel slighted by the way that man has treated me. Like I am just another thing to deal with on his list of daily chores.

I remember how my father had done that to me when I was growing up, and how much it had hurt me. Half the time, when he talked to me, I warranted so little of his attention that he didn't even look up at me. Dr. Murphy had inadvertently done the same thing to me in our session.

Logic tells me that he has most likely been thrown into doing the individual counseling sessions at the last minute. That still doesn't make me feel better though. Just as it hadn't made me feel better when my mom had tried to defend my father's constant dismissal of me as a child.

I feel horribly, inexplicably alone all of a sudden, even though I am in a room full of people. I remember the pay phone in the hallway, and picking up my journal I walk over to it. My heart races as I stare at the phone. Since I'm not allowed to have my cell phone in here, I can't remember any of my friends' phone numbers. I try to think of someone I can call.

I pick up the phone and carefully dial the only phone number I can remember. The phone rings and rings. Eventually, the familiar voice of my mother comes on the line.

"Hi, I'm not in right now. Please leave a message and I'll get back to you." The machine beeps for me to leave a message, but a lump has come to my throat, and I don't dare speak for fear of crying. I hang up the receiver and walk back, head down, to the group room.

I watch the frenzy of activity around me—people scurrying here and there, to the bathroom, to the doctor's office, to get something from their room, to rifle through magazines and old books with missing pages on the beaten-up bookshelf. Desperate, I look for Ricky and find him, playing checkers with some kid whose name I don't know.

I start to feel very sorry for myself. I remember going to school as a kid and how I could never seem to make many friends, or keep the ones I did make. Kids do stupid things to each other, like get into fights and call each other names. But for some reason I considered all of these things acts of treachery that should not go unpunished. I ended up isolating myself then, just as I have done here. The truth is though, I don't actually *like* anyone in this place. It's just that right now, I don't want to be alone. I am exhausted; tired of thinking, tired of pretending, tired of trying to trick people, and so *very* tired of the thoughts warring inside my brain.

I have a very bad headache that has come on quickly. I close my eyes and rub the bridge of my nose with my thumb and forefinger. I stop when I recall that I've seen Dr. X do the same thing. I feel betrayed by him not being here for me today. I know that he has to have some sort of life outside of the hospital, but I just expected that Dr. X would be there, working with me until I left. Now I am worrying that he won't be. It's a juvenile thought, but a genuine worry.

I have a curious mix of fear, revulsion, and respect for Dr. X. He has seen through me and demanded that I give him the truth. And I have argued with him, lied to him, and resented him for making me be honest with myself as well as him. I resent him for bringing up the past and for making me deal with it.

Now I'm blaming Dr. X for the way I am; stuck in here, isolated from everyone. I'm muttering to myself. Stupid doctor with his stupid speeches about getting well. I'm not really making any sense but still feel better, complaining about Dr. X and blaming my current state on him. In the end I let out a long sigh. I know I can't blame Dr. X for me being in this state. I'm just sulking.

After a while I tire of being alone with myself and walk over to the nurses' desk. I ask for drawing supplies and after a few moments get a plastic box filled with crayons, pastels and a few pencils. I sit in a chair, next to the dirty, cruddy windows with the steel inside them, trying to figure out what to draw. I frown. Nothing inspires me in here. I look out of the window again, and suddenly breathe in sharply. The sun is shining through a wet, leafless tree, in the middle of the courtyard. I have never noticed this tree before, since right across the courtyard is another wing of this hospital and usually I am trying to peer through the windows to see what's going on over there.

The tree looks almost black, and its branches, bare and almost skeletal, stretch up and out, toward the sun. I silently thank the tree for being there, and I grab a pencil from the box. I'm going to draw that tree.

I spend most of the afternoon sketching the tree, using swift strokes of the soft pastels to show more of the contrast between the darkness of the tree, and the green of the soggy grass around it. Finally, I stare at my picture. I frown. It sucks. It looks nothing like the beautiful tree outside. That tree, despite being bare and stripped down, seems to be reaching out for sunlight to a sky that has granted only rain for days.

I admire that tree and consider it my kin. That tree has probably struggled through dry seasons, and too much rain, and been stripped down by the seasons of life, but is still standing. And still reaching for the light.

Okay, so maybe I'm not an artist, but I *can* write, and I want to get that thought down. I tuck the crappy drawing of the tree inside of my journal and flip to a blank page.

December ??

So I was trying to draw this tree outside, and as I looked at it, something came to me.

This tree was beautiful. Even though it has been through the ups and downs of life, it is still standing, feet firmly rooted in the ground, and reaching for the light.

This sounds stupid, and I know it, but I want to be like that tree. I want to be able to weather the storms of life, and to keep reaching for light, even though right now I feel like I'm stripped bare, with nothing of me left.

So even though I'm sitting in a hospital right before Christmas, and I'm alone, I will look at the ugly ass picture I tried to draw of the beautiful tree, and remember how that tree was still standing, despite everything.

I turn to another page in my journal and, inspired by the tree, I realize that I don't have any hobbies that don't involve minor infractions of the law. Drinking, ditching school and having sex aren't considered healthy hobbies. Let's face it; they're not hobbies at all. But they have been my only interests.

I remember the generic list in one of the leaflets, of *healthy activities* to do if you get stressed out after you are discharged from the hospital. I decide to make up one of my own. The problem is, I can't really think of anything that I want to do. So I try to think about what I'm at least *interested* in.

Music. I love music. I spent hours listening to it when I wasn't in this place. Suddenly, I want to listen to music so badly that I feel like crying. I sigh, and sadly write the word *music* under my list of hobbies that I want to pursue when I get out of here.

I chew on my pencil, deep in thought. I am really, *really,* having a hard time figuring out what I enjoy doing. I note with some sadness that I can't remember the last time I really enjoyed anything. It is almost as if I've existed behind a plate of glass, watching other people live and laugh and feel, and being incapable of doing it myself. *That's what machines do. Machines do lots of things, but they don't feel.*

A new fear overtakes me, one that I can honestly say I can't remember feeling before. *What if I can't change? What if this is how I will always be? I've turned myself into a machine, but can I turn myself back? Can I become a human again?*

I am suddenly very worried that I am going to be stuck this way—miserable, alone, unhappy, and incapable of feeling much of anything. I think about the meds I am on, and realize that I've come to appreciate them for the sense of calm they are giving me. Am I just trying to drug myself so that I don't feel anything? Isn't that what the meds are designed to do after all?

I feel dizzy. Too many thoughts in my head and it's getting hard to breathe. Life suddenly seems to be a large, looming monster, one that I cannot deal with. Panic starts to overtake me as I begin to hyperventilate. Just as my erratic breathing is becoming noticeable to others, I happen to turn my head and notice the tree.

I make the slightest whimpering noise at the sight of it standing there, and I remember. I remember that the tree stands, despite the storms that it has weathered. My breathing slows back to normal, and I just focus on that tree until I feel calm again.

Okay Emma. You're okay. Everything is going to be okay. You're going to be like the tree, Emma, I tell myself. I whisper so that I don't look like a total weirdo to anyone who might be watching.

You're going to be just fine. You're going to get through this. If the tree is still standing, you can do the same thing...

It doesn't quite make sense; not in a linear, logical, *machine* sort of way, my fascination with this tree. But in a very *human* sort of way, my newfound love for the tree does make sense. I really *am* going to be like that tree.

I smile to myself. I, a *machine,* have fallen in love with a tree. I laugh softly when I think how silly it sounds, but it makes me happy. I have found something that makes sense to me, sets an example for me to follow. And even if it's just a tree, well, I like that. I have at least begun to think like a human again.

CHAPTER 14

"All good things…"

December ??

I don't deserve to live and breathe and feel. I ruin everything I touch.

So begins my journal entry this morning. I woke up in a bad mood, for reasons I am unsure of. I think it's a combination of mental and physical exhaustion, plus the fact that I woke, shivering, before the lights were on. The heating had gone off again.

Once again the familiar cycle of wake, shower, go to the main room, eat, take meds, and sit through group therapy has started. I am beginning to understand why anyone who has been in here for any length of time has turned into what I call a *zombie*. This place drains the life out of you; it is even becoming a chore to move. Certainly, it is taking much more energy than I had thought it would to pretend that everything is *okay,* and that I am doing *better*.

Truth be told, even though I have enjoyed the protective environment that being in the hospital has offered, that feeling has grown old and stale. I want my clothes back; I want my makeup and—most of all—I want my music back.

I sit in the chair, waiting for my meeting with Dr. X. Well, I hope it will be Dr. X, not the other doctor who had casually dismissed me yesterday. If it is going to be Dr. X, he is late—it is ten minutes past our meeting time and still he isn't here.

Just as I start to think that the meeting is going to be canceled, Dr. X rushes in, dropping files and folders along the way.

"Goddammit!" he says loudly, and I jump in the chair, startled.

I help him pick up the files and folders, and carry them to his desk.

"Thank you, Emma," he says to me, and hopelessly pushes the assortment of papers to one side of his desk. I assume he'll sort through them later.

He opens my file and takes a few minutes to read it. I sit across from him, on my hands to keep them warm, swinging my legs. I notice the picture of his family and remember that he hadn't been here yesterday because of a family emergency. I am suddenly worried about them, for some unknown reason.

"Hey Dr. X, um, is everything okay?" I ask him.

He looks up at me, startled. "Huh?" he says back. He hasn't heard what I said.

"They told me you weren't here yesterday because of an emergency. Is everything okay?"

Recognition crosses his face and Dr. X half smiles at me. "Everything is fine,. My wife slipped in the shower and bumped her head pretty badly. Thanks for asking, Emma."

I smile back and wait for him to finish reading. I suddenly become nervous and hope that Dr. Murphy has said good things about me. I start to chew on my fingernails.

Dr. X raises his eyebrows in surprise as he reads. I can only guess at what is written in my file. After what seems like an eternity, he looks up at me.

"Well. Seems you're doing much better, Emma. You're participating more in group sessions, focusing on your treatment plan, writing in your journal, doing your classwork. That's very good."

He pauses and adjusts his glasses before his gaze turns razor sharp, so that it seems to cut right through me.

I know what he is doing. He is trying

to see if I'm faking. I politely smile as our eyes meet.

"So, Emma. How are you feeling?"

For a split second, I want to tell Dr. X about the meeting with my father, and how my father had told me to say and do whatever I had to do to get out of here. But I don't.

"I'm doing a lot better, Doc. Really trying to, uh, you know, deal with my issues and stuff."

As soon as the words come out of my mouth, I want to kick myself. I'm not speaking with the poise and grace that I have practiced.

Dr. X continues to look straight at me. He leans back in his chair and taps his pen on the desk. He seems to be mulling something over.

"Well, that's very good," he says at last. "What do you think is helping you feel better?"

I open my mouth to speak, then think better of it. I hadn't really planned for this question. I haven't been expecting it. Damn him.

"Well, I think the medication is helping. I've been eating more, which, um, is helping. And I've been sleeping better, so that's good too. Um, I also talked to both of my parents, and they're very supportive of me and are going to help me when I get out of here."

Dr. X doesn't move. I'm not sure if I've messed up or not. I freeze beneath his icy stare.

"You've talked to *both* of your parents," he says. I think I know where he is going with this.

"Yes. My father came to visit me the other day."

"Yes, I know Emma. How did that go?"

Again, it occurs to me that I should tell the truth. That I am confused about my father; that I don't know what to think, and that I feel like a jerk for trying to kill myself and embarrassing my family. But, I didn't say any of that. I just tell Dr. X what I think he wants to hear.

"We both decided that we should let go of the past and start a new relationship together. He says that he wants to support me when I get out of here and spend more time with me."

"And is that okay with you, Emma?" Dr. X asks. He makes little notes in my file as we talk.

"Yep," I say.

Dr. X considers my answer. Then he flips through my chart and begins to re-read it. He's taking his time, reading and re-reading stuff, and making little notes. What the hell is he doing?

Dr. X looks at me again, and sighs. "Well Emma, it would *appear* that you are doing better. The nurses, orderlies and other hospital staff have made notes to that effect. You're cooperating more, and you're becoming more social as well."

Dr. X paused for effect.

"*However,* I must admit I am slightly suspicious of this sudden turn for the better."

He pauses again. I can't move. I want to scream. Instead, I'm just sitting here, silently. Dr. X continues.

"As a general rule it takes more than just a few days for a patient to show the level of change that your progress reports are suggesting. Makes me wonder..."

Dr. X pauses again. It's clear that there's more he wants to say, but he just sighs and shakes his head. Eventually he continues.

"The fact is, I cannot keep you here based on just a hunch, Emma. I've already spoken with both of your parents, and they do seem very supportive of you, and more than willing to continue to help you with your treatment plan when you get out of the hospital."

Dr. X watches me, looking for a reaction. I don't have much of one. I'm not quite sure what Dr. X is saying. One minute he seems to be implying that he doesn't believe me, the next minute he says that he can't keep me here. I'm confused, to say the least.

"Do you understand what I'm telling you Emma?" Dr. X asks.

I shake my head. "No. I don't."

Dr. X nods. "I'm sure this must be very confusing for you Emma. What I'm trying to tell you is that *personally* I think you should stay here a little bit longer. However, according to hospital protocol, you are ready to be discharged."

I'm sitting very still, not moving. Dr. X notices my lack of movement and continues to spell out to me what he's saying.

"Emma. I can't keep you here any longer."

I feel like a rush of cold air has hit me. I shiver as I take a deep, long breath. And I just can't help myself. I smile.

Dr. X doesn't return my smile however, so I quickly stop.

"Off the record, Emma, I'm very concerned about you. I know you haven't been honest with me since you've been here. I have my ideas as to why you hide your true self away, but I cannot prove anything. I really mean this in a nice way, Emma, but I hope I never see you again."

I frown when Dr. X says he doesn't want to see me again, before I realize what he actually means. He isn't stupid, he has seen through my act. But I'm not throwing trees at anyone or refusing to co-operate, so he's powerless to do much of anything to keep me from leaving the hospital. And when he says he doesn't want to see me again, it's just because if he does, it most likely means that I have tried to kill myself again. He really *does* mean it in a nice way.

"I understand Doc. You won't see me again."

Our eyes meet, and he's sending me an unspoken message. Something along the lines of *I know that you know that I know that you're still screwed up, and I'm trying to tell you to take care of yourself.* I want to laugh because that sounds like a line from some stupid sitcom or something, but I just nod quietly. Dr. X nods back at me. He knows that he's gotten his point across.

Dr. X breaks the silence. "I am going to recommend you for discharge, Emma. If everything continues to go well, your parents can most likely pick you up tomorrow morning. I will speak to them today and inform them of your progress and our intent to discharge you. You just take good care of yourself, Emma."

I am suddenly aware of the fact that I am going to miss Dr. X very much. My eyes begin to tear up. I am confused. I should be very happy, but instead I am afraid. And sad.

Dr. X smiles to reassure me. "You're as tough as nails, Emma. You'll be fine."

I can't talk. A lump is forming in my throat. I swallow hard and run a hand through my hair. And straighten my back. I am *not* going to cry.

"Thanks for everything Doc," I say, getting to my feet.

Dr. X is already sorting through the stack of papers on his desk. He looks up at me. "You're welcome, Emma. You can go now."

I feel I want to say something else to him, but I don't really know what. In the end though, I keep it simple.

"Bye Doc," I say. And that's it. That's all I can find to say to the man who has probably helped me more than anyone else in my whole life. Even so, I think Dr.

X understands what I am trying to say. I look at him and realize how tired he is. I'm suddenly more grateful than ever for having met him.

"Good-bye Emma," Dr. X answers. And then he's back to his mountain of paperwork, getting ready for the next patient.

I walk calmly to the bathroom and as soon as the door shuts behind me, I start to cry. I'm crying because I am afraid, and because I've never been very good at good-byes. And this good-bye is permanent. It has to be.

Slowly, my tears stop. Excitement begins to well up in my chest as I remember that I am getting the hell out of here. I smile and giggle to myself. It dawns on me that I have been in the bathroom for quite some time, so I quickly wash my face to erase any evidence of tears that might still remain.

When I walk back to the group room, Ricky walks over to me and sits down. It's okay though; not even Ricky's constant but well-meaning pestering can bother me right now.

"Well you look chipper today. What's going on Emma?" he asks.

A smile stretches from ear to ear across my face, and I know that I am going to be okay. I am tough as nails. I am going to make it.

"I'm going home, Ricky."

CHAPTER 15

Endgame

My mom and I are arguing. I think this one started over my refusal to wear clothing in any color other than black. I'm sitting on the bathroom floor and crying, with my head in my hands. My mom has hit me, and she tried to get me to hit her back. My refusal to do so has only angered her even more. I know she's going to twist the story to make it sound like it's my fault. She's screaming at me and I have my hands clamped over my ears to muffle the sound.

"What do you want Emma? What do you want? Do you want to go live with your father? I CAN'T DO THIS ANYMORE WITH YOU!"

I stop crying like a switch has been flipped. Very calmly, I lock eyes with my mother and I say what I need to say in a single simple sentence.

"If you send me to live with that abusive asshole again, I am going to kill myself..."

I wake up and frown. Why in the hell have I dreamed about *that* argument with my mom? I'm not really angry about it—I knew she'd never send me to live with him, and I know she is frustrated because her daughter is a depressed mess. I didn't blame her for her reaction then. So why am I dreaming about it now?

I don't have much time to ponder the reason for this unpleasant dream, because the lights are turned on and I begin the process of getting dressed. I shake off the memory as being just another nightmare and decide that I am *not* going to be in a bad mood today. Today is the day that I am going home and I am so excited I can barely stand it.

Of course, I am still nervous and unsure of what to expect when I get home. But whatever happens, it is bound to be better than being here. I mean, it *has* to be better than here, right?

I join everyone else in the main room and eat a breakfast that is just slightly warm—not burned or rubbery for a change. I consider it to be a good omen, a sign that things *are* indeed changing. And for the better.

I am practically humming to myself when I get in line for my meds. The water feels cool in my mouth, not tepid like it usually is. Yet another good sign that things are going to start going my way.

I sit in my final group therapy session, and even talk about my excitement at getting out of the hospital. And what it will be like to begin rebuilding relationships with my family. And how I'm going to explore healthy, creative outlets for my emotions when I get out of here. And you know what? I'm not pretending. I am completely serious about trying to become a healthy, sane human being. I've had enough of being sick, tired, and most of all, *a machine*.

After group therapy, when everyone is busy waiting their turn to file into Dr. X's office for their private therapy and assessments, a kindly nurse comes over to me. She explains that my parents are going to be picking me up at noon.

Excitedly, I go to my room to pack my few belongings into the plastic bag she's given me. Really, the only things I am taking are the Bible my father had given me and my journal. I think for a moment about *not* taking the journal, just throwing it away. But I decide against it. It is a testament to my decision to get better.

I finish packing and give the bag to the nurse. She takes it up to the front desk to hold for me until I am discharged from the hospital.

The last few hours before noon seem to drag by so slowly that at times it feels like the clock isn't moving at all.

At noon I am called to the front desk, where my mom is waiting for me. I smile, run up to her and hug her. She hugs me back, but it doesn't feel quite the way I remembered. I frown. She feels a little stiff and uncomfortable. She's never hugged me like that before. Or have I just been in here for so long that I've forgotten? God, is she mad at me for some reason? A twinge of nervousness runs through me, settling in my stomach.

"Hi Mom," I say, and it comes out almost like a question. To my relief, she doesn't seem angry at me. Maybe a little sad, but not angry.

"Hi Emma. Let's get you home, okay?" she says. She brushes my cheek softly with the back of a finger. For once, I don't care if anyone sees me being affectionate with my mom. In fact, I desperately *want* people to see it. Then they will see that I am loved, and that I am not a freak.

My mom has brought a change of clothes for me. I go back to my room to strip out of the hospital clothing and slip into something that is more, well, *me.*

My mom has brought me a black T-shirt, my favorite black hoodie sweatshirt and sneakers and blue jeans. I frown. Where in the *hell* had she found blue jeans that belonged to me? I don't even remember ever *owning* a pair of blue jeans. But still, it's better than the hospital clothing that I'm tearing off at lightspeed.

I dress in record time and run down the hall, throwing the dirty clothes in the laundry bin in the hallway. *Good riddance,* I mutter as I toss them in, running back up the hallway to meet with my mom again. She is busy signing my discharge paperwork.

I see the nurse hand her a folder of paperwork and a brown paper bag with my meds in it. The nurse is explaining what I am taking and how often. My mom glances at me briefly, just the once, and when she does, she wears an expression that I can't identify. Is she ashamed of me? I begin to chew on my fingers. I am anxious, just wanting to get the hell out of here. Suddenly I am overcome with a feeling that I am *never* going to leave this place; that this is all some elaborate trick, and that my mom is going to leave without me.

At last, when I can stand it no longer, the nurse is done talking, and my mom picks up the folder and the bag. My mom hands the bag to me.

"Hold these Emma," she says, all matter-of-fact. I peer up at her suspiciously. This is just not like her.

"Mom, why are you acting weird? Do you still love me?" I ask her quietly.

My mom stops walking and looks me square in the eyes. "Emma, I will *always, always* love you. That will never change, okay? I've just had a rough week too."

I feel only slightly relieved, because now I feel guilty as hell. I sigh and carry on walking down the hallway, next to my mom.

We walk out of the building, toward the parking lot. When we get to the car, I stop and turn to look back at the hospital. Then, I look up at the sky. There are some clouds, but there are beautiful streaks of blue, breaking up the monotony of the gray. I look to the distance and see dark storm clouds rolling slowly toward us.

My mom interrupts my thoughts. "Come on, Emma. It's supposed to rain again, and I want to get home before the weather gets too bad."

I get into the car. We drive home with the radio on, so neither of us has to talk. I fidget, nervously. Finally, I can't stand the silence between us anymore.

"I'm sorry Mom. Please don't hate me," I blurt out.

"Emma, I *don't* hate you honey. Please stop saying that. Just... you need to understand... that this is going to take some time to get over. And things are going to be different when you get home."

I had known that when I finally made it out of the hospital that things *were* going to be different. In most ways I am ready and waiting for them to be different. But I am still afraid. I remember Dr. X's words to me when he had sensed the fear inside me at our last meeting. "You're as tough as nails, Emma," he'd said. I smile a little bit, despite myself. I tell myself that everything is going to be okay, and not to be afraid.

"How's Rosemary?" I ask my mother.

My mom hesitates for a split second before she answers. "She's fine. She's at a friend's house right now."

I am slightly pissed off that my sister isn't at home for me to see, but I won't be making a scene about it.

Mom says she has to make a stop, and pulls into the parking lot of the liquor store at the bottom of the hill, before you come up to our house.

"Wait here," she says. She comes back a few minutes later with a bottle of wine in a brown paper bag.

We drive the rest of the way home in silence. I don't know exactly what I had been expecting, but I had hoped that she would be, I don't know, maybe excited to have me back home? It sounds silly I know, but I had been *so* excited to get home myself that I had wanted to find at least a *little* of that mirrored in my mom. But what I'm picking up on seems to be... what? Anxiety? Fear? Whatever it is, I can't quite place it.

I am beginning to make myself a nervous wreck before I finally decide that things cannot be rushed. Healing is going to take time.

We hit the gravel in the driveway and the sound jerks me out of my thoughts. Before the car even stops, I have unbuckled my seatbelt and I run up to the house. I pull up the mat on the front porch, and discover that the key I usually use to get into the house isn't there.

"Hey Mom, where's the key?" I ask.

My mom doesn't say anything at all. She just unlocks the door herself. I am starting to get creeped-out by my mom's behavior.

My mom goes into the kitchen and I follow her. She opens the bottle of wine, pours herself a glass, and quickly downs the whole thing. She has still not said a word.

"Um. I'm going to go to my room now Mom," I say.

My words seem to hover in the air, and my mom simply pours herself another glass of wine.

I walk through the house that is as silent as a tomb. I stop off at the door of Rosemary's room, hoping that she'd come home from her friend's house. Rosemary is not there. I sigh and continue walking down the hall, until I get to my bedroom.

I open the door, and my heart stops.

Unable to believe what I am seeing, I run back down the hallway into the kitchen. My mother is still silent as a statue, drinking her wine.

"Mom, what the hell did you do to my room? Where's all my stuff? Mom?"

I had opened the door to my room to find it an empty space. No posters, no pictures, no clothes in the closet, and not a stick of furniture in it. It is like I had never existed.

"MOM!" I finally shout. Slowly, like it is taking a great effort, her head turns toward me. Her hazel eyes finally meet mine. There is not a shred of emotion in them, and I realize that *that* was what I had been unable to identify in my mom at the hospital. And during the ride home. She was cold... no, not just cold... *mechanical.*

When my mother finally does speak, she speaks calmly and flatly, as efficient as any judge handing out a sentence to a condemned prisoner.

"I told you, things were going to change when you got home, Emma."

"Okay, so what the hell does that have to do with where my stuff is Mom?" I yell at her. I am afraid. Truly afraid. I have *never* seen my mom act like this.

My mother calmly continues. "I'm sorry, Emma," she says, pausing to pour herself another glass of wine. I just watch her drinking, stunned. Finally, I remember that I can speak.

"Sorry for *what* Mom? Did you throw my shit away?"

My mother's eyes meet mine, and though there is still not a shred of emotion in them, a single tear runs down her cheek.

"Emma. I can't do this anymore. I'm sorry. You're too much for me to handle."

I listen to her and can't believe what I am hearing. "So what the hell does that mean, Mom?"

My mother finishes her glass of wine and turns her back to me. Outside, sloppy wet drops of rain smack loudly on the car, on the pavement, over everything. My mother and I stand in the rapidly darkening kitchen in silence. Finally, I can handle it no more.

"Mom, what the *hell* are you saying?" I yell in frustration.

"Emma, I packed your things and sent them to your father's house."

"Well what the hell would you do *that* for?" I ask, not understanding—*refusing* to understand—what she is saying.

"Because Emma, you're going to live there."

I don't say anything. Just what can I say to that? I stare at her and she just keeps lifting that glass of wine to her lips, regular as clockwork, like she's a machine. It's funny that I had never seen it before. My mom as a machine. Through my frustration and fear, I'm beginning to see that perhaps just about anyone can become a machine. You just have to have the need to shut the world out.

But then I wonder, has my mom always been a machine and I've been so busy becoming a machine myself that I just never noticed? That could explain a lot about me. Perhaps it takes a machine to breed a machine.

I don't even want to think about it as I reach down deep within myself to find the switch that hides there in the darkness. If I'm going to survive, I'd better power up.